Praise for the MacDonald Family Trilogy

Under Scottish Stars

"In *Under Scottish Stars*, independent single mothe[...] [St]ewart returns to the beautiful land of Skye, looking for stabi[...] [for her] children—not romance with Malcolm Blake, who m[...] [...]na owns with her two brothers. Their [...] [...]ship is engaging, and Carla Laureano [...] [Ma]lcolm's vulnerabilities as they fall in love wh[...] [...]ed it. *Under Scottish Stars* is a satisfying romance that rem[...] [...] that love doesn't always go according to our agendas—and that [...] [...] a very good thing."

BETH K. VOGT, author of the Thatcher Sisters series

"*Under Scottish Stars* is a fabulous read, filled with compelling characters, a delicious setting, and a romance that can only be described as . . . swoon-worthy. Carla Laureano's third and final book in the MacDonald Family Trilogy exceeded all my expectations and truly shouldn't be missed."

JEN TURANO, *USA Today* bestselling author of *A Change of Fortune*

"Solid characters, brilliant dialogue, believable conflict, a setting you can taste—and, always, breath-stealing love scenes. No one writes a romantic hero like Laureano! *Under Scottish Stars* takes us back to Skye to explore poignant truths of single parenthood, family loyalty, the pursuit of dreams—and faith. A satisfying and stellar finish to the MacDonald Family Trilogy."

CANDACE CALVERT, bestselling author of *Maybe It's You* and *The Recipe*

London Tides

"Achieving an aching depth and a resounding trueness within a heated yet baggage-ridden romance, author Carla Laureano has proven herself a storyteller who is not afraid to take her characters into the darkest regions of their own hearts. An excellent follow-up to *Five Days in Skye*, *London Tides* tugs and churns every emotion . . . right up until the lovely, hope-buoying end."

SERENA CHASE, *USA Today*'s Happy Ever After blog

"At times lighthearted; at times heart wrenching. Laureano has penned a delightfully romantic tale about the importance of finding home. If readers weren't already smitten with the MacDonald brothers, they will be after *London Tides*!"

KATIE GANSHERT, award-winning author of *The Art of Losing Yourself*

"Another captivating story! *London Tides* is as compelling and engaging as Laureano's award-winning *Five Days in Skye*. It's deliciously romantic and filled with tension, wonderful characters, and vivid scenery. A must-read this summer!"

KATHERINE REAY, author of *Lizzy and Jane*

FIVE DAYS IN SKYE

"Sweet and scathing, lush and intimate. . . . This story has guts and heart as well as the depth and heat necessary to satisfy any romance reader's palate."

USA TODAY

"From page one, *Five Days in Skye* captured my imagination and every minute of my pleasure-reading time. With enviable finesse, author Carla Laureano weaves romance, hope, healing, and faith into a spunky and sparkling tale that made me sorry to say good-bye to the characters and the alluring Isle of Skye. I look forward to reading more from this author."

TAMARA LEIGH, author of *Splitting Harriet* and *The Unveiling*, book one in the Age of Faith series

"*Five Days in Skye* swept me away to Scotland! Against the craggy beauty of the Isle of Skye, author Carla Laureano weaves a story . . . of love between an American businesswoman and a Scottish celebrity chef. Fans of the movie *The Holiday* are sure to enjoy this contemporary romance. Laureano's voice is deft, seamless, and wonderfully accomplished. An exciting newcomer to the world of Christian fiction!"

BECKY WADE, author of *My Stubborn Heart* and *Undeniably Yours*

Under Scottish Stars

THE
MACDONALD FAMILY
TRILOGY

Under Scottish Stars

CARLA LAUREANO
RITA AWARD–WINNING AUTHOR

Tyndale House Publishers
Carol Stream, Illinois

Visit Tyndale online at tyndale.com.

Visit Carla Laureano's website at carlalaureano.com.

TYNDALE and Tyndale's quill logo are registered trademarks of Tyndale House Publishers.

Under Scottish Stars

Designed by Eva M. Winters

Edited by Sarah Mason Rische

Published in association with the literary agency of The Steve Laube Agency.

Under Scottish Stars is a work of fiction. Where real people, events, establishments, organizations, or locales appear, they are used fictitiously. All other elements of the novel are drawn from the author's imagination.

For information about special discounts for bulk purchases, please contact Tyndale House Publishers at csresponse@tyndale.com, or call 1-800-323-9400.

Library of Congress Cataloging-in-Publication Data
Names: Laureano, Carla, author.
Title: Under Scottish stars / Carla Laureano.
Description: Carol Stream, Illinois : Tyndale House Publishers, [2020] | Series: The MacDonald family trilogy ; 3
Identifiers: LCCN 2019058003 (print) | LCCN 2019058004 (ebook) | ISBN 9781496426291 (trade paperback) | ISBN 9781496426307 (kindle edition) | ISBN 9781496426314 (epub) | ISBN 9781496426321 (epub)
Subjects: LCSH: Domestic fiction. | GSAFD: Love stories.
Classification: LCC PS3612.A93257 U53 2020 (print) | LCC PS3612. A93257 (ebook) | DDC 813/.6—dc23
LC record available at https://lccn.loc.gov/2019058003
LC ebook record available at https://lccn.loc.gov/2019058004

Printed in the United States of America

26 25 24 23 22 21 20

7 6 5 4 3 2 1

*To my single-mom friends, who do the hardest
job in the world with grace and grit.
You amaze me.*

Acknowledgments

IF THERE WERE AN AWARD for the most circuitous route to publication, it would probably go to this book! As many of you know, *Under Scottish Stars* was originally scheduled to be published several years ago, but when I changed publishers, I took the MacDonald Family Trilogy with me. That began the long and complicated but gratifying process of getting these books back out in the world. It also meant a—*ahem*—rather long wait for this elusive third book, and it's hard to explain how glad I am to finally be able to share Serena and Malcolm's story.

The first acknowledgment must go to all the readers who embraced this series so warmly and hung in there for *five long years* for the final conclusion. I sincerely hope it was worth the wait! And if you've come to this series late, welcome. There's a small but dedicated community that would love to discuss the merits of the MacDonald Family Trilogy's heroes with you!

A big basket of thank-yous goes to:

The entire Tyndale Fiction team, who embraced this series and worked tirelessly to give it a second life and

ix

expand its readership. I'm so grateful for all your hard work and enthusiasm.

My original editor, Rachelle Gardner, and my Tyndale editor, Sarah Rische. Your combined efforts have undoubtedly made this book into the very best version of itself.

My agent, Steve Laube. There's no one I'd rather have with me in this crazy business. Your wisdom, humor, and integrity are always appreciated. Thank you for all you do.

My fabulous friends and partners in literary madness: Elizabeth Younts, Laurie Tomlinson, Evangeline Denmark, Brandy Vallance, Cindi Madsen, Lori Twichell, and Amber Lynn Perry. Some of you talked me off the ledge during the writing of this book, and some of you were with me during the re-edit/reissue, but many times that little chat icon is the only thing that keeps me going. That means my sanity—or lack thereof—is all on your shoulders. No pressure or anything.

My fantastic family: Rey, Nathan, Preston, Mom, and Dad. Your love and support mean more to me than anything.

My loving heavenly Father, who speaks to me most clearly through the pages of my own books. Help me listen.

CHAPTER ONE

THREE MINUTES INTO DESSERT, Serena MacDonald Stewart was checking the time on her mobile phone, concocting a quick escape. Half past eight. She'd already devoted two hours to the date that would never end. Could she pull off an emergency text message from her babysitter without tipping her hand?

"Is there a problem at home?"

Serena jerked her head up guiltily and gave an inward sigh at the disappointed expression on her date's face. "No, no problem." She returned her phone to the seat beside her and vowed to keep her mind on the man who had taken her out to this very expensive—and very long—dinner.

"It's hard leaving them behind, isn't it?" he said. "Is this your first date since—"

"Since Edward died? No, it isn't. But it doesn't seem to get any easier."

The patient understanding playing across his handsome features made her feel even worse. She'd met Daniel Cameron on a committee for the school that her daughter and his youngest son attended. He'd struck her as kind and thoughtful, and she'd not had the heart to turn him down when he'd asked her out to dinner. At least he was easy to look at: dark hair, green eyes, nice build for a man she figured was pushing fifty.

But there was absolutely no spark. Nothing. She couldn't muster one single flicker of interest.

Daniel leaned forward, lowering his voice. "I have to tell you, I haven't dated much since my divorce either. I know you're probably not supposed to bring up these things, but we both understand how it is."

Maybe not, considering she had no idea where he was going with this.

"At this point, I think we're simply trying to find someone we like and respect. You must be looking for a father for your children, especially with Max so young. Certainly, my children could use a better role model than their mother, especially considering my work keeps me so busy."

Oh no. *Now* she knew where he was going with this. She'd heard it too many times. *"I didn't ask you out because I thought we had something in common and find you attractive. I'm really looking for a mother for my children before it's too late and I mess things up on my own."*

Serena cleared her throat and made a show of glancing at her mobile again. "I really hate to cut this short, but my babysitter has to be home by half nine. Do you think we could—?"

"Oh, of course. Yes. I didn't realize it had gotten so late."

He signaled the server for their bill. "I don't suppose you have plans for next weekend?"

"Actually, I thought I might take Max and Em to Edinburgh. There's a Vermeer exhibit at the National Gallery."

He cracked a smile, which faded as soon as he realized she wasn't having a laugh. "You're really taking an eight-year-old and a three-year-old to an art museum?"

"Of course. You have to start these things early. Max simply needs to learn to keep his hands to himself, but Em's got a good eye for technique already. I think it would be an enriching experience. That's part of why we appreciate the art program at Highlands Academy so much."

"Certainly." Now he looked as uncomfortable as she felt.

Serena put two and two together. "You were part of the petition to cut the arts and music program in favor of more academics." Surely he knew she'd been lobbying against that very petition with the private-school board for the past month.

"I just think we're better off emphasizing math and science, especially for girls, given the current competitive business environment." He placed his credit card in the folder and handed it back to the server, seeming glad for an excuse not to look Serena in the eye.

"And I think we're doing the world a disservice by not emphasizing the development of creative thinkers. But of course, I have a master's degree in art history and worked as a gallery curator for years, so I might be a little biased."

"Oh?" His eyebrows lifted. "I'd no idea you worked."

She couldn't tell if it was simply a way to steer the topic away from his faux pas or if he was concerned about the fact she might want a career. "I gave it up before I had Em. It was somewhat . . . incompatible . . . with raising children."

Now he looked relieved. "I think that's admirable. Too many women put their own fulfillment ahead of their family's needs."

She should leave it alone. She knew she should. It wasn't as if this date were going anywhere. Yet she'd spent far too much time swallowing her opinions on the subject. She looked him directly in the eye and said, "It's probably not as common as men who bury themselves in the office and expect their wives to take on sole parenting responsibility."

And that was the nail in the coffin of a date already on life support. It made for an awkward drive home, though they both attempted a polite stream of chitchat. As they parted at her front door with a cordial handshake—he was smart enough not to go in for the kiss, at least—she figured it was for the best. Daniel wasn't a bad man, even if he did have rather conservative opinions on gender roles. He was intelligent, successful, and responsible. He simply lacked the level of imagination Serena required in a mate. She'd already had a marriage that felt like one long business transaction, and she wasn't about to jump into another.

"Did you have fun?" Allie, the teenage girl who babysat for Serena on occasion, popped up from the sofa in the reception room, a book in hand.

"It was nice, thanks." Serena reached into her clutch and took out several banknotes, which she handed to the girl with a smile.

Allie stuffed the money into her pocket and picked up her purse. "They were super easy tonight, by the way. Let me know when you need me again."

"Thank you, Allie. I'll ring you." Serena let the girl out the front door and watched until she got into her car and turned on the ignition. This little section of Nairn near the Moray Firth was quiet, almost rural, but her mum instincts wouldn't let her rest until she knew the girl was safely on her way. When Allie backed out of the drive, Serena stepped back into her house, locked up, and kicked her patent-leather heels onto the rug.

Nice dinner or not, that had been a waste of stilettos.

Serena quietly climbed the sweeping staircase to the upper floor and peeked into the first room she came to. Max was sleeping sprawled the wrong direction on his single bed, one pajama leg shoved up above the knee, his fine dark hair wild from his restless sleeping habits. She didn't move him— getting her three-year-old son to sleep was enough of a challenge without disturbing him—but merely covered him with his duvet, tucked his giraffe, Mr. Spots, in beside him, and pressed a kiss to his forehead. Next door, eight-year-old Em was hunkered under a purple floral covering, only the top of her head visible. Serena kissed her good night as well and tucked in the duvet more securely before continuing down the hall to her own expansive bedroom.

Serena's mobile buzzed in her handbag, and she yanked it out before it could go to a full ring and wake the kids. A quick glance at the screen showed a familiar number: the home of her younger brother, Jamie.

"Checking to make sure I got home safely from my date?" she said with a wry smile.

An American-accented female voice answered, "No, but the fact that you picked up answers my next question."

Serena laughed at her sister-in-law's wry tone. "Hi, Andrea. I just got back."

"So the hot date was not so hot?"

"Barely lukewarm." Serena shimmied out of her pencil skirt and peeled off the body shaper she'd worn to make the old garment fit, then kicked it halfway across the room. The date had been a waste of Lycra too. "He was nice, but—"

"No sparks."

"Not even a flicker. I'm beginning to think I'm asking too much." She yanked on her flannel pajama bottoms over her cotton knickers and grimaced at the marks the stiletto heels had made on her feet. "Maybe at my age, I should be looking for someone stable and boring."

"Oh, please. You're not even forty yet, so I don't want to hear 'at my age.' Besides, you're just going through what we all went through."

Serena put her mobile on speaker so she could slide off her jacket and wrestle out of her silk blouse. "Which is?"

"Dating the boring, safe guys while you're waiting for the one who curls your toes and sweeps you off your feet."

"Please stop right there. I don't need any more evidence of how you and my brother can't keep your hands off each other."

"I already apologized for that, and you really need to learn to knock." Andrea laughed. "It's not as if I came to Scotland intending to fall in love with a client, you know. Sometimes you have to go outside your comfort zone."

"I'll keep that in mind. What time are we supposed to be at your house tomorrow for supper?"

"That's why I was calling. Can we push it to seven? Jamie got delayed in London and missed his flight home, so he won't be back until tomorrow afternoon."

"That's fine. I thought I would take Em and Max to that new bakery that just opened in Old Town."

"Thank you. I offered to do Jamie's shopping to save him time, but for some reason he didn't take me up on the offer."

Now it was Serena's turn to laugh. Her brother the chef had managed to marry a woman who couldn't even boil water without ruining it, although Serena thought Andrea might be playing up the helpless routine to benefit from Jamie's amazing cooking. Then again, she'd once suffered through a lunch that her sister-in-law had prepared, so maybe not.

"Seven o'clock. We'll be there. Em is anxious to show you how much progress she's made on 'Für Elise.'"

"I can't wait. Tell her to practice hard, because as soon as she finishes this one, I have something really fun for her to try."

"I will. See you tomorrow." Serena ended the call and set her phone on the charger on the nightstand by her bed. What Andrea lacked in cooking ability, she made up for in musical talent, considering she had once been a concert pianist and now gave lessons to Em every Sunday before supper. And that was just something she did for fun while she ran her own hospitality consulting firm. By comparison, Serena filled her days with volunteering and teaching art at Em's school—the very program her date tonight was trying to eliminate.

How could Daniel have even asked her out, knowing that he was essentially lobbying against the one thing Serena really loved?

He didn't know, she realized. Because to men like him, art was something you dabbled in, not something you were passionate about or made a living from. Not something that had any real, tangible value. Serena removed her makeup and tied her hair up into a ponytail before heading downstairs to the kitchen to make some tea. She paused in the reception room to admire the collection of contemporary art on the white plaster walls. Unlike the rest of the modern interior, which had been selected by Edward's designer, these pieces held special meaning. She'd discovered and cultivated each of the artists, some of whom had gone on to be internationally recognized. The pride never failed to come with a pang of regret, a reminder that part of her life was long past. The regret deepened a degree when she moved down the hallway to a partially open door.

The space remained exactly as she'd left it: a blank canvas set up on an easel, plastic bins corralling paints and brushes on the small table next to it. She reached for the light, and her hand made a trail through the dust on the finger plate. Maybe she should turn this back into a storage room, as it had been when she and Edward moved in. She'd not used it for much else in the past several years. She clicked the light off and shut the door firmly.

Daniel and his ilk were going to win the argument, she knew, not because they were right but because she lacked the energy to convince the school otherwise. And she really couldn't blame them. How could she convince them of the value of art when she could barely convince herself?

Meals at Jamie and Andrea's house were always an event, partly because Andrea had a knack for making the simplest things elegant, but mostly because Jamie's idea of a low-key dinner was a mere four courses. It also might have had something to do with the restrained opulence of their renovated Victorian home, just a handful of miles from Serena's house. Right now, they were sampling Jamie's new spring recipes in the expansive all-white kitchen surrounded by gleaming stainless steel and Carrara marble.

"The lamb is good, but it just doesn't feel special enough," Serena said when she set down her fork and knife at last. "Maybe it's because beans don't say haute cuisine to me."

"She's right," Andrea said, "from one lima-bean hater to another."

"That's why we call them butter beans," Jamie said, but he seemed resigned to the pronouncement. "What about the sea bass?"

"Incredible," Serena said at the same time Andrea said, "Amazing."

"Sea bass it is," Jamie said. "I prefer it myself."

Serena nodded and sipped her wine—a good dry Riesling that Jamie had brought up from the cellar. Yes, they had a wine cellar. It still amazed her that the grand house managed to feel comfortable and inviting, something she attributed to her brother and his wife's impeccable sense of style.

"Can I go play the piano again?" Em asked, folding her napkin beside her plate.

"It's okay with me if it's okay with Andrea," Serena said.

"Be my guest, Em," Andrea said. "You can work on your new section."

"Can I go too?" Max piped up.

Serena smiled at her son. "Yes, you can go too."

The children half tumbled, half scurried to the parlor, where Andrea's baby grand lived, leaving the three adults sitting at the round glass table. It wasn't exactly like old times, but it was nice to finally have family nearby, good to have a regular routine. When she and Edward had moved from Edinburgh to Inverness for his work, the tiny city had felt impossibly lonely. The addition of her brother and his wife seemed, after eight years, to make it home.

"So, I've been meaning to talk to you about something," Jamie said.

Serena took another sip of wine with a smile. "Uh-oh. Sounds ominous."

"Not ominous. I wanted to see how you would feel about getting involved with the hotel on Skye again."

"Involved how, exactly? The renovations are complete and the new manager is in place."

"They are and he is. I'm asking if you would consider buying your way back in." Jamie reached for the wine bottle and refilled her glass. "Let's face it. Ian and Grace are hardly in country anymore with their new jobs. Andrea has a business to run, and I've still not found anyone to take over the chef de cuisine position at Notting Hill since Jeremy left. We're barely at our own homes, let alone the hotel."

"Why now? You and Ian have gotten over your differences. You don't need me to play referee anymore." Then Serena noticed Jamie's and Andrea's clasped hands beneath the table. "You're pregnant! That's why you want me to step in!"

Andrea's smile faltered, and she looked to Jamie. Serena's heart sank. "I'm sorry. I shouldn't have—"

"No, it's okay." Andrea took a deep breath. "We've only been trying about seven months, but the doctors all agree it's a long shot. There's just too much wrong for me to carry a baby."

Serena's stomach twisted with guilt. She'd just assumed they'd eventually start a family, but neither Jamie nor Andrea had mentioned that there might be barriers to that goal. She fumbled for a way out of her faux pas, but before she could speak, Jamie stepped in. "Which is why we're starting the process to adopt."

Serena blinked for a moment, and then a smile broke over her face. "I'm so happy for you! You'll make fantastic parents. I had no idea you were considering adoption."

"Blame Ian," Andrea said, her smile returning. "He and Grace are always talking about the children in India who need homes, and we realized that there are plenty of children in Scotland who need families as well. But we know it won't be easy, and we want to have as much time to devote to him or her as we can."

"Right. How are you going to work that?" Serena asked, looking to Jamie.

"Andrea's hired two new account managers so she can stop traveling and run her business from here. I'm going back to London next week to start interviews, but it could be a long process. I have my eye on someone, but I'm not sure I can entice him away from his current position."

"You mean you're trying to poach from the top," Serena guessed with a laugh. There were only a few restaurateurs in London with higher profiles than Jamie.

He flashed a quick grin that said she was right. "The point is, we don't feel that we can commit to being as involved in the hotel as we should be. Malcolm is doing a great job managing the hotel, but he's not an owner. We need to keep our offerings fresh, continue to bring in guests. After what you did with the gallery, this should be a simple thing."

"That was ten years ago, Jamie—"

"Skills don't expire."

"—and I have two children, one of whom is in school. I can't just pick up at a moment's notice like you can."

The tinkle of piano music from the other room stopped, followed by a crash and a wail. Serena put aside her napkin, but Andrea shook her head and rose instead. "Let me. It couldn't have been anything important. There's nothing truly breakable in the parlor."

She strode out of the room, leaving Serena sitting with her brother. "You two seem happy."

"We are." He smiled at her. "Don't change the subject."

"I don't know, Jamie. I need to think about it."

"If it's the money, we can—"

"It's not the money. I invested the proceeds of the sale. I can liquidate them if I have to. It's more the commitment."

"I never thought you'd be reluctant to visit Skye."

"It has nothing to do with that." Serena folded her hands on the table and lowered her voice. "I've tried to keep Em and Max's lives as stable as possible since Edward died. And now everything seems to be going smoothly. I'm not so sure I want to disrupt this."

"What's there to disrupt? You can work on the marketing ideas at home. Then you go out there one weekend a month, talk to Malcolm, check on Aunt Muriel. It's a mini holiday every few weeks."

What Jamie said sounded logical, but he'd never had to make the three-hour drive with two children. It might sound simple now, but after a few months, she could guarantee it would begin to wear on all of them. "I don't know. I'll have to think on it."

"Good. Think on it." Jamie's face brightened, and without even turning, Serena knew that Andrea had returned with the kids. He seemed to light up whenever his wife was in the room. Truly, they were so in love, it would have been nauseating if she didn't wish them so well. Max ran straight to Serena and climbed into her lap with his three-year-old enthusiasm. Em, on the other hand, quietly slipped into the chair beside her.

"Your 'Für Elise' is coming along nicely, Em," Jamie said. "When is your mean piano teacher going to let you move on to something else?"

"Stop." Andrea stuck out her tongue at her husband and gave him a nudge with her shoulder. "She'll move on when she's mastered it. And she's very close from what I just heard."

Serena looked between them and felt an answering pang in her own chest. The way they were working together so intently to give their future child what he or she needed only highlighted how suited for each other they were. She couldn't help feeling a twinge of resentment over her own situation—not that Edward had died and left her, but that she'd never had the opportunity to experience that kind of companionship in her ten-year marriage. But she'd gotten Em and Max out of it, and that far overshadowed anything she'd lacked personally.

"Dessert?" Jamie shoved away from the table. "I want your honest opinion of these."

Half an hour later, her honest opinion was that Jamie needed to hire the baker as his pastry chef. There was dense, moist almond cake; a chocolate-chili soufflé; and deep-fried zeppole filled with a light pastry cream. All were fantastic. Even Em, who hadn't been born with a sweet tooth, devoured everything set in front of her.

When they finally slipped on their coats to leave, Serena thought she might need to be rolled out the front entrance.

"Think about it," Jamie murmured when he hugged her. "Let me know."

"I will." Serena turned to Andrea and squeezed her tight. "Keep me posted on the adoption news. I'm so excited for you."

Serena stepped out onto the front stoop, holding tight to Max's hand as they descended the stairs to where she had parked on the drive. Her breath puffed out in front of her, hanging in the cold March air. The calendar might be clawing its way toward spring, but winter clung tenaciously to the Scottish Highlands. Even now, snow from a recent storm dotted the shady places beneath the hedges that marked off the formal gardens. Serena bundled her children into her dusty red Vauxhall and buckled Max into his car seat.

"What was that about, Mum?" Em asked as they pulled back onto the street and headed for their own home a few miles away.

"Nothing. Just some business matters."

"Are we going to Skye?"

Serena caught her daughter's eye in the rearview mirror. Exactly how much had Em heard? "For a visit maybe. But you have school and music lessons, and I have my art classes. We can't go for too long."

Em slumped back in her seat, disappointment evident in her young face.

Serena turned down the long drive to their home, the bright glow through its picture windows the only spot of light in the dark surroundings. Without the summer foliage in the front garden, the newer home's angled rooflines, white plaster, and Tudor detailing looked even starker than usual. She parked in the drive and twisted around to give instructions to her kids. But Max was already asleep, clutching his battered orange giraffe in one chubby hand.

"Get your rucksack and then go straight up to the bath," she whispered to Em. "I'll get your brother."

Em obeyed, grabbing the sparkly pink bag off the rear seat. Serena got Max out of the car seat and juggled her handbag as she fished her keys from her pocket. As soon as she pushed open the solid-oak entry door, she carried her son to his room, pulling off his tiny trainers as she went. She put him in bed fully clothed and pulled the duvet up over him. With any luck, he'd be so tired from the late supper and playing at Jamie's house that he would sleep all the way through the night.

Fat chance, Serena thought. He'd barely slept through an entire night since he was born, which meant that Serena had gotten good at pretending she wasn't sleep deprived and passing off her forgetfulness as busyness.

"Mum?" Em called. "Are you going to tuck me in?"

Serena slipped from Max's room and shut the door, then padded into the room next door, where Em was pulling on her pink pajamas. "That was the fastest bath in the history of baths."

"You didn't say to take a bath," Em said with a shrug, climbing beneath the covers. "You just said to *go* to the bath."

Serena chuckled and perched on the edge of the bed. "You know how much I love you, don't you?"

"More than chocolate?"

Serena pretended to think for a moment. "That's a hard one, but yes, more than chocolate. Now why don't you say your bedtime prayers?"

Listening to Em thank God for her blessings as she did every night—her family, her toys, their pretty house—Serena couldn't help the pang of disquiet that crept into her. She pushed it deep down while she pressed a kiss to her daughter's forehead, then turned on Em's desk lamp in the corner before turning off the overhead light. Still, the restlessness dogged her all the way down the hall to her stark, massive bedroom.

She sat on the edge of the bed, staring at her plush surroundings as though they were foreign. In some ways, they were. Edward had chosen this sprawling home, with its extensive grounds and water view, just as he'd hired the decorator to redo the interior in his particular contemporary taste. Had she been given a choice, she never would have chosen the sharp lines and bright-white walls that dominated the home, especially when her style leaned toward cozy wood and fluffy duvets that invited you to curl up in bed with a cup of tea. After her husband's death, Serena had considered moving into Inverness's charming city center, which was more in line with her own tastes, but by then they were firmly established in their suburban routine. There was no reason to inject any more uncertainty into their lives.

Even so, she couldn't deny that what Jamie had suggested intrigued her. She'd grown up on Skye, unlike her brothers, who had gone to boarding school, and she'd spent nearly as much time at the hotel as she had at her own house. If she were honest, she also missed working. She'd loved her job managing a gallery in Edinburgh before she met Edward. Loved finding talented artists. Loved marketing and promoting their work. Maybe the hotel wasn't the same thing, but it would be a challenge to both her mind and her creativity, something that had been sorely lacking in the past decade.

But what Jamie suggested required more than occasional visits, whatever he might say now. She would need to be there weekly, if not full-time. What would all that back-and-forth do to the kids? They'd already been through so much change in the past three years. Didn't she owe it to them to keep their lives as stable as possible?

No. No matter how much Daniel's assumptions had rankled last night, her most important job was to be a mother to her two children. They needed her even more now that she had to be both mum and dad. Just because the career change hadn't been entirely of her own choosing didn't mean she wasn't going to devote herself completely to the domestic life.

She managed to bury all thoughts of the hotel and art for the rest of the evening, but not long after she got home from dropping Em off at school the next morning, her mobile rang, flashing the school's phone number on the screen. Her heart seized for what felt like a full minute. She answered cautiously.

"Mrs. Stewart, this is Ada Douglass in the Highlands Academy office. Dr. Clark has asked if you would be able to come speak with him this morning."

"Is something wrong? Is Em all right?"

"Emmy is fine, Mrs. Stewart. May I tell Dr. Clark you're coming?"

"I'll be right there." Serena clicked off, her heart jump-starting to a hammer this time. It was the call she'd been dreading—the one that signaled the end of the art program and her employment at Highlands Academy—but that didn't make it any less painful. "Come, Maxie love. We need to go back to school. You can eat your biscuit in the car."

Max didn't protest when she hoisted him on her hip and carried him to the car, too focused on the biscuit's chocolate coating melting over his fist. The entire drive to school, she rehearsed her speech about why the school was making a colossal mistake by cutting their art and music programs, and how the arts were as crucial to the development of young minds as math and science. But deep down she knew it wouldn't do any good. This summons meant it was already too late.

Serena parked in front of the converted Victorian mansion that housed Highlands Academy and stared at the brownstone edifice for a long moment. Between teaching art, volunteering, and serving on several committees, she spent a good chunk of her life here. It was hard to accept that it was coming to an end.

"Mummy, my hands are sticky."

She twisted in her seat to see Max holding out his chocolate-covered palms, just before he gave one of them a lick. "Hold up, monkey." She rummaged in her handbag for some hand wipes and reached back to clean away the last traces of his snack. "Are you ready to go now? Can you be a good lad while Mummy has her meeting?"

Max grinned, an expression that meant either agreement or that he was hatching a plan decidedly incompatible with being a good lad. She chuckled. Her son possessed equal measures of mischief and charm, which made it difficult to discipline him as she ought.

Serena marched Max up the front steps, holding one of his hands while clutching the strap of her shoulder bag with the other. She proceeded straight to the wood-paneled office on the right, what would have been the house's parlor.

Ada Douglass, the school secretary, sat at a massive wood desk, the phone pressed to her ear. She held up a finger, but Serena thought she saw something akin to sympathy light in her eyes. When she put down the phone, she said, "Thank you for coming so promptly. You can go on through. Dr. Clark is waiting for you in his office."

"No need. I'm here." Dr. Eliot Clark smiled at Serena as he crossed the room, his hand outstretched. "I hope you haven't been waiting long. Please, let's speak in my office."

Sixtysomething with a full head of neatly combed white hair, the school's headmaster possessed a stern air that always made Serena nervous, even when he was being welcoming. She led Max into the small room with its glass-paned door and took a seat in the wingback chair before another massive mahogany desk. Her son immediately climbed onto her lap and began playing with his stuffed giraffe.

"Mrs. Stewart, I know you're familiar with the problems that Emmy has been having at school."

Serena blinked. They were here to talk about Em's behavior, not about Serena's teaching position? "I know there was an altercation with another girl earlier this year, but I was led to believe that it was resolved."

"So was I." Dr. Clark sighed and folded his hands. "We've been patient with Emmy because of all she's been through. It's not easy losing a parent, but I'm afraid we can't overlook physical violence."

"Violence? Em? I don't believe it."

"There were several witnesses, Mrs. Stewart, including her teacher. Emmy clearly struck another student and yanked her hair."

Serena just stared. That didn't sound like Em, the least violent child she'd ever met. Bookish, quiet, endured her younger brother's annoyances with admirable patience. "Who started it?"

Dr. Clark shifted uncomfortably.

"Right," Serena said. "Em claims that the other girl did, but you don't believe it."

"I'm afraid neither of them has been forthcoming about the situation. But regardless, this is an offense that would normally lead to expulsion."

Expulsion. Her eight-year-old daughter kicked out of school for fighting. Serena felt as if the chair had collapsed beneath her. She held more tightly to Max, who was squirming on her lap, and focused on the single word she had initially overlooked. "Normally?"

Another sigh, this one with a resigned smile. "Typically we would take disciplinary action. But we are not without sympathy for your situation. Out of respect for you and your late husband, we think it would be better that you have the opportunity to withdraw your daughter from Highlands Academy."

"And do what? Put her in another school for the last four months of the year?"

"Frankly, Mrs. Stewart, that's your concern now. But she will not be admitted back for the new term."

Serena swallowed hard. When they said out of respect for her husband, they meant out of respect for the massive donations that Edward and his company had made to the school. Sunspring Energy was the reason Highlands Academy even existed: it had been formed expressly for the families of executives who didn't want to send their children to Edinburgh or Glasgow for a proper prep-school education. She supposed she should be grateful for the consideration, but right now she merely felt numb.

"I'm very sorry there isn't more I can do. Emmy is a

delightful child, but we simply can't be seen to allow this kind of behavior. I'm sure you understand."

"What I understand is that neither girl is owning up to what happened, and yet you've singled my daughter out for punishment." Serena rose, hoisting Max with her. "Send Em down and we'll be going."

"There's some paperwork that needs to be—"

"I'll post it back to you."

Dr. Clark cleared his throat. "Then there's the issue of your classes."

Serena fixed him with a hard look, and whatever he saw there made him drop the subject. Whether he was going to fire her or say he expected her to stay on, she wouldn't be setting foot in this school again. She hiked her handbag over her shoulder and gave him a sharp nod. "Good-bye, Dr. Clark."

She carried Max from the office into the high-ceilinged foyer, assuming that the staff was hurrying Em down. When her daughter finally did arrive, dressed in her tartan pinafore and navy-blue cardigan, she wore a hangdog look that said she was expecting a tirade. "Mum, I'm sorry. I didn't—"

Serena put a hand on her shoulder and squeezed gently. "We'll talk about it later."

Em let out a long breath. "What happens now?"

They broke out the front doors, where the sun was struggling to cut through the gray clouds. Serena inhaled the frigid air, and all her excuses to Jamie, all the reasons she'd given for staying in Nairn, fell away.

"I think," Serena said slowly, "we're going to Skye."

CHAPTER TWO

A MONTH LATER SERENA STOOD on the shore of the Sound of Sleat beneath a steel-gray sky, the wind pulling tendrils from her plait and working its way beneath the hem of her field jacket. Somehow when she'd made the dramatic pronouncement on the steps of Highlands Academy, she'd thought their departure would happen more quickly. But the massive sheaf of paperwork involved in liquidating her investments and repurchasing her share of the hotel paled in comparison to the effort of extracting Em from school and enrolling her on Skye for the summer term, not to mention pausing activities and gym memberships and all the trappings of a life that she'd taken for granted in Nairn.

Now she watched the gentle lap of waves on the shore and breathed in the cold salt air, feeling the first measure of peace in weeks settle over her. The children were still up the road at Aunt Muriel's, sleeping off their late arrival and giving Serena a few unaccustomed moments alone. She'd been back to Skye frequently in the past few years, but this felt different—like a homecoming. Even with the changes to the hotel, the landscape was as familiar as her own features: the swaying grasses and scrubby brush from which the whitewashed buildings of Isleornsay's village sprang; the slim white lighthouse in the sound; the mysterious cover of fog that hovered over the water and reflected abstract patterns onto its dark, glassy surface. She inhaled the smell of the sea and damp foliage for a moment longer, then turned away from the water.

She cut through a field that was just beginning to show the first bits of green, its usual wildflowers delayed by the unseasonably cold weather; then she circled around the front entrance of the MacDonald Guest House. Even with the addition that had expanded and modernized the function of the hotel, it retained the old-fashioned charm inherent in the original whitewashed stone and mullioned windows. Andrea and Jamie had done a wonderful job transforming it from a modest regional guesthouse into an international holiday destination.

Serena stepped inside the hotel, where already the smell of food and the clatter from the kitchen spoke of breakfast being prepared, and the low hum of voices from the dining room to her left told her at least a few guests had found their way downstairs this early. The reception desk sat empty. From the looks of the car park, the hotel was full, and guests often checked out early in order to make afternoon flights from Inverness. Didn't they have a receptionist? Where was the hotel manager Jamie had hired?

While she was standing baffled in the foyer, a young couple appeared, dressed too warmly for a day of sightseeing, even considering the chilly temperatures outside. They brightened when they saw Serena.

"Do you work here?" the woman asked. "We've just arrived, and we don't want to miss anything."

Her pronounced Spanish accent explained the puffy down coats. Guests from southern Europe always regarded Scotland as one step below the Arctic Circle.

"I'd be happy to make some suggestions." Serena rounded the desk and found a paper tourist map of the island in one of the drawers. She highlighted a driving route in bright-yellow marker. "Since you're already equipped for the cold, you must do a little stargazing. We have more Dark Sky sites than anywhere else in Europe."

The couple exchanged looks, clearly intrigued by the idea.

"Why don't I print out another map and some star charts for you and leave them here at the desk? You can pick them up when you get back."

"Gracias," the man said. "Thank you for your help."

"Of course. I hope you enjoy your holiday on Skye." As soon as the couple left, Serena did as she'd promised, looking up several star charts and printing them out. Then she took out a fresh copy of the map and highlighted the locations of the nearest Dark Sky Discovery Sites. This hadn't exactly been her intention in coming to the hotel, but at least she could do something useful while she was here.

The dull thump of feet on the stairs made her turn to the

wooden staircase, where a couple, dressed for a day of hiking, carried down their trolley cases.

"Checking out?" Serena asked politely.

The young woman flipped her ginger ponytail. "We are. We're hiking the Quiraing today before we head back to Manchester."

"Ah, you picked a good day for it. We've a lot of fog today, but there's rain forecast the rest of the week."

The man fished his room key from his pocket and handed it to Serena. She hesitated, momentarily at a loss. Clearly she couldn't just take the key and send them on their way, but she had no idea whether or not they'd been given a bill when they checked in or if it had been slipped under the door. She sat down at the padded chair in front of the computer and quickly keyed in Muriel's password, blessing her aunt for suggesting she take it with her. The number on the door key helped her pull up the reservation, and she quickly printed the receipt for the account, which appeared to be paid in full. She handed the paper across the desk to them with a smile. "Thank you for staying with us. We hope to see you again."

"Cheers," the girl said brightly, and then they were out the front door into the gravel lot.

Serena turned back to the booking system and frowned. She could have sworn she had just checked them out of the room, but it still showed it occupied. Had she missed a step? She pressed a key, and the computer beeped obnoxiously at her. She tried again and earned another beep for her efforts.

"What are you doing?"

Serena swiveled in the chair, awash in guilt before she could remind herself that she had nothing to feel guilty about. "I was just . . ."

The rest of her sentence faded as she took in the man standing behind her, his arms crossed over his chest. He was taller than she—though who wasn't?—with the broad, muscular build of a rugby player and the scowl to match. Sandy blond hair, dark eyes, a couple of days' growth on his face that suggested he couldn't be bothered to shave, rather than a legitimate attempt at a beard. A tickle of memory at the back of her suddenly sluggish mind told her this must be the new manager, even if his jeans and battered leather jacket read more nightclub bouncer than sophisticated hotel supervisor.

Serena swallowed hard and dragged her eyes from the way his T-shirt stretched over his chest, cursing the flutter of attraction that started low in her stomach. Instead, she rose and stuck out her hand. "Malcolm Blake, I presume. I'm Serena Stewart."

He made no move to shake her hand. "I know who you are. We met last summer. What are you doing here?"

"At the moment, manning the front desk, which was conspicuously empty when our guests wanted to check out."

"*Our* guests?"

"Yes, *our* guests."

He stared at her, unblinking, and a little chill ran down her spine, not altogether unpleasant. "And why is that?"

"As of this week, I am once more part owner of the MacDonald Guest House."

"I don't understand."

"Jamie sold me back my share."

"Why?"

His hard tone finally loosened the logjam in her brain, and she drew herself up straighter. "I'm not sure that's any of your business."

He wiped a hand over his face. "What I mean is, James and Ian have been perfectly content to check in with me via phone and e-mail, and up until this point, they seemed satisfied with the way I run the hotel. Why, now, are you here, Mrs. Stewart?"

Somehow, on his lips, the title seemed dismissive, as if the fact she was a married—or formerly married—woman with children meant she had no business overseeing the health of her investment. "I imagine you know, Mr. Blake. I would appreciate if you could find some time in your busy schedule to take me through the inner workings of the hotel." She held up a hand. "Just so I understand everything that's being done here."

He gave her a bare, closemouthed smile. "Of course. I'd be delighted. Perhaps the first lesson should be on the proper way of using the booking system?" He nodded toward the computer. "Since you seem to be about to change one of my custom scripts?"

She turned her head back to the error message, behind which was a window filled with unreadable code. A slow flush heated her cheeks. She could hardly be angry with his tone when she had indeed been about to do that. Somehow. "Yes. I think perhaps that would be a good idea."

He gave her a suspicious look, obviously not buying her cooperative attitude, then leaned past her to the computer. The scent of a clean, outdoorsy cologne wafted around her, mixing with the scent of leather. Another unaccustomed pulse of heat slugged her in the stomach, choking the breath in her lungs. She leaned away from him while he closed the windows with a few keystrokes.

"May I?" he asked.

She practically leaped out of the chair. "Of course."

He barely looked at her as he plopped into the seat, his fingers flying over the keyboard with surprising accuracy. "Let's start with your own user account. Is 'sstewart' okay with you?"

"Fine," she murmured.

A few more clicks and keystrokes, and he stood again, gesturing back to the chair. "There you go. You're logged in."

"My password?"

"*Safezone*, lowercase, all one word."

"Oh?"

A slight smile tipped up the corner of his mouth. No, not a smile. A smirk. "I gave you the safest level of user privileges. There's no way you can delete anything important. As the new owner, I'm sure you realize how disruptive it would be if I had to take time out from my other duties to fix the booking module again."

He was laughing at her, and it made her want to smack that look off his handsome face. No matter what she might think of his manners, he was good-looking. "Yes, quite disruptive. And since you're so busy, I'm sure you won't mind an extra pair of hands around the hotel. You can show me every last detail of what it is you do here all day."

His smile faded. "Whatever you want, Mrs. Stewart, I'm happy to comply."

"Yes," she said, enjoying for a single moment the shift of power in her favor. "I'm sure you are."

Malcolm Blake knew when he was stuck, and by the satisfied little smile on Serena Stewart's face, he figured he'd have a better chance of prying a bear trap from his leg than shaking his new boss off his tail. Rotten timing too. The guesthouse was packed, and he hadn't even begun to address the two dozen issues that had met him the minute he walked in the door. No, the quickest way to get rid of her was to indulge her sudden urge to play innkeeper until she got bored and moved on to something else. With any luck, he could impress her with his work ethic and send her on her way by lunch. No matter what she might think of him, he took pride in his work. He wasn't going to let some snap judgment from the new owner negate everything he'd accomplished since he'd been hired.

"You might want to change first," he said finally.

"What's wrong with the way I'm dressed?"

Absolutely nothing, he wanted to say, but he wouldn't be able to keep the note of appreciation from his voice. Not to mention the fact it summoned his attention back to the very things he'd been trying to ignore. A man would have to be blind—or dead—not to notice how the fuzzy lavender sweater accentuated her lush curves or how the tight dark jeans hugged slim legs down to where they disappeared into the tops of her brown riding boots. He jerked his eyes back to her face, but that didn't help much, considering his enduring weakness for the contrast of pale skin and dark hair. Especially when it was paired with blue eyes the exact color of the sound outside.

He blew out his breath and hoped it could be passed off as irritation. Serena Stewart didn't seem the type to endure being ogled by the help, even if he could have sworn she'd been staring at his pecs. "Suit yourself. I've got to bring in a few cases of liquor to the bar later, and I'd hate for your nice clothes to get damaged." Especially considering those riding boots probably cost more than his car.

She frowned at him. "I'm fine. I'm not wearing an evening gown. But why exactly aren't the deliverymen doing this for you?"

"This is Skye, love. I am the deliveryman. I swung by the distillery this morning to pick up our order."

"Then I'm glad to help." She put on a sweet smile, beneath which he figured she was cursing his parentage and his very existence on the planet.

"I need to do a couple of things first. Think you can keep yourself occupied in the meantime?"

"I'll just shadow you. You can show me the ropes."

Make sure he met her standards, more like. But he only nodded and kept his sharp comments to himself. Irritating or not, this woman held his livelihood in her hands. And as much as he hated to admit it, this was the only decent-paying job he'd found since moving back to Skye. He couldn't afford to lose it. Pride, as important as it was to him, wasn't enough to pay the bills.

In the next hour he checked out four guests—without managing to erase anything vitally important—then started the task of cleaning the two rooms that would be occupied later that night. They did have housekeepers, one who worked weekdays and the other who worked weekends, but the weekday maid had called in sick just before he came to reception that morning. He grinned as he thrust a pile of dirty linens into Serena's arms, expecting her to suddenly remember an urgent appointment elsewhere. Instead, she helped gamely, not a single complaint escaping her lips, even when he directed her to scrub the sink and toilet. She might be a princess, but she was a stubborn princess.

Once the rooms were turned over, he led her out to the

car park, where his black Ford hatchback waited, the paint splashed with mud from the recent rains. He usually only stocked the bar on Sundays when it was closed, but last night's unexpected turnout to their live-music event had left them low on local spirits. No point in waiting on the delivery-men he'd pretended they didn't have when the distillery was just a few minutes' drive up the island.

"Grab a box," he said, "if it's not too heavy for you."

Serena shot him a challenging look and hefted a case of a dozen bottles from the boot, if not easily, then with far less effort than he would have expected from her. He picked up one as well and preceded her inside, nodding toward the polished bar. She was so short that she couldn't lift the box high enough to get it over the edge. She set it on one of the barstools. He fought a smile.

"Why are you laughing? You're not the only one who works out."

His grin broke free. She'd been checking him out all right. His snobbish princess of a new boss had been noticing him as much as he'd noticed her. Even if she didn't remember him.

That's the real issue, isn't it? She made an impression on you when you last met, but you're too far beneath her for her to remember your face. If he were smart, he'd abandon all the ridiculous thoughts that had plagued him since she walked through the door. But he wasn't that smart or that dis-ciplined, which meant his best bet was to stick to the original plan and send her on her way as quickly as possible, out of the realm of temptation.

As soon as they had carried all the boxes in from his car, she leaned against the mahogany bar top. "Would you show me the storeroom and your inventory methods now?"

CARLA LAUREANO

He nodded, even though he had to clamp his teeth down on a smart response before he did. By the time he was finished, he'd also shown Serena the point-of-sale system and cash drawer, the menu, and pretty much every minute detail she could think to ask about.

With each new question, his ability to keep his cool faltered. She might be fit, but she was most definitely a micromanager.

"You know, James and Ian seemed perfectly content to let me run the place," he said finally. "Why don't you just come out and say what concerns you?"

"Nothing concerns me. But if you've not noticed, James and Ian are rarely here, which is exactly why I bought back my share. It's a pretty poor business strategy to back away and let someone else make all the decisions."

"The help, you mean."

"Someone without a vested interest in the success of the venture." She drew herself up as if she could add inches to her tiny frame out of sheer will.

"You don't think I have a vested interest? If I don't do well, I don't get paid. I imagine that makes me more invested than you."

"Considering this property has been in my family for generations, I very much doubt that."

He flinched. Of course she was going to pull rank. She was an owner; he was just the hired help. And if he were smart, he would surgically remove his foot from his mouth and apologize. But the *I'm sorry* froze on his lips. He wasn't sorry at all. Instead, he cleared his throat. "What's the verdict then?"

She lifted her chin, and for the first time she looked uncomfortable. "I think you're doing a fine job."

"What?"

"You have everything under control. Your inventory methods are probably more stringent than necessary considering the size of the bar, but I appreciate the precautions you've made in locking down the stock. You clearly have a better grasp of the computer system than I do—" a faint self-deprecating smile surfaced on her lips—"and judging from the reviews of the hotel online, guests are perfectly satisfied with the service."

"Then why all the questions, if not because you thought I wasn't doing my job?"

"Because you're only one man, and from what I can tell, the hotel is understaffed. If I'm to properly assess personnel needs, I need to know every detail of the hotel operations. Unless, of course, you enjoy changing bed linens and scrubbing bathrooms?"

The hint of humor in her tone and the subtle lift of her eyebrows began to thaw his attitude toward her until he realized she'd played on his fear of being sacked to put him through the wringer today. He kept his own expression impassive. "I will defer to your judgment on that matter."

Her eyes narrowed slightly. "I'll get out of your way and let you finish your work then. I wouldn't want to be the one interfering with your ability to do your job."

"It was a pleasure, Mrs. Stewart."

"I highly doubt that, Mr. Blake."

Malcolm bit back his automatic response and gave her the most courteous nod he could summon. She flipped her ponytail over her shoulder and strode from the bar without a backward glance. He rubbed both hands through his hair with a groan.

He'd made a complete mess of that. He might be good with guests, but he was rubbish with authority. And like it or not, the new owner, Serena Stewart, had made it abundantly clear that she was in charge.

CHAPTER THREE

SERENA DROVE BACK to her aunt's house, a cold kernel of disquiet forming in the pit of her stomach. That hadn't gone at all as she'd hoped. She'd thought coming back to Skye to oversee the continued growth of the MacDonald Guest House would be a way to utilize her long-buried business skills, as well as a pleasant diversion from days that would otherwise be spent with household chores.

And yet she'd barely set foot in the hotel before Malcolm Blake had taken a dislike to her, greeting her with distrust if not outright hostility. What had she done to earn such a harsh reception?

The familiar sick feeling of worry washed over her as she began to catalog their interactions before she cut it off. No, this was not her fault. She had made a mistake with the booking system, but she'd done nothing to incite the level of ire he'd shown. The problem wasn't her; it was him.

And that problem was a big one. His surliness immediately put her back into a frame of mind she'd worked hard to break out of. Not to mention the little fact of her physical reaction to him. Even remembering how he'd inadvertently pressed up against her sent another shiver of anticipation through her.

Malcolm Blake might despise her, but she'd noticed him looking her over with far more interest than was proper to show toward one's boss. And she'd brought it on herself, simply because of her involuntary response to the scent of masculine cologne mixed with leather.

Nice one, Serena. The fact that he's good-looking and smells amazing doesn't mitigate the fact that he's a miserable git.

She pulled up in front of her aunt's house, a simple clapboard structure painted in soothing tones of white and gray, and slammed the gear lever into first before she turned off the car. The front door opened, and Max raced out at full tilt. She jumped from the car and caught him just as he sprang at her, then hoisted him onto her hip. He wrapped his arms and legs around her and smacked a wet kiss on her cheek. "Hi, Mummy."

"Hi, monkey! Did you have a good day with Auntie?"

"Mmm-hmm. We had shape sandwiches."

She shifted her son as she retrieved her handbag from the car, then nudged the door shut with her leg. Max was only three, but he was getting heavy. Adjusting her grip again, she trudged up the macadam walkway to the front door. "Shape sandwiches, huh? With cookie cutters?"

"Yes. I had a dinosaur. Em did hearts."

"Very nice. Auntie is a fun babysitter, isn't she?"

"Mmm-hmm. She gave us caramels too."

Serena chuckled and planted a kiss on top of his messy hair before she let him down on the front stoop. When she pushed the door open, the delicious smell of roasting meat drifted from the kitchen. She inhaled deeply. No matter how infrequently they came back to Serena's childhood residence, it always felt like home: the floral upholstery, the antique lace curtains, the scent of cooking food. It was as though time never passed in Muriel's presence.

"Mum, you're back!" Em looked from her spot on the sofa, where she was curled up with a thick book. "How's the hotel?"

"Fine." Serena perched on the edge of the sofa and gave her daughter a sideways hug. "Did you have a good day?"

"Yeah, Auntie let us collect sea glass and shells down by the water until it got too cold. And then Max and I helped with dinner."

"It smells delicious. I can't wait. Where is she?"

"I'm in here, dear," Muriel called from the kitchen. She appeared at the doorway, wearing trousers and a silky blouse, her silvery hair as perfectly coiffed as ever. She wiped her hands on a tea towel and accepted Serena's kiss on the cheek.

"Were the children good for you?" Serena asked, casting a mock-warning look at her kids, who donned *Who, me?* expressions in response.

"They were perfect angels." Muriel winked in their direction, and they grinned as if they were getting away with something. Serena's heart swelled. She'd hoped that the warm, homey atmosphere on Skye would be good for them, but she'd forgotten how much she herself had missed Muriel. Impulsively she reached out and hugged her.

"What was that for, dear?"

"I missed you, and I'm really happy to be back."

Muriel suppressed a smile. "Well. It's nice to have you back too. I could use some help in the kitchen. Come, child."

Serena's brow furrowed, but she followed obediently. Muriel never needed help in the kitchen. In fact, she was the one who had taught Jamie to cook as a boy, and she was almost as good as he was, which was why she normally waved everyone out of her way into other parts of the house. Clearly there was something on her mind.

"I had a little talk with Em today." Muriel retrieved two mugs from the cupboard and poured already-brewed tea into both of them. "Why didn't you tell me she was expelled?"

Serena deflated. She should have told Muriel the real reason they'd decided to come to Skye for summer term, but she'd not known how to broach the subject. It felt like something that was best addressed in person. "She wasn't expelled. I withdrew her because it was a hostile environment in which to learn."

Muriel's expression said she didn't make the distinction. "She told me she pulled a girl's hair because, in her words, 'Sophie is a stroppy cow.'"

Serena smothered a laugh. Em had told her the same thing, even though she had refused to elaborate further. "In my opinion, she's absolutely right. I have no doubt that Sophie began whatever caused Em to act out, but Sophie's father happens to be the one who took Edward's position after he died."

"You think that might have had something to do with it?"

"I don't know. But since Sunspring Energy is the reason the school even exists, you know they don't want to do anything to offend their biggest patrons."

"Same old story." Muriel looked at her sympathetically. "So she's going to be attending Sleat Primary."

"She starts next week. I decided to enroll her in the Gaelic Medium course."

"Even though she doesn't speak Gaelic?"

Muriel didn't mean the words as criticism, but they pierced all the same. Serena took a long swallow of her tea before she answered. "She speaks some. We've been working on it at home, and the head teacher assured me Em can be brought up to proficiency. She's so ahead of her class in academics, it won't have any long-term effects on her education. Besides, it's only one term, and then she'll be back to school in Nairn in the autumn."

"You know, Serena, you have nothing to feel guilty about. Skye is part of your heritage. It was unfair for Edward to make you give it up. Even though you abided by his wishes while he was alive, you have the right to make different choices now that he's gone."

"Who says I feel guilty?" Serena said sharply. Muriel just smiled in that kind, knowing way that made Serena feel bad for her response, and she moved on uncomfortably. "In any case, they've allowed me to enroll Max in the Gaelic nursery class, even though he's starting late. Then I won't need to rely on you to babysit him while I'm at the hotel."

"And how did that go?"

"Fine." Even to her own ears, her tone wasn't entirely convincing. "Mr. Blake seems to have things well in hand, even if he is somewhat . . . surly."

41

"Had a bit of a run-in, did you?"

"I wouldn't say that. I merely asked him to show me around the hotel, and he acted like it was a huge inconvenience. He assumes just because I want to know how the whole thing works that I'm questioning his judgment."

"Well, dear, you do like to be in charge."

"Aunt Muriel! Are you calling me bossy?"

Muriel shrugged, but there was a glint of mischief in her pale eyes. "I'm just saying that when you have two people who like to do things their own way, sometimes sparks are going to fly."

An involuntary flush crept up Serena's neck into her cheeks. "I would say mild irritation, not sparks. *Sparks* implies something else entirely. Besides, as far as the hotel's concerned, I *am* in charge."

"Of course. My mistake." Muriel sipped her own tea. "I certainly hope you two can come to an understanding, considering you're likely to be in close proximity to each other."

"Trust me, I plan to have as little contact with him as possible. He can stick to his regular management duties, and I'll work on marketing and guest satisfaction. There's no reason for us to have much contact at all."

"Whatever you say, dear." Muriel's tone was perfectly innocent, but something in her expression told Serena that the subject was far from dropped.

CHAPTER FOUR

BEING THE YOUNGEST IN THE FAMILY might have gotten Malcolm his way more often than not, but leave it to his sister, Nicola, to win in the end, even from the afterlife.

In fact, he imagined her looking down from heaven at him with a big "I told you so" grin as he pulled into her old house with its rutted, gravel-strewn drive. After all the ways she'd tried to get him to return to Skye, after all his excuses about it not being the right time, he'd never thought the words *legal guardian* would be the ones that finally dragged him back.

It wasn't that Skye wasn't beautiful—he could admit he enjoyed its expansive, ever-changing sky, the wildness of untouched grasses and deep-blue water. The landscape was one of the few things that could make someone like him wax poetic, even in his own mind. But with every stunning vista came a dozen bad memories, things he'd rather leave in his past.

Malcolm parked behind the red Volkswagen Polo already in the driveway and made his way to the front door of the two-story croft house in the fading light, noting the peeling paint on the shutters and the sinking patches in the stone pathway. He'd need to address those when the weather turned. Forcing his key into the sticky lock, he broke through to the dark-paneled mudroom, where he hung his jacket on a peg. The tiny space was meant to act as a buffer between the cold outside air and the inside warmth, but mostly it acted as a tripping hazard, cluttered with shoes and coats and rucksacks. He took a moment to straighten the pile of footwear before continuing into the hallway.

The entry was dark. From his vantage point in front of the stairs, he could see both the living room, with its scattered toss pillows, and the dining room table still covered with the morning paper, but there was no sign of his niece. "Kylee? Are you home?"

In response, a frantic scratching accompanied by jingling came from the kitchen as a fluff ball of a dog bounded into the hallway, its silly face twisted in an expression of ecstasy. Malcolm bent down and scooped up Kylee's Cavalier King Charles spaniel, and within seconds its pink tongue was slobbering all over his face.

"Don't lick, Ainsley," Malcolm said sternly, but he didn't have the heart to do much more. The silly thing barely even qualified as a dog, but the spaniel had decided to immediately adore him, going so far as to split his nights between Malcolm's bed and Kylee's.

He set Ainsley down, and the animal danced around for a moment, then cocked his head as if waiting for instructions.

"Where's our girl?"

Malcolm glanced at his watch, then realized it was Wednesday. Kylee's best friend, Lane, always picked her up before their practice for the high school's Gaelic choir. Kylee had chosen the activity less out of a desire to connect with her cultural heritage than because it was the closest she could get to a proper voice coach on the island.

On his way to the kitchen, he pulled out his mobile and texted Kylee: Home at the usual time? Dinner ready in an hour. If you could count putting a frozen lasagna in the outdated kitchen's old-fashioned oven as dinner. When it was Kylee's night to cook, they ate well, thanks to Nicola's thorough parenting. His nights were a different story. The best he could say was that they wouldn't starve.

With an hour on the timer and a quiet house, there was little to do with his time. He grabbed a sweatshirt and made his way out into the patchy back garden, where a large boxing bag hung from the wooden frame of Kylee's old play set, the swings long discarded. It was barely sturdy enough to take the impact, but he'd been too busy to make a proper stand or to reinforce the frame.

Only when he was already standing in front of the bag did he realize he'd neglected to grab his hand wraps and gloves on the way out. Never mind. It wasn't as if he were intending a full session anyway. Just some light contact to work out the kinks in his muscles and the lingering frustration over the new woman in his life who seemed determined to make him miserable.

He settled comfortably into his boxing stance—orthodox,

even though he was left handed—and circled the bag, throwing jabs and one-two combinations, just enough to touch the vinyl covering as if he were testing distance against an opponent. He'd done this as a warm-up drill so many times in the past twenty years that he didn't need to think about it, but he forced himself to concentrate and keep his eyes focused. It was too easy to get into bad habits when all he had to train with was a heavy bag—habits he'd have to unlearn if he ever got into the ring again.

Not that it was likely, considering the lack of a proper boxing club on Skye. He hadn't competed since his late teens, even though he had spent several evenings a week at a gym in Baltimore. It was a good way to work out the kinks that came from sitting in front of a screen all day. His girlfriend hadn't minded the effect on his body either. *"Hard to remember you're a geek when you look like that,"* she'd teased.

The thought of Teresa made him throw more power behind his next punch than he intended, and he cringed the second he made contact. He didn't need to see the smear of blood on the bag to know his knuckles had split open on the cold, inflexible vinyl. He dropped his guard and stepped back, breathing deeply while his heart rate returned to normal. It wasn't even that he missed Teresa, really. Not as he once had. She was just another reminder of how his plans had gotten derailed.

Malcolm fished his phone from his pocket to see if Kylee had responded—she hadn't—then walked back to the kitchen, where he soaked his injured fist under the cold tap for a minute. There would be no hiding this one. He was careful with his hands, considering he worked with guests all day, and now he looked as if he had gotten into a bar fight. It would be the perfect excuse for Serena to complain if she were looking for one.

The buzzer on the oven went off just as he heard the rattle of the front-door lock. Malcolm grabbed a folded towel from the countertop and yanked open the oven door. Even through the towel's layers, the heat from the foil pan singed his fingers. He juggled the pan to the counter, then grabbed a couple of plates from the cupboard. "Just in time! Dinner's ready."

Kylee's rucksack hit the floor in the lounge with a familiar thud, and his niece appeared in the kitchen doorway a minute later. "What are we having?"

"I made lasagna." Malcolm cut healthy portions from the tin and put them on stoneware plates.

"You mean you heated lasagna?"

"Same difference. Here, I'll take our plates if you'll grab the flatware."

Kylee rummaged in the drawer for forks and knives and followed him to the dining room, where he placed the plates on the table with a thunk.

"You know, you could serve something green on your nights," she said as she settled into her chair.

"Why? Tomatoes are vegetables."

Kylee rolled her eyes, but she was smiling. He watched her arrange her fork and knife properly beside her plate, struck by how much she looked like her mother at the same age. Dark-blonde hair; green eyes; tall, slim frame. Her mannerisms were even the same: her habit of tucking a piece of hair behind her ear, the way she smoothed the paper serviette into quarters. Not for the first time, he felt a pang of regret that he'd let his bad memories damage his relationship with Nicola. Being here with Kylee was almost like getting a second chance.

"Grace?" she prompted.

"You do it."

She bowed her head and said a quick prayer, then dug into her food. "You heat up a wicked frozen lasagna, Uncle Mal."

He chuckled. "I aim to please. Friday night I might defrost a shepherd's pie."

Kylee made a face. "No, thank you."

"So, how was your day?"

It was the obligatory parent question, and it always earned the obligatory teenage shrug. Today was no different, though it was followed by the ever-enlightening "Okay."

"Just okay?"

"Lane's decided to go to London for university."

Ah, now it made sense. Kylee had applied to a number of schools, both in the United Kingdom and in the States, but she'd received only one acceptance letter so far. None of her top choices were in London, where her best friend would be moving. He diverted the conversation away from friend drama and toward something he could actually help with. "What are we still waiting on?"

"Berklee, UCLA, and the Royal Conservatoire." She put down her fork. "What if I don't get in anywhere good?"

"You will." Also part of the script.

"But what if I don't?"

"I don't know, Kylee. I guess we'll deal with it when we come to it. But listen—" he nudged her hand across the table—"you are an amazing singer. I have faith in you. And you can always attend a junior college in America and transfer in somewhere as a sophomore. There are plenty of voice coaches in the States." If he got his old job back at the research institute at Johns Hopkins, he could actually afford to pay for it.

"I guess," she said doubtfully. He knew how she felt. When he was her age, he'd been desperate to get out of Glasgow and on with the rest of his life. Skye wasn't exactly the same, but it had to feel hopelessly small to a talented girl with dreams of being a famous singer-songwriter.

"Maybe I'll just study something boring like science," she muttered.

"Don't tease me, young lady. My old heart can't take the shock."

That earned a faint smile from her, which faded as she toyed with her fork. He recognized that look. It meant something was coming that he wouldn't like. "Can I ask you something?"

He was tempted to say no and avoid the issue, but that probably wasn't an example of good parenting. Cautiously he nodded.

"Do you remember that music festival I was talking about in Glasgow?"

"Mmm-hmm."

Kylee chewed her lip, then spilled out her words in one breath. "Lane actually managed to get tickets and her parents said she could go if she went with me. The term will be out and they were really hard to get—"

"Hold up. You want me to let two seventeen-year-old girls drive five hours to a festival that's as well known for its drug use as it is for its music?"

"I know, but Lane and I don't do any of that. I'm hoping that maybe you'll just think about it?"

"I'll think about it," he said, but her expression fell anyway, as if he'd said no. And he still might. He'd attended the festival a decade ago, and it had already been toeing the line between innocent fun and debauched hedonism. He could only imagine it had gotten worse over the years. Not someplace he wanted his sheltered, innocent niece and her even more innocent friend going alone, especially when Kylee looked twenty-two and already drew the wrong sort of attention.

Not that any male attention was the right kind when it came to his niece.

Kylee finished her meal in silence and piled her utensils on her plate. "May I be excused? I want to finish a song."

"Sure. My turn to do the dishes anyway."

As Malcolm filled the sink with soapy water a few minutes later, he heard the faint strum of a guitar from Kylee's room. He'd prepared himself for drama after her parents' death, and there had been no shortage of tears and bad attitudes, though like tonight, Kylee kept it mostly in check. He attributed it to the fact that almost immediately she had poured all her energy into her music and songwriting. But he always wondered if maybe it was just a way to delay the inevitable grieving, and it would explode in some unpredictable way.

Still, even if she was worried about her prospects, he wasn't in the least. He didn't need to know anything about music to recognize her determination. She might have lost both her parents, but he would do everything he could to make sure she didn't lose her dreams too.

CHAPTER FIVE

AFTER BREAKFAST THE NEXT MORNING, Serena left the children with Muriel and headed farther down the Sleat Peninsula toward Armadale. When she'd planned the temporary move to Skye, she'd known they wouldn't be able to stay with Muriel the whole time. Her aunt would have welcomed them, but considering Max's nightly awakenings and the fact that Muriel was a light sleeper, it was a better option to rent a holiday cottage. Unfortunately most of the options that would allow them to stay through August had already been booked, leaving only this little cottage about five miles away from Armadale Castle at the farthest end of the peninsula.

She drove slowly down the highway, taking care on the road left wet by the steady rain. Green was finally beginning to overtake the grays and browns of the winter-dormant foliage, a sure sign that spring was on its way. While she'd always secretly loved winter on Skye, when its rustic beauty was highlighted by a fine dusting of snow, the slow forward creep of the seasons held a particularly appropriate promise: a new beginning, bright life springing from a long, cold winter.

Serena followed the directions she'd scribbled on the back of an envelope, looking for the tree with the broken branch that would mark the otherwise-unsigned turnoff to the cottage's long drive. Her car's suspension thudded over the ruts in the road, jolting her all the way to her teeth. Water pooled in the little worn channels on the side of the road and filled the potholes left behind by winter ice, their glassy surface broken by a fine fall of rain.

She followed the winding drive up a gentle slope and parked in front of a tiny cottage. The structure's exterior was encouraging: neatly whitewashed stone, a fenced garden, a picnic bench on a gravel pad along one side. Clearly the owner had gone to some trouble to make it an inviting accommodation for holidaymakers.

She stepped out of the car and zipped her waxed jacket against a sudden frigid gust. For all her romantic thoughts about spring, the wind still held winter's bite.

The cottage door opened and delivered an older man in a heavy corduroy jacket and a dark watch cap onto the stoop. "Mrs. Stewart?"

"Mr. Brown."

He nodded and gestured for her to follow. "Come inside and have a look, then."

Not one for small talk apparently. Serena squeezed past

him into the tiny cottage and looked around. It was bare but neat, with rag rugs and pine furniture, just enough room for two or three people. More than adequate for their temporary needs.

"One bedroom down the hall and a loft," he said.

She nodded and examined the perimeter of the room. "Where are the rads?"

"No radiators, dear."

"Excuse me?"

He jerked his head in what she assumed was an invitation to follow and led her to a wood-burning stove in the small kitchen. No radiators or proper appliances, just this old-fashioned stove for both heat and cooking? She wasn't even sure she knew how to use one.

"There's a woodpile out back. More than enough to last you the summer."

Her hopes deflated as quickly as they had risen. She could bring in an electric hot plate and mini-oven for cooking, but Skye's summer nights remained cool. Even if she were willing to keep the stove constantly burning, the idea of hot iron around curious three-year-old fingers seemed like a bad idea.

"I'm going to have to give some thought to this," she said slowly. "I'd not known this was the only source of heat."

He shrugged and ushered her outside, where the rain had shifted from a fine mist to a steady patter. She pulled up her hood, shook Mr. Brown's hand, and hightailed it back into the warmth of her sedan.

So that was a bust. She might not have many requirements, but reliable heat that didn't involve an open fire was certainly one of them. What was she going to do now?

Find another place, clearly. Yet she'd had enough difficulty finding this cottage within the school's catchment area. Even if she could find an available rental, it wouldn't necessarily be within the prescribed boundaries—which meant her plans of having Em ride the bus home each day were for naught.

Serena had planned on going straight to the hotel, but instead she drove all the way back up the Sleat Peninsula and then an extra fifty minutes to her favorite coffee shop in Portree. Not only did the shop make an excellent latte, but it had free Wi-Fi and a community noticeboard on which locals often posted room and cottage rentals. Her avoidance had nothing at all to do with the fluttery feeling in the pit of her stomach when she thought of Malcolm Blake. Finding a place to stay was her first priority.

And yet after a fruitless scan of the board and an hour on the Internet, Serena had to admit it might be a futile hope. She even navigated the guesthouse's reservations system to check availability of the self-catering cottages, which were of course booked solid through September. Just as well, she supposed. Staying on-site would make her plans of keeping clear of the hotel manager that much more difficult. In fact, if she weren't loath to let him think he had scared her off, she would implement that plan today.

She tossed her paper cup in the bin and ventured back outside to her parked car. Time to put on her big-girl pants and make it clear she had as much right to be there as he did. As part owner, it was her responsibility to review the books and see how the hotel's money was being spent. She couldn't force him to be pleasant, but she could refuse to rise to his bait. This wasn't personal, after all.

The rain shifted to a steady downpour on the drive back to Isleornsay. At the rate it was going, the hotel grounds would be ankle deep in mud by morning. She parked in front of the structure, zipped up her coat again, and took a deep breath to prepare herself for battle.

———⚬⚬⚬———

Some days the hotel clicked along like a well-oiled machine. The guests were happy, the facilities operated as they should, and everyone showed up for work.

Today was not one of those days.

By two o'clock, Malcolm had already cleaned four rooms—after the housekeeper called in sick for the second day in a row—unclogged two toilets, retrieved a wedding ring from the P trap of a guest room sink, and spent twenty minutes on the phone with technical support to determine why the website had crashed. That in turn led to an hour restoring the site from backup and then making arrangements to switch it to a dedicated server, something he'd been considering since he came on board last year but hadn't gotten around to doing. He settled into the desk chair in his office and massaged the back of his neck. Done. Surely that meant he'd covered all possible disasters and annoyances he was due for the day.

Almost as if the thought had summoned her, the door opened and delivered Serena Stewart.

"Can I get the last two quarters' P and Ls?"

"Good afternoon to you too, Mrs. Stewart." He sat back in his chair, enjoying the view of her in those snug jeans and a zip-front Scandinavian sweater that opened a little too low to be considered work appropriate. He'd have thought it was on purpose if not for the fact she wasn't wearing a lick of makeup and she'd plaited her hair back tightly against the falling rain. Not exactly the kind of thing a woman did when she was trying to be seductive.

He definitely shouldn't be thinking along those lines about his boss anyway.

"Sorry. Good afternoon. How are things going today?"

"Two steps short of Armageddon," Malcolm said, exaggerating just a touch for effect. "Now that it's pouring down rain, I expect to have guests blame me for my lack of control over the Scottish weather as well."

To his surprise a faint smile passed over her lips. "Do people do that?"

"Frequently."

She shook her head, and the smile faded. "The P and Ls? Please?"

Well, she had said please, but he needed more information than that. "Why do you need them?"

The walls went back up, and she stiffened. "Because I asked you for them."

"I meant, what do you need them for, so I know what files to give you?" He studied her defensive expression and decided to take a different approach. "I know we didn't get off on the right foot yesterday. But it would be a lot easier if you would stop instantly assuming I'm trying to make your life difficult. I'm just trying to do my job."

The only change in her expression was a lifted eyebrow. "That goes both ways, you know."

She wasn't going to budge an inch. And he didn't have any choice but to comply. He rose and circled the desk. "Listen, love—"

"No, just stop right there." She held up a hand. "I'm not sure if your problem with me comes from the fact that I'm a woman or that you don't want someone encroaching on your territory, but I don't appreciate the implication that I'm not capable of running a business. I can and I have. So I suggest that you shove down whatever argumentative tendencies seem to spring up in my presence and give me what I want."

He couldn't help it. A grin broke over his face, his anger evaporating. And even though he knew it would make matters worse, he let his gaze travel down to the expanse of cleavage exposed by her sweater's wandering zip.

She followed his attention and flushed crimson, yanking the zip up almost to her neck. He could see her processing how her words could have been taken as an innuendo, her color deepening even further.

She crossed her arms over her chest in a uselessly protective gesture. "Charming. Either you have no sense of self-preservation or you're trying to force me to fire you. Which is it?"

He cleared his throat and forced an expression of seriousness back onto his face. "The former, I think. Mrs. Stewart—Serena—I'm not trying to be argumentative, and I'm not trying to make your life difficult. But I've run this hotel fairly successfully for the past nine months with no help and too little staff. What exactly do you think I'm doing wrong?"

"I already told you, you're not doing anything wrong." Her ire seemed to dampen a degree. "Let's put aside the fact that I'm an owner and have every right to be here. By your own admission, you're overworked. If this hotel is going to be the success I know it can be, you need my help."

She looked sincere. And perhaps he had been overly defensive since her arrival. "Okay."

"Okay?"

He turned away, pulled open a file drawer, and yanked out the folder that contained the reports, holding it out. "Take a look. I think you'll find everything is in order."

She slowly took the file. "Thank you."

"You're welcome." It nearly killed him to say the words. "Before you go, I do have a question. What exactly did you say to the guests while you were here yesterday?"

"I just gave them some ideas about what to do on Skye. Nothing special. Why?"

"A couple of them asked for you this morning. The Avilas were particularly appreciative of your stargazing tips."

A slow smile spread across her face. "I'm glad it cleared up last night for a bit before the rain came in. You can't come to Skye this time of year and not appreciate our night skies. It's practically sacrilege."

"Indeed it is," he said slowly.

She held up the folder like a parting salute. "I'll get back to you about this."

"Fair enough." He watched her swivel on her heel and disappear out the door, not entirely sure what had just happened.

CHAPTER SIX

MALCOLM BLAKE KNEW what he was doing. At least she could cross that concern off her list.

Serena flipped through the last page of the report and stacked it neatly in the file folder on Muriel's dining-room table. The hotel was doing well. They were within range of the revenue goals and occupancy rates Jamie and Andrea had laid out in the business plan, and customer satisfaction was high, judging from both online reviews and the comment cards guests left upon checkout. Malcolm was managing things exactly as he ought.

On the other hand, their high spring occupancy was due to an unexpected article in a London-based travel magazine. It was a huge break, but one they couldn't count on to be repeated. That meant Serena had to come up with creative publicity ideas to keep pulling in new customers while they recovered the repeat guests they'd lost during the renovation closures.

Serena opened the next report and scanned the payroll statement. They were indeed understaffed. She ran her finger across the row that contained Malcolm's information and sighed at the figure there. Not only would she *not* be firing him, but she might actually have to give him a raise. Not right away, of course—doing it now would only reinforce his arrogance at a time when she needed him to act like a team player. They might have agreed to a cease-fire, but the whole situation involved far more tension than she liked, especially considering the way he'd drawn attention to her wardrobe malfunction to gain the upper hand.

Heat rose to her face at the recollection. She shoved the file folder back into her satchel and reached for a notepad and pen instead. Several minutes later, a cup of tea appeared just beyond her right hand.

Muriel slid into the seat beside her, mild curiosity playing over her face. "What are you working on?"

"Some ideas for the hotel, though I doubt Malcolm will be pleased with me adding to his responsibilities."

"Malcolm, hmm? When did you two get to be on a first-name basis?"

Serena blinked. She had always thought of him as Malcolm, though she'd been very careful to address him as Mr. Blake. "We're not."

"Does this mean you've decided that he's not quite such a boor after all?"

Serena set her pen neatly on her notepad. "No, I still think he's a boor. But he's doing a good job."

"Well, that's a start. I hate to see you two at odds. He's a good man. I think you probably have a bit in common."

"What do you know of him anyway?"

"What has he told you?"

Serena shrugged and took a sip of her tea. "Absolutely nothing. It's not like we've been spending all our time giggling and plaiting each other's hair."

Muriel narrowed her eyes. "Serena Marie."

"Sorry." Serena buried her smile. Muriel hated sarcasm, and the fact that Serena was thirty-nine years old did not exempt her from the rules of the house. "I don't feel the need to get to know him on a personal level as long as he's doing his job."

"If you say so." Muriel nudged the notepad beneath Serena's hand. "What's this about?"

Serena told her how she had made sightseeing suggestions to several guests, and they'd come back looking for her. "I'm thinking we should offer self-guided tours to hotel guests."

"That's an excellent idea. What sort of tours?"

She turned the notepad so Muriel could read her list. "Driving tours, walking tours, stargazing outings. I'm sure we could do more, but these are the ones that come to mind. We would offer routes, maps, perhaps boxed lunches. Most visitors to Skye want to be in nature but have a luxurious room and good food at the end of the day. We've got the second part, so it makes sense that we get involved in the first."

Muriel pushed away from the table and stood, then squeezed Serena's shoulder. "You're a smart girl. This is a wonderful idea. You should talk to Malcolm, though. He's the one who will have to keep these going after you're gone."

"I'll talk to him once I have a full plan in place," Serena said. "Right now it's just a sketch."

"Good. I'm going to sleep now."

"Pray that Max stays asleep, or it won't last long," Serena said wryly.

"Ach, child, he's fine. It won't last forever; I promise. You may not think so now, but one of these days you're going to look back on these years and wonder how they passed so quickly."

"Right, because without a full night's sleep, the entire decade felt like one long day," Serena said. Muriel just chuckled and bid her good night, leaving her alone in the quiet dining room.

Muriel was right, though. Her children were growing up fast, and she was somehow missing it. She'd been thinking of this trip merely in terms of responsibilities and duties and, yes, reclaiming some part of herself that she'd lost along the way. But it could be more than that. This was her chance to give Em and Max a taste of an island childhood, even if it were just for a little while.

◦⟨⟩◦

Serena stayed away from the hotel for the next couple of days, which Malcolm inexplicably regretted. He'd only meant to push some buttons, considering how determined she seemed to push his, not to scare her away completely. Since he had resented her presence from almost the moment she arrived at the hotel, he shouldn't have been wishing his plan hadn't worked so well.

He felt equally daft for his wash of relief when she popped her head into his office on Sunday afternoon. "May I speak with you?"

"Of course," he said. "Please come in."

She stepped inside and shut the door behind her, a leather satchel dangling from the crook of one elbow. Her sweater today lacked a zip, and he had to fight to keep a grin from bursting onto his lips as she seated herself in front of the desk.

"I have an idea."

"Why do I suddenly feel a chill running down my spine?"

One corner of her mouth lifted into a wry smile. She removed a sheaf of papers from her bag and passed them across the desk. "You have only yourself to blame. You're the one who got me thinking along these lines."

He took the stack and flipped through it. It was a supplemental marketing plan, laid out like the one with which Andrea had tasked him when she hired him to manage the hotel. "Self-guided tours?"

"A value-added offering for our guests. It should cut down on your having to answer the same questions for each guest, and it gives us one more advantage over other area accommodations. We've already started to draw high-end travelers. This will appeal to the luxury-adventure set."

She held her breath, and he realized that she was actually nervous about his answer. "I like the idea. But why are you asking me? You're the owner. You can do whatever you want."

"I'm not here all the time. You're the one who has to make it work. I want to be certain you're on board with the idea before I go any further."

He continued flipping pages. There were walking tours, driving tours, even a stargazing outing. "So you really are interested in astronomy?"

"Hard to grow up on Skye without at least having some

interest. And that's one of the reasons holiday goers come here in the winter. It's certainly not for the weather."

"No, it certainly isn't. If we advertised a 'Winter with the Stars' package, I bet we could get our off-season occupancy rates up even higher." He looked up from the plan. "This is a great idea, Serena. Let's do this."

She looked surprised. "I've included some mock-ups of brochures in the back. I thought you might want to offer some input on the copy before they go to print."

He flipped to the back, where indeed there were three full-color trifold brochures, professionally designed and laid out. "You did these?"

"I did." A hint of pride hung in her voice, and she raised her chin as if daring him to say something critical about them.

"They're perfect. Really impressive. I had no idea that you could do this."

"That stands to reason, since you know absolutely nothing about me."

The jab struck. Maybe he really had hurt her feelings by being so combative. But the conflict hadn't been one-sided: she'd taken one look at him and assumed he was incapable of running a hotel. Not that he wanted to bring that up, especially now that they were finally having a civil conversation. "That's true. I don't suppose you happen to write as well?"

"Why?"

He leaned back in his chair. "We have Facebook and Instagram accounts set up, but there's really nothing on them. We could use someone to take over the hotel's social media. "

"What did you have in mind?"

"Posts about Skye. Things to do, things to see, what

makes the island unique. What makes the hotel unique. Really give the flavor of the guesthouse and the location. I can tie them into the website so new posts appear next to the booking form."

"I like that idea. We could highlight local events, the bands that play at the bar." Her voice gained excitement as she talked about it, her eyes sparkling. In that moment he realized just how pretty she was when she wasn't giving him a hard time. Well, she was pretty even then, but now she was downright magnetic. His thoughts must have shown on his face, because her voice trailed off midsentence. "What? Why are you looking at me like that?"

"Sorry, was I? I was just thinking I'm glad you agree, because technical papers are the extent of my writing ability and I don't think 'great view' is really going to cut it. So what do you think? Will you do it?"

Serena hesitated, then gave a single nod. "I'll do it." She paused, then added, "It's a really good idea, Malcolm. We should have done it a long time ago."

"Well, this—" he held up her papers—"is a great idea as well. So thank you."

She didn't seem to know what to do with his gratitude, so she rose and gestured to the marketing plan. "You can keep that. It's a copy. I'm going to run the ideas past Jamie and Ian to make sure they're okay with the changes. Andrea might have some ideas to contribute as well."

"Perfect. I'll let you know when I have the changes made to the website."

"Thanks." She gave him a faint smile, nodded, and then hightailed it out of his office as if she were on fire.

He stared at the door as it closed behind her, both unsettled and intrigued. The more contact he had with the new owner, the more he wondered if the high-handed, spoiled-princess persona had been simply an act. What would he find if he made the effort to dig a little deeper?

CHAPTER SEVEN

Serena returned to her aunt's house, feeling simultaneously pleased and confused. She should have been happy that Malcolm not only had accepted her ideas enthusiastically but had come up with an excellent one of his own. Already her mind whirled with topics. She might not consider herself a writer, but she knew Skye. She loved Skye. It would be easy to come up with a post every day on the things that made it so special to her.

And yet there had been a moment when they were talking, when Malcolm had looked at her—really looked at her—and she had felt a current of . . . something. Not that she should read too much into it, because he had been as open about his appreciation of her appearance as he had about his utter dislike of her personality. He could despise her but still find her attractive.

No, more disturbing was the fact that the little spark had gone both ways. Call it attraction or interest or chemistry, there was something about him that made her off balance and breathless. Yes, objectively he had plenty going for him in the looks department—deep-brown eyes, full lips, and a strong jaw that prevented the first two from daring to look feminine. But she was far too sensible, her taste too refined, to be taken in by something as visceral as muscles or annoyingly scruffy facial hair.

Whatever it was, she needed to get a handle on it. She could fill a notebook with reasons why being attracted to Malcolm Blake was a terrible idea, and not just because he was an employee.

As soon as she set foot into Muriel's house, her children rushed her.

"Mummy!" Max wrapped his arms around her legs as if she had been gone the entire day and not just half an hour. She lifted him, groaning from his weight, as Em threw her arms around her waist.

"What a greeting!" Serena planted a kiss on top of Em's head, then a loud smack on Max's cheek. "What have you been up to? You don't have Auntie Muriel tied up in the kitchen, do you?"

"No, Mummy," Max said with a giggle. "Come look."

She lugged him into the kitchen, Em trailing behind, to where Muriel stood at the counter with a large bowl, mixing brightly colored pink dough. "What's this? Biscuits?"

"Salt dough," Muriel said. "Do you remember making this when you were a child?"

"Of course I do." She'd always thought it was even better than clay, because the shapes could be baked like cookies.

She plopped Max down on the counter and then leaned over to kiss her aunt's cheek. "Great-aunties are the best, aren't they?"

"Mmm-hmm," Max said, his default answer. As Muriel turned away to grab two smaller glass bowls off the countertop, Max darted a hand in and pinched off a piece of dough, then shoved it into his mouth. He shuddered and immediately spit it onto the counter.

Serena laughed. "It's not cookie dough, monkey. And I know for certain Auntie already told you that."

"I did, and now you know why." The look Muriel bestowed on Max was downright doting. She had helped raise Serena and Jamie, and now she filled the role of grandmother that Serena's mother should have held. Marjorie was the kind of grandmother who sent gifts from afar and then wondered why the children didn't run to her during their single yearly visit. Muriel, on the other hand, cut paper dolls on the kitchen table and made salt dough out of baking supplies and food coloring.

"Will you play with us, Mum?" Em asked hopefully.

"Of course I will." Serena helped Muriel divide the dough into four equal pieces while her aunt started mixing the ingredients for another batch.

"What do you think, you two? Blue or green?"

"Blue," Max said at the same time Em said, "Green."

"Turquoise it is," Serena said.

Muriel went to the cupboard to get the food coloring, but as she opened the door, she swayed on her feet. Instantly Serena was at her side, grabbing her elbow. "Are you all right?"

"I'm fine," Muriel said. "Just a little dizzy for a moment. Nothing to be concerned about."

Serena frowned and looked closely at Muriel. Her aunt had dark shadows beneath her eyes, but Serena had attributed that to the fact Max had woken them in the middle of the night again. Was there something else going on? Muriel was as stubborn as her father had been, which was part of the reason his cancer hadn't been discovered until it was too late to treat it. Serena wasn't about to encourage that sort of behavior, especially since Muriel had been having odd symptoms on and off for the past year.

"Perhaps you should go to the surgery this week," Serena said softly, outside the children's hearing. "Just in case."

Muriel fixed her with a stern look. "I'm fine, Serena, dear. Now mind your own business."

Okay, then. Muriel wasn't going to take any advice from her niece. Still, Serena made a mental note to check up on her more often and force her to see her physician if she seemed to be worsening.

"How did Malcolm take your suggestions?" Muriel asked.

Nicely played, Auntie. "Shockingly well. He also asked me to take over the hotel's social media."

"Sounds promising. So you two are getting along?"

"For the time being. Don't hold your breath."

She ignored Muriel's knowing look and seated herself at the counter with her lump of salt dough. For the next hour she concentrated on making little animals and letters—Max already knew most of his alphabet—putting thoughts of the frustrating hotel manager behind her.

"So, Em," Muriel said, "first day at your new school tomorrow. How are you feeling about it?"

"Nervous," Em said. "My Gaelic is really bad. What if I can't understand anything?"

"Your Gaelic is not *that* bad," Serena said. "Besides, all the teachers speak English. The students too."

Em nodded, but the way she smashed the misshapen figure she'd been sculpting told a different story. A thread of doubt crept into Serena. Was this really the best thing? Maybe she should have homeschooled Em for the rest of the year. It was a big enough adjustment to come for the last term without the instruction being in a language in which Em wasn't even close to fluent. She probably should have gone into the English Medium course, after all.

"You'll be fine," Muriel said firmly, catching Serena's eye. "Your mum wouldn't have put you in that class if she didn't think you were more than capable of excelling there." She nudged the girl with a conspiratorial look. "Besides, both your mum and I speak Gaelic, and despite his protests to the contrary, so does your uncle Jamie."

Em perked up. "I know. He taught me loads of insults when I told him my schoolmates were being mean."

Muriel struggled to look stern, and Serena smothered a snicker before saying, "Well, perhaps you should keep those to yourself, cupcake. These schoolmates will understand them. Though you could see if your teachers would count it as extra credit."

Em narrowed her eyes suspiciously, then let out a giggle. "I'll tell them it was all my mum's idea."

"That's the spirit." Serena put her arms around Em and gave her a squeeze. "You'll do great, love. Promise. Just be patient with yourself."

Despite her brave words, Serena didn't sleep much that night, tossing and turning in the room she shared with Max. And for once, it had nothing to do with her son, who didn't stir the entire night. The quiet gave her too much time to think—about the new school, about being on Skye, about how far they'd deviated from the life she thought she was supposed to give her children. For that matter, her own life didn't much resemble her naive plans.

"Stop your whinging," Serena whispered to herself in the dark.

She had no cause for complaint. She had a beautiful house and healthy, intelligent children. She might not have a career, but she had something to keep her occupied, at least for the time being. She'd already learned how hollow the "loving husband" part of the dream could be. Maybe the reason she'd had no luck dating since Edward's death was simply because she couldn't imagine ever falling in love again. And that was fine. She might not have wanted Em and Max to grow up without a father, but she'd come to realize it didn't have to be all bad.

The next morning, despite her bleary-eyed state, Serena put on a cheerful face when Em entered the dining room. "Special first-day-of-school breakfast. Tea, scones, oatcakes, scrambled eggs, and sausage."

"Is this all for me and Max?" Em asked, wide-eyed.

"For the four of us, yes. It's a special day." Serena knew she was overdoing it, but baking settled her nerves, and today they felt especially raw.

Muriel entered the dining room, already dressed, and favored her with a knowing smile. "Couldn't sleep?"

"Thought I'd get a start on the week's baking," Serena said, though there was no fooling her aunt.

Once they had made a good dent in the breakfast spread, Muriel volunteered to clear away the dishes and wrap up the leftovers so Serena could supervise the process of getting Em and Max dressed. Serena managed not to break down while Em put on her new school uniform—navy trousers and a light-blue polo embroidered with the school crest—but she had to swipe at her eyes when Max wanted to wear dark jeans and his blue sweater so he could be just like his sister.

"Mum? Are you all right?" Em stared at her as if she were a complete stranger.

"Sorry, sorry." Serena dabbed at her eyes. "I cried when I sent you to school, Em, but it's doubly difficult now that Max is going."

Max climbed into her lap and put his hands on either side of her face. "It's okay, Mummy. Do you want to keep my giraffe while I'm gone?"

Serena chuckled and kissed her son's nose. "That is the sweetest offer I've ever heard, but I know for a fact that Mr. Spots would be very disappointed not to go to nursery school." She pulled him close and gave him a hug, then tugged Em over to do the same. "You are the best kids anyone could ask for, you know that?"

Max squirmed out of her grip, but Em looked her in the eye and said seriously, "We'll be okay, Mum. Don't worry."

"All right. If you say so." She planted kisses on the tops of their heads and then straightened. "Let's grab your rucksacks and get going. Don't want to be late on the first day, do we?"

Maybe she should get emotional more often, Serena thought as she bundled them through the frigid air to the car. Em and Max were so determined to prove that she had no reason to be sad that they seemed to forget their own nerves. That is until they turned off the highway to Sleat's tiny primary school.

"You know, this is where I went to school," Serena said brightly as she found a parking spot. "And I loved it. I think it's cool that you get to come here too."

Em looked unconvinced, so Serena took both children by the hand and walked with them toward the entrance. Several buildings lay nestled in the gently sloping countryside, their walls whitewashed in the traditional Skye manner below steeply slanted gray roofs. Just beyond lay the pitch, struggling into green through the puddles of water from the past week's incessant rain, and a thick swath of woods separated the schoolyard from the sound beyond. Em's doubtful look highlighted just how far removed it was from the Victorian brownstone of Highlands Academy, with its manicured gardens.

"Relax," Serena whispered to her outside the school doors, pressing a kiss to the top of her head. "This is going to be a wonderful adventure." And it would be. She was certain of that. But the conviction didn't change the wobble in her stomach as she left her children in the capable hands of the primary school's teachers and drove back to her aunt's house. Muriel had gone to Broadford to do the grocery shopping, so Serena rattled around the house, doing laundry and dusting already-pristine surfaces. She was so desperate for a distraction that she actually considered going down to the hotel to check in with Malcolm. In the end she settled for finalizing the brochure design and creating a calendar for her social media posts.

When Muriel finally returned, Serena jumped up from the dining room table. "May I help with the groceries?"

"Serena Marie, you're not sitting here fretting over the children, are you?"

"Of course not," Serena said. "*Stewing* would be a more accurate description." She took the bags from Muriel with a sheepish smile and carried them to the kitchen. Wasn't it a mother's prerogative to worry about her kids on the first day at a new school?

She needn't have worried about Max, though. When she met him at the school doors at the end of the morning session, he ran to her, beaming.

"Did you have fun, monkey?"

"Mmm-hmm. I'm hungry."

Serena lifted him onto her hip and gave him a tight hug. Clearly he was more than ready for school. And with any luck, she had been worrying about Em for nothing.

———❦———

"I don't want to talk about it! Why did you make me come to this dumb school?"

Em slammed the car door and raced up the drive to Muriel's path while Serena looked on, stricken.

"I still like school, Mummy," came Max's voice from the backseat. Serena sighed and leaned her head back against her car's headrest. So much for her hopes of a smooth transition. She couldn't even get Em to tell her what had happened, and forcing the issue had only earned another outburst. "Come on, Maxie, we better go inside."

She retrieved her son from his car seat and deposited him on the reception-room floor with a bin full of trucks, then went after Em. She knocked softly on the closed bedroom door. "Em? Can we talk?"

"I'm doing my homework," Em's sullen voice came back.

Serena hesitated, then turned and went back to Max.

Despite all her instincts telling her to press, she couldn't make Em talk until she was ready.

Sure enough, a few minutes later, a sniffling, swollen-eyed little girl emerged. She'd already changed out of her uniform into jeans and a pink sweater.

"Do you want to talk about it?" Serena prompted.

"I didn't understand anything," Em said. "The teacher just told me to follow along the best I could. And then she asked me a question and I said something stupid in Gaelic. I got my words all mixed up and everyone laughed."

Serena sighed. She'd known it would be an adjustment, but she'd underestimated how much her intelligent child wanted to have all the right answers. She put her arm around Em. "I know it's hard at first to not understand what's going on. But the more you pay attention and the more you try, the clearer things will become."

"But Mum—"

"No buts. I know you can do this, Em. And I know you are not a quitter. You can't let one bad experience convince you to stop trying."

Em looked unconvinced, but she nodded anyway.

"Isn't there anyone who might be able to help you out?"

"Well, there is this one girl, Felicity. Her mum is Scottish, but she was born in Australia. She's only been here two years, and she speaks Gaelic almost as well as the Scottish kids."

Serena smoothed back Em's dark hair. "Then maybe you just need to be humble and ask for help. What do you think?"

Em sniffled, looking slightly less morose. "I guess so."

Serena hugged her again and offered to look over her homework—also in Gaelic—until it was time to help Muriel with dinner. But doubt still dogged her as she went through the familiar motions of making dinner rolls.

"You're chewing on something," Muriel said from the other side of the kitchen. "You never work dough so hard unless you're worried."

"I'm not worried. I'm . . . thinking."

"Well, you just thought all the air out of that dough. You're going to have to give it a second rise before you shape them now."

Serena stopped what she was doing and stared down at the mangled lump before her. She was supposed to be working it lightly before dividing it into individual pieces, and instead she'd undone all the work of the first rise. She gave it a frustrated punch before looking back at Muriel.

"Did I make the right decision coming back here? Em hates school. We still don't have a place to stay—"

"You most certainly do. I've told you that you can stay here as long as you like. Through the summer even."

"We both know that will begin to wear on all of us." Serena sighed. "Maybe I was too hasty coming here. I was running away, and I somehow believed Skye would solve all our problems."

"Serena, dear, look at me." Muriel stared at her until she complied. "Stop fretting. Yes, it may take some adjustment for everyone. But you need to stop second-guessing yourself and worrying about making a mistake. You are an excellent mum and an intelligent woman and more than capable of making your own decisions. I know that. Your children know that. Your family knows that. The only person who needs to believe it now is you."

The words trod too closely to something Serena had

barely admitted to herself, let alone to her aunt, and she felt an uncomfortable flush creep across her chest. "I just want things to be perfect for them. I don't want them to look back and resent decisions I made for their own good."

Muriel placed a gentle hand on her shoulder. "Serena, darling, sometimes you just have to have a little faith."

"Faith. Right." She swallowed and plopped the ball of dough into the oiled bowl, then covered it with cling film. Faith was an easy thing to talk about but hard to hold on to. And even harder to regain once you let it slip through your fingers.

Out in the lounge, Max and Em were huddled in the middle of the rug, surrounded by board games that Muriel had unearthed from a cupboard. "What are we playing?" Serena asked, kneeling down beside them.

"Chess," Max said.

"I see." It was a chessboard, all right, but instead of chess pieces, the board was set up with checkers and Candy Land figurines. "Maybe I'll watch the first game so I can pick up the rules."

She quickly learned there were no rules, or perhaps they changed too quickly to grasp. After a quick break to form the rolls from the rested dough and let them do their final rise on the warmth of the hob, she returned to find that her children had switched to straight checkers. Em could clearly wipe Max off the board, but she pretended not to see all the moves that would let her win until it was clear Max had an unshakable lead.

"I won!" Max crowed, holding up his fists like a prizefighter.

"Well done, Maxie." Serena ruffled her son's hair and gave her daughter a knowing smile. Em was a good big sister. A lovable girl in general, which made her school difficulties past and present all the more baffling.

"Let's build a castle now!" Max swept the checkers exuberantly into a box, then dove on a bag of wooden blocks beside him, which he began to form into a wobbly tower. "This is where the dragon lives."

"I see. Are there people in the castle?"

"No. Just dragons. And sheep. Dragons eat sheep."

Now the building project was making more sense. She'd let him talk her into playing one of his favorite films after school. Serena was about to make a comment about Scottish Vikings when a knock shuddered the front door.

"Serena, will you get that?" Muriel called from the kitchen.

Serena frowned and pushed herself to her feet. Who on earth would be calling on a rainy night? She opened the door cautiously, and her heart took an upward leap into her throat when she found herself face-to-face with Malcolm Blake. "What are you doing here?"

"Muriel invited us to supper." He ran a hand through his hair to catch the raindrops that perched there and on the shoulders of his jacket. "May we come in? It's cold."

"We?" Serena stood aside as he moved into the reception room and then blinked as a pretty young woman followed him in. She resembled him so strongly there was no doubting the family connection. Malcolm had a daughter? And a teenage one at that?

"Serena, this is Kylee. Kylee, meet Serena Stewart, one of the hotel owners and Muriel's niece."

"Nice to meet you, Mrs. Stewart." Kylee shook her hand with a smile and an impressive amount of poise for a teenage girl.

"Nice to meet you too," Serena said automatically, still stunned. "These are my children, Em and Max."

Kylee immediately went to Em's side, where the girl had begun to assemble a puzzle. "Oh, that's pretty. Is it Sleeping Beauty? Can I help?"

"Here, you can do her dress." Em shoved a few pieces in Kylee's direction. She was obviously dazzled by the older girl if she was giving her the good pieces instead of passing off the boring blue sky.

Serena put on a smile that probably looked as fake as it felt. "Have a seat and I'll let Aunt Muriel know you're here."

She practically ran to the kitchen and leaned over the counter. "Why didn't you tell me you invited him?"

"Oh, did I forget to mention that?" Muriel said innocently. "Must have slipped my mind."

"Of course it did. If this is your idea of making us get along—"

Muriel shot her a stern look that made the protest die on her lips. "Malcolm and Kylee often have dinner here on Monday nights. I didn't think it was hospitable to tell them they weren't welcome just because you seem to have taken a dislike to him."

The words made Serena feel like a selfish three-year-old, but the anxious feeling remained. Her nerves were stretched thin enough without the prospect of dealing with Malcolm tonight. "I just wish you'd given me some warning."

"Why, dear? So you could fret over that too? It's time to put your rolls in the oven so we can get the food on the table. Unless of course you'd like to sit and make small talk."

"No, thank you." Serena slid the pan into the oven beneath

the chicken, which had exactly twenty minutes left on the timer. She contemplated whether she could believably plead last-minute dinner preparations as a way to hide out, but everything was done, down to the place settings on the dining table. Had she only noticed the two extra plates, she'd have known that Muriel was up to something.

Serena pulled an elastic from her wrist, fastened her hair back into a ponytail, and took a deep breath before marching into the reception room.

Malcolm was sitting on the floor building an addition to the castle with her son. "You see, if you're going to have dragons, you have to have a runway, right? Because some of them need to have space to take off and land, like aeroplanes. Don't you think?"

Max's eyes lit up as if Malcolm had come up with the most brilliant plan in the history of dragon-castle building. "I forgot! Because they're big."

"Exactly. Really big." Malcolm's eyes flicked up to meet Serena's, but they didn't linger before he went back to paving the new runway with bright-red blocks.

Fine. So he's good with kids. Probably because he has the mentality of a three-year-old himself.

Kylee perked up. "Hey, Uncle Mal, I think we have some old blocks like these in the attic or something. We should bring them for Max."

"Yeah, I'll look tonight when we go home. I put a bunch of boxes up there after Christmas."

Serena looked between Malcolm and Kylee. "This is your niece?"

Now he finally focused on her. "Yes. My older sister's daughter." He put subtle emphasis on *older*, as if to call her out for being foolish enough to think he could have a teen-ager of his own. "She lives with me."

"Technically you live with me," Kylee said.

"Hey, watch it, kid. Remember who feeds you."

"I do," Kylee said. "You can't cook."

Serena laughed out loud, which earned her a look from Malcolm that held much less affection than the one with which he'd favored Kylee. Somehow she'd be disappointed to find out that he was good in the kitchen. It would completely blow the picture she'd formed of him.

Then she sniffed. What was burning?

"Blast! The rolls!" She darted back into the kitchen and yanked open the oven door. It let out a small puff of smoke that carried with it the distinct smell of char. She grabbed a pot holder and pulled out the baking dish in dismay. The tops were a perfect golden brown as always, but a peek through the bottom of the glass dish showed the undersides were completely black.

And then she realized that not only had she placed them on the lower rack under the chicken but she hadn't double-checked the oven temperature. At least it hadn't been enough to entirely destroy them.

"I guess we're cutting off the bottoms," she muttered to herself. "Maybe no one will notice."

That hope proved to be a vain one. Muriel and Kylee didn't say anything as they added their rolls to their plates along-side the chicken, but Malcolm flipped his over. "That explains the char smell."

Heat rose to Serena's face, which irritated her even more. Since when did she care whether he thought she could cook?

He was an employee, barely an acquaintance. It wasn't as if she felt any need to impress him.

"Serena is a talented baker when she's not distracted," Muriel said.

Malcolm flashed her a grin. "Distracted? Why are you distracted?"

Curse the man. He probably thought he was the distraction. Serena scrambled for a plausible answer and landed on one that was at least partially true. "I've been thinking about our rental."

"Rental? Of what?"

"I'd planned on renting a cottage in Armadale through the summer," she explained, "but when I arrived, it wasn't suitable."

"Too rustic?"

"Its only heat was a wood-burning stove, and I'm not comfortable with Max around fire."

"Understandable. There's nothing else available?"

"Not that I've found so far. And nothing that would let us stay for the entire season."

"Uncle Mal, what about Mrs. Docherty's croft house?" Kylee asked.

Serena looked between Kylee and Malcolm. "Mrs. Docherty?"

"Our neighbor," Malcolm said. "There are two houses on the property beside us. Mrs. Docherty spends summers in the modern house in the back, and she rents the old nineteenth-century croft house in the front. It's been vacant since last autumn."

"The bloke who was living there went to jail," Kylee said, her eyes bright with excitement.

Malcolm gave her a warning look. "That's just gossip. In any case, the house is very simple. I'm not sure it's what you're looking for."

It was in close proximity to him, he meant. Well, that didn't exactly commend it to her either. But Kylee didn't seem to pick up the subtext.

"What do you mean? It would be perfect. It has two bedrooms downstairs, plus a loft, and I know it has radiators because you helped winterize them when it went vacant."

"I could make the enquiry for you if you like," Malcolm said slowly. "It does have a rather nice view of Broadford Bay if you don't mind driving from the Breakish area."

"Oh, would you, Malcolm?" Muriel laid a hand on his forearm. "That would be lovely."

Malcolm looked at Serena, obviously waiting for her response. She waffled for a long moment. Hadn't she just been worrying about their accommodations? And Aunt Muriel had told her she had to have faith. Somehow, though, Serena didn't appreciate God's providence coming in the form of another source of stress.

Yet it did sound like an option—possibly her only option. She swallowed her reservations and something that felt suspiciously like pride. "Yes, would you ask, please?"

"It would be my pleasure," he said with a twinkle in his eye.

Muriel looked perfectly satisfied by the turn of events, unaware of the undercurrent in the polite conversation. But from the looks that Malcolm kept shooting Serena across the table, he was enjoying this far too much. He wouldn't let her forget that she'd needed him.

CHAPTER EIGHT

MALCOLM CALLED AND LEFT A MESSAGE for Mrs. Docherty first thing the next morning, secretly hoping she'd make a quick reply. Maybe it was simply his contrary nature that liked the idea of playing hero to a woman whose worst nightmare was being a damsel in distress, or maybe it was the notion that Serena would have to use a little more humility in their future interactions.

Or perhaps it was simply the anticipation of being able to see her in a less formal setting as his next-door neighbor. It was useless to deny that she intrigued him. She was a puzzle, and he'd never been able to resist the urge to take something apart and learn how it worked. Despite her obvious shock at seeing him—and her assumption that Kylee was his daughter—she'd been subdued last night. Perhaps troubled. What exactly did Serena Stewart have to be worried about?

He didn't get a chance to pry because she didn't set foot in the hotel for the next few days. Was she avoiding him? No, that idea was ridiculous. She had children, after all, and motherhood came with an additional set of duties.

On Thursday afternoon, his direct office line finally rang. "Malcolm, dear, it's Anna Docherty."

"Mrs. Docherty! You got my message. I thought you were too busy sunbathing to call me back." The owner of the croft house next door spent winters with her daughter in the south of France, claiming the Scottish weather was too hard on her arthritis. Mostly he thought she just liked to be waited on by young French men. She had a reputation for being a saucy old lady from what he'd heard.

Her delighted chuckle filled the line. "You know me so well. You said you have a tenant for my croft house?"

Malcolm told her about Serena, mentioning that she had two children and needed a place through the end of summer, but as soon as Mrs. Docherty realized he was talking about Duncan MacDonald's daughter, she was sold.

"You know Duncan taught my youngest son fiddle, don't you? Not that he kept up with it as he should—doesn't even speak Gaelic anymore since moving to Edinburgh—but it's good to keep the old music from being lost, don't you think?"

Malcolm pulled out a file folder of invoices as Mrs. Docherty rattled on about her son. She seemed to think he had become a successful hairstylist simply because he was too lazy to hold a "real job," as she liked to call it. Malcolm read over the line items on the last produce invoice, inserting murmurs of agreement in appropriate places. When she'd gone on for a full ten minutes without any input, he finally interjected. "Should I tell her it's available?"

"What's available? Oh, the house. Right you are. You have the key, dear. Go ahead and show it to her and let me know if she wants it. You can collect the rent for me until I come back in June."

"It would be my pleasure. I have to get back to work now. Give those French girls a chance, will you?"

Malcolm hung up with a laugh. He'd have thought the eccentric-old-lady act was a put-on if Kylee hadn't told him all the stories that had circulated around the village over the years. As blunt as she was dotty, she had inspired her own saying: plenty of things were now referred to as "pulling an Anna Docherty." He suspected she did them just to keep the village humming. And why not? When you'd outlived three husbands, birthed six children, and made it to the ripe age of eighty-nine, you were within your rights to have a little fun.

He shuffled through a pile of paperwork until he found the laminated sheet that contained Serena's mobile number, then picked up the phone and dialed.

She picked up immediately, her tone surprised. "Malcolm! Is there a problem?"

"No problem. The croft house is available. I have the keys if you'd like to come over later tonight and take a look."

"Couldn't we do it tomorrow?" The sounds of young voices rang from the background.

"I'm at the hotel all day," he reminded her. "Unless you want to come by before I leave in the morning."

"That would be better, I think." Her voice turned muffled, but he heard her say clearly, "Max, that does not go in the toilet. And you can't run around without pants. Come back here."

Malcolm chuckled. "Come by at half seven then. I'll text you the address later. I'll even bring coffee."

"I'll be there," she murmured. "Thank you."

"You're welcome." He set the receiver carefully in the cradle. Her words had surely been reflex, but they sparked an unexpected warmth in him all the same.

CHAPTER NINE

SERENA STOOD ON THE FRONT STEPS of the address Malcolm had texted her, shivering even though she was wearing her quilted jacket and shearling-lined boots. Mid-April on Skye should not have been this cold, but there had been one storm after another, this one bringing a socked-in fog and a freezing drizzle that stuck like ice chips to her coat and hair.

As minutes passed, she wondered if she had somehow gotten the address or the time wrong. She pulled her mobile from her pocket, ready to call Malcolm, when the outline of a figure appeared in the fog at the end of the long, muddy drive. Details resolved as he trudged toward her, wearing a thick sweater and mud-splattered wellies, a black knit cap pulled down over his ears and forehead. She cursed herself silently at the sudden jig happening in her insides. *Rugged* had never described her taste in men, but it worked for him. A little too well.

"I'm sorry I'm late." Malcolm handed her an insulated mug. "Does bringing coffee make up for it?"

"I might be able to overlook it. Busy morning?" She was pleased by how level and dispassionate her voice came out.

"A bit of an incident involving Kylee's dog, muddy paws, and every piece of upholstery in the house," he said with a crooked grin. "The pup's lucky he's cute."

Serena reluctantly returned the smile. "Em's been begging me for one, but I can't be responsible for keeping one more creature alive right now."

"I understand that." Malcolm dug his key ring from his pocket and brushed past her to fit the key into the door. "The house has been shut up for a bit, so it'll be cold. But the rads worked in the autumn."

Serena moved past him into the foyer that led directly to a lounge. The outside had been a traditional croft house style, a scaled-down version of the hotel with a whitewashed stone exterior and newer mullioned windows. The inside surprised her with its bright and modern cast. The original wide-plank floors covered the entire interior, and the walls were painted a clean and bright cream. Comfy slipcovered furniture stood opposite a small flat-screen television.

"No dining room, but there's an eat-in kitchen." Malcolm delivered the words with the practiced composure of an estate agent, so incongruous with his appearance this morning that she smiled. She followed him down the hallway into a somewhat dated but functional kitchen, complete with a washer/dryer unit beneath the countertop.

Her smile widened when she saw the vintage enameled AGA range. "It's charming."

Malcolm seemed surprised by her response. "Have a look at the bedrooms then. There are two downstairs, which I imagine you'd want for the children, and one double upstairs."

The two bedrooms on the main floor were small but equally appealing, with antique single beds, freshly laundered linens folded at the foot of each. Just down the hall was a minuscule bath with a tankless water heater built into the stand-up shower cubicle. A steep flight of stairs off the center hall led to a tiny wood-paneled loft beneath the eaves, barely wide enough for a double bed. Malcolm pressed himself back against the wall so she could pass, but it wasn't far enough to ignore the waft of that outdoorsy cologne or his solid presence as she brushed by him.

She stopped in front of the window, drawing in a breath. "The view is incredible!"

He moved in behind her to take a look, and once more every nerve in her body snapped to attention. She needed to move before she gave away her reaction, but there was barely enough room for one person to maneuver, let alone two.

"I have that same view from my bedroom," he said. "At least here they've raised the bed frame so you can see outside while lying down. You'd have an amazing view of the stars, if it would stop storming."

Something about the intimacy of the observation made heat crawl up her neck and spread across her chest. Her coat suddenly felt uncomfortably stuffy, despite the house's cold interior. She cleared her throat. "The radiators and the boiler work?"

"They did when I winterized the place, but I can turn them on for you if you want."

"That won't be necessary," she said. "I'm sure I can manage on my own."

Malcolm looked down at her, a thoughtful look on his face that was far more unsettling than his usual arrogant smirk. "Is it really that hard for you to accept help?"

Serena flushed deeper, not sure whether it was guilt or offense she felt. "No, I just don't need any help. I've turned on radiators before."

"I don't mean that. It's eating you up that I was the one to find you a house, and you can't even let me turn on the rads. That chip on your shoulder must get heavy after a while."

Her guilt fled as quickly as it had come. "Me? That's amusing coming from you."

"Oh, I earned my chip honestly. What I want to know is what you have to be so angry about."

The assumption was so astoundingly blind that for a moment she was speechless. "You mean besides the fact that my husband died and left me with two children to raise on my own?"

"Besides that, yes. I would think that you would be grateful for the help, considering the situation."

She glared at him. "Maybe I've had my fill of men telling me what I should be grateful for, as if I'm too weak or stupid to know my own mind."

"If you think that's what I'm doing, you've spent too much time with the wrong sorts of men." Malcolm crossed his arms over his chest, his expression once again superior. She wanted nothing more than to wipe that smirk off his face.

No, scratch that. She wanted nothing more than to be

able to revel in her righteous indignation without being distracted by the way his sweater clung to the muscles in his arms and shoulders, the sudden desire to know what it felt like to be pressed against that hard body.

What on earth was wrong with her?

Serena forced a flippant smile to match his own, though her heart now beat so hard she was sure he could see it through her sweater. "I suppose you consider yourself the right sort of man, then?"

"I was just making an observation. You're the one who made it personal." He took another step toward her, and she forced herself to stand her ground, even though they were nearly toe to toe in the narrow space between the bed and the window.

"There is nothing personal between us."

"No?" He reached out and twisted an escaped lock of hair around his finger, his eyes never leaving hers. Energy hummed between them, electrifying every last nerve ending, paralyzing her ability to move away. When his gaze dipped to her mouth, her breath stilled in her lungs. She wavered between wanting to kiss him and wanting to push him away, teetered while she waited to see which impulse would win out.

But instead of lowering his mouth to hers, he dropped his hand and lifted one eyebrow. "Do you want to change your answer?"

A rush of irritation burst up in place of her earlier butterflies. What kind of game was he playing? She straightened and fixed her gaze somewhere over his shoulder so she didn't have to look him in the eye. "Move, please."

He stared for several seconds, then shifted into the corner

so she could slide by. When she was halfway to the door, he said, "I didn't take you for the type that ran away from a challenge."

She froze. All her best intentions disintegrated as she turned and marched back to him, so close that he backed into the wall with a thump. "Let me make one thing clear. I'm not some naive girl who doesn't know what she wants and needs to be enlightened. Not by you. Not by anyone. And just because I'm attracted to you doesn't mean I feel any need to act on it."

She spun on her heel and took the stairs as fast as she dared, her heart still slamming against her ribs. His footsteps thundered down the wooden treads after her.

"So you admit it! You are attracted to me."

Serena didn't answer as she let herself out and climbed into the front seat of the car. Curse her temper. It wasn't as if she'd told him anything he didn't already know—he'd turned her into a puddle by touching her *hair*, for heaven's sake—but now that she'd owned up to it, he would be relentless. She flipped down the visor and tucked those stray pieces back into her ponytail, trying to ignore the brightness of her eyes, the color in her cheeks.

A knock on the window startled her. She flipped the visor back up and turned the key in the ignition so she could roll down the window.

Malcolm bent down to her level, his forearm braced along the top of the car. "Have dinner with me. You can't say something like that and not let me make a case for myself."

"I'm not interested."

He studied her closely. "I don't believe you."

"I'm sorry, did you think we had a moment back there? I didn't notice."

His eyes narrowed, and he smoothed his hand over the lower half of his face as if he weren't sure what to do next. She took advantage of his silence to put the car in gear, and he had to jump back as she began to reverse down the driveway.

"Wait!" he called after her. "Do you want the place or not?"

She braked, but she didn't even have to consider. It was perfect—in every way but the next-door neighbor. Sticking her head out the window, she called back, "I'll move in tomorrow."

Serena refused to look at him as she backed out, and she certainly wasn't going to peek in the rearview mirror as she accelerated down the road. The frigid air rushed in through her open window, cooling her overheated skin. There was no doubt this was turning into a power struggle, and to her everlasting irritation, the balance had subtly but undeniably shifted to Malcolm's side.

———— ⚬⚬⚬⚬ ————

The exchange with Serena well and truly wrecked Malcolm's concentration for the day, and he had only himself to blame. Occasionally he gave in to reckless impulses against his better judgment. He should just be relieved that Serena had responded as she had, instead of firing him on the spot.

Of course, as soon as he began helping her find a place to stay, their professional relationship had strayed into the personal. He'd be lying to himself if he said he didn't want it to remain there. It was only one last shred of self-preservation that had kept him from taking the invitation in her eyes and kissing her senseless.

And yes, there had been invitation, no matter what she

had tried to tell him. But there had also been fear. It was the fear that had checked him at the last moment.

He barely listened as Liam, the night clerk, gave him the morning update before leaving. Malcolm moved through his duties at the hotel with half a mind, conducting inventory, checking out guests, reviewing time sheets so he could submit them to the payroll company that issued their pay packets. But Serena still nagged at the edge of his mind.

Why the fear? Not of him. She'd stood up to him since the minute she walked through the hotel's front door, and when she let herself, she actually seemed to like him. It was more as if she wasn't willing to give up her unfounded assumptions about him. At least she'd owned up to the attraction between them, even if she had inadvertently tipped her hand. Her confidence that she would never act on her feelings felt like an outright dare. He never could resist a dare.

The door to his office opened on cue, and in walked the woman in question. If this kept happening, he'd start to think they had some sort of psychic link.

"You're back to finish what we started?"

She was clearly prepared this time, because she stared at him coolly, not even a flicker of an eyelash to betray her thoughts. "Hardly. You forgot to give me the keys for the croft house."

"You forgot them on purpose so you could see me again."

"Have you ever read any psychology? They call that projection. You're imposing your own desires on me."

Was that a hint of flirtation? A slow smile spread over his face. "That's probably true. But if I recall, you were the one who started it."

Her lips twitched in what he could swear was an attempt

to hold back a smile. "*You* were the one who started it. But considering you're my employee, anything else would be improper."

"Improper, you say?"

"Highly. Sorry."

Malcolm stood and circled the desk, then perched on the edge while he studied her. "You're not sorry. You're scared because we did have a moment back there, and you don't know what do about it."

Serena's cheeks immediately pinked, but she lifted her chin and stared him down. "You don't scare me."

"Then prove it. Go out with me. On a real date. No games. Just dinner and wine and two people who happen to find each other attractive. You never know. We might actually have something in common."

Her stubborn look faltered, just for a moment, as if she were testing his sincerity. Then the calculating look came back. "That was very good. Does that line work on most women?"

"You really are determined to think the worst of me, aren't you? It's not a line. I just think it's time we acknowledge there's something between us."

She wavered again, catching her lip briefly between her teeth, and he almost groaned at the sudden impulse that little movement summoned within him. He should have kissed her when he had a chance. Now it would be the only thing he could think about in her presence.

"There's nothing between us but your imagination," she said firmly. "And even if there were, I'm going back to Inverness in the autumn. I don't indulge in meaningless flings."

"I asked you to dinner, not bed."

"I'm not interested in either."

"You'll change your mind."

"I wouldn't hold my breath if I were you." She gave him a swift nod and then turned on her heel.

"Don't you need this?" He pulled the key from his pocket, the very reason she'd come here in the first place. Oh, he was getting to her all right.

She plucked it from his hand, but he closed his fingers around hers before she could pull away. "I'd be happy to help you move in tomorrow after work. All you have to do is ask."

Serena stared at him, unwavering, until he released her hand and the key with it. "I already told you. I can manage on my own."

He called after her as she slipped out the door, "You don't have to, you know."

She just kept walking, the echo of boot heels fading with each step. Malcolm plopped back down on the edge of the desk. He had no idea what went on in that woman's mind, but now that she'd issued the challenge, he had no choice but to accept.

⟡

Despite the bitterly cold wind sweeping across the Sleat Peninsula, Serena gave in to the children's begging to play by the shore after school. It was Friday afternoon, after all, the end of a long week, and it gave her a much-needed distraction from the thoughts buzzing insistently through her head.

She might have tried to play it cool with Malcolm, but the truth was, even the touch of his hand made every rational thought evaporate. The more she tried to prove he didn't affect her, the deeper in she dug herself.

"Max, stay out of the water!" she called as her son darted for the shoreline. She sighed as he plowed straight into the water up to his calves, sloshing it over the tops of his wellies.

"Sorry, Mummy," he yelled back, all earnestness, but by then the damage had been done. Em looked to Serena for approval, then darted off to join him.

By the time they trudged back to the house, the children were shivering and wet, covered in sand to their knees.

"Maybe after supper we can look at the stars. It's finally starting to clear. I might even make hot chocolate. But only if you go take a bath right now."

That was enough incentive to make Em dart for Muriel's en suite, though Max still pulled every excuse he could concoct to avoid the tub in the guest bath. The stargazing idea had been a shameless bribe, but Serena needed something to settle the distracted, squirmy feeling in her middle every time Malcolm came to mind. Which he did with irritating frequency.

Muriel begged off stargazing to turn in early, so as soon as the final glow of twilight faded from the horizon, Serena bundled her children out the door to her car. She hoisted Max up onto the bonnet and gave Em a hand to climb up beside him, then settled herself in between.

Compared to the mainland, there was no light pollution on Skye, just the broad expanse of black overhead, the stars sparkling in the darkness like the scatter of glitter that covered most of Em's wardrobe.

"Mum?" Em held up her plastic mug, and Serena carefully poured her some of the rich chocolate, decanting more into a lidded cup for Max. He took a sip and then curled up beneath the blanket on the car bonnet as if it were his own bed.

Em lay back against the windscreen and looked up at the stars. "We haven't done this in a long time. I miss it."

"Me too. There's too much light where we live to see anything but the brightest constellations. It's one of the best things about Skye."

"No, I mean . . . this. Doing nothing. Together."

Serena turned her head and studied her daughter. When had she gotten so old? Life hadn't been easy since Edward died, but Serena had been mostly focused on maintaining their busy calendar and dealing with school issues. Now, seeing the thoughtful look on her daughter's face, she realized Em had somehow become a young woman far ahead of schedule.

"It has been a hard few years, hasn't it? I'm sorry if I've not been as present as I should have been."

Em looked surprised. "I didn't mean it like that."

"I know you didn't. But I also know that I've been trying to be both mum and dad to you, and I don't always do it perfectly."

Em glanced away, focusing instead on the stars overhead. "You always did that. Nothing's changed since Dad died."

The bitterness in Em's voice surprised Serena. Her daughter didn't like to talk about Edward, but she had thought it was out of grief and finally acceptance. "Well, I miss him. I miss being a family."

"We were never a family," Em said, "at least not like that. It was always just you and me. And then Max, of course."

Tears pricked Serena's eyes, and she lay back on the car,

a heavy sense of failure sweeping over her. She couldn't have predicted that once they'd had Em, Edward would be more interested in work than in his own family. She couldn't have predicted that he would die of a heart attack at the age of forty-two and that her daughter wouldn't get to say good-bye. But somehow she still felt responsible. As though she had failed to give her kids the life she'd been robbed of when her own parents divorced.

She couldn't say anything, so instead she put one arm around each of her children and hugged them tight to her sides. Max scooted around to get comfortable, a light snore coming from his open mouth, but Em laid her head on Serena's shoulder.

"So which ones have we not done?" Em asked after several seconds of silence.

"Hmm." Serena focused on the section of the sky in front of them. "We've done Perseus and Ursa and Cepheus—"

"Isn't Draco around there somewhere?"

"It is. Look. Twisted between Ursa Major and Minor. There's some debate about the origin of Draco, but I like this story the best. Do you remember the tale of the 'Twelve Labors of Heracles'?"

"I don't know."

"Well, Hera tricked Heracles into killing his family, which he deeply regretted."

"That's gruesome."

"Most Greek myths are," Serena said wryly. "Heracles asked for labors to atone for his sin. The Oracle of Delphi told him he had to serve at the pleasure of King Eurystheus for twelve years. And while he was in the king's service, Eurystheus commanded him to perform twelve labors—"

"Actually, it was ten."

"But the king claimed Heracles had help with two. Right. Anyhow. The eleventh task was to steal the golden apples from the garden of the Hesperides. But the apples were guarded by a great serpent beast, Ladon, which twined around the tree that held the apples. And that's why the constellation is positioned with its head beneath the foot of Heracles."

"That's cool," Em said softly. "But kind of sad when you consider the dragon's job was to protect the apples, and he got killed for it."

"I think Sir Frederic Leighton might have agreed with you. He painted the Hesperides singing a lullaby to the serpent." Serena paused, then added, "Leighton is the painter who did all the ladies in the apricot-colored Greek dresses, like the ones we saw at Tate Britain."

"Where is this one?"

Serena thought. She'd studied the Victorian classicists in great detail, but she no longer knew the locations of all the paintings. "Lady Lever, I think."

"Where's that? Have we been there?"

"No, we haven't been there. It's in Liverpool."

"We should go there. You'd like to see it. Your voice sounds happy when you talk about art."

Serena smiled. "You're right. It does make me happy. Maybe we'll take a trip this summer. There are a lot of good museums in Liverpool."

"I don't trust Max in a museum."

"We'll keep him on a short leash." Serena grinned at her daughter, but she took a moment to brush a hand over the soft hair of her sleeping toddler. Moments like this made her grateful for the balance between her two children: her thoughtful, intellectual daughter and her headstrong, active son. "We're doing pretty well on our own, aren't we? I just want you two to be happy."

Em's expression turned uncertain. "Mum? I'm sorry for all the trouble I caused. I didn't mean us to have to leave Inverness."

"Is that what you think? That we came to Skye because of school?"

"Isn't it?"

Serena hugged her tightly. "No. We could have stayed in Inverness. But I wanted you and Max to know what it's like to grow up on Skye and speak Gaelic and just relax. At least for a while." She grimaced. "I guess I miscalculated a little, didn't I?"

Em shrugged. "It's not so bad. A couple of the girls at school are nice."

"And you're just now telling me? You know I've been worried this whole time."

"Sorry. But I'm okay. So just stop worrying for a minute, will you?"

Her heart full, Serena smiled again. "Okay. What next? I don't think we've done Pegasus in a while, have we?"

They lay there, Serena telling the Greek myths behind the constellations while Em interjected the bits she knew and made wry comments that reminded Serena so much of Edward. Pretty soon Em's voice started to get sleepy, her body slack against her. Serena nudged her and whispered, "Let's go to bed now. It's starting to get cloudy again anyway."

"Mmm," Em mumbled, but she pushed herself to a sitting position while Serena slid off the bonnet. She scooped Max up in her arms and carried him inside, while Em stumbled along behind her, half dragging her blanket.

Once Serena tucked both of them in bed with a whispered prayer and a kiss to the forehead, she went back out to the car and retrieved their chocolate container and the extra blanket. The night was dark and still, the drifting clouds above her obscuring the moon.

It was good to be reminded why she was here in the first place. For her children. To regain a bit of herself, to remember who she was without a man. Not to jump right into the same mistakes she'd made last time, no matter how appealing Malcolm might be.

CHAPTER TEN

THE NEXT DAY MALCOLM WOKE UP EARLY to his alarm and rapped sharply on Kylee's door to wake her. "Time to get up, Ky. We need to get going." He waited until he heard a sleepy acknowledgment inside and then rustling that indicated she was getting out of bed. It was her voice lesson that necessitated the early wake-up call, but she was a teenager after all. They'd rushed out the door far too many times, something that grated on Malcolm's precise, orderly concept of time.

By the time Kylee came downstairs, dressed in her weekend clothes of jeans and a hoodie, her long blonde hair tied in a ponytail, the porridge was ready and waiting to be spooned into bowls. It was just about the only thing Malcolm could make without burning.

"What a surprise!" Kylee said. "I would never have expected porridge for breakfast."

"Clam up, girlie," Malcolm said, gesturing to the table. "You can make your own breakfast if you don't like it."

Kylee had heard this same routine before, so she rolled her eyes and slid into the chair with her bowl in hand. "You know, you don't have to drive me. I do have my own car."

"A four-hour round trip is too far for you to be driving alone at seventeen. I feel better taking you myself."

"Has anyone ever told you that you are way overprotective?"

"Only you, about twenty times. And I have good reason to be overprotective." He fixed her with a stern look and instantly regretted it when a shadow of grief passed over her face. He didn't mean to remind her about Nicola and Richard's passing any more often than she already thought about it, but surely she could understand that he might be reluctant to send her off by herself when it was an auto accident that had taken her parents' lives nearly a year ago. The weather in Scotland was too unpredictable. All it took was an unforecasted storm to turn rain to snow and create driving conditions that she was too inexperienced to handle. As long as he was in charge of her, he would err on the side of caution.

As soon as Malcolm finished his porridge, sweetened with honey, cream, and butter, he put his bowl in the sink. "I'm going to get dressed, and then we can go."

As he climbed the stairs, he wondered what Serena was doing at this moment. Was she already moving into the croft house next door, or was she, too, having breakfast with her children? He and Serena weren't as different as she seemed to believe. They were both single parents doing the best they could with the circumstances they'd been given. Of course, she had the resources to spend time with her children; but then again, Kylee was at an age where she needed Malcolm's guidance and support far more than his constant attention. She was also incredibly responsible for her age. He definitely had the easier job of the two of them.

Not that Serena would acknowledge their similarities. Like it or not, things had gotten personal between them, but she seemed to believe that if she ignored it, pretended the spark didn't exist, it would go away. Maybe she could flip the switch that easily, but he couldn't stop thinking about how inviting her lips had looked and wishing he'd made a move, consequences be hanged.

Malcolm combed his hair and trimmed his beard, which was looking more like a proper beard than the scraggly mess it had been before, then donned a heavy fisherman's knit sweater with his jeans. His laptop went into a ballistic nylon case along with a small notepad and a reference book on web design. He'd have a couple of hours to work while Kylee was in her voice lesson, and even though the coding to add the social media feed to the site hardly compared in difficulty to his old work of analyzing astronomical data, he was out of practice.

"We're going to be late!" Kylee yelled from downstairs.

"I'm coming." He slung the case over his shoulder, descended the stairs quickly, and took his coat from the front hall. "Grab your keys. You're driving today."

Kylee looked surprised, but she took her rucksack and followed him outside to where her Volkswagen was parked behind his Ford Focus. The tiny cars in the United Kingdom had been a surprisingly difficult readjustment after years in

UNDER SCOTTISH STARS

the United States. He'd tried to talk Kylee into something a little bigger and a little safer, but she had insisted on this supermini in case she moved to the city center at some point. A reasonable plan, but it still meant feeling like a sardine squeezed into a can whenever he rode with her.

He didn't complain when she turned the radio to a pop station the minute they crossed the Skye bridge—those were the rules: the driver chose the music—and instead cracked open the web-design book.

After a few minutes she glanced over at him. "What are you reading?"

"XML and CSS. Thrilling, right?"

"Sounds like good *craic*. My next question is why?"

"I asked Serena to take over the hotel's social media. I'm working on tying it in to the hotel website."

"That's a good idea!"

He shot her a wry smile, even though she missed it because she was responsibly keeping her eyes on the road. "Don't sound so surprised, Kylee. It does happen every once in a while."

"Sorry. You know that's not what I meant. I didn't know you even had an Instagram account."

"Well, now that I've retired my eight-track and you've shown me those newfangled things called MP3s, I figured I'd go all the way with the technology."

Kylee snorted, but she didn't apologize. With typical teenage centricity, she assumed that anyone over the age of twenty had no idea what was going on in the world, never mind the fact that Malcolm had made a career of writing software for cutting-edge technology. He just smiled to himself and returned to his reading. Despite the adjustment inherent

108

in the move back to Skye and taking on a responsibility he'd thought was still years in the future, he liked Kylee. She was smart and funny, just like Nicola. When she started singing along with the radio, he reminded himself to add *talented* to the list. God only knew where she had inherited her singing ability, because when the rest of the family sang, the neighborhood dogs joined in.

He'd refreshed his cascading style sheet knowledge and gotten a disturbingly thorough education on the Top 40 by the time Kylee made the turnoff to the small commercial section of Fort William, where her voice teacher was located. She made a quick detour and pulled up in front of a pub called the Blooming Fuchsia. "Pick you up in two hours?"

"I'll be waiting. Have fun." He climbed out and watched the red car drive off before heading inside.

It was early to be in a pub, but the Blooming Fuchsia opened at seven o'clock and served an excellent breakfast. As soon as he set foot in the clubby interior, with its dark paneling and polished mahogany bar, a young blonde woman appeared from the back, wearing a bright smile.

"Morning, Malcolm! Your usual?"

"If you wouldn't mind, Janine. I'm going to grab a booth."

He settled in at one of the large corner booths, knowing the pub didn't start picking up steam until after noon on Saturday, and took out his laptop. He nodded his thanks to Janine when she left his tea, mixed with milk and sugar, and then he brought up a code editor on-screen. He'd already found some open source social media widget code; all it would take was a few tweaks to make it work with their existing site and save him hours of coding and testing.

"Kylee at her voice lesson?"

Malcolm looked up as Janine set his Scottish breakfast order on the table. "She is. How have things been around here?"

"Not bad. My mum's moving to Aberdeen with her new boyfriend. Just been helping her pack."

"Do you still have family in the Highlands?"

"My dad, but I don't see him much. Leaves me lots of free time." She looked flattered by the question, which made him regret that he'd engaged. She always seemed to leave openings as if she were hoping he'd ask her out. Which wasn't going to happen. Not only was she at least ten years younger than he—he guessed about twenty to his thirty-three—but she wasn't his type. He'd never gone for the slender blondes, especially when they reminded him so much of his niece.

Unbidden, Serena's image rose in his mind by means of comparison. Hard to pretend that he didn't at least have a little bit of a thing for his boss when that happened with such regularity. He cleared his throat. "Nice to see you, Janine, but I need to finish this before Kylee comes back."

"Oh, right. Sure. Just let me know if you need anything. I'll be right over there."

Definitely flirting. Malcolm smiled vaguely. "Thanks, I will."

He hadn't finished the changes by the time Kylee walked into the pub, but he was close. He saved his work and shut the laptop. "How did it go?"

"Good. We're working on one of Rosina's arias from *The Barber of Seville*. Which is brilliant, because it's for a coloratura mezzo-soprano, and I'm almost a true contralto."

He only understood about five words of that sentence,

though he was pretty sure the opera was an Italian comedy. He remembered because he'd thought it was funny that a story set in Spain was written in Italian. Still, he gave her an encouraging smile. She wasn't at all an operatic singer—she wanted to be a singer-songwriter, after all—but she threw herself after anything that would help her reach her ultimate goals. He wanted to encourage that kind of work ethic. "Ready to go, then? You can tell me all about Rosana in the car."

"Rosina."

"That's what I said." He ruffled her hair, knowing it irritated her, then waved good-bye to Janine behind the bar.

They walked out to where the Polo was parked at the curb, dodging a foursome on their way into the pub. Kylee grinned at him. "You know that girl has been wanting you to ask her out for the last six months."

"The fact you called her a girl is exactly why I would never do it. She could be one of your friends."

"You know, you could totally date. It would be okay with me."

Malcolm got into the car, hoping that she would drop the subject on her way to the driver's seat, but she persisted.

"Really. I mean, I feel bad that you and Teresa split up when you left—"

"That was Teresa's doing," Malcolm said, "not yours. So don't waste any thought on that. Besides, there's no point in dating when we have no idea where we'll end up next."

He expected her to turn on the ignition, but she just sat there. "What if we stay in Scotland? The University of Glasgow has a good music program, and I've already been accepted."

He frowned. "What's this about, Kylee? I thought you were keen on going to America."

She swallowed hard and reached into her pocket, then brought up an e-mail on her phone. His stomach sank as he read the return address: UCLA. He read only as far as it took to see it was a flat rejection. She reached over him to swipe to another message, this one from Berklee College of Music, her first choice. He steeled himself for the bad news.

"Wait, this isn't a rejection," he said. "You're on the waiting list."

"Same thing. It's not like any spaces are going to open up. Everyone who gets in attends."

Malcolm clicked off the screen and handed the phone back to her. "I'm sorry, Kylee. I know how much you wanted this."

She shrugged, her throat working and her long lashes fluttering as she blinked away tears. "It's okay. I knew it was a long shot. I mean, at least they didn't reject me, right? They thought I had talent, but it's not like I've had the world-class training here that some of the other kids had. I've heard the program is hellishly competitive."

Malcolm hesitated and then put an arm around her and gave her a tight hug. "I'm proud of you, Kylee. You're so talented, I have no doubt that you'll end up where you're supposed to be. You can always try a couple of years at Glasgow, and then if you still want to go to America, transfer in as a junior. Or you can do your undergrad program here and then apply for a diploma program at Berklee. You told me admissions for that are less competitive."

"You'd do that? Stay here in Scotland?"

"Of course I would. We're a family. That means we look

out for each other." He gave her a little nudge. "Now let's get going. It looks like rain."

Kylee was quiet on the way home, but not mopey. He was proud of her maturity. He would have had difficulty dealing with that kind of disappointment at her age, but here she was considering all the options. With her determination, there was no doubt she would make her way in the music business one way or another, even catch the eye of a record label. She had her father's brains, her mother's tenacity, and plenty of God-given talent. Malcolm might not be able to claim any credit for that, but at least he could give her every opportunity within his power.

CHAPTER ELEVEN

SERENA FIT THE KEY INTO THE LOCK, balancing a box on her hip as she pushed the door to the croft house open. Even though clouds still threatened overhead, the ever-present rain had finally tapered off, giving her a small window in which to move her trunkful of possessions into their new, if temporary, home.

She wandered into the kitchen and set the box on the table, where she found a note in Malcolm's messy scrawl: *Welcome home. I'll be back at 8 if you need any help getting warmed up.*

Very funny. Leave it to him to lace an innocent welcome note with innuendo.

Except maybe he didn't mean it as innuendo. Serena

shivered and rubbed her arms. The outside temperature had risen several degrees, but the inside remained as cold as it had been when she first looked at the croft house. Hadn't he turned on the heat as he said he would? She went to the unit on the far side of the kitchen and touched the radiator coils. Frigid.

Too late she remembered her insistence that she could handle the job herself. She knelt before the unit and searched for the knob that would open the valve to let the hot water in. And realized that there was no knob, only a screw that required a spanner to open.

She sat back on her heels, frustrated. She could wait for Malcolm to come home from work and do it for her as part of his duties as landlord. Or she could drive to the hotel and get a set of adjustables. Both of which felt like letting Malcolm win. No doubt he was expecting her to do one of those very things.

Instead, Serena got back into her car and turned toward Broadford, where the nearest hardware store was located. She really should have tools at hand anyway, especially this far away from the nearest handyman. Forty-five minutes later, she was back with a full set of adjustable spanners in different sizes. After checking that the boiler had been filled—it had been—she turned it on to heat the water while she put away the few kitchen items she'd brought from home. This croft house, unlike the cottage rental on Sleat, had only a handful of pots, utensils, and plates in the kitchen cabinets. She would have to go home for the rest. No point in owning a spare set when this was just a temporary arrangement.

Serena had their clothes hung in their small wardrobes

and folded into the narrow chests of drawers when the boiler finally came up to temperature. She went around to the main radiator in the lounge and bled out the air from the system until water spurted into the catch bowl she placed beneath it. Then all there was left to do was open the rest of the valves.

Malcolm had to think she would be waiting on him to come home and turn them on for her. He probably imagined her shivering in her winter coat and cursing her own stubbornness. Clearly she didn't need him, evidenced by the heat beginning to radiate from the metal coils.

She spent the next several hours cleaning every surface of the kitchen and bath with supplies she'd brought from Nairn, until she was satisfied she had banished every last germ. Only then did she allow herself to plop onto her sofa and sit back contentedly. The croft house was perfect. Quaint and traditional but still comfortable. It was just what she'd had in mind when she envisioned their island interlude on Skye.

There was enough time to go to the co-op for groceries before she had to pick up Em and Max from Muriel's. Maybe there would even be time to bake some of her signature shortbread together before supper.

When she brought her children to their new home, their reactions were exactly as she'd hoped. "This is it?" Em asked, jumping out of the car the instant Serena parked. "It's so tiny and cute!"

Serena retrieved Max from the car seat, and both children bolted for the front door. "You each have your own bedroom. Go have a look." They darted inside as soon as Serena unlatched the door, but she lingered on the front porch for

UNDER SCOTTISH STARS

a moment, her eyes drawn to the house next door, barely visible through the bare trees on the property line. The drive was empty. She didn't expect to have much contact with Malcolm outside of work anyway.

"Mum, look!"

Serena dragged herself inside toward Em's excited voice. After the children explored every corner of their new home, she set them up at the table to help her measure and mix ingredients for shortbread.

"I love it here," Em said, her eyes shining over the dusting of flour on her nose. "It's like a little fairy-tale cottage, isn't it?"

Serena smiled over her shoulder. "It certainly is. Our own little place in the woods, just the three of us."

———— ∽◯◯◯∾ ————

Serena started awake, her eyes snapping open and searching the dark. Her alarm clock showed it was just after eleven. What had woken her? Was it simply the unfamiliar sounds of their new accommodations, the settling of the old house? As she listened, she caught the sound again, faintly: Max, calling her name.

She threw aside her duvet and took the stairs as quickly as she dared in the dark. Once she reached the bottom floor, she knew something was wrong. The cold damp hit her like a physical force, the contrast between her toasty loft and the icy lower floor causing gooseflesh to break out over her bare arms and legs.

When she entered Max's room, he was sitting up in bed, his eyes wide. "It's really cold, Mummy!"

She placed a hand on his radiator, even though she knew the answer. Frigid.

"Mum?" Em poked her head into Max's room, her duvet wrapped around her shoulders. "My room's cold. What happened to the rads?"

"I don't know, sweetie, but the one upstairs is working. Why don't you climb into my bed while I figure it out?"

They immediately scampered out of the room, their feet pounding up the wooden steps. Serena leaned against the wall with a groan, then jerked away when her bare skin hit cold plaster. Clearly the insulation in this old house left something to be desired if the temperature had dropped so quickly after the radiators turned off.

Blast Malcolm. But no, she had only herself to blame. Had she taken his offer of help, he would have turned them on and tested them thoroughly on Friday. Could they wait it out until tomorrow? The sprawl of her already-sleeping children across her bed answered for her. If she were to get any rest tonight, she'd have to swallow her pride, no matter how bitter it tasted. Maybe Malcolm would still be awake. She found her mobile phone and dialed his number. It went straight to voice mail.

Serena wavered for a long moment. Then she yanked on flannel bottoms and her cardigan, thrust her feet into her wellies, and marched next door. Light glowed through the upstairs window. He'd said they had the same view through their bedroom windows, so that had to be his. He was still awake.

This is a bad idea. A very bad idea. I should just leave.

She forced herself to raise her hand and knock.

The porch light flipped on, and moments later Malcolm opened the door, dressed in a T-shirt and flannel pajama bottoms not unlike hers, his feet bare. He looked over her disheveled state, a lazy smile stretching his lips. "Why hello, Mrs. Stewart. I didn't expect a middle-of-the-night visit from you. At least not so soon."

Serena resisted the urge to roll her eyes. Like it or not, she needed his help. "The radiators died. It's getting cold in the house."

"Is that right?" He braced a muscular arm against the doorframe, his smile widening to full amusement.

The infuriating man was going to make her say it. "The kids' rooms are freezing. Can you . . . will you come over and take a look?"

"All you had to do was ask." He straightened and dropped his arm. "Go on back. I'll get my tools."

Serena had to swallow down a lump that tasted like pride and gratitude mixed, neither palatable. "Thank you."

"Was it that hard?"

For once he seemed serious, not as though he was baiting her. She gave him a lopsided smile and stepped off the stoop. "You have no idea."

"I'll be right there."

She walked quietly back to the house, her chest feeling tight for a reason she couldn't pinpoint. She should be grateful, and she was. He could have given her a much harder time about rousing him in the middle of the night. He could have refused. But he'd done neither.

When she let herself into the croft house, she wavered before giving in and heading to the bathroom to brush her teeth and smooth her hair into a ponytail. She was just checking on Em and Max again when a light knock sounded at the door.

Malcolm had dressed in jeans and a heavy jacket, and his

toolbox was in hand. When she let him in, he pitched his voice low. "All the rads are cold?"

"All but the one in the loft."

"Okay then." He flicked on the lights as he went and knelt before the radiator in the lounge, feeling the coils. "They were working earlier?"

She nodded.

"In that case, they probably just need to be balanced. The hot water likes to stay upstairs, and it can't get back down to the ground floor."

"Max and Em are sleeping in my bed, though."

"I'll be quiet." He pulled a torch and a spanner from the toolbox, then gestured for her to precede him up the stairs.

She stayed out of his way on the other side of the bed while he knelt beside the radiator, shining the torch's beam on the valve. Ten seconds later, he stood.

"That was it?" she whispered in disbelief.

"That was it. You had the valve completely open. It really only needs a quarter turn."

Serena followed him down the stairs, muttering to herself, "I should have had you do this in the first place."

"Do my ears deceive me, or did Serena Stewart just admit defeat?"

Serena made a face. "Not defeat. I did turn them on; I just never knew radiators needed to be balanced."

"Sorry about that. I should have insisted on doing it."

"You wanted me to come running for help."

"And you did. You simply lasted twelve hours longer than I anticipated." He threw her a grin, but his tone was almost self-deprecating. An answering smile rose to Serena's face. He could get some serious mileage out of this one, but he was being kind. He packed his tools again, then stood. "I'll wait a couple of minutes to make sure the other ones are heating."

"Thank you. I'm sorry I got you out of bed in the middle of the night."

"Don't worry." His smile flashed, just as mischievous and suggestive as ever. "I can think of several ways you can make it up to me."

She quelled the answering jitter in her middle before it could get started. "I wish you wouldn't do that."

"Serena, why do you keep pretending this thing between us doesn't exist?"

"I'm your boss, and apparently now you are my landlord. Other than that, we don't have a *thing*."

"We have a thing, whether you admit it or not. But if the fact that we have a work relationship bothers you, we can set some ground rules."

"What would those be exactly?"

"Work stays at work. Home stays at home. And while I do have a certain responsibility as a landlord, I doubt midnight repair calls are part of the job. So I think you might owe me."

The teasing tone was back, but something unsettlingly intense had crept into his eyes. She swallowed. "You're very persistent."

"You have no idea." He held her gaze a moment longer, then nodded toward the bedrooms. "Why don't you check the other rads so we can go back to bed?"

It was the escape she'd been waiting for. She rushed to Em's room first, then Max's, both of which were beginning to heat. Thanks to Malcolm. As much as she hated to admit it, she really did owe him.

"Good?" he asked when she returned.

"Yes, thank you." She paused. "I mean that."

"You're welcome. Sleep well."

She closed the door behind him and resisted the urge to peek out the window. He was right, though. They did have a thing. She just had absolutely no idea where it would lead.

CHAPTER TWELVE

SERENA HADN'T BEEN IN THE CROFT HOUSE for two days before Muriel called to summon her and the kids for dinner. It didn't take much to figure out why: it was Monday, and Muriel had invited her usual guests. Serena's attempts at declining met with little success.

"What do you mean you won't be able to come?" Muriel said. "I've made two whole chickens. I know you're not asking me to waste an entire chicken."

So at ten minutes before six, Serena parked her car in front of Muriel's house and let herself in. As expected, her aunt was bustling around in one of her old-fashioned aprons over a tailored dress, looking like a 1960s housewife. "I'm here. What do you want me to do?"

Muriel shoved a wooden bowl of mixed salad greens

across the island to Serena. "I'll take your reluctance to come tonight as a sign you like the croft house."

No, it was a sign that she didn't want to see Malcolm after their oddly intense encounter, but she couldn't say that. She picked up the salad tongs and began to toss the greens in the dressing. "It's actually perfect. Very peaceful."

"And your new neighbor?"

She should have known this was where the questioning was leading. "I haven't seen him much, though he was kind enough to come turn on the radiators when we moved in." Serena repressed a smile at her revisionist version of the truth.

"Oh, he did, did he?"

Serena ignored Muriel's amusement. "The croft house isn't fully stocked, though, so I'll need to make a trip back to Nairn sometime this week."

"Why not just have Jamie get your things? They'll be here in another few weeks."

Serena fixed her aunt with a reproving look. "That's not until June. I can't do without my pots for two months. Besides, do you really think he would bring me the right items?"

"Jamie? If they're cooking or wardrobe related, yes."

Serena chuckled. There was some element of truth in that. Her younger brother had a better sense of style than Serena did, and most of her kitchen equipment had been gifts from him. Still, she wasn't going to have him riffle through her unmentionables. "Best I do it myself, Auntie."

"Why don't you leave Em and Max here, then? No reason to subject them to six hours in the car."

"I'd thought I'd make it an overnight trip. You don't want to chase Max by yourself for two days . . ."

Muriel fixed her no-nonsense gaze on her. "May I remind you that I survived you and your brothers? I imagine I could handle your very well-behaved children for two days."

It *would* be convenient to make the drive alone, without the inevitable stops that came with a recently potty-trained toddler. Just as Serena opened her mouth to agree, a crash and a scream from one of the bedrooms cut her off.

Serena raced to the source of the sound, where she found Max sobbing amidst a pile of books, the shelf above him listing precariously on one bracket. "I want the book!" he wailed, pointing a finger at a volume two shelves up before bursting into more piteous crying.

Serena scooped him up, wiping away the tears trailing down his chubby cheeks. "But, Maxie love, you shouldn't have climbed the shelf to get it. Ask Sister next time."

Max directed a glare in Em's direction with all the three-year-old fury he could muster, to which Em simply gave an innocent shrug. Too innocent. Em had likely told Max to get it himself, with predictable results.

"I'll get it for you now, and then we'll go read in the lounge. Em, please pick these up, and we'll fix the shelf later."

Em complied without argument, confirming Serena's suspicions. Serena took the volume down—a board book about trucks—and walked Max out to the lounge. With the exception of a little red patch above one eyebrow, he looked none the worse for wear. The tears seemed mostly born of indignation, considering how quickly they disappeared when she started reading about all the different kinds of trucks and lorries.

By the fourth time through, Serena was about to shed some tears of her own. When a knock sounded at the front door, she was halfway to it before Muriel called, "Serena, dear, will you get that? Malcolm must be early."

Sure enough, Malcolm stood on the front porch, a toolbox in one hand, Kylee behind him. He gave her a slow smile, which quickened her heartbeat with annoying alacrity.

"You know," she said as she stood aside for them to enter, "most men bring wine, not a toolbox."

"Who says I don't have a bottle stashed in the bottom of this?"

"Do you?"

"No, but I'm insulted by the assumption." He winked, and she rolled her eyes at him. He pushed by her and went straight to Max. "Hey, little man. What's up?" He ruffled her son's hair before continuing into the kitchen.

"Hi, Kylee," Serena said. "Dinner will be in a few minutes. You can watch some telly while we wait if you want."

"That's all right. I can help." Kylee followed her into the kitchen, where Malcolm was standing with Muriel.

"Malcolm is going to look at the sink in my bathroom," Muriel said. "It's been draining slowly. Could you show him where it is, please?"

Serena shot a reproving look at Muriel, who gave her the same innocent expression Em had tried earlier; then she jerked her head at a still-grinning Malcolm. "Follow me."

She took him through Muriel's old-fashioned but pristine bedroom to the small, updated en suite. "That sink right there, in case you were unable to surmise that on your own."

Malcolm set down his toolbox beside the pedestal sink. "You seem uncomfortable, Serena. I thought you appreciated my ability to fix things. At least you did the other night."

"Very funny. Are you all set in here? I'm going to go help set the table."

"You mean you don't want to stay and be my lovely assistant?"

"I'm sure you can manage without me. And while I'd love to see you try to make unclogging a drain look sexy, I don't think you can pull it off."

"You underestimate me." He unbuttoned his shirt and shrugged it off to reveal a snug black T-shirt that most definitely did show off his muscular upper body to advantage. Whether it was by calculation or an accident, she had to clamp her lips together in order not to laugh.

"I think I've estimated you exactly right. Don't take too long. We'd hate to start dinner without you." She went back to the dining room, where Muriel had already put Kylee to work setting the table.

"Need any help?" Serena asked.

"No, I've got it." Kylee set down all the forks and knives in the proper order, the water glasses set precisely at the upper right of the plates. "My mum was a bit of a stickler for manners and table settings and such."

"She taught you well."

"It's not like we have much of a chance to use it. We don't have guests." She shot Serena a crooked smile. "And Uncle Malcolm can't cook."

Serena returned the smile. There was no reproach in the girl's voice, just a simple statement of fact. But it did make Serena wonder about the arrangement. Clearly Malcolm loved his niece and was doing his best for her, but what had happened to her parents? How had she been left in the care of a bachelor uncle? She'd meant to ask Muriel more than once, but she'd been afraid her aunt would take her interest to mean something else entirely.

"Did I miss dinner?" Malcolm popped his head into the dining room. He was wearing his button-down again, though he hadn't fastened it up.

"Just in time. Did you repair the sink?"

"Simple fix." He moved past Serena and lowered his voice so only she could hear. "And I looked sexy while doing it. Shame that you missed it."

The laugh bubbled up inside her again, but she managed to capture it just in time, even if she couldn't control her smile. "I'll have to learn to live with the disappointment."

Malcolm left the room, and she heard him talking to Muriel in his usual cheerful tone. When she turned back, Kylee was watching her.

"You like my uncle?"

"Yeah," Serena said brightly. "Of course I do."

Kylee just looked at her with an expression that said she was too smart to believe that evasion. Serena cursed her carelessness. It wouldn't do to flirt openly with Malcolm if she didn't want to answer a bunch of embarrassing and irrelevant questions. Not that she'd intended to flirt. It had just sort of happened.

When they finally all settled around the table, six of them circling what looked like enough food to feed a dozen people, Serena found herself sitting directly across from Malcolm. She tried not to focus on him, but every time she looked up, he was watching her with that thoughtful expression, as if she were a mystery to be solved. Serena volunteered to help clear the table, just to get away from him, but on her second trip back to the dining room, Em called to her from the reception room. "Mum, come play Snakes and Ladders with us!"

"As soon as I finish here." A touch of mischief welled up. "You could ask Malcolm. I know for a fact that he loves to play games."

"As appealing as that sounds," Malcolm said from the doorway, "I have to drive Kylee home before I head back to the bar. Owen rang in sick."

There seemed to be a spate of that lately. Even considering the unseasonably cold weather, Serena would have hoped their staff would be more reliable. She needed to address the personnel situation soon. "If you want, I can take her home when we're finished. It's no trouble."

Malcolm looked surprised. "You wouldn't mind?"

"Of course not. I owe you one, after all."

"That's not exactly what I had in mind," he murmured, his gaze once more sending a tingling to her toes. "But I'll take what I can get." He settled at the table with Em and Max, and Serena took the only open space beside him on the floor. Immediately she realized that Malcolm had a completely different set of rules for Snakes and Ladders, and his were much more fun. He made his pieces tumble down the snakes, screaming in a high-pitched cartoon voice while Max squealed with childish laughter. Every time the kids looked away, he switched their pieces. When it was her daughter's turn, he counted loudly to distract her, earning a giggle from Em. Even Kylee and Muriel were smiling at his unconventional rules.

After some questionable scorekeeping by Malcolm, Max won the game and proceeded to jump on the couch to celebrate his victory. Malcolm straightened and made a big show of stretching. "I need to go to work now, but you owe me a rematch, Max."

"What's a rematch?"

"It means he wants to play again so he can try to win." Serena guided Max off the sofa before he managed to tumble onto his head.

Max looked pleased with the idea. "Okay."

"You're still fine with driving Kylee home?" Malcolm asked.

"Of course. We'll leave in a few minutes."

"All right. I'll check in later. Kylee, come get your bag and guitar from my car before I go."

Em looked at Kylee with excitement. "You play the guitar? I play the piano."

"Do you? I'd like to hear that."

"Okay! Maybe you can play your guitar too."

"It's a deal."

Kylee slipped past Malcolm, who looked uncertainly at Serena. "I really hate to ask you to do this."

"Now who's having trouble accepting help? Just say thank you. And that we're even."

"Even, huh?"

She stared him down until he chuckled.

"Fine, we're even."

"Was it that hard?" she asked, throwing his own words back at him.

Mischief sparkled in his eyes, and he moved close enough to murmur in her ear. "Careful. Someone might get the idea you have a sense of humor."

"I have a sense of humor. I just don't find you all that funny."

"Liar."

She was preparing a retort when Kylee came back in with her schoolbag and sticker-decorated guitar case. Instead, Serena simply said, "Go. I'll get her home."

"Thank you," he mouthed, then gave Kylee a quick hug.

Em bounced on the sofa impatiently, her attention fixed on the teen girl. "You go first."

Kylee took out her guitar and strummed it a few times, making an adjustment to a peg or two. Then she began to play. Kylee's voice was undeniably good, with a smoky quality that Serena associated with folk singers. She began to listen to the lyrics, and it was all she could do not to let her mouth drop open. When the girl was finished and the group was done applauding, Serena asked, "Did you write that?"

Kylee nodded with a shy smile. "I played it at the school talent show last year. Though I keep changing it up a little."

"You are very talented. Are you going to study music at university?"

Kylee shifted in a way that made Serena think it was a sore subject. "I hope so. I'd like to record a demo this summer too, though."

"I think you're smart to keep all your options open." From what Serena could tell, the girl had loads of natural talent, but it wasn't likely to get nurtured to its full potential on Skye. Impulsively she said, "If it's all right with your uncle, I'd like to introduce you to some friends of mine—they're professional musicians. Davy fronts a band and runs her own record label, and Glenn is a session player. They were both my dad's students at one time."

Kylee stared at Serena with an expression of wonder and suspicion. "You don't even know me."

"I know talent when I hear it, and I know artists need to

be developed. Davy and Glenn might be able to give you some practical advice." They would be encouraging, Serena knew, but realistic. The music industry was a difficult one, and they would undoubtedly urge Kylee to take her education as seriously as her songwriting.

Em jumped in to show off her newly mastered "Für Elise," cutting off the rest of the conversation. Serena watched Malcolm's niece and hoped she hadn't just overstepped her bounds.

CHAPTER THIRTEEN

"MUMMY. MUMMY, WAKE UP."

Serena pried her eyes open as a hand softly patted her cheek and found herself looking straight into the eyes of her son. The filtered light pouring in through the uncovered windows said it was early.

"Morning, lovie." She lifted the covers so Max could climb into the warmth beneath the duvet with her. "What are you doing up already?"

"There's someone at the door."

"You probably dreamed it." Serena closed her eyes, praying that Max would get the hint and go back to sleep.

"Mum! There's someone at the door."

Serena sighed as Em bounded into the room and flung

herself onto the end of the bed. So much for going back to sleep. She pushed herself upright, shivering at the cool air that nipped the skin left uncovered by her skimpy pajama top. "Who is it?"

"I don't know. I didn't open it to look."

Serena swung her legs over the side, reached for her oversize cardigan, and wrapped it around herself as she descended the steps to the ground floor. She yanked the front door open and found herself looking straight into Malcolm's deep-brown eyes.

Serena reached up to smooth her hair before she could stop herself. "Good morning. What are you doing here?"

"I brought you breakfast." He held up a vacuum carafe and a white bakery bag, wearing a grin that gave her heart a somersault. Then it faded into a strangely uncertain expression. "Can we talk for a moment?"

"Mum, who is it?" Em thundered down the stairs, Max only steps behind.

"It's Malcolm. I need to talk to him for a second. Why don't you two get dressed for school?" She stepped out onto the porch and pulled the door closed behind her, glad she had worn long pajama bottoms. Just as quickly she realized her top was showing indecent amounts of cleavage and clutched the cardigan's lapels together.

"Coffee." He handed her the carafe, then held out the bag. "Pastries."

She'd woken in an alternate universe, clearly. "Thank you, but . . . I don't understand."

"Well, you called me to the door in my pajamas, so I figured I'd return the favor. At least I brought you coffee."

"Very funny. Really, though, why are you here?"

He cleared his throat and thrust his hands into the pockets of his leather jacket. "Kylee told me you offered her an introduction to some musician friends."

"I hope I didn't overstep. I offered before I thought about asking you."

"No, that's not it at all." The uncertainty flashed once more. "That's a rather large favor. I was just teasing when I said you owed me one."

Now, this was an interesting turn of events. He'd given her a hard time about accepting help, and now he was squirming because she'd done his niece a favor. "I didn't do it for you. I did it for Kylee."

"Why?"

"Because I know what it is to be an artist with the limited opportunities on Skye. And I know how fast dreams die when they aren't nurtured. Kylee is too talented to watch that happen."

"Then thank you. You have no idea what this means to Kylee. And me."

"Sure," she said softly. He began to turn, and before she could think better of it, she asked, "Malcolm?"

"Yes?"

"What happened to Kylee's parents . . . your sister? Why does she live with you?"

Malcolm's expression closed, and Serena instantly regretted broaching the subject. Then he met her eyes, his pain evident in the tense lines of his face. "They were killed in a car accident last year."

It was the sort of answer she had feared. "That's awful. I'm so sorry."

"Yeah, me too." He glanced down the drive, toward his

house—what had to have been his sister's house. "I'm not half the parent Nicola and Richard were, but I'm all Kylee has left."

Serena swallowed, everything she could come up with feeling woefully inadequate. "She's a remarkable girl, Malcolm. And for what it's worth, I think you're doing a great job with her."

Their eyes met and held for a long moment, beginning the most peculiar ache in her chest. Then he smiled faintly and stepped backward off the porch. "That means more than you know, actually. Thanks again, Serena." She watched him stride to the end of the drive, where he turned back with a wave before heading to his house. Serena slowly opened the door to her own, where she was instantly peppered with Em's excited questions.

"What was he doing here? What did he bring you, Mum?"

"I don't know." She was about to suggest they share whatever it was, until she peeked into the bag and found mini cranberry bannocks. Three of them.

"We get one too?" Max asked, wide-eyed.

"Yes, you get one too." Somehow that was a degree of thoughtfulness she hadn't expected from Malcolm.

Serena set the kettle on the stove to heat for the kids' tea and then sat down with them at the kitchen table, where they dug into the lightly sweet fruit-studded bread as if it were their first meal all month. All the while her mind continued to circulate around Malcolm Blake.

What was she to make of him? He was a puzzling mix of bluntness and sensitivity. He had no compunction over hassling her and slinging innuendo, but he also played Snakes and Ladders with her children with as much enthusiasm as if they were his own, not to mention the way he advocated for his niece. He made a big show of his blue-collar, work-for-a-living ethics, but glimpses of how he managed the hotel made her think he possessed far more experience than he let on. Plus, there was still the whole engineering career that she couldn't fit into what little she knew of his background.

You could always pull his personnel file. Or you could just ask him. But that was dangerous because once he knew she was curious about him, he'd press her even harder for that date. Her willpower was already beginning to crumble. Bad enough that she hadn't felt this kind of primal pull toward a man in years. Even worse that these glimpses of the deeper, thoughtful person inside powerfully tempted her to give in and see where this *thing* might go.

She couldn't do that. She had a life in Nairn. Skye was merely a detour. And unless she was looking for a quick, casual fling—she wasn't—it made no sense to even dip a toe into those waters.

Plus, she was his boss. Maybe they could be friends, or at least cordial coworkers. But anything else could only lead to disaster.

She managed to get the children off to school with some semblance of concentration, then sat down at her kitchen table to begin her work for the day. First, she dialed Davy. When the call went directly to voice mail, she left a message and then opened her laptop. It was high time that she took a look at the staffing situation. Malcolm might act as though filling in at the bar was no big deal, but he routinely worked eleven-hour days during the week and another six or eight hours on the weekends. That was far too much on a regular basis; she certainly didn't think it was fair to make him pick up the slack for the bartenders and housekeepers as well.

But there was also the matter of payroll budgets and staff schedules, not to mention hiring reliable people. By the time she went to pick up Max from preschool, her head ached from staring at columns of numbers. There was no doubt about it— it would cost them to bring on extra staff, and it would cut into profits. But it needed to be done. They didn't want to become known as a business that took advantage of its employees. James and Ian would have to understand that.

Serena drove Max home, then settled him with cookies, milk, and a puzzle while she drafted her proposal to her brothers. She sent off the message with a copy of a spreadsheet, hoping they would agree with her proposed allocation of funds. She would have to get moving on the new marketing plans to help make up for it.

Those would have to wait, though, since it was nearly time to pick up Em from school. There never seemed to be enough uninterrupted time in her day to finish a task. When she and Max arrived at the front of Sleat Primary, the little girl sped out of the school building with a wide smile. "Mum, Felicity invited me over to her house after school tomorrow. Can I go?"

Em's beaming face brought a wash of relief. "I'd like to talk to her mum first. Does Felicity ride the bus?"

"No, they're over there." Em pointed to a little girl and a woman with identical blonde ponytails, already starting toward the car park. Before Serena could say anything, Em abandoned her rucksack and sprinted after them. "Felicity! Wait! My mum wants to talk to your mum."

Serena retrieved Em's bag with a wry smile and led Max

to the waiting woman, who smiled and put out her hand. "I'm Alice Quinn, Felicity's mother."

Serena shook Alice's hand. "Serena Stewart."

"You're new to the school. I was going to ring you and invite you and Emmy for tea, but I see Felicity beat me to it."

"That's very kind of you. We'd love to. As long as it's okay that I bring Max."

"Naturally." Alice smiled warmly. "We live at Elm Cottage in Tokavaig. Do you know it?"

"I do. Close to Dunscaith Castle, isn't it?"

"Precisely. Tomorrow, then?"

"Tomorrow. Thank you again."

"We're looking forward to it, truly." Alice and Felicity gave identical waves good-bye and turned toward their car.

"Thanks, Mum." Em's eyes were bright, and she was barely able to keep from skipping back to their own vehicle. "I think you might like Andrew's mum too. They just moved back last year from Fort William. Sort of like us, I guess. Andrew doesn't speak Gaelic very well either."

Serena smiled and ruffled Em's hair. "I'm sure I will. I'm glad you've made some friends." Maybe they were finally settling into the change at last.

In fact, there was something so ordinary about the night— Em doing schoolwork at the table and Max playing with cars on the floor while she cooked—that she felt she could take a deep breath for the first time in weeks. This was what she wanted for her family, at least for a season—relaxed afternoons free from lessons and pressure and bustle. When the weather finally turned, they would rush through their work to play outside in the increasingly light evenings.

They had just finished supper when Serena's mobile beeped.

She picked it up and saw Davy's number on the screen. Missed call. The mobile signal here in Breakish was still somewhat dodgy, even if it was far better than in Isleornsay. She tapped an icon to play the message, and a female voice with a very thick Highland accent poured from the speaker.

"Hi, Serena; it's Davy. I just got home. Glenn is in LA right now, and I have a gig in Inverness on Saturday, but perhaps you could bring Kylee by the following Saturday? We're happy to give her some guidance. Tell her to bring her guitar too, if she wants."

Serena deleted the message with a smile. Davy—short for Davina—had been one of her dad's most talented students, which also meant she'd been around the house a lot growing up. She'd been right between Serena and Jamie in age, a year behind Serena in school, so they'd had their share of girl talk. It was one of those friendships that had endured despite the fact they had seen each other only a handful of times in the past fifteen years.

Serena called back and left another message, then hesitated a moment before dialing Malcolm's mobile. He picked up immediately, the sound of voices and laughter ringing out in the background.

"I knew you'd come around." His voice warbled over the bad connection. "Admit it, it's because of my coffee-making skills. What time should I pick you up on Friday?"

Serena laughed. "Not so fast. I wasn't calling because I'm agreeing to the date idea."

"And this is the sound of my heart breaking." A horrible sound came on the other end of the line.

Serena couldn't suppress her laugh. "That's paper crumpling."

"How do you know? Are you so skilled at breaking men's hearts that you recognize the sound?"

Her smile stretched wider, making her face ache. "Be serious, please. I did have a legitimate reason for calling."

"Okay." His voice sobered. "What's up?"

"I heard back from Davy tonight."

Static crackled on the other end of the line. "What's that? You're breaking up."

"I said—Wait, where are you?"

"At the bar."

"Again?"

"Again." His tone said he was no more pleased than she was. "Owen . . . sick . . . I said I'd . . ."

Serena pulled the phone away from her ear, though clearly it wasn't going to help. She was fortunate her call had even connected in the first place. Even though she didn't know if he could hear her, she said, "Hold tight. I'm coming over."

The phone went dead before she knew whether he caught her last words. She lowered the phone and looked at her children. "Shoes on. You're going to visit Auntie while I head to the hotel for a few minutes."

"Why?" Max asked.

Because your mum has gone completely mad. She also felt a little guilty that once more Malcolm was pulling a second shift while she had enjoyed supper at home with her family. No wonder Muriel invited Malcolm and Kylee over on Monday nights.

While the children put on their shoes, Serena packed a healthy portion of the still-warm shepherd's pie in a plastic container with utensils. After she dropped Em and Max at Muriel's—something her aunt declared a wonderful surprise—she drove down to the hotel, her heart beating a little harder than the trip warranted. This gesture definitely took them over the line of business association into the realm of personal.

Serena parked at the end of the lot near the bar, then crunched to the heavy oak door. Light and laughter and the sound of music drifted from inside, signs that the place was crowded, even on a Tuesday night.

The heat and noise hit her like a blast when she pulled the door open. Almost every table was filled, even though few of the barstools at the mahogany slab were taken. In the far corner of the dark-paneled room, several men set up traditional Scottish instruments. No wonder it was packed.

She let her eyes go back to the bar, where Malcolm pulled draught beers and poured drinks while chatting personably with the patrons. He'd ditched the leather jacket in favor of a checked shirt unbuttoned over a T-shirt, the sleeves rolled back past the elbow.

He looked surprisingly comfortable in the role, not like he was only filling in for the night.

The sudden flush of attraction shocked Serena into stillness, and for a brief moment she considered turning around. But before she could put that thought into action, he saw her and gave her a surprised smile she felt down to her toes. No turning back now.

"What's this?" He gave the already-clean bar a reflexive wipe as she approached.

"Dinner. Have you eaten?"

"I have not. I hardly expected you to bring me dinner after you hung up on me."

"I did not—" she began before she realized he was baiting

her. "It only seemed fair, since you are once again stuck here instead of home."

"I don't know about fair, but it's appreciated. Can I get you something?"

"No thanks. I don't drink if I'm going to get behind the wheel."

"Very sensible of you. But it doesn't have to be alcohol. Here. Try this." He found a highball glass beneath the bar, scooped ice into it, then filled it with seltzer from the hose. Then he poured something from a clear glass bottle and added a splash of cream from the under-counter fridge. He slid it across to her. "Italian soda."

"In a bar in Scotland?"

He grinned. "I make them for the designated drivers. Better than a bottled fizzy."

She took a sip and smiled. "Ginger."

"Yes." He cocked his head. "Come down and keep me company while I eat?"

She should just tell him about Davy's call and leave, but instead she found herself sliding onto a stool at the end of the bar while he opened the container.

He took a bite and nodded in approval. "This is good. Thank you."

"You're welcome." Serena sat there silently for a few minutes, then said, "You look pretty comfortable back there. I take it you've done this before?"

"I tended bar to put myself through grad school."

"Grad school?"

"You'd be surprised how many overeducated bartenders and hotel managers are out there. I don't mind it, actually. I like the people."

She gave him a sideways smirk. "All this time I thought you weren't a people person. But it was just me."

He leaned forward onto his crossed arms, his eyes never leaving her face. The proximity made her heart pick up speed. "I probably owe you an apology for that, don't I?"

"No. Well, yes, but I don't expect one." Why was her brain suddenly working so sluggishly? "You work hard, and I know that. Which is why I'm talking to Jamie and Ian about increasing our budget for payroll."

Malcolm straightened, the smile fading. "Why?"

"Because you clearly have other responsibilities, and it isn't fair that you're constantly asked to fill in for employees. That's not your job."

"I don't mind."

"But I do. I don't want to be responsible for the fact you're not home for Kylee."

He cleared his throat. "Serena. I can use the extra hours."

Too late she realized she should have led with the other half of her news. "I'm not surprised. Considering your responsibilities, you're being underpaid. I'm giving you a raise."

He blinked. "Come again?"

"I'm waiting for Ian and Jamie to approve the final numbers, but it's clear to me that we can't do without you. And you don't underpay indispensable staff."

Malcolm stared at her as if he weren't sure what to say: the pitfalls of crossing that line between professional and personal. She rushed on before the silence could get truly uncomfortable. "Anyhow, the real reason I'm here is because I heard back from Davy tonight. She says they're free Saturday after next. Do you think that will work for Kylee? You're not on the schedule here until two."

"For this opportunity, we'll make sure it works." For a moment that unexpected vulnerability surfaced in his eyes. "Thank you. For . . . both things."

Her heart gave a little tug, and she buried the feeling as quickly as it had surfaced. "That's what friends do, isn't it?"

"Are we friends now?"

"I think it's preferable to enemies."

He studied her face. "I never thought of you as an enemy."

The way he looked at her was starting to go to her head far faster than alcohol ever could have. She rushed on. "In any case, it's the least I can do. We need to start implementing the new marketing ideas soon, especially if I'm adding to the overhead. Starting next week I'll probably spend mornings at the hotel while Em and Max are at school. If I'm not going to be in the way, that is."

"You won't be in the way." He snapped the lid onto the container and pushed it toward her. "Thank you for dinner."

"It's my pleasure. See you on Monday, then?"

"I'll be looking forward to it."

She took the container with an uncertain smile and turned away from the bar. Just before she pushed through the door, she darted a glance behind her, expecting to see that Malcolm had gone back to work. Instead, he stood in the same place, watching her.

There was no other option. It was time to get out of town.

CHAPTER FOURTEEN

EVEN THOUGH LEAVING her children with Aunt Muriel felt a bit like leaving behind a limb, Serena felt a rush of relief as she crossed the concrete bridge from Skye on Friday afternoon. She wasn't running away. Precisely the opposite. She needed some distance to consider the thoughts that wouldn't leave her alone day or night.

It wasn't exactly that she regretted making peace with Malcolm. She was beginning to like him, and his way with her children was undeniably endearing. The idea of spending time with him was becoming more and more appealing. When was the last time someone had made her laugh so much, feel so alive? And yet if they did start dating, what happened when the summer was over and it was time for her to go back to the mainland? She was far past the age where she believed she could keep her heart out of it. It was either go for it or stop everything right now before it got out of hand.

Unfortunately she was afraid to do one and didn't want to do the other.

"Oh, for heaven's sake," she muttered. She twisted the dial on her radio to drown out her annoyingly persistent thoughts.

By the time she walked through the front door of her home in Nairn, Serena was both exhausted and thoroughly disgusted with herself. She locked the door behind her and proceeded into the kitchen. After two weeks on Skye, she'd expected to feel the relief of coming home after a long trip, but the space felt empty and foreign. If she hadn't been dead on her feet, she might have considered driving back tonight so she could be home when the children woke up.

She immediately started a kettle on the boil, then surveyed the contents of her cabinets. Plates, bowls, servers. Flatware, some mixing bowls. The croft house's kitchen was so sparse she needed to transfer the entire contents of her tableware cabinet back to Skye. She began stacking items on the kitchen table and then poured herself a cup of tea while she considered what else she might need. She'd been making do with a single ancient baking sheet, so pans and tins went into the pile as well.

Once she'd packed up the items in a heavy cardboard box, she went upstairs to her bedroom to pull out the few pieces of clothing she'd decided she wanted to bring back with her. They were mostly comfy sweaters and long-sleeved shirts, considering she'd slanted her packing more toward the summer than the spring, an overly optimistic move if ever there was one. She hesitated with her fingers on the hanger of one of her favorite items: a clingy wool-cashmere sweater-dress in a gorgeous moody violet. She'd left it behind because on Skye, where would she wear it? After a moment's consideration, she pulled it from the closet along with a coordinating scarf and a pair of black high-heeled boots. Just in case.

She'd forgotten how little time it took to do things without interruptions, so she returned to the kitchen to make herself a sandwich for dinner, then plopped in front of the television in the lounge. The first movie she turned on was an odd, quiet film that first seemed to be a drama about infidelity, then veered into a murder thriller. Not exactly what she wanted to watch while home alone. She changed the channel and settled on *Bridget Jones's Diary*. She didn't know whether it was better or worse: a woman of a certain age making a fool of herself in the pursuit of love? Maybe a little too close to home, all things considered.

When the film ended, she found herself once more at a loss. What now? It wasn't even ten. She opened a bottle of white wine, took a glass up to her bathroom, and ran water in the tub. Even after a long, luxurious soak with scented salts, she was tucked between crisp sheets before eleven.

My exciting life, she thought wryly just before she drifted off to sleep.

Serena had been sure she would be up at the crack of dawn, ready to drive back to Skye. Max's idea of letting her sleep in, despite the multiple night wakings, was barely seven o'clock in the morning. Yet when she pried her eyes open to the bright wash of light through her bedroom windows, the angle was all wrong. It wasn't the dim morning glow that followed first dawn. It was the full glaring brightness of an unusually sunny spring day.

She jerked her eyes to the clock: 11:05. What? No, that couldn't be possible. She grabbed her watch from the night-stand, but the always-reliable perpetual motion confirmed her bedroom alarm clock to be perfectly accurate. She threw back her covers and was halfway to the bathroom before she realized she actually had nowhere to be. Muriel didn't expect her until tonight. So why was she rushing?

The mattress crushed beneath her weight as she sat heavily on the edge. If she left by two o'clock, she would be back in time to feed the kids and tuck them into bed. The car was already packed, and she didn't need more than a few minutes to dress. So what was she going to do with her unexpected windfall of time?

Her feet carried her downstairs to the converted pantry almost without realizing where she was going. The canvas still sat on the easel where she'd left it, and foil tubes lay on the table beside it with a clean palette, waiting. For what, she didn't know—inspiration, maybe, or courage. For a moment, an idea tickled at the edge of her mind, unformed and begging to be given shape. But even before she picked up a brush, it choked somewhere inside her. She couldn't do it. It was this place, the weight of the past that had seeped into the walls. Edward might be gone, but the memories remained: his irritation at coming home to find her still in her paja-mas, cloistered in this tiny space instead of making dinner; the little jabs about getting older and holding on to childish dreams; the fact he had never once said anything complimentary about her work.

Tears pricked her eyes. Maybe Edward had been right. Maybe it was time to pack this away for good. Be sensible. Art was something from a former life, a part of a person who no longer existed. She was a widowed mum of two, after all. To make great art—to make art at all—she needed passion, and that was something so far in her past, she barely remembered what it felt like.

Unbidden, Malcolm popped into her mind, bringing up a fresh wave of nervous anticipation not unlike the feeling she'd once had while incubating a new idea. Until she'd met him, she thought that part of her was dead too, the irrational part that wanted more despite all the reasons she should be satisfied with her life. And if that part was still there, however deeply buried, didn't it mean the ability to paint might remain too?

She hesitated only a heartbeat before she grabbed a cardboard box from the corner and began packing up her supplies: oil paints, brushes, watercolors, canvases. Everything she would need to work should the inspiration hit. As the room emptied of its contents, piled into first one box and then three more, the tight band around her chest began to loosen.

Her boxes of art supplies joined the kitchen utensils and clothes in the boot of her car. Then Serena took a deep breath and looked back at the house. Divested of her most prized possessions and void of the children she loved, the structure became what it had always been and she'd never noticed: merely a house. Never truly a home.

It was time to do what she should have done three years ago. She had to sell it. She couldn't make the kind of life here that Em and Max deserved, not when every wall and every room was steeped in negativity and bad memories.

She would break the news to the children while they were still on Skye so they could get used to the idea, and when they returned to Nairn, she would put it on the market.

Serena locked the front door behind her and walked to

the car with a new lightness in her heart. It lasted all the way across the upper part of Scotland, and it may have been to blame for the way she answered the phone when Malcolm's number rang through half an hour from the bridge. "You missed me already, did you? It's only been two days."

"I did, but that's not why I'm calling."

The seriousness in his voice immediately washed away her good mood. "What's wrong?"

"Muriel is at hospital right now."

"What? What happened?" She sucked in her breath as a wave of fear hit her. "Where are Max and Em? She was watching them—"

"I've got them; don't worry."

The relief was so strong, for a moment she swayed behind the wheel.

Malcolm went on. "I had Kylee take them to our house. I hope that's okay. I gave her my key to your place so she could get some clothes and toys for them. I'm here at Broadford Hospital with Muriel."

"I'm still about an hour out. Do they know what's wrong?"

She could hear the hesitation on the other end of the line, but his voice was neutral when he answered. "They're not sure yet. She was apparently feeling unwell all morning, and she collapsed up at the house. Em called 999 and then dialed me. She's a brave little girl."

Thank You, God, for Em's quick thinking.

"We've got everything under control here, so don't feel like you need to rush. We were lucky that we got here before the doctors left for the evening, or they would have sent her to Inverness. They might still, depending on what the test results show."

"Thank you, Malcolm. I appreciate it."

"Of course. See you soon."

Serena hung up and shoved her phone into the cup holder beside her, her chest tight. She should have known something was wrong. Muriel had been acting more tired than usual for at least a year, which was why Jamie and Andrea had hired Malcolm in the first place, to take the workload of the hotel from her. And Serena herself had noted how weary she'd looked right after they'd arrived, but she'd just attributed that to the fact that Max had woken them up multiple nights in a row. Why hadn't Serena pushed her harder to see her doctor? Why hadn't she left immediately when she woke this morning?

No, she couldn't blame herself. Had she left Nairn early, she might have picked up her children, and Muriel would have been alone. It was a blessing that Serena had been delayed, or who knew how long her aunt would have lain there?

Still, it didn't stop the creeping sense of sickness in her middle over the next hour. She had to consciously hold her speed down. When at last she parked at the tiny white-stucco building that was Broadford Hospital, her trembling legs would barely hold her. She moved quickly across the car park to the outdated brown steel-and-glass entrance, where she was met with a warm blast of antiseptic-scented air.

The deserted reception area was old and faded, just linoleum floors with some chairs and a wood-paneled reception desk marked *Enquiries*. Movement to her left caught her attention, and she nearly wilted with relief when Malcolm rose, putting aside the magazine he'd been reading.

She met him in the center of the room, clutching the strap

of her handbag like a lifeline. "What's going on? Have you heard anything?"

"They will only tell me that she's stable, but since I'm not family, I can't find out any information. Let's find a nurse, and maybe you'll be able to learn more."

Serena was relieved when Malcolm stepped up to the empty reception station and called for a nurse. A moment later a woman strode down the hallway, and he introduced Serena as Muriel MacDonald's niece.

"Can you tell us anything about what happened?" Serena asked.

"We're still waiting on test results. But for the time being, she's stable and doesn't appear to need to be transferred."

Serena blinked. They still didn't have any idea what caused her collapse? How was that possible?

"The doctor is with her now," the nurse continued. "We'll let you know when you can go back and see her."

"Thank you." Serena moved back to the chairs with Malcolm and sank into one beside him. After a moment she said, "Thank you for being here. And thank you for making sure Em and Max were taken care of."

"Do you want to call them? I can ring Kylee. They'd probably like to talk to you."

She nodded, and Malcolm dialed his mobile phone, greeted Kylee, then handed it over to Serena.

"Hi, Kylee. How are they?"

"Eating an early supper right now," Kylee said. "I made them soup. Max is mostly playing with it, but Em seems to like it. After they're done, I'm going to get Max washed up and in his pajamas. Em's already in hers, but I thought it was safer to wait until he was done."

Serena laughed. "Yes, probably so. Are they behaving for you?"

"So far." There was a hint of amusement in Kylee's voice. "I promised them that if they were good, they could fall asleep on the sofa to the telly. I hope that's okay."

"That's a perfect distraction. You're doing great. Thank you, Kylee."

"You're welcome," Kylee said. "Is Auntie Muriel okay?"

"We don't know yet, but she's stable. We'll keep you posted on when we'll be home. I hope you didn't have to cancel your Saturday night plans."

"Just homework. Tell Auntie hi when you see her."

"We will." She waited while Kylee gave the phone to Em and then Max, spoke with each of them for a few minutes, then clicked off and handed the mobile back to Malcolm.

"Everything's okay?"

"They sound like they're having a grand time." Impulsively she reached for his hand and gave it a squeeze. "I don't know how to thank you for being here for my family."

"It's my pleasure."

It was his usual answer, but his tone held no hint of humor or irony. When she tried to withdraw her hand, he held it fast, and after a moment of consideration, she left it in his. It felt nice to have the support, even if she'd never expected it to come from Malcolm.

It seemed as if hours passed as they sat there holding hands over the arms of the chairs, Serena staring at the opposite wall, Malcolm flipping awkwardly through his magazine one-handed. It would have been far easier for him to just let go of her, but he didn't seem inclined to do that. Only when a white-coated doctor emerged down the hall and called her name did he finally release her hand, rising with her.

"Yes? I'm Serena Stewart."

The physician shook her hand. "I'm Dr. Lee. I just spoke with your aunt. You can go back and visit her now."

"Thank you. Do you know what happened?" She fell into step with him, aware of Malcolm following at a respectful distance.

"The labs just came back. Her symptoms weren't from a heart attack but from hyperthyroidism. I strongly suspect an autoimmune disorder called Graves' disease, but our sonographer won't be in until tomorrow so we can confirm. Right now your aunt is on a beta-blocker as an emergency treatment until the antithyroid medications take effect."

Serena swallowed. She'd never claimed to have any medical knowledge, but everything he was saying to her sounded frightening and complicated. The only way it could be worse was if it occurred to one of her children. When she spoke, her voice came out sounding small and anxious. "Will she be okay?"

Dr. Lee smiled. "Yes, she'll be fine. I'm admitting her overnight as a precautionary measure, but assuming she continues to respond well to treatment, she should be discharged tomorrow. Had it been worse, we would have transferred her to Raigmore by helicopter, but I don't believe that's necessary." He stopped in front of a closed door. "You can go in and see her now."

"Thank you, doctor." Serena smiled at him and then pushed into the small room, trying to mask her dismay at seeing her aunt in the hospital bed, hooked up to monitors and tubes. An IV dripped fluid into one arm, and leads coming from beneath her hospital gown connected her to a cardiac monitor. What Serena assumed was an oxygen monitor was clipped to one finger.

"How are you feeling, Auntie?" Serena perched on the chair beside Muriel's bed. Malcolm stood quietly at the door.

"Oh, child, don't give me that look. I'm not dying." Muriel's voice was a shade weaker than usual, but it held her familiar no-nonsense tone. "Didn't the doctor tell you?"

"He did tell me, but it was still bad enough for Em to call emergency services!"

Muriel actually looked abashed. "How is she doing? She was pretty frightened. Max was too, but he was more interested in the paramedics when they arrived."

"Em is fine," Malcolm said from his post by the door. "Kylee volunteered to watch them until Serena got home."

"She's a good girl," Muriel said. Serena wasn't sure whether she meant Em or Kylee. "You should go home and see your children. There's no need to keep me company here. I have my telly and a book. Malcolm brought me one."

"I had one in the car," he said. "I didn't expect her to be a fan of military thrillers."

"I'm not, but it's better than staring at the wall, isn't it?"

With that level of spunk still intact, Muriel had to be fine. Serena finally managed to take a deep breath. "You must ring me as soon as you know you're being discharged. I'll come get you. I'm only ten minutes away."

"I will. Now go. Stop fussing." Muriel waved a hand, clearly embarrassed to be the center of attention. Serena bent to kiss her cheek, surprised when Malcolm did the same thing.

"Go, you two. And make sure you grab some supper before it gets too late."

Malcolm escorted Serena out of the room. Once they were halfway down the hall, he let out a low laugh. "If there were any doubt that she's going to be fine, that should eliminate it."

"She is a rather tough lady," Serena admitted. "Thank you again, Malcolm. I'm glad you were here."

Pleasure registered on his face before he dipped his head in acknowledgment. He ushered her toward the reception area. "After you. I know two children who are going to be happy to see their mum."

<hr />

As it turned out, Em and Max were not happy to see Serena, because they were already asleep on the floor of Malcolm's lounge, curled up with pillows and their favorite soft toys under a thick blanket. As soon as Serena and Malcolm entered the room, Kylee jumped up from the sofa and put a finger to her lips.

"They tried to stay awake for you, but they were tired out by all the excitement. They've been asleep for almost an hour. They didn't even make it through their program."

"Thank you, Kylee." Serena put her arms around the girl and squeezed her hard. "You have no idea how much I appreciate this."

"It's no trouble, really. They were perfect angels."

"Honestly?"

Kylee smiled. "Honestly. Even Max, though he convinced me to give him a piggyback ride through the house for an hour. I think I'm more tired than they are."

"I'd believe it. I'm sure they had a wonderful time. You must allow me to pay you for your babysitting time."

"No, you don't have to do that."

"I insist."

Kylee's eyes went to her uncle. "No, really . . . I . . ."

"I told Kylee if she did it, she could go to a music festival in June," Malcolm said. "I think she's proved she can be responsible." He raised his eyebrows and gave his niece a pointed look. "Right?"

"Absolutely. I promise."

"Well, a concert is better than cash, but you still have my thanks."

Kylee gave her another shy smile. "Their clothes are in that bag over there."

"I suppose we should wake them up," Serena said.

Malcolm stopped her. "If you can carry Max, I'll carry Em, and we'll just put them straight to bed. It's not that far between our houses."

"Are you sure?" Em was small for her age, but she wasn't that small, even if Malcolm did look as if he could lift plenty of weight without breaking a sweat.

"I'm sure."

"Okay, if you say so." Serena threw him a grin, then hooked the bag of clothes over one arm before lifting Max and his giraffe together. Even in his sleep, her son wrapped his arms and legs around her, burying his head against her neck.

Malcolm lifted Em, who flopped like a rag doll, and groaned under the deadweight.

"Still time to change your mind."

"No, I'm fine," Malcolm said, his voice slightly strained.

Serena chuckled to herself and carried Max out the front door while Malcolm struggled to find the most comfortable way of carrying her daughter. "I warned you she was heavy."

"She's not heavy; she's just like carrying bags of cement," he threw back as they crunched down the gravel driveway toward the paved road. "I can't believe she hasn't woken up yet."

It was only about three hundred feet between the driveways, but his lack of conversation told her Malcolm was finding Em harder to manage than he'd thought. When they finally made it to the croft house, Serena shifted Max while she retrieved her keys and let them in. Kylee had even thought to leave the porch light on for them.

"Em's room is on the right," Serena whispered. "Just put her on the bed, and I'll come tuck her in." She veered off to Max's room and placed him on his own mattress, where he immediately rolled over and clutched his giraffe.

When she emerged, Malcolm waited for her in the hallway, looking none the worse for the burden. She slipped into the other bedroom to wrestle Em's unruly arms and legs beneath the covers, then shut the door behind her.

Out in the hallway again, Serena gestured for him to follow her to the kitchen, where she fell back against the countertop with a sigh. "Some day, huh?"

He thrust his hands into his pockets. "Yeah. You could say that."

She wiped a hand over her face, and unexpected tears rose to her eyes. She swallowed hard and blinked them away.

"Hey, what's this about?" Malcolm moved to her side and rubbed her arm reassuringly.

"It's just—it was too much. I'm closer to Muriel than my own mother, and seeing her that way—"

"Makes you realize she won't be around forever. I know. It's hard." He slid his arms around her, and Serena stiffened before she yielded to the embrace. For a moment she just stood there, soaking up the warmth from his body, appreciating being held for the first time in . . . she couldn't remember how long. It was time to face the facts: she really had read Malcolm wrong. He was a good man. Responsible, trustworthy, caring. She let herself sink against him a bit, tightening her arms around his middle, and her heart started thumping harder despite her best efforts to stay detached. Just from personality alone, it would be difficult to keep him at a distance, but the fact that he was also attractive and strong and always smelled like an amazing mix of leather and cologne—

"Serena?"

"Mmm?"

"If you don't want me to take advantage of the situation, I probably should be going."

His voice was teasing, but when she looked up at him, there was no mistaking the heat in his eyes. "And if I ask you to stay?"

He chuckled. "You're cruel."

"I'm not cruel. I'm simply rethinking my earlier decision about you."

He ran a hand through his already-tousled hair, messing it up further. She had the sudden urge to do the same. "Serena, you're going to have to tell me exactly what you want from me."

She slid her palm up his chest, feeling the hard muscle beneath her fingers, the heavy thud of his heart that matched her own. His breathing quickened, but his hand remained unmoving on her waist. He was waiting, she realized, letting her make the first move. To decide if this was the moment that their relationship was going to shift from flirtation to something more. Despite all his teasing, his love of innuendo, he was trying not to take advantage of her emotional state.

Serena gave in to the urge to comb her fingers through his hair, felt the tremor that went through his body at her touch, and at last, she knew exactly what she wanted. She stretched up and brushed her lips over his. He responded slowly and gently, and she sank into the kiss with a sigh, even as desire hummed to life throughout her entire body.

He pulled back much too soon, and a spike of uncertainty shot through her. Had she somehow misunderstood him? Had he just been trying not to hurt her feelings? "Malcolm, I—"

In one swift movement, he lifted her onto the countertop so they were level, his eyes darkening and his expression intent. And then his hands were in her hair, his mouth claiming hers completely, every last fear and uncertainty and conscious thought swept away in the power of their connection. It was all she could do to simply hold on, lost in the sensation of his hands, his lips, the frantic thump of her own heart.

Just before she lost herself entirely, Malcolm broke the kiss. He didn't move away, though, instead pressing his lips to her cheek and her neck and the top of her shoulder, sending shivers over her skin with each movement.

Serena twined her arms around his neck, a little breathless laugh escaping her. "Had I known you could kiss like that, I wouldn't have waited so long."

Malcolm pulled back, humor flashing in his eyes. "Does this mean you'll finally let me take you to dinner?"

"When?"

"Friday? Shall I ask Kylee if she can babysit?"

"I would love that. She did a wonderful job with them

tonight." Part of her was amazed she could carry on a normal conversation when she still felt lit up like a Roman candle from his kiss, when it was taking all her self-control not to grab him by the collar and do it again.

"I will." He studied her face for a moment, then stole one more quick, soft kiss. "Maybe I should stay a little while longer."

She laughed, even though she wanted to say, *Yes, stay. Don't leave when things are getting good.* "I think that's exactly why you should go."

"All right, all right. Need to set a good example, don't we?" Malcolm sighed, but the warmth in his expression radiated into her.

"Sadly, yes." She slid off the counter and walked him to the door, where he took one more kiss from her before she half nudged, half shoved him out onto the stoop. "Good night."

"See you soon. That's a promise." He gave her a devilish smile and then clambered down the front porch. She waved before she shut the door. Quickly. Before she could invite him back in to snog in her lounge like teenagers.

The thought made Serena grin as she walked into the kitchen and set the kettle on the stove. Only then did she remember the boxes of belongings she had brought from home, still packed in the boot of her car. Never mind. She could get them tomorrow. Right now she just wanted to have a cup of tea in her quiet house and enjoy the fluttery little feeling she got from the promise of this new step in their relationship.

And no matter how much she was tempted, she would not think about the future.

—◦◦◦◦◦—

Malcolm took his time walking to his house from Serena's while he shook off the memory of that kiss. Or rather, he made his walk much longer than it truly needed to be by turning the opposite way down their road, around the back of the croft, and then across a well-worn path that ran alongside his property. By the time he let himself into his house, he'd managed—mostly—to shake the desire to turn around and kiss Serena some more, for as long as she'd let him.

Kylee was sitting at the table, books spread open in front of her, her head bent over a composition notebook. He pulled up a chair to the right of her. "Homework on a Saturday night?"

"I have a paper due a week from Monday, but I don't want to be worrying about it when we go see Davy and Glenn."

"That seems sensible." He paused, then added, "You know, Kylee, I'm proud of you. You stepped up in a difficult situation, and you did great with Max and Em."

"Muriel has been really nice to me," Kylee said. "Is she doing okay?"

"She will be. I think she'll be discharged tomorrow, and then it might be a matter of her being on medication for the rest of her life. But there are worse things."

"Right." Kylee swallowed, and he knew she was thinking of her parents. She closed the cover of her composition book. "I think I'll go to bed now."

"Wait. I have a favor to ask of you."

"Yes?" A tinge of suspicion colored her tone.

He almost laughed. "Can you babysit again on Friday night?"

A crafty little smile came to her lips. "Why? You want to take Serena out on a date?"

No point in denying it. "Yes. I do."

"Well, now. I guess that all depends on what it's worth to you." She leaned back and crossed her legs in such a perfect imitation of her mother that it made Malcolm grin even while his heart ached from the similarities.

"What exactly did you have in mind? You already got your festival."

"You let us drive ourselves."

"You go right for the throat, don't you?"

"You've been here for almost a year, and she's the first woman you've even looked at. You really want this date."

He narrowed his eyes at his niece. "Since when are you keeping track of my love life?"

"First, eww. And second, I'd have to be blind to miss the embarrassing way women flirt with you. Seriously, you are really thick."

Malcolm shook his head. This was not a conversation he wanted to have with a seventeen-year-old. And what women were flirting with him besides the waitress in Fort William? Yes, everyone was friendly, but this was Skye, and even more than twenty years away didn't change his local status. "Does that mean you'd be okay with me dating someone?"

"I don't care what you do," she said, but she didn't meet his eyes. "Less time to butt into my business."

"You're not exactly making a case for getting what you want here, Ky."

"Fine. I already told you I'm okay with you dating someone, especially if it's Serena. She's really nice. And she likes you."

"How do you know?" Not that the kiss had left many doubts about that fact.

Kylee shrugged. "Girls know these things. So, what do you say? I'll babysit on Friday, and you let me and Lane go by ourselves."

"You drive a hard bargain."

"You really like her."

"Okay, now *I'm* not having this conversation with you. I'll make you a deal. I still drive, but I'll just drop you off and pick you up. There is to be absolutely no drinking and no drugs. If you look the least bit intoxicated, you will never leave the house again. I will follow you around your university campus and walk you to every class as punishment."

Kylee looked at him in horror, but she finally shook his outstretched hand. She didn't need to know that he'd already anticipated this argument and decided on a compromise. She would be off to uni by herself in a few months. He had to give her a little freedom sometime, and better she try it out while he was still there to watch over her.

She cleaned up her books and shoved them into her rucksack, then took the stairs two at a time up to her room. Even though it was still early, Malcolm took a moment to turn off all the lights and lock the doors before he went upstairs to his own room.

Only then did he allow his mind to wander back to Serena. He had no idea what he was doing with her, or what she wanted from him. She liked kissing him, clearly, and the feeling was mutual. But there was still the fact that she was here on Skye only temporarily.

Regardless, he had a date to plan on Friday. Now the question was, how did one impress a woman like Serena

Stewart? There was nothing he could plan on Skye that she hadn't done and nothing he could give her that she couldn't buy herself.

In that case, he'd just have to give her something that money couldn't buy.

CHAPTER FIFTEEN

SERENA STAYED CLOSE to the croft house on Sunday morning in case Muriel called to say she was being discharged. She took advantage of the time to put away the items she'd brought from home while Max and Em played in the garden; all the while she thought of Malcolm. How sweet and supportive he had been. How if she closed her eyes, she could still remember the feel of his lips on hers.

How much she was looking forward to their date on Friday.

It had been inevitable, she decided, as soon as she'd seen him playing with her son on Muriel's rug. Any man could put his best foot forward on a date, but one who would abandon his dignity to make a three-year-old laugh proved himself worthy of serious consideration.

Before she had much time to follow the thought to its inevitable conclusion, her mobile rang. She picked it up from the kitchen table and pressed it to her ear.

"I'm being discharged," Muriel said immediately. "I'm just waiting for the doctor to sign the paperwork."

"Let me get Em and Max cleaned up, and we'll come get you. They've been playing outside all morning."

"I owe my girl a special treat," Muriel said. "Is Malcolm coming with you? I want to make sure I get to thank him too."

"When I see him, I'll be sure to tell him you'd like a visit." Just hearing his name started a flutter in Serena's stomach. She really needed to get that under control before she went to hospital. Her aunt had an uncanny way of reading her thoughts through her facial expressions, and she was pretty sure that right now she'd be giving away more than she wanted to share.

She hung up and hesitated over the phone for a moment before she dialed Malcolm's number. What would it hurt? Muriel wanted him to know that she was being discharged.

But rather than the call going to voice mail as she expected, he picked up on the second ring. His quiet greeting gave her a jolt of pleasure. "You have excellent timing. We just got home from church."

"You go to church?" Serena asked, startled.

"Don't sound so surprised."

"I didn't mean . . . You just don't seem the type."

"If I weren't the type, I wouldn't have left so willingly last night."

The sudden huskiness in his voice raised a shiver on her skin. She had to swallow to regain her ability to speak, considering the way her mind barreled down that track. "I called because I wanted to let you know Muriel is being discharged today."

His tone immediately changed. "That's fantastic news. Do you want me to come with you?"

She was all set to say no, to tell him there wasn't any reason to disrupt his day, but Muriel would be pleased if he was there. And if she were perfectly honest, she wanted to see him again. "Would you?"

"Of course. Give me a few minutes to change, and I'll come over."

Serena clicked off the line and shoved her phone into her pocket. He hadn't even asked for details; he'd simply agreed. That shouldn't have surprised her. That's what normal people who were friends and maybe dating did, right? It had been so long since she'd been in this situation, it caught her off guard.

She called the kids in from the backyard, gave them a quick spray-off in the bathtub, and got them dressed in clean clothes. She was just finishing Em's pigtails when a knock came at the front door.

"That's Malcolm. Get your shoes on, and we'll go."

"Malcolm?" Em brightened so quickly, Serena wondered if she was the only one who had a little crush.

Em dogged her heels to the front door, shattering any hopes Serena had of a hello kiss. "Hi, Malcolm!" Em said brightly as Serena yanked open the door.

"Hello to you, Miss Emmy." Malcolm smiled at Serena over her head. "Ready to go?"

"Let me get my handbag."

"And Max," Em said.

"That kind of goes without saying, cupcake." She gave one

of Em's braids a tug, then smiled back at Malcolm. "I'll just be a moment."

"Take your time." He stuck his hands in his jacket pockets and rocked back on his heels, perfectly comfortable in her foyer while her eight-year-old daughter smiled adoringly up at him.

She went to Max's room, where her son had gotten distracted by a pile of cars on the rug. "Come on, my little monkey. Let's go see Auntie, shall we?"

He held up a police car in one fist. "I'm going to give her this to make her feel better."

Serena kissed him on the cheek. "I think that's very sweet. She'll love it."

Out in the hallway, Malcolm's and Em's voices drifted to her. "... do you think about Kylee watching you two again?"

"Are you going to take Mum on a date?" Em sounded excited, and Serena almost groaned aloud. There could be nothing worse than an eight-year-old trying to arrange her love life. She bustled into the room before Malcolm was forced to answer.

"Sorry," she said to Malcolm with a grimace. "Em, don't be so nosy."

"It's okay," he said. "Unless you didn't want them to know I'm taking you out, in which case, the cat is out of the bag."

"Hey, guys, why don't you run out to the car. Em, help Max get buckled in, would you?" She set Max down, and Em took him by the hand. As soon as the door closed behind them, Serena began, "I'm sorry. She's—"

She didn't get out the rest of her apology before he took her face in his hands and kissed her. She wrapped her arms around his midsection beneath his jacket, momentarily forgetting anything but his lips on hers. When he stepped back, she felt a little dazed.

"There. That should hold me. I can play the family friend today, and no one will have any idea I'm actually seducing you with the promise of several hours of adult conversation."

Serena laughed, though she was still feeling the effect of that kiss. "Are you now?"

"I am. Kylee will come over here to babysit on Friday, and you get to relax for a few hours."

"You have no idea how wonderful that sounds."

"I think I do. Now come, let's go before we have to answer questions about what's taking so long."

Serena grabbed her handbag from the hallway and produced the keys to lock the door behind them. How did he manage to do that? He lifted her spirits by his very presence and put her children at ease. He didn't even seem uncomfortable with Em's prying questions. And yet her daughter's tone when she questioned him made Serena think Em wasn't looking at him as a crush but as something potentially much more problematic.

She sighed as she walked to her car and checked Max's seat belt. She'd tried so hard to keep her children out of this, but when it came to Skye, business and personal matters inevitably got entwined. For all their sakes, she needed to be careful. She might be realistic about the relationship—if she could call it that—but her children were much too young to understand. They looked at Malcolm and, at least in Em's case, hoped for a daddy.

"Is something the matter?" Malcolm asked, and she realized she was sitting in the driver's seat with her hands curled around the steering wheel, staring out the windscreen.

"No, sorry." She turned the key in the ignition and backed down the drive, silently chiding herself for being so distracted.

"She'll be okay, you know. They wouldn't be sending her home today if not. The fact they didn't transfer her last night is reassuring."

"Right. I know you're right." Bless him for not picking up on the real reason for her odd behavior. And the words did ease her fears about Muriel. Her aunt had always been such an anchor in her life, Serena didn't know how she would cope if something were to happen to her. It would be even more crushing than when her father had died. Certainly worse than losing Edward, even if she felt too guilty to admit that out loud.

At Broadford Hospital, the nurse waved her straight back, and Serena cautiously traversed the hallway with Em, Max, and Malcolm behind her. She knocked lightly before pushing open the door.

In contrast to how they'd found her last night, Muriel had been disconnected from the monitors and looked as she always did, dressed in her own clothes and reading a book in the chair by the bed.

"Auntie!" Em flung herself across the room at Muriel and immediately started crying.

"Ah, none of that, my brave girl." Muriel squeezed Em tight and then opened her arms to Max, who couldn't stand to be left out of a hug. She held her great-niece and -nephew for a few moments, then looked over their heads at Serena and Malcolm. "I thought Malcolm wasn't coming?"

He looked questioningly at Serena, who shrugged. "He was home. How's the book?"

"Violent." Muriel didn't seem to mean it as a criticism. "I'm just waiting on my prescriptions, and then we can go."

"Am I interrupting a family reunion?" A good-natured female voice came from behind Serena, and she stepped out of the way for a white-coated doctor.

"I'm Dr. Goran," she said, shaking Serena's hand.

"Serena Stewart, her niece."

"A pleasure to meet you. As I was just telling your aunt, she's very lucky. Even considering the severity and sudden onset of her symptoms, she's responding very well to her medications. As long as she's diligent about taking her pills, I would expect her to feel like herself in a couple of weeks, if not less."

"So it is Graves' disease?"

The doctor looked to Muriel as if to gain her permission to speak, then said, "It is. It's not unusual for the condition to develop later in life, perhaps triggered by her case of bronchitis last year. Her primary physician will want to monitor her closely to make sure the antithyroid medications are working as they should." She moved to Muriel's side and handed her several slips of paper. "Make sure you follow up with your primary-care physician tomorrow and fill your scripts in the morning."

"Thank you, doctor." Muriel nudged aside Em and Max and stood. "Let's go, then. I'm anxious to get back to my own home."

Muriel wobbled a little bit, and Serena made an immediate move to her side, but Malcolm stopped her with a look. Smoothly he stepped beside Muriel and tucked her hand into his elbow as if he were escorting her instead of steadying her. "Now, Auntie, you have to promise me that you're actually going to rest, especially until you see your regular physician."

His stern look elicited a smile from Muriel. "If you insist. Em, dear, will you get my handbag?"

Em sprang to action, taking Muriel's bag and book while Serena held tight to Max's hand so he wouldn't bolt. Malcolm kept up a running commentary all the way out to the car park, then helped Muriel into the front seat of Serena's car without seeming like he was helping her. Apparently, not only had Muriel adopted Malcolm, but the feeling was mutual.

When they reached Muriel's home, he again escorted the older woman inside. The house looked as neat as always, except the coffee table had been pushed up against the piano, Serena assumed to make room for the paramedics. Em's eyes welled up again when she took in the scene.

"You did great, Em." Serena hugged her daughter tightly and pressed a kiss to the top of her head. "I'm so proud of you."

"Thanks, Mum," she whispered.

Muriel patted a sofa cushion beside her. "Ah, my favorite girl. Come sit next to me for a minute."

Em obliged, curling up on the sofa next to her, while Max claimed her other side. Muriel put an arm around each of them. "How could I not feel better with such attentive helpers?"

"Since you're in such good hands, I'm going to go see what we have for lunch," Serena said.

In the fridge she found a container of roast chicken still on the bone, some fruit, and the usual condiments. Chicken salad it was. She was in the process of cubing the chicken breast when Malcolm entered the room. He settled at the island to watch her.

"So you *can* cook."

"Chopping doesn't qualify as cooking," she said. "But yes.

How do you think I've managed to feed my family all this time?"

"For all I know, you had a personal chef in Inverness."

She started to make a retort before she realized he was just teasing her. "Well, if Kylee is to be believed, you're the one who needs one." She dumped the chicken into a mixing bowl, then began to cut the grapes and apples into uniform pieces, which she added to the mixture with a handful of walnuts and a healthy dollop of crème fraîche.

Malcolm leaned over and stole a piece of chicken from the bowl with his fingers. "This is good. But I probably shouldn't stay. I'm overdue at the hotel already."

"Surely you have time," Serena said. "Unless you have something better planned than delicious chicken salad on whole-wheat bread."

"I most certainly do." He stretched across the island for a kiss, and she happily obliged him.

"This explains quite a lot."

Serena jerked back at Muriel's voice, her face flaming.

"Don't mind me," Muriel said blithely. "I'm just getting myself a drink of water."

Serena looked at Malcolm, who shrugged, completely unperturbed. Surely Muriel would have questions that Serena didn't yet know how to answer. But her aunt only filled her glass at the sink, took a long drink, and then returned the way she'd come.

"Do you think that means she approves or not?" Malcolm asked.

"Considering she's been making oblique comments every time your name comes up, I'm fairly certain it's not disapproval." Serena retrieved a loaf of bread and began to put together sandwiches on the cutting board. Malcolm word-lessly retrieved a stack of plates from the cabinet and set them on the island beside her.

"I'm going to take these out to Em and Max," he said when she put half a sandwich on each of two plates.

She stopped him with a hand on his wrist. "Thank you."

"For carrying sandwiches?" He flashed a wicked grin. "What do I get if I pour them milk too?"

"I wasn't talking about that."

He leaned down and kissed the tip of her nose. "I know."

CHAPTER SIXTEEN

DATING WAS COMPLETELY DIFFERENT when you had two children, Serena thought at ten minutes until seven on Friday. When she'd started seeing Edward, she'd spent hours getting ready—soaking in a bubble bath, styling her hair to perfection, redoing her makeup until it was runway perfect. Now she was putting on mascara as quickly as possible, while Max splashed in the bathtub beside her. After she got him dried off and into his pajamas, she would change from her robe into her date clothes—once the imminent danger of sticky fingers was mostly past.

"Mummy!"

Serena turned toward Max just as he slammed his hand onto the surface of the water, sending up a splash that sprayed across the room and splattered everything in its path: the wall, the mirror, her newly made-up face.

"Max! Stop that!" She grabbed a towel and dabbed her face, trying not to smear her work.

"Sorry, Mummy."

"All right, monkey, it's time to get you out. What pajamas do you want to wear?"

"Dinosaurs!"

Of course. Everything was dinosaurs lately. She grabbed a towel and lifted him out onto the mat, then gave him a good rubdown before she carried him down the hall to his bedroom. As soon as she pulled out his pajamas from the built-in drawers, though, he yanked them out of her hand. "I'll do it."

"All right, Mr. Independent. You do it. I'm going to get dressed."

She left him wrestling his legs into his underpants and climbed the stairs to her own bedroom, where she'd already laid out her clothes. Her patterned lace tights and slinky sweater-dress required nearly as much wiggling as Max was doing downstairs. She checked her reflection in the full-length mirror she'd picked up at a big-box store in Fort William this week, giving her rear view a critical once-over. Well, nothing to be done about that; she'd had two kids. At least the deep V of the faux-wrap front made her waist look small and her other assets impressively perky.

"Not bad for thirty-nine years old," she murmured to herself.

"You look pretty, Mum."

Serena looked away from the mirror to where Em stood in the doorway, wearing the T-shirt and tracksuit bottoms she'd selected for her pajamas. "Thank you, cupcake. Are you okay staying with Kylee tonight?"

"Yeah. She's fun. And she said she would help us make blondies."

"Good. We won't be too late."

Serena zipped up her knee-high boots, then grabbed her watch from the nightstand and fastened it on her wrist. As she followed her daughter down the stairs, Em asked, "So, is this a date?"

"Well . . ." Serena still hadn't decided what she was going to tell the kids. "Kind of. He asked me if I wanted to go to dinner, and I said yes."

"That's a date," her daughter said with all the certainty of an overly romantic eight-year-old.

"I suppose it is. But Malcolm and I are friends. We like to spend time together."

"You know, it's okay, Mum. If you want to date, I mean. Even if you want to get married again someday." Em looked up at her earnestly, her eyes shining, and Serena's heart gave a clench.

All this time she'd devoted herself completely to her kids, thinking she would be doing them a disservice otherwise, and Em was worrying about her mum's lack of a social life. She gave her daughter a hug and kissed the top of her dark head. "Thanks, cupcake. Let's not get carried away, though. It's only dinner."

"Okay." But Em's look said she believed otherwise.

A knock sounded at the door, and before Serena could respond, Em ran for it. "I'll get it!" she yelled as she yanked the door open. "Mum! Malcolm and Kylee are here!"

Serena shook her head. Her foot touched the last stair as Malcolm walked into the house. He wore a pair of dark trousers, a light wool pullover, and his signature leather jacket, though his hair looked a little less tousled than usual and he'd given his beard a trim. She'd never thought she'd like a rugged, outdoorsy look on a man, but her heart gave a little leap when she saw him.

"You have purple hair!" Em squealed. Serena dragged her eyes away from Malcolm when she realized that Em was talking about Kylee.

The teen shrugged sheepishly. "It's just chalk. Is it okay if I do some in Em's hair?"

Em turned puppy-dog brown eyes to Serena. "Please, Mum? Pleasepleaseplease?"

"If it washes out," Serena said, earning a round of cheering from her daughter.

"Uh, Serena," Malcolm said, "I think you have an escapee."

She turned just in time to see a bare three-year-old bum disappear around the corner, Max's delighted laughter trailing down the hall behind him.

"Excuse me while I deal with my little nudist." Serena strode down the hall after her son. "Max, how is this getting yourself dressed? Come on, Son."

After a short game of tag with Max darting out of reach each time, she wrestled him to a stop long enough to get both his underpants *and* his pajamas on his body and then gave him strict instructions to stay fully clothed. He clung to her as she walked back into the lounge.

"Are you ready? Or should I have made the reservation for three?" Amusement sparkled in Malcolm's eyes, and the relief rushing through Serena's body surprised her. Any other man would have been halfway out the door if he walked in on this display.

"Hey, Max," Kylee said, "I've got something for you in my bag. Do you want to go into the kitchen and see what it is?" Kylee held out her arms, and after a moment's hesitation, Max went to her instead.

"Thank you," Serena mouthed to Kylee. She gave Em one last hug and then grabbed her handbag off the console table.

"Ready?" Malcolm asked.

"Finally. Let's escape while we can."

They slipped out the front door, Serena pausing to lock it behind them, and then she followed him down the drive to where his black compact was parked. He opened the door for her, and she spent the time it took for him to circle to the driver's side to draw in a few deep breaths. In and out. In and out. Turn mum mode off. Turn woman mode on. If she could even remember what that was. And then Malcolm leaned across the console, took her chin in his hand, and kissed her, and she had no problem at all remembering.

"All right, so this is a little embarrassing," he said when he sat back again.

"What? That you couldn't wait until the good-night?"

His smile flashed, accompanied by an irresistible crinkle of his eyes, and her heart did another little leap. "I'm not embarrassed at all about that. I hope you're not going to make me wait until the good-night to kiss you again either . . ."

"Hmm. We'll see. What's embarrassing? Did you forget to make reservations? This is Skye. It's not like everything will be booked."

"Best you see for yourself, I reckon." He buckled his seat belt and then backed down her drive. By the time they turned down the Sleat Peninsula, she thought she might know the source of his embarrassment. When he pulled up in front of the MacDonald Guest House, it was clear.

He turned sideways on the seat to face her. "Listen, I asked around for opinions on what the best restaurant on Skye was, and every single person said—"

"This one." She laughed. "Blame my brother. At least we know the food is good."

"Chef Villarreal is about to try out a new menu, and I convinced him to give us a preview. So other than Jamie, you will be the first person to sample these dishes."

He looked so simultaneously uncertain and eager to please that she leaned across the seat and kissed him again. "It's perfect. I've only eaten here once, if you can believe that."

"I hoped that might be the case. What's the use of all your hard work if you can't enjoy it?"

If anyone thought it was odd that the owner and the hotel manager were having dinner in the dining room like regular guests, no one let on. Serena did notice that they were shown to the best table in the back corner, dimly lit and away from even the small amount of noise that came from the cozy restaurant. Every detail was simple and perfect, from the white linen tablecloths to the lushly upholstered chairs to the candlelit ambience.

Almost immediately after they were seated, the hostess brought a bottle of wine to the table. "Spanish cava," she said quietly, pouring with flair into their two glasses and then slipping away just as unobtrusively. Being on the receiving end of the restaurant's service, Serena could see why everyone had pointed Malcolm in this direction.

"Was this your idea?" she asked as she reached for the glass of sparkling wine.

"No," he said. "I considered it, but it felt a bit . . . presumptuous."

"I appreciate your restraint. But it doesn't mean I won't enjoy the wine now that it's here." She took a sip and gave a nod of approval. "I'm guessing by the fact we have no menus that it's chef's choice?"

"Exactly."

Serena reached for the bread basket and spread butter garnished with pink salt on a dark slice. "This is pumpernickel, I think. Rather nice pumpernickel, actually. I'm typically not much of a fan. It's usually too sour."

"We get this from an artisanal bakery in Portree," Malcolm said. "They supply us and a few other restaurants on the island, as well as their own store."

"It's very good."

"So this wasn't a horrendous idea after all?"

His insecurity was endearing, particularly considering how cocky and overconfident she'd thought him when they first met. "It was an excellent idea."

He leaned back in his chair and studied her. "I'm curious. Why did you sell your interest in the hotel if you were just going to buy back in?"

Serena considered how much to tell him. "I know it's hard to believe now, but after our father died, my brothers were at odds. Ian worked for Jamie, but they barely spoke to each other outside of business matters. If one said black, the other said white. As the third partner in the hotel, I was always having to play tiebreaker." She shrugged. "I was more interested in maintaining my relationship with my brothers than I was in staying involved with the family business. Jamie offered to buy out my share to keep it in the family. Now neither of them really has the time to be as hands-on as they'd like, so Jamie asked me to buy back in. And here we are."

"Here we are." He smiled warmly, seeming comfortable just to look at her, even though she squirmed under the scrutiny.

"My turn to ask a question. My brothers said you were an engineer. What kind of engineer are you exactly?"

"That's what you wanted to ask? You know you could have pulled my CV from the employment files a long time ago."

"I thought about it," she said, "but enough time had passed, and our relationship became not so strictly business, so it felt as if I'd be spying on you."

"It's a bit hard to explain, actually. I work with telescopes."

"Telescopes? Like the ones you can buy for stargazing?"

"No, the space-based ones like the Hubble."

She blinked at him. Of all the answers he could have given, she never expected anything so . . . technical. "How does one go about doing that for a living?"

He chuckled. "I'm not sure how most people do it. I went into it backward. I've always had a talent for figuring out how things work, especially if they involve power of any sort. I was the lad who was always trying to make an electromagnet out of car batteries and the like. I ended up getting a degree in electrical engineering and then going to work for an aerospace contractor, but I hated it. I'd always had an interest in astronomy, and I had a fair amount of programming knowledge, so when I learned there was work in the field outside of astrophysics, I decided to go back to school for a graduate degree in computer science."

That was completely unexpected. She associated the hotel management and the repair skills with something more blue-collar, like mechanical engineering. But to find out he was somewhat of an academic? "So you quit your job and tended bar to support yourself?"

"Exactly. It was too hard to get my courses while keeping the day job."

"I'm impressed. But I still don't understand what that has to do with telescopes."

"I am—I was—a software engineer for a space research institute at Johns Hopkins in Maryland. Basically I wrote programs that analyzed and interpreted the data that came back from the telescope so astronomers could use it."

"So the whole time I was on about Dark Sky sites and star charts and all that, you not only knew what I was talking about, but you actually worked in the field. Why didn't you say anything?"

Malcolm had the grace to look abashed. "You were so excited about it and you wanted to take on the work, so I didn't want to burst your bubble. Would you have continued on if you knew I worked in astronomy?"

"Maybe not." She sat back from the table. "But now I feel foolish."

"You shouldn't. Most of our guests want to know the best place to see Cassiopeia and the Big Dipper, not the algorithms scientists use to classify an object as a star or a galaxy."

"That's true," Serena said with a little smile, "but I still feel somewhat at a loss. Scientific people are my natural enemy."

"Why is that?"

"Because I read art history. Which, before you say it, I realize is the degree for people who don't actually need to work for a living."

"I gave up a high-paying job to look at star data and play

with telescopes," he said. "I hardly think I'm in a position to judge. Why art history?"

"I've always loved art, ever since I was a child. But fine art seemed just too—"

"Unemployable?"

Serena smiled. Somehow when Malcolm said it, it didn't make her feel defensive. "Something like that. I was able to get an internship at the Tate Gallery in London after I finished university."

"How does one do *that*?" he asked.

"Well, first one has to have a nearly useless degree from a very good university. And then one uses her family connections to call in favors to get a coveted position." Voiced aloud, she realized how snobbish and privileged she must sound. At the time it had merely seemed sensible. "However, it was my qualifications that landed me a permanent position there, and then later a job managing artists at a rather prestigious gallery in Edinburgh."

"So deep down, you're an academic like me," he said.

"I can't tell whether you think that's a good thing or a bad thing."

He laughed again. "It's a good thing."

"So why do you hide the fact that you're obviously very intelligent? Why didn't you say anything about all this?"

As soon as the words left her mouth, she realized they could be taken as an insult. But his eyes just sparkled as if her fumbling amused him. "I don't hide my intelligence. I just don't go on about my education."

"Why not?"

"I don't know. Why don't you?"

A slight smile crept onto her lips. "You are very good at

turning things around so I forget what I'm asking you. If you want a real answer from me, I expect you to answer first."

Now he looked a little uncomfortable, which she found endearing. "I suppose I didn't tell *you* because I wanted to know if you liked me for me, not just because you thought I had a suitably impressive collection of diplomas at home."

She leaned forward, holding his gaze. "And once more you didn't entirely answer my question."

He thought for a long moment before he answered. "We are from completely different worlds, Serena. In yours, a good education is assumed—demanded even."

"We both grew up here on Skye."

"Except I moved away when I was eleven. And even then, you can't compare our experiences here."

"What happened exactly?"

He drummed his fingers on the table. "Before or after my dad emptied out the bank account and left us destitute?"

A mixture of horror and sympathy washed over Serena. She suspected that reaction was exactly why he hadn't told her. "I had no idea."

"How could you? You probably didn't know that my mum used to clean this hotel either. But it still wasn't enough to make ends meet. My aunt invited us to come stay with her in Glasgow and got Mum a job cleaning a hotel there. You see, she dropped out of school at fourteen to work her family's croft, so it wasn't as if she had marketable skills."

"But she did what she had to do to support you and your sister. That's admirable."

"My sister was seven years older than me, and she stayed on Skye to get married," Malcolm said. "So it was just me and Mum. And the place in Glasgow—well, the city usually gets a bad rap, but where we lived deserved its reputation. It wasn't exactly a place you wanted to be seen as a bright and innocent lad, fresh from the country, if you know what I mean. I went to school and got perfect marks and spent my afternoons trying to not get my face bashed in."

He told the story with a light tone, but she sensed the deep scars beneath the words. For a moment she could see beyond the swagger and the humor to the little boy who had been terrorized by bullies.

"I did pretty well until I won a science fair at thirteen and ended up in the paper," he went on. "Couple of blokes waited for me outside my building and gave me a pounding I still haven't forgotten. I was black and blue for weeks. Loads of stitches." He pushed his hair away from his temple to show a jagged scar at his hairline, now faded to a silvery white.

She winced. "What happened then? What did your mum do?"

"Well, after she was done vowing to kill the delinquents— this woman who couldn't have weighed more than seven stone dripping wet—she made me promise that I would lie low and avoid trouble. I hadn't been looking for trouble in the first place, so this advice wasn't exactly helpful.

"I was determined that my mum wasn't going to fight my battles for me, so I found a boxing club and convinced the owner to let me train there in return for sweeping floors and cleaning bags and scrubbing toilets—whatever I could do. Mum worked two jobs sometimes, and my aunt didn't care what I did, so I managed to keep it a secret. It didn't take long for the owner to figure out what was going on. See, this bloke—Reginald—he'd grown up similarly in Glasgow, and he recognized a skinny kid with too little food, too much intelligence, and no supervision. So he started paying me a little. He just 'happened' to have extra food around when I came over from school, just 'happened' to be short a sparring partner for one of the more skilled lads."

"It sounds like a movie," Serena said, caught up entirely in the story. "Are you sure you're not embellishing for effect?"

"I swear, it's God's honest truth. I got good in the ring pretty quickly, so the next time I was confronted, I didn't run away. I stood my ground."

"What happened?"

"I got my—ahem—tail kicked. Badly. I might have been good at boxing an opponent, but it's a lot different when they don't wear gloves and they bring their mates. When I showed up at the club the next day, I thought Reg was going to congratulate me on my bravery, and instead he laced into me like I'll never forget."

"Because you got cocky?"

"Because he wasn't teaching me to be a street brawler. He was trying to keep me out of trouble and give me a chance to make something of myself." Malcolm smiled. "My mum would probably have been horrified had she ever met the man, considering his vocabulary mostly consisted of four-letter words, and his idea of discipline was a sharp slap to the head, but he was the only one looking out for me at a time when I could have really gone down the wrong path. He told me I was too smart to be acting like a prat . . . except he didn't say *prat*, of course. And if I really cared about my mum, I would go to university, find a good job, get her into a safer part of Glasgow. In short, he told me I needed to make good choices if I were to be a better man than my father was."

"That's some story," Serena said softly. "Where is your mum now?"

"Well, I got her out of that tenement building that she hated so much and into a safer flat. I moved to America to work at the Space Telescope Science Institute, and while I was gone, she up and married a greengrocer."

"Do you like him?"

He seemed surprised by the question. "I do, actually. He doesn't care for me too much. But that might have something to do with the fact I told him I'd knock seven bells out of him if he ever hurt my mum the way Dad did. He took it to heart, I think."

"Would you have done it?"

"In my twenties, without hesitation. Now, I honestly don't know. Does that concern you?"

Serena studied him. Despite Malcolm's rough edges, his physicality, there was still something calm and steady at the core that made her feel safe. "Not a bit. I've never thought of myself as a violent person, but if someone laid a hand on one of my kids, I don't think I could be responsible for my actions."

"It does change your perspective, doesn't it? When I was just the uncle, I could get in trouble with Kylee. Drove Nic crazy. Now I worry about Kylee all the time."

She knew exactly the feeling. After Edward died, she'd felt the weight of her responsibility double. She raised her glass and clinked it together with his. "To the part of being a parent no one ever warns you about."

"Didn't exactly come about how I expected it," he said wryly.

"It never does."

The first course of their meal arrived then, an exquisitely plated scallop starter that tasted as good as it looked. Serena took her first bite and then set down her fork with a sigh. "My brother is a genius."

"No arguments here. But this dish is Chef Villarreal's."

"Really? Very impressive."

"I think so too."

The conversation turned to lighter subjects finally, recollections of the peculiarities of growing up on Skye, funny stories about her children and his niece, current television programs. And with each passing minute, Serena's admiration for Malcolm grew. She had made so many misguided assumptions about him. He was intelligent, funny, well read. And he looked at her as if there were no one with whom he'd rather share his evening, that singular focus fixed with laser precision on her. She found herself talking too much, even though anytime the topic turned to her marriage or what came before it, she steered it away. There were some things she just wasn't ready to tell him. He simply listened, refilling her wineglass and asking questions.

By the time he paid the bill and they rose to leave, the growing feeling of connection with him had become more unsettling than the ever-present current of attraction.

"Thank you for a lovely evening," Serena said when they returned to the car park. "It's been so long since I've had a good, uninterrupted meal in pleasant company, it feels like a holiday."

Malcolm opened the car door for her. "The evening's not over yet."

"And you're not going to tell me where we're going next?"

"Oh no. But you're welcome to try to guess."

"I don't think so," she said slowly. "I'll just sit back and enjoy the surprise."

CHAPTER SEVENTEEN

SERENA COULDN'T BEGIN TO GUESS their destination until Malcolm turned off the highway down the neatly paved road that led into Kinloch Forest. The headlamps swept across the trees that crowded the drive, illuminating them in patches as they passed through the gate into the forestry area.

"Really?" she asked, unreasonably giddy at the prospect. "We're going stargazing?"

He glanced over at her, the light from the car's instrument cluster illuminating his pleased expression. "Indeed. Even in the village there's too much light pollution to see anything. I thought you should be able to enjoy what you've put so much work into. Especially since we have only a couple of weeks of dark skies left."

"I love this. We've been out only one night since we arrived. I was telling the kids the stories behind the constellations. Well, I was telling Em. Max never makes it much past the first few minutes."

Malcolm smiled at her in the dark, something she felt more than saw, as he pulled into the dirt car park. "There's a flat spot where we can sit up there—not that I need to tell you that. You literally wrote the brochure on it."

Serena suddenly wished she had worn jeans and low-heeled boots, because even though the ground had dried out from an unaccustomed week without heavy rain, the ground still sloped unevenly upward from the car park. She buttoned her coat while Malcolm went to the boot and began rummaging through the packed items.

"I don't suppose you would mind carrying some things, would you?"

"Of course not. What have you got in there?"

He pulled out a picnic hamper and handed it over first. "Dessert, naturally. A couple of blankets—I wasn't sure how warm you would dress, but I didn't want to spoil the surprise. And this, which I will carry." He pulled out a hard-sided case and a padded black bag that was shaped like the case for a hunting rifle, but shorter. It took her a second to puzzle through what they could be until she put it together.

"Really? You brought a telescope?"

He chuckled. "You are the first woman to consider that a positive. Not that we really need a telescope, but I thought it could be fun."

"It is fun." She slid the picnic hamper to the crook of her elbow and then took one of the blankets while he gathered the rest of the gear. Then he withdrew a torch fitted with a red filter—to preserve their night vision, she knew—and slammed the boot.

"Shall we?"

"Lead on."

When they reached the flat-topped grassy area, he spread out one of the blankets. She lowered herself to the center of it, already chilled by the cold night, her breath puffing out in front of her. He knelt before her and draped the second blanket around her shoulders, then got to work assembling the telescope on its tripod while she rummaged through the hamper.

Besides the stainless-steel carafe of something she assumed was coffee or tea, it contained little paper boxes of all sorts of pastries: cream puffs, tiny individual almond cakes, mini lemon and fruit tarts, and what looked like chocolate truffles. "I like your style," she said. "Which one do you want to try first?"

"I've already tried them all." She sensed his smile in the darkness. "And by now your children probably have as well. What do you think Kylee had in her rucksack?"

"Oh no, poor Kylee. Giving those two sugar before bed practically guarantees they'll be running circles around her."

"She can handle it. Besides, she was quite the negotiator when I asked her to do this. It's going to be worth any amount of hyperactivity."

Serena laughed. "I'm really beginning to like that girl."

"She's something all right." He lowered himself to the ground beside her and delved into the hamper. "So, which will it be?"

"Chocolate. Definitely chocolate."

He removed one of the ganache truffles from its fluted paper cup and held it for her to take a bite. She licked the chocolate from her lips and gave him a teasing smile. "First you ply me with wine, and then you feed me chocolate in the dark. Are you trying to seduce me?"

"Do you want me to?" His tone was serious, almost sultry, but even in the red glow of the torch, she could see the humor dancing in his eyes.

"Not just yet." She laughed at the look of surprise on his face. Had he been a different sort of man, she'd worry that she was hinting at something she didn't plan to deliver.

They sampled all the pastries in the box and drank their coffee while Serena pointed out the constellations overhead and told the stories behind them. Then he pulled her to her feet and rearranged the blanket over her shoulders.

"My turn. Come look." He made a couple of quick adjustments to the telescope and then stood aside as she bent to look through the eyepiece.

She drew in her breath. "What is that?"

"Jupiter," he said. "If you look closely, you can see two of its moons. Do you see those bright starlike dots?"

"I do." A smile spread over her face. The planet was a bright disc, two tan bands clearly visible through the telescope's high-magnification lens. It put an inexplicable sense of awe into her heart. "I've never seen it in such detail."

"It's a little humbling, the extent of what we can't see and what we still don't know," Malcolm said. "I always think of it like the universe's heartbeat. Or God's fingerprint. You can see it when you know where to look."

"You're very poetic for an engineer."

"I blame it on the present company." For a change his humor was absent, and the seriousness in his voice made her heart thud.

"What else can we see?" she asked, quickly backing away from both the telescope and his mood.

Malcolm squinted up at the sky, then made a few more adjustments. He stuck to the stars after that, telling her their facts, even though he took every opportunity to touch her.

It only got colder as the night went on, and Serena began to shiver despite the blankets and coffee. Malcolm rubbed her arms for warmth. "Let me pack up, and we'll get you inside."

She wasn't sorry to get back to the shelter of the car, but she hated to think about the evening drawing to an end. It had been so long since she'd been on a date that was so normal and enjoyable and romantic in its simplicity. He'd not tried to impress her. Rather he'd sought to give her an evening without worries, filled with things he knew she enjoyed. And he'd thoroughly succeeded.

When he at last pulled into her drive and parked, they just sat in the dark for a few seconds. "You know the minute we come to the door, Kylee will be peeking out, trying to catch us at something," he said.

"So if I'm going to take advantage of you, I should do it now?"

"Something like that."

"Then come here." Serena tugged his jacket to bring him closer, then lifted her face for a long kiss that started an ache in her rather than satisfied it. When they parted, she brushed her fingers across his whiskered jaw. "This was one of the nicest nights I can remember. Thank you."

"So what do you think? Can I see you again?"

She smiled coyly. "You'll see me at work every day next week."

"But I can't kiss you at work." He pulled her close again, but this time he kissed only her cheek and her jaw near her ear.

She leaned into him with a sigh of pleasure. "Who says you can't?"

"I think I did. Remember? Work stays at work; home stays at home?"

"Then you can't complain about your own rules. However, the answer is yes. I would love to go out with you again."

"Good." He kissed her one last time, lingering too long for it to be called quick, then brushed his thumb over her bottom lip. "Now let's go inside before we have to explain to Kylee what was taking us so long in the car."

"Oh, Kylee is seventeen. She knows."

Malcolm fixed her with a reproving look. "I do *not* want to hear things like that. Kylee hasn't even thought of kissing a boy, let alone doing anything else."

"Congratulations, Malcolm. You can officially consider yourself a father."

It was nice not having to downplay that part of her life, Serena thought as he took her hand and walked her to the door. Even when she'd dated in the past, she'd spent the whole time either wishing the man she was with could see her as a woman and not simply as a potential mother for his children or trying to pretend she wasn't worrying about her kids at home. Malcolm didn't make her feel she had to choose between her two halves.

The minute they reached the front step, though, Kylee yanked the door open, wild eyed and upset. From behind her came Max's all-too-familiar inconsolable scream. "Thank God you're home. He's been crying for ten minutes, and I don't know what to do!"

"It's okay. It's night terrors. He probably doesn't recognize you." Serena fumbled in her handbag for a moment and then pressed several banknotes into Kylee's hand. "Thank you, Kylee." She turned to Malcolm. "I'm sorry. I'm going to go take care of this. Can you let yourselves out?"

She didn't wait to hear their answer, just dropped her bag by the door and darted for Max's room. He was bouncing on his bed, screaming at the top of his lungs while staring at nothing on the opposite wall. Immediately her heart rate ramped up, blood pumping through her veins as if she were facing an attack and not just her inconsolable son. She climbed on the bed beside him, knowing that it probably wouldn't do any good.

"Hi, monkey," she murmured. "Mummy's home. I'm here."

"No!" he screamed, still not looking at her. "Go away!" He lashed out at her as if she were attacking him, and she backed off a little. Some nights she could hold him and he would calm down. Nights like this, he could scream for hours, and all she could do was make sure he didn't hurt himself.

She kept up a steady stream of soothing words, but they didn't seem to penetrate. He just kept screaming and thrashing, throwing himself around on the bed. Serena had no idea how long it lasted; she just knew that the longer it went on, the more tense she became. Frustrated tears swelled in her eyes as she kept her distance and made sure he didn't pitch himself off the bed.

Then suddenly the tears subsided, and he looked at her, his eyes clear. "Mummy?"

"Yes, sweetie, I'm home. Do you want to go back to sleep?"

He nodded and lay down on the bed, clutching his giraffe as if the incident had never happened. Serena heaved a sigh of relief and drew the covers up over him, then tiptoed out of the room.

In the hallway, though, she paused as the tears that had been threatening finally spilled over. It had been ages since Max had had a night terror that bad. Was it the universe's way of balancing things out because she'd enjoyed one blissful night of worrying only about herself? Or was God punishing her because she'd dared to have something in her life besides motherhood?

No, God didn't work that way. It was only guilt over the feeling that Max had ruined what was up until that point a perfect night. But this was her life. The children would always be her first responsibility. There were no do-overs for her younger and more carefree years, even if she didn't exactly wish for one. But a full night's sleep . . . a few minutes to herself to smile over what had been a perfect date . . . was that too much to ask?

She wiped her damp face with her sleeve and walked into the kitchen, intending to make herself a cup of tea, then stopped short. Malcolm stood at the counter pouring water from the steaming kettle into two cups.

"He's asleep?" he asked in a hushed voice. He took the cups and set them on the table.

"What are you doing here?"

"Do you want me to leave? I realize you said to let ourselves out, but I thought you might need me. I had Kylee take my car back to the house."

It was so thoughtful and so much more than she would have expected that the tears came back in full force. He didn't hesitate before enfolding her in his arms. She sniffled against his chest, battling against the swell of conflicting emotions.

"It's okay, Serena. You're a good mum. It's not your fault."

"I know, it's only—" She pulled away and dabbed at her eyes, aware of how watery her voice sounded. "It's hard sometimes. So hard to do it by myself. And you're being very sweet, but I can't let myself rely on you."

He pulled her into him again and held her tightly. His voice was muffled in her hair. "I would like to be someone you could rely on."

"Please, Malcolm. Just stop."

"Why?" Now it was his turn to pull away and look her in the eye. "Why is it so hard to let someone care about you and maybe help a little?"

Because it won't last. Because when this is over—and it will be over at some point or another—my life will be that much harder. But she couldn't say that to him. It would sound as though she were asking for a commitment, and she wasn't. Not when they'd just had their very first date. Not when they still knew so little about each other.

"Can't we drink our tea and enjoy the quiet?"

He looked disappointed, but he kissed the top of her head and let her go. She sat down with one of the cups, and Malcolm settled across from her. After a few moments of sipping their drinks, he asked, "How often does this happen?"

"Once a week, sometimes more. He wakes up every night, but most of the time he goes right back to sleep when I tuck him in. This one was really bad, though. Maybe because I wasn't here."

"Don't do that to yourself," he said.

"I know. It probably would have happened anyway. He's been having night terrors for more than a year, for no reason

I can determine. At least he won't remember it in the morning. If I tell him he woke up in the night, he'll deny it."

Malcolm chuckled. "Just as stubborn as his mum, you're saying?"

"I am not stubborn."

He drilled her with a comical squint.

"Okay, fine, maybe I'm a little stubborn. And maybe I just got spoiled with Em. She's always been an easy child."

"Except for getting kicked out of school." Malcolm shrugged at her surprised look. "Sorry. I was wondering why you changed schools midterm, so Muriel told me."

"I still don't know what to make of that." She'd almost forgotten about it, considering how peaceful their stay on Skye had been. "She'd never had a problem with a single person her entire life. Literally. Everyone loves her. So why was she picking fights at school? And why won't she tell me the reason?"

"Maybe she's protecting someone," Malcolm suggested. "Em doesn't strike me as a girl who would be purposely stubborn, unlike her mother."

Serena made a face at him, but his joking was beginning to lighten her heavy heart. "She seems to be doing really well in the Gaelic Medium course here, but I still don't know what I'm going to do for next year. Do I find another independent school? Public school? I refuse to send her away to boarding school, even when she's older."

"Serena." Malcolm took her hand across the table and squeezed it. "Maybe just this once you should sit back and trust. I understand wanting to have everything planned out, but some things in life you just have to take on faith."

"Blind faith has led me into some very bad decisions. I prefer to keep my eyes wide open." She hadn't meant to say that, hadn't meant to come so close to a truth he wouldn't want to hear. He seemed to have the idea that everything would work out if one just stayed the course—including their relationship. He was too smart not to pick up her reticence toward him and know the things were linked.

But instead of pressing the issue, he circled to her side and pulled her to her feet. "I'm going to let *you* go to sleep now. I'll see you tomorrow?"

"Tomorrow?"

"You're taking us to meet Davy and Glenn. Right?"

Serena shook free of her melancholy. "Yes, of course. Sorry. I have to bring the kids, so I'll drive if that's all right with you."

"Perfectly fine."

He tugged her against him and gave her a lingering kiss. Her tension slowly melted away, and she slid her arms around his waist.

"Just let me do what I can for as long as I'm able to do it, okay?"

She swallowed and nodded. "I'll try."

There were a couple more kisses on the way to the door and one on the steps, but as she closed the door behind him, Serena couldn't help but feel as if things were slipping fast out of her control.

CHAPTER EIGHTEEN

MALCOLM WOKE BEFORE HIS ALARM went off, overtaken by a feeling of anticipation he couldn't place until he remembered the plans for the day. Kylee had spoken of nothing else when he got home last night and then spent far too much time in her room picking out today's outfit. Sleep had come more slowly for him than he liked to admit as he went over every moment of his date with Serena like a lovesick fool.

He still wasn't sure what to think. She liked him, was certainly attracted to him, but she still held him at arm's length when it came to anything remotely serious or personal. Maybe it was simply concern over her children, and if that were the case, he couldn't blame her. She just seemed far more comfortable letting him get close to her physically than emotionally.

He was pretty sure blokes shouldn't even be thinking this sort of rubbish.

He shook his head in annoyance and threw aside his covers, then strode to Kylee's closed door and rapped sharply. "Time to get up, Kylee. You don't want to be late."

"I'm up," she replied. Of course. She'd probably been fine-tuning her look since daybreak.

Twenty minutes later, he'd already showered and dressed in jeans and a nice shirt, and Kylee still hadn't emerged from her room. The strains of her stereo drifted into the hallway this time. That seemed somehow like progress. He knocked again and called through the door, "I'm going to grab breakfast for us. Be ready to go by half eight, okay?"

"Okay!" she yelled back over the thump of the bass.

Downstairs he grabbed his keys from the hook in the mudroom and hopped in his car. He wasn't sure how this whole meeting would pan out, but Kylee was at least taking it seriously. Learning from working recording artists was an opportunity she would never pass up. They owed Serena for setting it up.

There were a number of cafés and restaurants in Broadford that served breakfast, but instead he went to a tiny bakery shack just across the road from the bay, little more than a lean-to with peeling paint and hand-lettered signs. In addition to making some of the island's best fish-and-chips, it also served fresh pastries and rolls in the morning.

"Malcolm!" The owner, a pretty twentysomething with dyed black hair and a ring through her septum, smiled when he stepped up to the counter. "What'll you have?"

"Morning, Amy. Half dozen of the raspberry brioche and two large coffees. The dark roast."

"Have guests this weekend, do you?"

"Day trip with friends." It wasn't exactly accurate, but it was vague and innocent enough to not require additional explanation.

Amy went to one of the trays on the back counter and placed six of the red-jam-swirled buns in a white paper bag, then pumped the coffee from an industrial carafe into two takeaway cups.

She favored him with a sympathetic look when he handed over his payment. "How is Kylee doing, by the way?"

"Good, considering. It's a bit of an adjustment all round." Amy had known Nicola—in fact, that was how Malcolm had learned about this place—but he had the feeling that her questioning had little to do with actual concern over his niece.

"Well, if you need anything, you know where to find me."

"Thanks for the offer. I think we're doing okay. Cheers, Amy."

He raised the cup in a half salute good-bye, then returned to where he'd parked on the verge. Her interest both amused and surprised him. How long had she been flirting with him and he hadn't even noticed? Kylee was right. He really was thick. But he'd been so wound up about doing a good job with his niece and the hotel, it had taken Serena and her adorably prickly attitude to catch his attention.

Malcolm smiled to himself as he slid the coffees into the cup holders and put the car in gear. He'd convinced himself that nothing was going to happen between him and Serena before she'd kissed him that first night. And while he might have been careful not to push things too far in the days since, she certainly didn't hold back. He was getting the feeling she was the type of woman who, once you finally earned her trust, would give everything for the man she loved.

A man needed to be worthy of that sort of devotion.

He parked behind Kylee's car and carried the coffees and pastries into the house. "Ky, are you ready yet?"

She thundered down the stairs almost immediately, a fringed bag slung over her shoulder. He did the now-automatic scan for appropriateness, but other than a little extra makeup and some jewelry that read more rock star than her everyday style, she looked as she always did.

"Ready to go?" he asked.

Her throat worked. "Sure."

"Relax." Malcolm tousled her hair, earning him a scowl in return. "If they're friends of Serena's, they'll be nice. Do you know what you want to ask them?"

"Kind of." Kylee drew a deep breath.

It was good practice for her. Because of the distance to most of her university choices, she'd been able to audition by video, but if she wanted a real music career, she would have to get used to putting herself out there. Kylee took her guitar case from where it waited near the door, and then they walked down the road to Serena's house. Before he could even knock, the door opened.

"Morning!" Serena addressed both of them, but her gaze quickly slid to Malcolm. "Come on in. There's extra porridge if you two are hungry. We don't have to leave for a few minutes yet."

"We actually brought breakfast," Kylee said as Malcolm passed a coffee cup to Serena. "I really owe you way more than coffee and buns for setting this up."

Malcolm repressed a smile at the implication that the

food had been Kylee's idea. He saw amusement in Serena's eyes that mirrored his own, but she just said kindly, "It's my pleasure, Kylee. Davy and Glenn should be a great source of information for you."

"Malcolm!" Em came running from the kitchen, followed by Max close at her heels. "Did you bring us something?"

"Manners," Serena scolded, but Malcolm laughed.

"Into the kitchen. I don't think your mum wants you to eat in the lounge." He surreptitiously opened the bag so Serena could peek in before they entered the kitchen. "I didn't get anything too sugary. Is it okay?"

"It's fine." From her smile, one would have thought he'd brought far more than a couple of brioche buns. Or maybe it was the fact that he'd let her peek before he offered it to them.

Serena went to the cabinet and stirred sugar into her cup, then pulled out a small carton of milk from the fridge. "You want some?"

"I take mine black."

"How very American," she said teasingly.

"Is it? I have my tea with milk and sugar, so I'm still a proper Scot in all the important ways." He reached past her to take a plate from the cabinet, purposely pressing up against her for a second while his hand rested on her waist. The sidelong glance she gave him made him wish for a couple of minutes away from prying eyes. Instead, he took the plate and set it on the table. "Dig in while they're still warm." The three kids descended on the food like starving prisoners.

Malcolm grabbed two buns and put them on plates, presenting one to Serena with a flourish.

"Raspberry is my favorite." She took a bite and rolled her eyes in ecstasy. "This is amazing."

"I thought chocolate was your favorite."

"Close second. I like anything sweet. You know you have a baking problem when your children groan over a full biscuit jar."

"Somehow I don't believe that." He shifted his glance to Max, who had a smear of raspberry jam over his lips and down his chin.

"Em doesn't have our sweet tooth. She actually asks for vegetables." Serena grabbed a paper serviette and wet it under the tap, then swooped in to wipe Max's face before the mess got transferred to his clothes. "Five minutes, everyone. We don't want to be late."

Malcolm watched Serena wipe her children clean and clear the table with practiced movements. She was a good mother. He had never thought that would be a quality he'd notice, even though he'd admired Nicola's seeming ease in raising Kylee. It also made him realize exactly what Serena's life must be like: always busy, often thankless. She could afford an au pair, but she chose to do everything herself, something he admired immensely. The recollection of how he'd challenged her right to have a chip on her shoulder made him feel vaguely guilty. On the surface, perhaps, she had nothing to complain about, but he also remembered how she'd dissolved into tears in his arms last night. She'd probably endured a lot of long and lonely nights, bearing the burden of raising two children without any support. She deserved to have someone to ease that burden. Max and Em deserved a father.

In that moment he realized with frightening clarity how serious he was about this woman.

"All right, everyone ready to go?" Serena clapped her hands, and Em and Max reluctantly slid from their chairs.

She wrestled them into their jackets, then led them all out to the car.

"Sorry, Kylee, you're going to have to squeeze in the back. I moved Em to the middle so you could have the window, but your guitar needs to go in the boot."

Once the instrument was safely stowed in the rear compartment and everyone was seat-belted in, Serena backed out of the drive and turned toward Portree. It wasn't long before Kylee had both Serena's children engaged in a game of I Spy, even though she had an unfair advantage from driving this route every day to school.

"She's a good girl," Serena murmured to Malcolm.

"I can't take credit," he whispered back. "Nicola and Richard were excellent parents."

"I'm sure. But considering all she's been through, she's doing really well. I think you've done right by her. I know what you had to give up to make it happen."

He placed his hand briefly over Serena's on the gearshift and squeezed before letting go. He was just doing what needed to be done, but her acknowledgment of the sacrifice made him feel good anyway. In truth, he'd initially resented the responsibility, especially after Teresa had made it clear he wasn't worth moving to Scotland for and she wasn't willing to wait for him. To think he had actually believed they might get married at some point . . . Now he realized their priorities had been far too different for a long-term relationship to ever work.

Davy and Glenn's house lay by a rutted road in Portree just off A855, one of many similar rows of townhomes, indistinguishable from one another in their white-plastered uniformity. This was the Skye that most holiday goers didn't know about. Brochures showed only quaint old buildings with sweeping views of the bays or the sound, not this modern rural neighborhood studded with television aerials and blue plastic rubbish-collection bins.

Serena pulled up in front of an end unit, before which was parked a silver Vauxhall estate car. Malcolm stifled a smile. This should eliminate any get-rich-quick fantasy Kylee harbored about music. Davy and Glenn were clearly solidly middle class, making a decent but not luxurious living. In his opinion, that was a positive sign. Teenagers might dream of wealth and fame, but parents and guardians had nightmares of insect-infested flats and busking on the street for 20p coins.

Serena hopped out of the car and retrieved Kylee's guitar from the boot before she took Max from his car seat. Kylee took her instrument and followed Serena slowly toward the front of the townhome, obviously nervous. Malcolm nudged her forward with an encouraging smile.

Serena was already knocking confidently at the door, which opened almost immediately. Malcolm wasn't sure what he had expected of Davy, but this utterly normal-looking woman was not it. She was tall and pretty, with short-cropped dark hair, dressed in jeans and a 1940s-style printed blouse.

"Serena!" Davy said warmly, giving Serena a squeeze before she turned to the kids. "I can't believe this is Em and Maxie. I almost didn't recognize you two, you were so young last time I saw you." She straightened and directed a warm smile toward the newcomers. "And you must be Malcolm and Kylee. Please, come in."

Malcolm nudged Kylee up the two steps and into a very modern town house. The walls and high ceilings were all painted a bright white, the small reception room decorated in contemporary furnishings and large color-splashed canvases.

"Have a seat." Davy waved her hand toward a boxy leather sofa. "I'll go let Glenn know you're here."

Kylee gingerly perched on the edge of the sofa while Max made a beeline for the tabby dozing on the arm of a chair. "Kitty!"

The cat was still trying to decide whether to tolerate the boy when Davy returned with a tray of tea accoutrements, followed closely by a slender man with a shaved head. He fit the musician stereotype better than his wife with an earring in each ear and several tattoos on the insides of his forearms.

While Davy set the tea things down on the table, the man held out his hand to Malcolm. "Glenn."

"Malcolm. Nice to meet you. This is my niece, Kylee."

"Hi, Kylee." Glenn gave her a friendly nod, but he didn't approach her. "I'm glad you could come visit us. Serena said you had some questions about a career in music."

"If you don't mind." Kylee's voice came out as little more than a squeak.

"Ach, Glenn." Davy shot her husband a sharp look. "Tea first. And biscuits. Come sit by me, Kylee. You'll love these. They're lavender shortbread. I thought Serena was mad when she gave me the recipe, but they're actually lovely."

Serena and Davy poured tea and dished out the biscuits to the whole crowd. After they'd nibbled on the shortbread, which was indeed very good, Davy set down her cup and turned to Kylee. "So, tell me a little about your music. Serena says you're a singer-songwriter?"

Malcolm could see all the tension return to Kylee's body. "Yes."

"If you could pick one artist to model yourself after, who would it be?"

Bless Davy, Malcolm thought. Within seconds, Kylee was chatting enthusiastically about her favorite singers. Minutes after that, she was pulling out her guitar as an illustration, and Glenn brought out his own to accompany her.

Malcolm pulled Serena aside. "They're fantastic," he whispered. "I don't know how to thank you."

"Davy and Glenn will give her good advice. I'm going to take Em and Max outside to play, though. They're getting restless."

"I'll stay here."

"I would too." She touched his arm before she gathered up her children and ushered them out the front door. Malcolm settled back with his tea and watched Kylee, her eyes bright, her expression fully engrossed in Glenn's words.

Yes, there had been sacrifices, but he couldn't doubt that they were absolutely worth it.

———— ⌒♁⌒ ————

Serena sat on a low cement wall watching Em and Max play an improvised game with sticks and rocks they had found in Davy and Glenn's front garden.

After she'd been outside for perhaps half an hour, Davy came out the front door and plopped onto the wall next to her. "You're right. She's good."

"I thought so. But I'm not the best judge of musical talent."

"Glenn is a better judge of singers than I am," Davy said. "But considering she's largely self-taught on the guitar and already so proficient, there's no doubt she has natural talent."

"He's in there talking to her?"

"Giving her a realistic idea of what she can expect in a university music program and what she'll need to do if she wants to make it as an artist."

Serena threw Davy a wry glance. "I hope he doesn't terrify her. He can be a little intense."

"It's a brutal business. If she's that easily frightened off, best she knows now while she can still choose to do something else. Making a living from art doesn't offer much security in the best of times."

Even though Davy's words weren't meant for Serena, they still stung. Serena simply nodded. "I owe you one. Thanks."

"Sure." Davy cocked her head and studied her. "So, what's this Malcolm to you? Don't tell me he's your employee like you did over the phone."

Serena smiled. "He is my employee."

"But not just."

"No, not just." When Davy stared expectantly, she shrugged. "We're seeing each other. Nothing serious."

"So 'not serious' that you're calling in favors on his niece's behalf?"

Serena considered her words carefully. "I like him. A lot. But I'm just supposed to be here for the summer, and we both have obligations. I don't know what's going to happen."

"When Glenn and I met, he was living in Edinburgh and I was here on Skye, and we somehow made it work. Not that I'm pushing, mind you; just saying that these things have a way of sorting themselves when you're motivated." Davy fell quiet for a moment, watching as Em pretended to run away from her gleefully squealing little brother. "How's everything else going?"

"You know. We're fine, all things considered." She didn't

go into the details that had brought them to Skye. She and Davy were still friends, but they were no longer sharing-deepest-secrets sort of friends.

The door to the town house opened again, revealing Malcolm standing beneath the frame. Even though he was probably supposed to be retrieving Davy, his gaze rested longest on Serena, making her heart give another one of those silly little squeezes.

"Looks like I'm being summoned." Davy hopped off the wall, then looked between Malcolm and Serena and smiled. "I have a feeling you might be able to work something out."

Serena stood, but before she could follow Davy, Malcolm joined her on the low wall.

"How are they doing in there?" Serena asked.

"Now that Kylee has gotten over her terror of sitting with some real musicians, she's in her element. Especially once she learned that Glenn played on April Chaos's last studio album."

Serena laughed. "I'm glad it's helpful. Amazing all the talent we have on our little island, isn't it?"

"Absolutely." Malcolm squeezed her hand before standing. "I should go back inside. I wanted to let you know we'll be ready to leave in a few minutes."

"We'll be right in." Serena watched him saunter back across the garden to the house, but she didn't immediately leave her seat on the wall. *Our little island,* she'd said. It had been so long since she'd lived here that she'd ceased to claim ownership, but the past month had made her realize what she loved so much about Skye. The friendliness, the small community. Would it really be so bad to stay?

Up until this point, she'd been holding herself back from

really exploring where her relationship with Malcolm could go because she was so sure it had to be limited to a summer romance. But what if it didn't? It wasn't as if she had a job demanding her return. Em's school no longer dictated where they lived, and she'd already decided to sell her house. What if she stopped using that as an excuse not to get attached?

The idea simultaneously thrilled and terrified her. The only time she'd fully abandoned caution and given her heart away, she'd ended up in a troubled marriage for ten years. But Malcolm wasn't Edward in any respect. Besides, they weren't to that point anyway. She was just considering giving this *thing* a chance to develop naturally. There couldn't be any harm in that. Could there?

<hr />

Kylee didn't stop talking the entire way back to Breakish, giving Malcolm and Serena a play-by-play of everything Glenn and Davy had said to her, plus an analysis of the imagined subtext.

"I'm pretty sure they meant just what they said." Malcolm turned in his seat to smile at her. "If Glenn said you're talented but could benefit from a conservatory education and some courses from the music-production track, that's probably what he meant."

"Right." Kylee fell silent for a moment. "But the music program at Glasgow is almost strictly classical. I don't want to be an opera singer." Now Malcolm understood what this was about. The type of program about which Glenn had spoken mirrored Berklee almost perfectly, but the University of Glasgow was structured far differently. No doubt Kylee felt she'd damaged her future career chances by not getting into the school of her choice.

"I happen to know that you can study abroad for your third year, so don't count those schools out yet." At Kylee's surprised look, he laughed. "What? You didn't think I'd read the catalog? I'd venture to say I know your future coursework better than you do."

A tiny smile crept back onto Kylee's lips. As Malcolm turned forward, he saw Serena was smiling at him as well. He hadn't even realized he needed validation of his parenting skills, but her approval warmed him. Maybe understanding how dedicated he was to Kylee would help Serena realize that he was worthy of her trust.

Kylee picked up where she had left off, punctuated by a little hero worship from Em, who was apparently a burgeoning pianist herself. When they pulled into the drive of Serena's house, Kylee's exuberance once again won out. As soon as Serena got out of the car, Kylee threw her arms around her. "This might be the nicest thing anyone has ever done for me."

"You're welcome," Serena said with a laugh. "I'm glad it was helpful."

"Hey, Ky, why don't you head home," Malcolm said. "I'll be there in a minute."

"Okay." Kylee must have been too preoccupied with the events of the morning to shoot him her usual knowing look, because she just gave a wave good-bye before heading down the drive.

Serena unbuckled Max from his car seat, and the little boy immediately clung to her with arms and legs, killing Malcolm's hope of a private conversation and a good-bye kiss.

He cleared his throat. "I was wondering . . . would you like to go to church with us tomorrow?"

She seemed startled by the invitation. "Church?"

"You know, big building with stained glass, lots of singing—"

"I know what it is. I just haven't—Where do you go?"

"Same place Muriel goes . . . where you used to attend. You don't remember, do you? Mum and Nicola and I sat a few rows behind you every weekend for years."

Now color bloomed on her cheeks, and she looked embarrassed. "I can't say I noticed. I vaguely remember Nicola, but you must have been a few years behind me."

Right. Their age difference. "Does that bother you?"

A slow smile spread over her face. "No. At least not as much as it should."

"Good." Despite the fact that she was holding her son and Em lingered a few steps away, he was tempted to kiss her right there. Instead, he asked, "So you'll come?"

She still looked reluctant, but she nodded. "Okay."

"Great. It starts at nine. I'll save you a seat."

Malcolm winked at her, then turned away. He was halfway down the drive before she called after him. "Wait! Kylee's guitar!"

"Oh, right." He waited while Serena opened the boot with her key fob and then reached in for the guitar case. He paused at the open boxes pushed to the side. "What's all this?"

She circled around beside him, looking suddenly uncomfortable. "It's nothing."

"It doesn't look like nothing." There were stacks of blank stretched canvases and boxes of paints and brushes and wood-handled instruments he didn't recognize. "You paint?"

"I used to paint."

"Former painters don't generally carry around art supplies," he said gently.

She didn't meet his eye. Instead, she retrieved the guitar case and handed it to him, then slammed the boot. "I'll see you tomorrow morning, then."

"Good. You won't stand me up, will you? It's church, after all. I'm just thinking of your eternal soul."

She cracked a smile, the tension of moments before gone. "My eternal soul is safe, thank you very much. Or it was before you came along. Now go. We'll see you there."

He grinned at her, then turned on his heel. He got only a few steps down the drive before he turned back. "Serena? Thanks again. You have no idea what this meant to Kylee."

That little smile surfaced again. "I think I do."

As he walked home with his niece's guitar in hand, Malcolm wondered if Serena's encouragement of Kylee's musical pursuits came from more than just the desire to do a friend a favor.

CHAPTER NINETEEN

THE PARISH CHURCH that Serena and her family had attended for years sat on a quiet street in Portree, an eighteenth-century stone building with the arched stained-glass windows that had fueled Serena's daydreams as a child. She had attended Sunday services elsewhere after leaving Skye, but there was something about this tiny village building, which had been the site of her spiritual education, that seemed particularly holy to her.

She took Max first to the crèche, expecting some sort of objection from him, but he immediately joined a little girl on the rug and began playing with plastic dinosaurs. Em went to her Sunday school class with surprising enthusiasm. Instead, it was Serena who felt awkward standing at the back of the aisle, looking for Malcolm and Kylee among the pews. Almost as if he sensed her presence, Malcolm turned to scan the church and then raised a hand. She quickly walked down the aisle and slid into the space beside him.

"Good morning," he said warmly. "You made it."

"You were worried about the state of my eternal soul."

"And you made a rather daring accusation against me."

Serena leaned forward so she could greet Kylee, who wore a dress and cardigan that were far sweeter than the ripped jeans and studded belt she had worn yesterday. "Good morning, Kylee."

"Hi, Serena," she said. "I'm happy you came."

"Thank you for letting me tag along." She'd practically been bullied into it, but then Malcolm couldn't know that she and God had been on sketchy terms lately. If she could call almost a full decade "lately."

The service was just as she remembered, beginning with a performance by the children's choir. Then an unfamiliar minister took the pulpit for the morning's message. The entire time she was aware of Malcolm beside her. He was so engrossed in the message that she thought he had forgotten about her until he brushed his finger against the back of her hand where it rested on the pew between them.

She stared at the stained-glass windows, mesmerized by the colors and patterns as she had once been as a girl, the words of the minister fading into the background. An unexpected bubble of emotion welled up. She'd hoped being back here would be comforting, but she'd underestimated the strength of her memories. Staring through her tears at the windows in the months after her parents' divorce, aware of her mum and Ian's conspicuous absence on the pew next to her, ignoring the sympathetic stares from other parishioners. The self-consciousness had been relieved only by her fascination with the church's art, her daydreams about what she would draw or paint when she got home.

There had been so much she couldn't express in words, especially not to the well-meaning church folk who saw her either as a part orphan, abandoned by her mum, or as a cautionary tale about the evils of divorce. She'd saved it all up inside, until it could be spilled out in oils, charcoal, watercolors. To their credit, Dad and Aunt Muriel hadn't pushed, even when the subject matter of her work was disturbing.

And then, somehow, somewhere, that well of emotion had dried up, been locked away like an abandoned church, its colors never to be seen again.

"You okay?" Malcolm whispered in her ear.

She realized she was biting her bottom lip so it didn't quiver. She gave a terse nod and straightened, determined to keep her attention on the sermon.

By the end of the service, her emotions felt strangely raw. She put on a pleasant smile as she walked into the vestibule with Malcolm and Kylee, but her hopes of making a clean escape evaporated when she saw the light of recognition in several older parishioners' eyes. A gray-haired woman detached from the group and came her way. "Serena MacDonald?"

"Hello, Mrs. MacDonald," Serena said, aware of the strangeness of the address. They might share the same last name, but if she was related to the woman, it was only distantly. There had been MacDonalds on Skye for a thousand years. "It's Serena Stewart now, actually."

"Right, right, of course." The woman's expression changed

to one of sympathy and she patted Serena's arm. "I heard about your husband, you poor dear. Why have you not been back? You know, Jamie came to visit us, even if he did make noise about lightning striking him."

Serena smiled. There probably wasn't a longtime church member who didn't remember the time that Jamie wrapped the reverend's car in cling film—or any of the other pranks that had him in constant trouble. "He's actually quite a responsible adult now, I assure you."

"Oh, I know he is, dear." Only then did Mrs. MacDonald seem to notice Malcolm standing behind Serena with Kylee. "Oh, my! Hello, Malcolm. Did you two come together?" Her eyes took on a calculating light as she looked between them.

"Not exactly," Serena said at the same time Malcolm said, "Yes."

"We're neighbors," Serena explained. "And of course he works at the hotel. He thought it was high time I came back for a visit."

"Well, he's a good boy. You know, you could do much worse than a fine man like Malcolm here. Why, I told my granddaughter Eisley that she really should get to know him better—"

"Eisley fancies the fellow at the co-op," Malcolm cut in smoothly, shaking the old woman's hand. He lowered his voice, but it wasn't low enough, because Serena heard him say, "Don't worry, though. I'm working on this one."

He was working on her? Serena frowned at him, said her good-byes to Mrs. MacDonald, and then left the vestibule without explanation to Malcolm. When she returned with Max and Em in tow, he was waiting for her alone, his expression puzzled.

"You're angry at me."

"I'm not angry at you." She tugged her children toward the door, hoping he wouldn't follow, but he trailed her down the steps into the sharp morning wind.

"Why aren't you talking to me, then?"

She paused at the bottom and pitched her voice low. "I just would have liked to discuss . . . us . . . before we talked about it with other people."

Malcolm looked amused. "I never said we were together. In fact, I implied I was pursuing you but you were resisting. I thought that seemed pretty accurate."

"But . . ." That was true. He hadn't said they were together. It had just made her feel exposed, especially when she didn't even know how she felt about him yet.

"Unless you're ashamed of me."

She blinked at him. "What?"

He moved closer and whispered in her ear. "You're embarrassed to admit that you're dating someone who works for you. Who has to work at all."

She jerked her eyes to his face. "No! That's not true."

"Then what is it?"

She hesitated. "My parents' divorce was a spectator event at this church. I just don't like the idea of anyone involved in this . . . thing of ours . . . before we've figured it out ourselves."

He considered a long moment, then nodded soberly. "I'm sorry. I didn't think it was a big deal. But I guess we've really not made anything official." He leaned close. "I'd kiss you good-bye, but—"

"Right." She gave him a vague smile that felt wholly inadequate and watched him go with a lump in her throat. They were still okay, weren't they? He didn't seem angry, and he'd even apologized, which she hadn't expected. But she still couldn't help feeling as if she'd somehow made a huge mistake.

Serena put on a happy face when they parked in front of Muriel's house and she ushered the kids inside, even though she still felt sick to her stomach. This was exactly what she hadn't wanted to happen. Weren't men supposed to be all aloof and insensitive?

That's what you had the first time, and look how happy it made you. But Malcolm was nothing like Edward—in looks, in attitude, or in any of the ways that actually mattered. He seemed to be a genuinely caring person. The idea that she had hurt his feelings ate away at her relentlessly.

"Auntie, we're here!" Serena closed the door behind them and followed the delicious smell of cooking roast to the kitchen, where Muriel was sitting at the counter cutting potatoes. "What's this?"

Muriel lifted her face for Serena's kiss on the cheek. "We're having mash with our roast today."

"No, I mean why are you cooking? I told you to leave all the side dishes for me."

"Oh, nonsense. Stop fussing over me like I'm an invalid."

"Auntie," Serena said sternly, "they took you to hospital by ambulance a week ago. You actually skipped church for the first time in forever. Of course I'm going to fuss over you."

Muriel waved her hand in her trademark dismissal. "I'm feeling fine. Now that I'm on the medication, things will be better. I'm just a wee bit tired is all."

"Which is why you should let me take over here."

Muriel sighed heavily, but she pushed the cutting board toward Serena, who washed her hands and got to work.

"So, how was your date Friday?" Muriel asked.

Another pang, straight to her heart. "Good. It was nice."

"Then why do you look like your dog died?"

Serena jerked her head up. Here she thought she'd been doing so well at hiding her feelings. "I don't have a dog."

"Is Malcolm not a good kisser? I've always imagined he'd be a good kisser."

"Aunt Muriel!"

"Oh, sweetheart, I'm old, not dead. I know a man with passion when I see one."

Serena smiled despite her heavy heart. "He's a very good kisser."

"So what's the problem, then?"

Serena stopped chopping and put the knife down. "I think I mucked things up. I got angry with him at church for implying we're dating."

"Are you?"

"I don't know."

"Why not?"

"Okay, I think I liked you better when you were playing the invalid. You were less nosy."

Muriel chuckled and put one thin-skinned hand on Serena's wrist. "Serena, darling, that man has had his eye on you from the moment he met you. He was just too cautious to do anything about it until you showed some interest back. Do you really think he's going to miss his chance to claim you?"

Serena shook her head. "I'm not his to claim, for one thing. I'm not anyone's to claim. One date is not a promise of commitment."

"When two people have as many responsibilities as you two do, making that leap to an actual public date is something of a statement." Muriel headed off her next protest with a gentle smile. "I'm not telling you to marry the man. I'm just saying that if you finally went out with him—if you're letting him spend time with your children—then there's something about him that appeals to you. Something that's worth exploring. I know you, Serena. You're not going to let your heart leap before your head has fully considered all the angles."

It was so on the nose that it irritated her. Was she so predictable that everyone knew what she wanted before she did? "Maybe we're just messing around. Did you ever think of that?"

"Wheesht, Serena. Now you're simply trying to be shocking. And it won't work. You were a good girl then, and you're a good girl now. Besides, you underestimate Malcolm if you think that's what he's looking for."

Muriel hadn't been on the receiving end of that first kiss in her croft house. Then again, he hadn't pushed matters at all after their date, and he'd left early. All his talk about church and setting a good example seemed completely sincere.

Serena shook her head as if it would jolt the thoughts out, but it was too late. They were imprinted in her brain. Try as she might to tell herself she was just feeling things out with Malcolm, her heart was getting more involved each day. Had she ruined things with him with her carelessness this morning?

The urge to see him and put matters right built with the passing hours, but when they finally returned home, Malcolm's car was still absent from his drive. She pushed down her disappointment and hustled the kids inside. He was working, of course, while she enjoyed a leisurely Sunday with her family. It was impossible not to feel the inequity.

She finally got the children tucked into bed and pulled out her laptop, only to find half a dozen messages from Jamie and Ian in response to her e-mail. She scrolled through the discussion until she got to the bottom line: they authorized her to make any decisions about personnel she deemed necessary, including allowing Malcolm to hire an assistant manager.

She smiled to herself and stepped out into the night, finally armed with an excuse to go next door and talk to him, but his car wasn't back yet. Instead of going straight inside, she wrapped the lapels of her cardigan around herself and leaned against the side of her car. A steady breeze blew off the water, carrying Skye's signature scent of salt and peat and smoke and pushing clouds across the night sky in alternating patches of gray and diamond-studded blue. She tilted her head back and tried to pick out the visible constellations, their stories running through her head. All tragic, it seemed, though a few were laced with triumphant melancholy, such as Callisto, the sworn virgin seduced by Zeus and turned into a bear by his jealous wife, Hera, then placed in the stars for her safety.

That tickle in her mind began again, like the shreds of a fast-fading dream. She grasped them, reeled them in until the prompting became too strong to ignore. Armful by armful, Serena transferred her art supplies from the car's boot to her lounge: canvases, paints, her collapsible easel. In a near daze, she set up the frame, placed a stretched canvas on it, and began to squeeze out pigments onto a clean palette. She remembered to strip off her cardigan and shove up the sleeves of her long-sleeved T-shirt before she picked up the brush.

It had been so long since she'd held one that the weight of

it felt unfamiliar in her hand. The paint went on the canvas tentatively at first, then with increasing confidence. With each stroke, the gap between then and now seemed to close, her focus narrowing to nothing more than the square of paint-covered canvas before her and the vision in her head that seemed to come to life a little more with each moment.

A knock startled her out of her trance, and she glanced at her watch. After midnight. She'd been at this for nearly four hours already? Who would be knocking at her door this late?

She peered out the side window, her heart giving a painful lurch at Malcolm's familiar form on her front step. He was practically giving her a medical condition with all the odd things his presence did to her. She flipped the latch and pulled the door open.

"Hi," he said, hands thrust into his jacket pockets. "Am I disturbing you?"

"No, not at all. Do you want to come in?"

He stepped past her tentatively. "I just got home, and I saw your lights were on."

"Yeah, I lost track of time." She purposely didn't look in the direction of her easel, but she saw his gaze flick toward it anyway before he focused on her.

"I wanted to apologize again. You've made it clear we're just feeling things out, and the last thing I want you to think is that I'm pressuring you."

"I may have overreacted a little," Serena said. "I haven't dated in thirteen years. It feels—"

"Strange?"

"Strange. And good. And a little nerve-racking."

He stepped closer and lifted a hand to cradle the side of her face. "Serena, you've nothing to fear from me."

The sincerity in his expression and the intensity of feeling in his eyes twisted her insides up into one big confused muddle. Then he kissed her with such gentleness, she felt something break, as if his presence were causing actual physical barriers to crumble.

He pulled back and smiled at her, then touched a finger to her cheek. "Do you know you have paint on your face?"

Serena reached up to wipe it away, but it would take scrubbing to remove it. She bit her lip. "Do you want to see?"

He nodded solemnly, and she crossed her arms over her chest as she moved around to the front of the canvas. She held her breath while he stared. And then after what seemed like forever, he said, "Wow."

"Really?" Relief left her in a whoosh. "It's not finished yet."

"I know, but—" He reached out, then dropped his hand before he could touch the wet paint. "Wow."

"You said that already."

"It's the only thing I know how to say. This is going to be incredible. It's already incredible."

She looked back at the canvas and tried to see it through his eyes. It was a starry night sky—not Van Gogh's, but an ancient's—the swirl of color just beginning to outline the figure of Callisto in her process of transforming from human to bear among the stars. She knew too much not to see all its flaws, the places where her technique was weak or the reality diverged from her vision. But maybe, just maybe, it looked like art.

"Is this Cassiopeia?" he asked.

"Callisto. Do you . . . I mean, is it . . . ?"

He looked down at her, his expression sending her body into a whole new series of jitters that surely couldn't be healthy. "It's going to be amazing, Serena. Even I can tell you are an extraordinarily talented artist."

She swallowed the tears threatening to rise again. "You're not just—"

"—trying to get back into your good graces? No. I mean, I do want back in your good graces, but I'm not just saying what you want to hear." He took her hand and squeezed it. "I don't know what made you stop, but you should be doing this."

She stared at him for the space of several heartbeats. Then she wrapped her arms around his neck and kissed him.

He laughed. "If I knew that's all it took to get on your good side—"

"You said that's not what you were doing!"

"It wasn't, but I like the end result." He tipped her face up to his and kissed her again. "Does that mean I'm forgiven?"

A surge of mischief swelled up inside her. "I don't know. I should think about it more."

He closed his hands on her waist and bent to nip her bottom lip. "How about now?"

"Still not convinced."

"Now?" He pressed her back, dropping little kisses on her lips with each step, until they fell to the sofa in a laughing tangle.

She slid her fingers through his hair as she looked up into his face, and time seemed to slow, locked in the intensity of his deep-brown eyes. She could have sworn her heart stopped beating altogether.

"I think this is the part where I excuse myself for the night," he murmured.

She swallowed and moistened her suddenly dry lips. "Probably a good idea."

He levered himself off the sofa and pulled her to her feet, where she ended up right back in his arms. He was getting harder and harder to resist, when he lifted her spirits with his mere presence, when she was beginning to crave his voice and touch more than she'd ever thought possible.

Still, it wasn't until Serena woke the next morning and he immediately sprang to mind that she realized her intentions to keep him at a safe distance had failed entirely. She lay in bed and stared at the ceiling, trying to reconcile the twin thrills of terror and elation that surged through her at the mere thought of him. They barely knew each other, after all, and other than the strength of their chemistry, what did she really know about him?

She rolled over, crumpling her pillow beneath her head. Maybe that wasn't entirely true. She saw how much he loved his niece and what he had sacrificed to put Kylee's needs first. He was kind and patient with her children. He was utterly determined to be a better man than his father, caring for his mother when she'd had no one else.

No, she might not know all the details of his life before her, but she knew who he was as surely as she knew how she felt about him. Malcolm Blake was a good man, a trustworthy man. If his actions could be believed, he cared for her. His tenderness seemed to say what words didn't.

And she'd actually shown him her painting. For that matter, she was painting, period. Just thinking about the half-finished canvas made her want to jump out of bed and get to work. It wasn't a stretch to say that her feelings for Malcolm had awakened parts of her that she thought were gone forever.

"Are you awake, Mum?"

She pushed herself up onto one elbow to find Em hovering

in the doorway. "Why are you up so early, cupcake?" Max had woken them at three this morning, so she'd assumed she would have to drag them both out of bed for school.

Em perched on the edge of the bed, her expression conflicted. "Is Malcolm your boyfriend?"

Great. The one question she didn't know how to answer. "I don't know, sweetheart. We haven't really talked about it yet. Would it bother you if he was?"

Em thought, then shook her head. She crawled under the covers with Serena and lay on her back, staring at the ceiling. "No, I really like him. He's nice and he plays with me and Max. And he told me I could look through his telescope."

"When was this?"

"At Glenn and Davy's house. I told him how you told us the stories in the stars, and he said he liked the stars too."

Serena smiled, torn between being touched by his kindness toward her daughter and afraid that Em was already getting too invested in this relationship. It was one thing to risk her own heart, but another to put her child's heart on the line.

She turned to Em and laced their fingers together. Wide brown eyes, so much like Edward's, stared back at her. "Here's the thing, cupcake. Malcolm and I are just dating. That means we're still getting to know each other, to see if we really like each other. And it's possible that after some time, we might realize we're not right for each other."

"Mum," Em said patiently. "I know what dating is."

"How do you—Never mind." Girls these days seemed to understand romance from birth. She still remembered when Em had come home from school at five years old and announced she was going to marry Tommy Wade. "I just don't want you to get your hopes up. Malcolm is a really good person, and I'm glad you like him, because I couldn't date someone you didn't like. But that doesn't mean we're going to get married or that we're even going to keep dating. Does that make sense?"

Em looked a little disappointed, but she nodded. "Okay. But it would be okay if you did marry him."

Maybe it would, her traitorous heart sang. Serena simply gathered her daughter to her and gave her a tight hug. "What do you say we go make breakfast? Just us girls before Max wakes up?"

"Okay." Em threw aside the covers and bounded out of bed, the conversation already forgotten. Serena followed more slowly, her earlier giddy mood tempered by her daughter's words. She couldn't forget that she wasn't the only one whose heart was at stake here. Even if she were willing to depend on Malcolm a little, she had to spare her children the potential fallout if things went wrong.

After peeking in on Max, who was sound asleep in his bed, one leg sticking out from beneath the duvet, she went to the kitchen and began pulling canisters from the cabinets. This oatcake recipe was one of her favorites, her take on a Scottish classic, sweetened with honey and lightened with the addition of a little flour to the soaked pinhead oats that the original recipe called for. They were just rolling out the dough on the cutting board when a knock drew her attention.

"Here, why don't you start cutting them out?" She handed Em a large biscuit cutter and strode to the front door, pulling it open without checking to see who it was.

"Did I wake you?" Malcolm stood on the front steps wearing a mischievous grin, a vacuum carafe in his hand.

Serena pulled the lapels of her robe tighter together and tried not to let on that his mere proximity sent a tingle down to her toes. When she didn't immediately answer, he held out the carafe. "Coffee. I know you could make your own, but I wanted to see if I could catch you again in a state of undress. Mission accomplished."

Serena's cheeks warmed, even though the twinkle in his eye said he was just having a laugh at her expense. She took the coffee with a smile. "I would invite you in for breakfast, but the ladies of the house are not yet prepared to receive guests."

"Fair enough. I shall be a gentleman and let you return to your morning repast." He delivered the last words in a stuffy English accent—at least the best he could manage, considering how his Highland accent managed to intrude—and gave a formal bow.

"Thanks for the coffee," she said as he stepped off the stoop.

"Thanks for the view," he shot back with that same mischievous smile.

Serena's own smile lingered after she closed the door and padded barefoot back to the kitchen. Em looked up from her baking sheet of oatcakes. "Was that Malcolm?"

"Brought me coffee," she said.

Em sighed. "That's so romantic."

Serena wanted to correct her, but she couldn't bring herself to chide her daughter. Nothing she said at this point would save their hearts if things went wrong. Both she and Em were goners.

CHAPTER TWENTY

MALCOLM DROVE TO THE HOTEL, his smile still lingering. He hadn't truly shown up early to try to catch Serena in her nightgown, though he wasn't above teasing her. He'd wanted to do something small to let her know he was thinking about her, even if it was something she could have easily done herself.

The fact was, he couldn't get her out of his mind. Last night seemed to have catapulted their relationship to another level. He could see how difficult it had been for her to show him her painting, how badly she'd wanted his support. She'd almost seemed braced for condemnation, as if she'd been doing something wrong. But he'd also seen a new spark in her, a passion he wouldn't have thought she possessed if it weren't for her enthusiastic response to his kisses. There were depths to this woman that he hadn't yet explored, and he wanted to know everything that they contained.

And somehow, that thought didn't worry him. He rubbed a hand thoughtfully over his jaw. He might be able to love Serena Stewart.

If he didn't already, he was getting there fast.

The last thing he wanted to do was force the issue, especially after the way she'd reacted at church yesterday. He was more likely to scare her away by admitting he had serious feelings for her than just holding steady and waiting for her to come around.

There would, of course, have to be plenty more kissing. He could be persuasive in ways that had nothing to do with words. That thought summoned a grin that lasted all the way to Isleornsay, into the hotel, and right up to his first crisis of the morning.

By the time Serena showed up just after nine, Malcolm's jaw ached from clenching his teeth. He'd dealt with nothing but complaints since he arrived, all things that were far beyond his control, like the fact that guests in one room had played their television too loud and that the breakfast room served only Scottish breakfast tea and not Darjeeling. Both guests demanded a discount for the inconvenience.

The minute he saw Serena, all those annoyances faded into the background. "Hi."

"Hi yourself. Do you have a few minutes? I want to talk to you about something."

"Sure. Come back to my office." He led her down the hall and held the door open for her, slightly puzzled by her serious tone. Was there a problem with the hotel? Or with them?

"I forgot to tell you last night." She gave him a mischievous smile, no doubt remembering the previous evening's exchange in her lounge. So it wasn't about them. He shifted and fought to keep his attention away from those memories and on the present, where she was still talking.

"Jamie and Ian agree it's time to hire someone else."

He blinked, jerked back to the present. "What?"

"You knew it was coming; I mentioned it in the bar."

"What? No." Clearly he'd missed something important. "You're firing me?"

She stared at him as if he'd begun speaking another language. "I said I wanted you to hire an assistant manager and another bartender. Weren't you listening?"

"Uh, apparently not." He let out a breath of relief and gave her a suggestive grin. "I was thinking about other things."

A smile flickered at the corners of her mouth. "Well, try to think about this for now. I'd like to meet your final choices before the official hire, but the decision is yours." She pushed a piece of paper across the desk. "Here's the revised payroll budget."

Malcolm lifted the sheet and scanned the lines. When he came to his own name, he did a double take. The figure beside it was much larger than what he currently made in the course of a year. "Serena, I know you said you were giving me a raise, but this is . . ."

"I'm putting you on salary. We would like you to still be here in the afternoons and early evenings on Friday, Saturday, and Sunday, since those are our busiest times. As for the schedule, you can work that out among you, Liam, and the new assistant manager. You'll have more flexibility for Kylee at least."

"I don't know what to say, Serena. This isn't because we're . . ."

"No." She didn't flinch, didn't hesitate. "I checked pay rates for managers of hotels of the same quality as this one—or at least the rating we're aspiring to—and this is competitive. Even if it is somewhat high for Skye."

"I don't know what to say." It didn't sound like a favor because they were dating, but it still felt odd to be given a raise by a woman he'd just kissed rather thoroughly last night.

"Say you agree and you'll put out the job listing immediately."

"Yes. To both."

"Good. I'll go sit at the front desk until I have to pick up Max from school." She retrieved her bag and headed for the door.

"Wait. When can I see you again?"

A tiny pleased smile returned to her lips. "Since Muriel still isn't up for dinner tonight, you can come over for dessert instead. Say, nine o'clock?"

"I'll be there." He rose and moved toward her. "One more thing?"

"Yes?" She stepped back inside.

He shut the door, threaded his hands through her hair, and kissed her. It took her only a moment to switch gears and respond with abandon, her hand gripping the collar of his shirt. When she finally pulled away, she laughed. "Pace yourself, Casanova. Unless we want the entire staff whispering about our relationship."

He pretended to grumble, but inside he felt downright elated. "Casanova?"

"Do you prefer Don Juan?" she asked. "Lothario?"

"None of the above." He tugged her back into his arms and looked directly into her eyes. "In case you missed it, I'm a one-woman man. And I'm completely devoted to you."

Serena stared up at him, breathless and wide-eyed, a tinge of pink coming to her cheeks. "I believe you."

Then with a secretive smile, she ducked out of his arms and slipped from the office.

Malcolm stayed behind for a moment. He'd certainly been persuasive. He just hadn't expected that the one he'd convince was himself.

———— ∘⊷⊶∘ ————

Something had changed. Maybe it was Malcolm's declaration after he'd pulled Serena back into the office for that kiss—not words of love but of devotion, which considering the context was plenty. Or maybe it was the ever-present realization that however she'd planned on holding herself back, she'd fallen for him anyway.

Now Serena supervised Em and Max's bedtime routine, her entire body humming with anticipation. Baking short crust perfumed the house with the delicious aroma of Irish butter and freshly ground spices.

"Can't we have dessert too?" Max asked, giving her the puppy-dog look that usually preceded him getting exactly what he wanted.

Serena wiped a smudge of strawberry sauce from the corner of his mouth. "You had dessert already, monkey. Time for bed now." *And please stay asleep for a change,* she added silently.

Max finally relented and snuggled under the covers while Serena said his bedtime prayer, his eyes closing before she was even finished. She repeated the same process with Em in her bedroom, then closed the door and tiptoed into the hall.

Blissful silence. She loved her children more than anything in the world, but some days she couldn't wait to have the nighttime quiet to herself.

She paused in the kitchen to remove the pastry from the oven and then moved into the lounge, where the half-finished painting stood, taunting her, beckoning her. Malcolm wouldn't be here for a while yet. It couldn't hurt, could it? She squeezed fresh paint onto the palette and began to define the details of the Callisto figure, which was still merely broad strokes of background and highlight, a suggestion of shape.

An insistent knocking brought her back to the present. She blinked away the image in her mind's eye and opened the door for Malcolm.

"I've been knocking," he said. "Did I wake you?"

"No." She held up her paint-stained hands as explanation and stepped aside for him to enter.

He dropped a light kiss on her lips and wrapped his arms around her waist. "If you're in the middle of something, we can do this some other time. I don't want to interrupt your work."

"No, stay. I can stop now. Besides, I made a berry crostata for dessert, and it's never as good the next day."

He pulled back. "Wait, you meant dessert literally?"

Serena gave him a little nudge. "Stop. You knew very well what was on offer."

He grinned, and she rolled her eyes as she moved into the kitchen to wash her hands. The crostata had cooled, leaving the crust of the rustic tart crispy and flaky, the berry filling just warm enough to ooze over the sides when she cut them each a slice. She handed Malcolm a plate and fork and poured them cups of tea.

"I could get used to this," Malcolm said when they were seated on the sofa and he took his first bite. "Culinary skill really does run in your family."

"Jamie got the cooking ability, and I got the baking. It pretty much skipped Ian altogether. Fortunately his wife is an excellent cook, or he'd continue to live like a bachelor on takeaway."

"Like me, you mean?"

"So Kylee was telling the truth?"

"I can make porridge, toad-in-the-hole, and anything from a tin."

"So you're saying I shouldn't expect a dinner invitation anytime soon."

"I wouldn't do that to you. I kind of want you to stick around." Malcolm smiled warmly at her, the humor still glimmering in his eyes.

"Is that right?" She took a teasing tone, but her heart was once more thudding dully against her ribs.

"That is right." He took her hand and held it tightly, his eyes never leaving hers. "I meant what I said before. However we might have started, this isn't just a casual thing to me."

"No," she murmured, even though fear threatened to overtake the wonder. "Not for me either."

From the look on his face, she expected him to kiss her, but he just squeezed her hand and went back to his crostata. When they finished their dessert, Serena curled up against him on the sofa, cradling her mug between her hands while they talked about everything and nothing: growing up on Skye, Malcolm's boxing, the children. Somewhere along the line, that turned into kissing like teenagers while their parents weren't home, which then led to a fit of giggles that Serena couldn't stop.

"I'm not sure whether I should be insulted or not," Malcolm said, his fingertip tracing the line of her collarbone.

"Oh, no need to be insulted." She forced herself to sober. "You just make me feel young again. I can't remember the last time I snogged on the sofa. Don't you find it funny?"

"No, *funny* wasn't the word I was searching for." The sexy timbre of his voice gave her shivers, but the sparkle of mirth in his eyes made her smile again. "However, speaking of teenagers, I need to get home. Kylee is obsessing over her Advanced Highers, and she'll stay up all night studying if I don't make her go to sleep."

"Pity," Serena said.

He leaned in to kiss her one more time. "Indeed it is. But likely a wise idea. I'm not sure I can resist you and your temptress ways much longer."

"You just say that because you want me to send the rest of the crostata home with you."

"Not at all. Because then I wouldn't have an excuse to come back." He enfolded her in his arms and dipped his head to whisper in her ear, "Without a doubt, you are the best part of my return to Skye."

Serena flushed to her roots as they said their good-byes and she closed the door behind him. Her heart hiccuped again in a disturbing fashion.

There was no use denying it any longer. She was well and truly in love with Malcolm Blake.

CHAPTER TWENTY-ONE

OVER THE NEXT COUPLE OF WEEKS, Serena and Malcolm fell into a pleasant routine. Sunday mornings were spent together at church with Muriel and the kids, followed by afternoon roast dinner before Malcolm had to return to the hotel. During the week, Serena spent each morning at the hotel setting up ads, finalizing the boxed-lunch menu additions, and taking photos for the new blog while Max was in preschool. Most of the time Malcolm let her handle the front desk while he did maintenance- and inventory-related tasks, but that didn't prevent him from pulling her into the supply cupboard whenever he had an opportunity to get her alone. Say what she might about the dangers of interoffice romance, it had its perks.

Malcolm found her one afternoon standing in the parlor and staring at the wall with her hands on her hips.

"You look deep in thought." He rested his hands on her waist and pressed his lips to the top of her head.

"This room is underutilized. We originally intended to use it for afternoon tea, but guests rarely attend."

"What are you thinking instead?"

"Art."

"I don't understand. We have art."

She turned and he released her. "No, we have decor. I mean fine art. What if we were to leave the furniture but turn the space into a display for local artists?"

Malcolm stared past her at the walls, now covered with reproductions of old masters, trying to catch her vision. "Like a gallery?"

"In a sense. But shown in a way that people could envision it hanging in their homes. Rotated frequently. We could put small cards about the featured artists in the guest rooms. What could be a better memory of a romantic holiday than artwork created right here?"

Her excitement was irresistible: the sparkle in her eye and the flush in her cheeks made him want to kiss her then and there. "Where would you get the art?"

"That's not a problem. Do you remember the big canvas hanging in Davy's lounge? That's by a local painter. The artist community is small and tightly knit, so as soon as word gets out, we'll be flooded with interest. Especially considering we draw a demographic that would actually buy fine art."

"I really think you have something. Are you going to clear it with Jamie and Ian?"

"I'm thinking about setting it up before they come into

town for Muriel's birthday. That gives me a little more than a month, but it's possible if I start immediately."

"Right. Jamie e-mailed to confirm their rooms."

Serena's expression turned guarded, and Malcolm knew what she was going to say before it left her lips.

"I understand if you'd like me to keep a low profile," he said. "It's a family gathering."

"No! I was going to ask you if you would like to come. As my date."

His eyebrows lifted. She was ready to make their relationship public? To her family? "Are you sure?"

"Well, the staff knows already—"

"Thanks to the supply-cupboard incident."

"And it won't stay a secret for long once Jamie starts talking to the employees. But even so, I want you there. It's time."

Maybe a family dinner was a normal event for some couples, but he knew this was a major step for Serena. Despite the fact they were in clear view of whatever guests might enter, he bent and kissed her. "I'd love to. Thank you for asking me."

"You're welcome. Now I have some calls to make if I'm going to put this together before they arrive."

Malcolm reached for her. "I take it back. I don't like this idea at all."

She grinned and ducked out of his grasp. He watched her go with a renewed sense of wonder. Maybe it was that he had finally gotten to know the real Serena Stewart, or maybe she had changed, but this vibrant, flirtatious, passionate woman who got excited over new ideas hardly resembled the uptight owner who had chewed him out a month ago. Dare he think it had something to do with him?

She'd certainly made an impact on him. He'd returned to Skye out of necessity, and he'd made the best of it out of pride and self-protection. But only now did he feel like he was making a life.

A life that was about to have more free time, apparently. He'd forgotten to tell Serena he'd found a strong candidate for the assistant-manager position. Soon he'd have more time to spend at home with Kylee . . . and Serena.

That was probably a good thing, because the minute he walked through his door that night, Kylee practically descended on him. "I can't do this! It's hopeless!" She paced the lounge with furious steps, an open textbook in her hand. "Why did I ever think this was going to work?"

Malcolm put his hands on her shoulders to stop her pacing. "Back up. What exactly is hopeless?"

Kylee snapped the book closed. "This. I'm going to flunk the exams, and my offers will be rescinded."

Now it made sense. The first of her SQA exams—the Scottish exit examinations—was in only three days, and Kylee's offers to the University of Glasgow and the Royal Conservatoire hadn't been as flexible as she'd hoped, requiring her to pull one A and two Bs to keep her spots. Privately, Malcolm would be surprised if she didn't earn all As, but that didn't make the pressure any less real for her.

"What can I do?"

She froze, clearly not expecting that response. "I—I don't know."

"The study halls are open for the next couple of days, right? And they have tutoring available through term break. Would it make a difference to have someone else help you prepare?"

"Maybe," Kylee said slowly.

Malcolm didn't think she really needed the extra help, but at least now she was thinking past irrational panic to solutions. "Why don't you go wash, and I'll make you something to eat. Okay?"

"Okay." She brightened a little. "Thanks."

"That's what I'm here for." He went to the kitchen to put on water for tea and rummage for a snack, wondering if he was doing the right thing. Should he be insisting that she would be fine instead of validating her worry? Once more, he regretted missing so much of her life by staying away from Skye and realized how little he actually knew about his niece. It should be Nicola here to reassure her and make midnight snacks. Maybe the fact he wasn't as close worked in his favor because she thought he'd be honest with her. He had no idea. But his focus had to be on Kylee.

He cut up some fruit and placed it on a plate along with leftover slices of Irish cheddar, then took it up to her room. Once she was back to the books, he took out his phone and dialed Serena.

"Just couldn't stay away, could you?" The mere sound of Serena's voice lifted his spirits.

"Something like that. Actually I wanted to tell you I might be a little scarce the next few weeks." He related his conversation with Kylee and the impending exams.

"I completely understand. Kylee comes first."

"Thank you." Relief rushed through him, making him glad once again that Serena wasn't the demanding sort. "I did forget to mention before you left, though. I've found someone for the assistant-manager position. Can you be there at ten tomorrow to meet her?"

"Her? How very egalitarian of you."

Malcolm chuckled, remembering how Serena had accused him of chauvinism soon after she'd arrived on Skye. "Don't sound so surprised."

"Your surprises are a good thing. In fact, it's one of the things I love most about you."

He held his breath at the word *love*, even though it was clearly out of context. "Maybe I should come next door and—"

"Kylee, remember?"

"Right. Kylee. I'll see you tomorrow, though?"

"It will be the best part of my day. Good night, Malcolm."

Malcolm smiled as he ended the call. He might surprise her, but she still surprised *him* with the place she had taken in his life. For the first time since he'd returned to Skye, he actually felt at home. Serena's presence, and that of her children and Aunt Muriel, filled the blank spots in his life he hadn't noticed were empty.

He couldn't help thinking what it would be like to not have to say good night by phone, to have her here in his home, in his bed, every night for the rest of their lives.

Serena saw Malcolm at the hotel each morning, but she couldn't deny that she missed their nightly routine of tea and dessert after the children went to bed. Of course she understood that Kylee came first, and with only six weeks left until the gallery's soft opening, she had plenty of work to occupy her time. The cards for the room binders needed to be finished by the end of the week if they were to be printed in time, and the plans for the grand-opening reception still needed to be finalized.

By Thursday night, though, she couldn't resist the urge to go next door regardless of what she'd said about Kylee being the priority. She packed a shopping tote with a couple of packages of biscuits, as well as a fresh batch of shortbread she and Em had made after school. At the last minute, she threw in a couple of pieces of fruit. Who knew if Malcolm's sketchy culinary skills extended to buying fresh produce?

She left Em and Max in front of the television with coloring books, then walked next door in the fading evening light, shivering in the cool breeze. She'd forgotten her jacket again.

Dull, rhythmic thuds drifted toward her when she approached the front of the house. Frowning, she changed direction toward the back garden, avoiding the water-filled potholes in the gravel walk. A few dozen meters away, Malcolm, dressed in ratty tracksuit bottoms and a long-sleeved thermal shirt, circled a large boxing bag hanging on the frame of an old play set. More thuds rang out as his gloved fists impacted the vinyl surface of the bag.

Serena leaned against the corner of the house, transfixed by the sight. He'd said he'd only been an amateur and now simply boxed to stay in shape, but there was something in the rhythmic, confident way he threw punches that suggested he was nowhere near a novice. A smile came unbidden to her lips. No sense in denying it: his ability to work a punching bag like a pro was about the sexiest thing she had ever seen.

Malcolm never looked up, but his teasing tone drifted to her on the breeze. "Did you need something, miss, or did you just come to watch?"

Her smile widened to a full-fledged grin. "Don't mind me. I'm just enjoying the view."

He gave the bag one last hard shot with his right hand, then straightened and started in her direction, his half smile driving a twist of anticipation into her stomach.

He stripped off his gloves and tossed them aside when he reached her, then caught her around the waist with his still-wrapped hands. "Like what you see?" he murmured in her ear.

She shivered again, this time not from the cold, as his lips found her neck and finally her mouth. When they came up for air, she gave him a playful—and ineffectual—shove. "You're all sweaty."

"You didn't seem to be complaining."

She laughed and ducked out of his reach. "How's the studying going? I brought Kylee some snacks."

"That's very thoughtful." He bent to retrieve his gloves from where he'd discarded them and inclined his head toward the back door in invitation. "According to her, she failed her first exam today. Which I expect means an A is forthcoming."

Serena laughed and moved with him into the outdated kitchen. Supper dishes were still in the sink, but otherwise it was cleaner than she'd expected. She began to unpack the biscuits and fruit onto the table. "I understand that. I panicked over my exams too. Good food helps."

"That it does." He moved to the stairwell in the hall outside the kitchen, unwinding his hand wraps. "Kylee! Serena brought you something."

"Be down in a minute!" she called back.

Malcolm came back to rummage in the fridge and emerged with a carafe of juice. "Do you want something to drink?"

"No, thanks. I need to get back in a minute. I only trust Em and Max alone for so long." She watched him surreptitiously from across the kitchen, distracted by the way the thermal outlined every muscle in his lean torso to where it disappeared into the waistband of the low-slung track bottoms. "You still seem really serious about the boxing. But you don't ever intend to compete?"

"No, those days are long past. Besides, there's no proper club on Skye. I wish there were. It would have been good for me when I was a kid. I had a lot of spare time on my hands."

"Maybe you should start one."

He frowned. "A boxing club? I was just an amateur with a handful of fights. I'm no trainer."

"Maybe not a proper club, exactly, but an after-school program. You're excellent with kids."

He looked intrigued by the suggestion, but before he could say more, Kylee burst into the kitchen. She stopped short in the doorway. "Those are for me?"

"They are," Serena said. "I thought you could use more brain fuel. When are your other exams?"

"Two next week, and then two more the week after that."

"I'm sure you'll do well. If you need anything, I'm right next door."

Kylee smiled shyly. "Thanks, Serena."

Serena glanced at her watch. "I should get back now."

"I'll walk you," Malcolm said.

Serena said her good-byes to Kylee and then stepped outside with Malcolm. As they walked to her house, his hand found hers in a gesture that felt at once ordinary and perfectly right. They lingered on her front step with a long kiss.

"Thank you for thinking of Kylee." He still held her close,

his head tilted down to hers. "She may not show it, but those things mean a lot to her."

"I like doing it," Serena said. "I was thinking . . . if it's okay with you, maybe you two could come over to celebrate after she's finished. Muriel always made a big deal out of it for us. I'd like Kylee to have that memory too."

"That sounds perfect."

He stole a kiss, then another, then a third before Serena laughed and shoved him away. "Family responsibilities call. Go."

"Yeah, yeah, I'm going." His playful look threatened her resolve. "Good night."

"Good night," she said, so softly she was sure he didn't hear her. She watched until he disappeared down the drive, wishing for things she had no right to expect, things she'd promised herself she wouldn't want.

Two weeks later, on the evening following Kylee's last exam, Serena pressed Em into service to help with the bread and gave Max the task of setting the small kitchen table for five. She'd chosen a menu she knew everyone liked: herb-roasted chicken and potatoes, a spring bean salad, and trifle for dessert.

"The food smells good," Kylee said as soon as she and Malcolm arrived. "It's really nice of you to do this for me."

"It's my pleasure," Serena said. "How were they?"

"Not as difficult as I expected. You were right."

"Then we really do need to celebrate," Serena said. "Take a seat. I'm about to put everything on the table."

Em, Max, and Kylee immediately pulled up chairs, but

Malcolm stepped up behind Serena, slipped his arms around her middle, and pressed a kiss to the spot just below her ear. She sighed and leaned back against his chest for a moment. It felt good to be open with their relationship, to show affection in front of their families, even if Em always wore a hopeful look when they did.

"Why don't you grab the chicken," she murmured, "while I finish with the salad."

"Buzzkill," he whispered back, but he let go and took the platter to the table. She succumbed to the pull of the domestic scene, the fantasy it brought to life. What would it be like to have a real family? A husband who came home after work and sat down to dinner and played with the kids? Who helped with schoolwork, tucked the children in for the night, and then pulled her into their bedroom to make love to her, even though toys still littered the lounge and dishes were soaking in the sink?

She'd convinced herself that was just a foolish fantasy while she was with Edward, but looking at Malcolm now, teasing Max and Em at the table, she actually believed that sort of marriage might exist.

After dinner, which they devoured in record time, Serena served up the trifle. "This might be our last chance to look at the stars before we lose full dark. What do you think?"

"Can we, Uncle Malcolm?" Kylee asked.

"I don't see why not," he said. "I did promise Em a look through the telescope."

The sky was still light, though, which left hours to fill. Kylee helped with the dishes while Malcolm entertained Em and Max, and then they all settled around a board game on the lounge's coffee table. At one point Serena caught

Malcolm watching her with such a transparent look of longing that it caught her off guard. This wasn't the flash of desire she saw so often from him, the wish he didn't have to leave her with only a kiss, but something that made her think he was as affected by the happy picture of domesticity as she was.

And then it was gone, swallowed by laughter until it was time to make the hot chocolate and take blankets into the back garden. Serena let Em tell the constellation stories that she knew, and then Max took his turn making up nonsensical tales that made everyone giggle even when they tried to remain serious. Malcolm retrieved his telescope from next door so they could look at distant stars.

It didn't take long for their stargazing companions to dwindle: first Max fell asleep, followed by Em, and soon Kylee began stifling yawns behind her hand. The teenager excused herself with a tight hug for Serena, then cut across their adjacent back gardens. Malcolm helped Serena carry the kids inside to their beds, and then they returned to the blanket spread out on the cool, damp grass.

Serena stretched out on the blanket and rolled to her side so she could view him in the dim light. He was watching her with a tenderness that made every part of her ache.

"What are you thinking?" she asked softly.

"I was just thinking I could get used to nights like this."

"Me too. It was perfect. Sad to think we might not have another one."

"Why not?" His voice turned guarded.

"It will be September before the stargazing gets good again."

Relief washed over his face. Only then did she realize he'd

thought she referred to either their relationship or her plans to leave at the end of the summer.

Her heartbeat accelerated, but she forced herself to speak. "There's something I wanted to talk to you about. You know I originally planned to go back to Inverness in August."

"I'm trying not to think about that, but yes."

"Do you think Mrs. Docherty would let us stay on if we didn't go back in the autumn?"

"Is that something you think you might do?"

"I'm considering it," Serena said. "I know not all your memories of Skye are good, but I think I want Max and Em to have the kind of childhood I had here. I didn't realize how much until we came back."

He was moving closer to her on the blanket. "Is that the only reason you'd consider staying?"

"No." A teasing smile came to her lips. "I'm also concerned with what might happen to the hotel if I left. You clearly need me."

He dipped his head and kissed her cheek, his beard tickling her skin and sending a delicious thrill through her body. "I most certainly do need you."

His lips were wandering lower, and she wrapped her arms around his neck, not caring that they were exposed beneath the starlit sky. She didn't particularly want him to stop what he was doing. "Does that mean you're okay with me staying around and micromanaging you for the foreseeable future?"

He looked into her eyes and smiled. "It wouldn't be the same without you."

CHAPTER TWENTY-TWO

SERENA REMAINED SO FOCUSED on pulling together the first gallery display before the arrival of her brothers and their wives that she managed to forget what this visit would mean. Telling Jamie and Ian about her relationship with Malcolm had seemed like an easy thing when it was still weeks in the future, but as the moment of truth arrived, she couldn't prevent the occasional moment of panic from seeping in.

Muriel was thrilled, of course, having been rooting for the match since Serena and Malcolm's first spark-filled clash. But to Serena's brothers, Malcolm was an employee, and she was their sister. Even if her family weren't snobs, there was no guarantee her overprotective relatives wouldn't decide he wasn't good enough for her. Fortunately neither

Jamie nor Ian was much for physical intimidation, because she sensed Malcolm wouldn't respond well to those types of challenges.

Serena took the day of her aunt's birthday off from the hotel to make Muriel's favorite Black Forest gâteau, a three-layer affair with chocolate cake, whipped cream, and the German cherry *Kirschwasser* liqueur that gave the confection its name. She let the layers cool until after she picked Em up from school and then settled both children at the kitchen table to make special birthday cards with colored paper, glue, and glitter. She assembled the cake layers with the cream-and-jam filling and then carefully transferred it all to a plastic carrier.

"All right, time to get ready to go to Aunt Muriel's. Are you looking forward to seeing Uncle Jamie and Uncle Ian?"

"Yay!" Max exclaimed, but Em's brow furrowed. "Will Aunt Andrea be mad I've not been practicing?"

"You have been practicing, every Sunday after church."

"Yes, but she says if I want to be a great pianist like her, I have to practice every single day whether I feel like it or not."

Inwardly Serena wondered if Em's continuing fascination with the piano had more to do with her adoration of her new aunt than a dream of becoming a musician, but her desire for lessons had started long before Andrea had come along. Who knew but that there might be some great musical talent lurking beneath Em's surface, just waiting to be unleashed?

"We have been neglecting your practice a bit, haven't we? We'll have to see what we can do about that." If they decided to stay on Skye, she would have to bring the piano from their home in Nairn, and it would never fit in the croft house's tiny lounge. There were all sorts of consequences to a move that she hadn't yet fully considered.

She got Em and Max suitably outfitted—Em in a pretty wool dress and polished patent-leather shoes, Max in proper trousers and a knit waistcoat—then turned to her own wardrobe. Dinner was supposed to be somewhat formal, though she wasn't sure whose idea that had been. Em followed her up the stairs and plopped on the bed while Serena considered her clothing options. She held up two different sweaters. "Which do you think? The cream cowl-neck or the blue scoop?"

Em considered seriously, her brow furrowed like she was solving a maths problem. "The cream. It looks pretty with your hair."

Serena pulled the angora sweater over her cotton tank and wide-legged trousers and selected a pair of sizeable diamond earrings as a finishing touch. She was just sliding her feet into low-heeled boots when she paused and asked the question had been spinning around her head for the last three weeks. "What would you think about staying on Skye?"

Em's expression turned suspicious. "Are you serious?"

That was not the reaction she'd expected. "Maybe. You and Max seem so happy here, and I know that Auntie likes to have us around . . . Would it be so bad to stay?"

"What would happen to our house back home?"

"Well, I imagine we would sell it and find a place here." Serena sank down on the edge of the bed and smoothed her hand over Em's hair. "Would that bother you? I know it's the only home you really know." *It's also the last reminder of your dad,* she thought, not sure whether that was a plus or a minus for her daughter.

Em chewed her lip. "I don't know. I don't think so . . . but it's weird."

"You don't have to tell me now. Think about it. I think it might be good for us, but I don't want to make any decisions without consulting you."

"And Max?"

"And Max. Even though I don't think he much cares as long as he has his cars."

Em grinned suddenly. "True. And his giraffe." She barreled down the stairs, her concerns of moments before apparently forgotten, and Serena followed her to where Max was playing in the lounge. "Ready to go, monkey? I got a text earlier that Uncle Ian and Aunt Grace made it to Skye this afternoon."

Max cheered, and Serena ruffled his hair. "Come on, then. And don't forget your giraffe."

Max rushed off to retrieve his ratty stuffed animal where it lay on the sofa and tucked it into the crook of his arm. She hustled the children out the door to the car, her stomach starting to quiver. It was silly, really. This was her family. They already liked Malcolm. It would be fine. It had to be fine.

Serena thought she would be the first to arrive, but the familiar silver Audi parked in Muriel's drive told her that Jamie and Andrea were already there. Em and Max took off the minute they got their seat belts off, pounding up the stairs to the front door. Serena followed more slowly and stepped through the door to the distinct aroma of cooking.

As always happened when her brother was around, everyone was gathered in Muriel's kitchen, where Jamie was busy cutting vegetables at the island. Andrea hoisted Max to give him a big smack on the cheek, while Em hugged her around the middle. Favorite-aunt status looked to be safely assured.

"Some greeting, huh?" Serena grinned as she gave Andrea her own hug.

"I love it. I missed my favorite Scottish niece and nephew!" Andrea said.

"We're your only Scottish niece and nephew," Em said.

Andrea gave Em's hair an affectionate ruffle. "And you're way too smart for your own good."

Serena circled to give her brother a quick hug, and he planted a kiss on the top of her head with barely a pause in his chopping. "Hi, Sis. Want to grab the platter and arrange these for me while I take the asparagus out of the oven?"

"Sure. But why are you cooking? We're having dinner in two hours."

"Appetizers," he said, though it should have been obvious. No matter the occasion, Jamie would find a food-related task for himself.

Serena found the platter in the cabinet and began to arrange the raw vegetables in an artful starburst pattern. "Why do I get to be your sous-chef tonight?"

"Because I'm useless in the kitchen," Andrea said. "He's all but given up on me."

"Clever, Andrea. I should have done the same." Serena glanced around. "Where's Auntie? And what happened to Ian and Grace? I thought they were supposed to drive with you."

"Auntie is still getting ready, and Ian and Grace are going to meet us at the hotel. They flew straight from Mumbai and barely made their connection in London this morning, so they needed a nap first."

"Oh, good. At least they won't miss dinner." Serena had

spent little time with Grace since she'd come back into Ian's life, but she liked the effect the woman had had on her formerly conservative—even stiff—older brother. Ian would never have dreamed of a bicontinental lifestyle before. Then again, who would have dreamed they'd go from estranged to married in a mere six months? By those standards, they were still newlyweds.

Now that the subject had been broached, she had the perfect opening. She tried for a casual tone. "I asked Malcolm to join us tonight."

"Oh, good," Jamie said. "We owe him much more than dinner for how he took care of Max and Em when Muriel was ill."

This was the moment she should say, *"That's not why I asked him,"* but the words stuck in her throat. Why was she so reluctant to admit they were dating? No matter what Malcolm had accused her of, she wasn't ashamed or embarrassed. Maybe she simply didn't want to subject him to scrutiny. Or maybe it was that introducing him to her family as someone important to her made the relationship real.

"Serena? Vegetables?" Jamie nudged her with his elbow, and she realized she'd been staring absently at the platter.

"Right, sorry." She went back to work, diligently focusing on the crudités and not on the prospect of bringing a man she had just started dating to a family function where he would be questioned and scrutinized. Maybe that had been the wrong thing to do.

"I'm not sure I've ever seen you this quiet," Andrea said. "Is something wrong?"

"No, just tired. Max has been sleeping even worse than usual these days. I swear, I would have thought we'd be through this two years ago."

"That's rough," Andrea said. "I'm a complete nightmare when I don't sleep. Just ask my husband."

Jamie held up his hands. "I didn't say anything."

"Hey, Em," Andrea said. "We've missed a bunch of lessons. Do you want to see if you still remember your last piece?"

Em brightened and trailed off behind Andrea to the piano in the reception room. The thump of the fallboard was followed by tentative notes from Serena's daughter on the piano keys.

"So, now that they're gone, what's the real story?" Jamie asked.

"Excuse me?" Serena scattered cherry tomatoes all over the countertop. "About what?"

"About Muriel. She's been all bright and chipper like nothing happened, but she's still really sick, isn't she?"

"I don't know, honestly. Besides a little tiredness, she seems to be doing well. They took her off the beta-blockers as soon as the thyroid meds kicked in, but she hasn't told me much else. She's been surprisingly close-lipped about the whole thing."

"Just like Dad. Doesn't like to admit that she might be human."

Serena chuckled. Muriel did always have a superhuman efficiency about her, but the fact she'd been allowing Serena to cook suggested that she knew her limits and was for once abiding by them.

No matter what she said, the incident had to have scared her.

"Serena, you're here!" Muriel breezed into the kitchen, looking so energetic and alive that it made the concerns they'd just expressed seem unfounded.

Serena hugged her aunt tightly. "Happy birthday, Auntie. What is it, forty-nine?"

"Oh, hush." Muriel chuckled. "You know very well I refuse to age past forty-five."

Serena grinned and grabbed the plate of appetizers Jamie shoved in her direction while he rearranged the last of the crudités on a platter. There were prosciutto-wrapped asparagus bundles—a family favorite—along with bite-size goat-cheese tarts and some sort of tomato-and-salmon construction. As usual, Jamie prepared for a family birthday as if it were a catered event.

"These are the last of it," Jamie said. "Now why don't you take the guest of honor in there?"

Muriel smiled and made her way into the reception room with Serena, where Andrea broke into an impromptu rendition of the birthday song on the piano as soon as they entered.

Max was instantly at Muriel's side with his homemade card. "Open your gifts now!"

"Max, why don't we wait until later when everyone is here?" Serena said.

Muriel gave her a subtle headshake and patted the sofa cushion beside her. "Come sit next to me on the sofa, Maxie." He climbed up beside her, ripped open the envelope, and "read" his card to her.

Em's card came next, also opened by Max, followed by Serena's gift of a small flower pendant carved from mother-of-pearl. Muriel immediately removed her necklace and replaced it with the flower. Jamie and Andrea went last, presenting her with an ivory wool shawl big enough to wrap around her several times.

"These are just lovely," Muriel said, clasping her hands to

her chest. "But the best gift of all is having my family together in one place."

Serena cleared her throat. "Speaking of that—and no final decisions have been made yet—I'm seriously considering staying on Skye."

"Really?" Jamie asked at the same time Andrea exclaimed, "That's wonderful!"

Muriel watched Serena with a knowing expression: she knew what her real motivation was.

"What about Em's school?" Jamie asked.

"Highlands is no longer an option, and it's the only private day school of that caliber in the area. If I were going to send her to public school, there's no reason why she couldn't do the same here. At least she would be using Gaelic regularly, which I've been somewhat lax about at home."

"I think it's a wonderful idea," Andrea said quickly. "I would move here in a second if our careers allowed."

Serena knew Andrea was telling the truth: she'd originally come to Skye on business, and she'd fallen in love not only with Jamie but with the island as well. Serena wouldn't be surprised if Andrea wanted that slower pace for her future children, much as Serena did.

"Whatever you decide," Muriel said, "I hope you'll spend as much time here as possible. I've missed you. It's good to have you back."

It only made sense. Muriel's recent health scare had proven that someone should be close by as she got older. And if it allowed Serena to continue to explore her relationship with Malcolm, all the better.

They barely made a dent in the food Jamie had prepared before it was time to go down to the hotel. Muriel volunteered to ride with Serena. As soon as Serena closed the car door, she said, "You're just going to spring Malcolm on them?"

Serena grimaced. "I meant to tell them. I just lost my bottle."

"They're going to figure it out soon enough."

"I know, I know." Serena cast a quick look at Muriel. "Do you think I'm mad to consider moving us all back here?"

"Mad? No. And selfishly I'd love nothing better. But you need to ask yourself if you would be happy living on Skye if Malcolm weren't in the picture."

"Of course," Serena said. "But is it terrible that I don't want to find out?"

Muriel smiled in that way she had, that look Serena thought of as her older-and-wiser expression. She just didn't know what it meant in the current instance. But she didn't have long to dwell on it as she pulled up at the hotel beside Jamie's sleek sedan.

Moment of truth.

Serena unloaded Max and Em, who ran ahead and let themselves into the hotel foyer. Serena took a deep breath and waited for Muriel to unfold herself from the passenger seat, then walked with her straight into the commotion of a family reunion.

"Serena!" Ian was the closest and grabbed her for a hug, dwarfing her with his full-foot height advantage. "There you are! Max was just telling us he drove here himself."

Serena laughed and pulled back. Her older brother looked tanned and happy, the usually serious lines of his face softened by a wide smile. She looked past him to his wife of six months. Grace was as petite as Serena, her cherubic blonde looks contrasting with her short, choppy hair and the colored tattoos covering her right arm. She wasn't at all the type of woman Serena would have expected her brother to marry, but it was clear from the way he looked at her that he adored her. Serena gave her a hug and a kiss on the cheek.

"You're looking well," Grace said, her words colored by a faint Irish accent. "Enjoying being back on Skye?"

"You could say that. I heard you had some problems getting here."

"Our flight from Mumbai was grounded for mechanical problems, so we had to rearrange everything. I'm sorry we didn't make it to the house earlier. We were completely knackered."

Ian slid his arm around Grace's waist and pulled her close. "Wouldn't have missed this, though, especially since we couldn't make it back for Easter."

"Are we ready, then?" Jamie asked, looking around the group. "Just waiting for Malcolm?"

"He'll be along in a few minutes," Serena said. "He's training the new assistant manager."

Jamie nodded, though Andrea gave her a faintly puzzled look, as if she had picked up on something in Serena's voice. Well, what did it matter? They would all know soon enough. She followed her family through the double doors to the restaurant, where several tables had been pushed together along the far wall.

"I want to sit next to Aunt Andrea," Em said. They shuffled around to accommodate the request. Serena put Max in the chair on her left and placed her handbag beside her to the right, a subtle cue that she was holding it for Malcolm. Andrea tried to hide her smile. The woman was definitely perceptive, even if Serena's brothers were completely clueless.

The server came to the table—the same one who had served Malcolm and Serena on their first date, as a matter of fact—and provided them with bottles of sparkling water as well as their menus. Serena cast a glance behind her at the open doors, wondering what she was supposed to do about her date.

As if she had summoned him, Malcolm appeared in the entryway. There was no other way to describe how he looked but breath-stealing—smartly turned out in a dark suit but no tie, looking so appealing that she was sure her reaction showed on her face. He gave Serena a private look that made her catch her breath, then crossed the room to the table. "Sorry I'm late," he said to the group, then bent to kiss Serena lightly on the lips.

Dead silence settled over the table, but Malcolm didn't seem to notice, or maybe he didn't care. He sat in the empty chair and reached for her hand before he met their stunned gazes. "I take it that Serena didn't tell you we're dating?"

Something about his utter assurance made her nervousness settle.

She smiled at him. "I hadn't gotten to it."

"Mmm. I can see that." Malcolm flipped open his menu and scanned the dinner options unconcernedly. He wasn't going to make it easy on them. Serena repressed a smile.

"So when did all this happen?" Ian asked, looking between the two of them.

Serena looked up at her brother. "A couple of months ago, I suppose."

Ian looked past her to Malcolm. "For the sake of the occasion, do you suppose we can just skip over the part where Jamie and I threaten violence if you hurt our sister?"

"I'm sure I can use my imagination," Malcolm said with a wry twist of his mouth before turning his attention back to the menu. "If you don't mind the recommendation, the salt-crusted sea bass is excellent. And believe it or not, we make a fantastic steak here. All locally sourced and organically raised."

"You know the menu as well as I do," Jamie said.

"Of course I do." It wasn't cocky, just confident, and Malcolm seemed completely comfortable at the table with her family. After the initial surprise—and the smiles the women sent her way—her family seemed to be taking to the idea just fine. Maybe she was the only one who felt the awkwardness surrounding dating again after having been widowed. Or maybe she'd made such a point about her life being her own business that they no longer questioned her. She never should have allowed Edward to separate her from the people she loved.

After the server came back to take their orders and the wine was poured, Jamie leaned forward. "Andrea and I have an announcement to make."

Everyone's eyes snapped in their direction.

"We just received our approval to adopt."

"That's marvelous," Muriel said immediately, reaching for Jamie's hand.

"Congratulations," Ian said. "How long will it be before you're matched?"

Andrea looked to her husband. "A few months perhaps? Our agency thinks it could be fairly fast."

She and Jamie looked so pleased that Serena felt a rush of anticipation for them. They'd made the best of what had to have been a very painful situation, and they would make amazing parents. She reached over to smooth Max's hair. No matter how difficult her marriage had been at times, she couldn't regret it when it had given her two beautiful children.

The conversation continued on the topic for a bit longer, and then Ian said, "Well, that makes my news a little less exciting, but I might as well mention it."

"You're pregnant?" Jamie said, deadpan.

Laughter rang out around the table. "No, fortunately, and neither is Grace." They'd made it clear there would be no children of their own in their future, just nieces and nephews. "My contract at the Children's Advocacy Fund is up in October, and we have another candidate who is better suited to the position in Mumbai. I've agreed to move instead to a full-time fund-raising role in London in the autumn. My official title will be director of strategic partnerships, but it really means soliciting ongoing corporate donations."

"I thought you enjoyed being a program coordinator!" Serena said.

"I do. But I only took it because the last person backed out of his contract, and they were in a tough spot. This new candidate speaks Hindi and Marathi, which I don't. Besides, Grace and I have been married for six months, and we've only managed to be in the same country at the same time for about half of it."

Serena grinned. "I understand *your* reasoning, but what does Grace get out of it? Isn't that a bait and switch?"

"Very nice, Sis, thanks." Ian sent her a look, but it wasn't without affection.

Serena stifled a chuckle. "Seriously, though, how does your new line of work appeal to you, Grace?" she asked.

"Humanitarian work has to be a big change from war photography."

"It is," Grace said, "though of course the biggest difference is spending most of my time in an office. I never thought I would enjoy art direction so much, but it helps that I have some truly talented staff photographers."

"Tell them about the exhibit," Ian prompted.

Grace shot him a wry look that made Serena think he wasn't supposed to mention it. "I've been invited to contribute to a big open-air exhibit outside the Natural History Museum. Fifty years of London street photography."

"That's brilliant news!" Serena said. "I hope you'll let us know when it is. We'd love to come. I hate that we missed your last exhibition."

And then the attention focused on her. She raised her hands with a laugh. "Don't look at me. I do have something to show you all, but it can wait until after dinner."

As conversation flowed around the table, Malcolm stretched his arm across the back of her chair, a comfortable, affectionate gesture she realized she'd missed. Serena chatted with Andrea over Max's head, while Malcolm talked to Ian and James about his amateur boxing days. Once the food arrived, the conversations tapered off: all the dishes were unequivocally excellent. Malcolm acted like the doting boyfriend, refilling her wineglass, offering her tastes of his meal so she could sample other dishes. She admired his poise, how seamlessly he settled into his place beside her. She could tell that not only did her sisters-in-law like him but her brothers respected him, which was a far more difficult thing to earn.

"Malcolm, are you coming back to the house for dessert

with us?" Muriel asked, and Serena realized she'd lost the thread of the conversation somewhere.

Malcolm looked at Serena questioningly.

"Please do. You don't want to miss out on my famous Black Forest gâteau."

"I'd love to, then. Thank you. But first I think Serena has something she'd like to show everyone."

"I do." Serena folded her napkin next to her plate and rose. The rest of her family followed suit, and they poured out into the foyer. She took a deep breath, inexplicably nervous, and led them into the parlor. "You're looking at the soft opening of the Isleornsay Gallery, currently located at the MacDonald Guest House."

She stepped back to watch their reactions as they wandered through the parlor, taking in the new room. Rather than setting the paintings in stark linear arrangements, she'd placed the colorful abstract canvases as she would show an eclectic collection in her own home: loosely fit together like puzzle pieces. She'd made use of the existing picture rail by hanging them from a fine chain for an effect that was simultaneously traditional and funky.

Malcolm slid an arm around her and whispered in her ear, "You did an amazing job here, Serena. Truly."

Jamie was the first of her family to speak. "This is great, Serena. Really unexpected. Local artists, I presume?"

"Yes." Serena handed out the finished cards, thick vellum stock that gave details about the artists and the individual works. They might be a tiny gallery, but she was determined to give the artists their due respect.

Grace was standing close to one painting, scrutinizing it carefully. Serena moved in beside her. "What would you think about doing a small exhibit here someday, Grace? I mean, we're not the Natural History Museum . . ."

Grace smiled. "I'm experimenting with platinum and palladium prints right now. Maybe a series of landscapes? I've got film from our last trip to Skye that has yet to be printed. I think some of them might suit."

"You name it and we'll do it," Serena said.

Ian came up behind her and slung an arm around Serena's shoulders. "I'm proud of you. This is wonderful."

"I thought it was a promising marketing idea."

"It is, but not because of that. It's good to see you doing what you love again. Think you might ever show some of your own?"

"I don't think so," she began, but she didn't finish the sentence because she caught a glimpse of Max climbing on top of a wingback chair. No doubt he intended to test his flying ability. She started toward him, but Malcolm beat her to it.

"No, you don't, you little daredevil." Malcolm scooped him off the back of the chair and tossed him over his shoulder. "Leave the flying to Superman, why don't we?"

Serena watched the two of them, her heart swelling to bursting. Em was by Malcolm's side now, clamoring for his attention, and he hoisted her with his other arm, pretending to stagger under her weight.

"So. Malcolm. Serious or not serious?" Andrea appeared at Serena's side and followed her gaze. "Or is that a silly question?"

"Undefined right now." Technically it was true, but there was nothing casual about the way she felt about him.

"Is this the reason for your sudden interest in moving back to Skye?"

"It's one of them." Serena suddenly felt pummeled by uncertainty. "Am I being completely foolish here? We've only known each other for a few months, and we spent part of that fighting."

"I'm not sure I'm the best person to answer that question," Andrea said. "I moved to Scotland for a man I'd known for only five days."

Serena chuckled. Jamie and Andrea certainly redefined the meaning of the words *whirlwind romance*, even if it had taken them more than a year after they met to tie the knot. But there hadn't been kids involved in their situation, and Serena had to take Em's and Max's feelings into account.

Malcolm caught her attention from across the room. Max was now riding on his shoulders, and Em had claimed one of his hands. "Are we ready to go? The natives are getting restless."

"I'm ready if everyone else is. Dessert is waiting. And it's good, even if I do say so myself."

"I can't wait." Malcolm smiled warmly at her, then gave her son a bounce. "C'mon, Maxie. It's time for your mum's cake, and I don't want to miss that."

Serena watched Max giggle as he clutched Malcolm's head, and Malcolm gave her an uneven grin beneath the little boy's fingers. Her earlier doubts melted away. And from the knowing glances her family leveled in her direction, everyone else knew it too.

CHAPTER TWENTY-THREE

MALCOLM FOLLOWED SERENA back to Muriel's house. That had gone well. He hadn't been concerned, but he could tell that Serena had been. Rather than be insulted, he was flattered. She wouldn't be so worried about what her family thought if he wasn't important to her. He'd always been a good judge of people, though, so he'd known Jamie would be impressed by the personal interest he'd taken in the workings of the restaurant. Ian, the former Olympic rower, would respect the fact that he'd been a competitive boxer in his time.

Of course, it was sheer luck that Ian had waived the usual "right to threaten" reserved for older brothers everywhere.

Malcolm chuckled to himself as he parked behind Serena's

sedan and climbed out quickly so he could help Muriel from the car.

"Such a nice young man," Muriel said, patting his arm. "Thank you for spending my birthday with me."

"I can't think of anything I'd rather be doing." He smiled at Serena over the top of the car as she retrieved Max.

James and Andrea pulled up with Grace and Ian then, and they moved en masse into the house.

"I'm going to make coffee and cut the cake," Serena said.

"I'll help." Malcolm followed her into the kitchen, looked around, and then tugged her to him for a kiss.

"And here I thought you were actually volunteering to help," she said. "Silly me."

"Oh, I am. Doesn't mean I can't do both." He went to the cabinet, found a stack of dessert plates, and brought them to the island. "How am I doing so far? Do they approve?"

She produced a serrated knife and made the first precise cut of the cake. "I would say they do. The fact that you're here in the first place means you score big with them."

"I don't understand."

Serena looked startled, as if she hadn't meant to say those words.

He could see the conflict in her eyes. "Serena, what aren't you telling me?"

She didn't look at him, instead drawing the knife through the cake again. "My family didn't like Edward. Not least because he hated Skye."

"I can't say I was thrilled to come back myself."

"You had a good reason. You had bad memories of the place. Edward disliked it because he didn't want to be reminded of my roots here. He preferred focusing on the English side of my family."

Malcolm settled on the stool across from her. "I thought he was Scottish."

"He was. But most of his colleagues were English. He went to school in England. As did Ian, of course—but Ian doesn't look down on the islands as being somehow inferior."

"So Edward never came here with you, I take it?"

"Not often, and he did everything he could to keep me from coming back. Insisted on having birthday parties and holidays first in Edinburgh and then Inverness. My family, bless them, went along with it, or Em would have grown up without knowing them."

Malcolm stayed silent, trying to reconcile what sounded like a very controlling man with Serena's no-nonsense, take-charge attitude. He couldn't imagine her taking well to anyone telling her she couldn't come home for a visit. Was that why she was so reluctant to trust him?

"I'm sorry you went through that," he said finally. "No one deserves to be cut off from the people they love. And maybe it sounds terrible, but I'm glad you don't have to deal with that anymore."

Serena picked up the knife and paused, her expression raw. "Honestly, so am I."

Then she blanched. The knife clattered to the countertop. Malcolm followed her gaze and felt the blood drain from his face when he saw Em standing in the doorway, her expression stricken.

"Em—" Serena began, but the little girl darted from the room. "I have to go talk to her. Can you do this?"

Sick over what he'd just witnessed, Malcolm nodded. He'd

had no idea that Em was there or he wouldn't have said anything about her father. Clearly the little girl hadn't known about the problems in her parents' marriage, and this was undoubtedly the last way Serena wanted her to find out. He trailed her into the reception room in time to see her disappear out the front door.

"What was that about?" Muriel asked, wide-eyed.

"I think Em overheard something she shouldn't have about her father," he said.

Muriel exchanged a glance with Jamie and Ian. There was more to this story than simply Serena's late husband's dislike of Skye.

"Is there something I should know about Edward?"

"Best she tell you herself," Muriel said. "It's not our story to share."

Except Serena had backed away from the topic every time it had come up. This was the most she'd told him about her marriage the entire time they'd been dating.

Since Malcolm wasn't going to get an explanation from her family, he went to the kitchen and finished cutting slices of cake, which he brought out in pairs to the group. There he sat listening to the conversation while he wondered inwardly about what else Serena had not told him. Perhaps her caution toward their relationship had nothing to do with him.

———⌾⌾⌾———

Serena followed her daughter out the front door, her heart rising into her throat. How much had Em heard?

The little girl was sitting on the front step, shivering with what could have been cold or emotion. Serena slowly lowered herself down beside her, only then realizing that tears streamed down Em's face.

"Hey," she said softly. "Do you want to tell me what that was all about?"

Em looked up at her, eyes still brimming. "Did you tell Daddy to leave?"

The question pierced Serena through the heart like a shot. She took a second to catch her breath and make her voice level. "Why would you ask that?"

"Sophie said she heard her parents talk about it. She said he died because you kicked him out. Is it true?"

Now everything was beginning to make sense. Sophie's father was an executive at Edward's company, the man who had moved into his position after his death. It was entirely possible that Edward had confided his marital problems before he died, and in true eight-year-old fashion, Sophie had drawn her own conclusions from an overheard conversation. Was that why Em had been fighting? Defending her mother?

Serena took Em's hand between both of hers. "Daddy wasn't leaving us, sweetheart. And I didn't kick him out. He and I were arguing, and we decided it would be best if we had some space while we worked things out."

Instead of brightening, Em just sobbed harder. "But I heard you yelling at him about me. I didn't mean to be bad. If I'd have been better, you wouldn't have argued and he might still be alive."

"Look at me." Serena took Em by the shoulders and turned her to face her. "None of this is your fault. Daddy and I were married for a long time. And we had some problems. But we did love each other. We didn't want you to think that you had anything to do with our arguing, so we agreed it was better that we live apart for a little while. But that wasn't why he died. He had a heart problem that nobody knew about, and it could just as easily have happened while he was on his business trip. The two things aren't related. And neither had anything to do with you."

Em looked uncertain, but the tears weren't falling anymore. "Do you promise?"

"I promise. I wish you'd told me the first time Sophie said something. You wouldn't have had to worry about this by yourself the whole time."

"I didn't want to hurt your feelings," Em said with a sniffle. "Besides, if I told you, we wouldn't have come to Skye and you wouldn't have met Malcolm."

Serena couldn't argue with that logic. She put her arm around her daughter and gave her a tight squeeze. "I love you, cupcake. You know that, right?"

Em nodded.

"And you know that you can tell me absolutely anything? No matter what it is? You and I, we're in this together."

Now Em managed a watery smile and leaned her head against Serena's shoulder. Serena heaved a sigh, her heart aching. This was never what she'd wanted for her family. But now that Em knew the truth, the only thing she could do was be honest and reassure her that it hadn't been her fault, that Serena's first priority would always be her and Max.

They had to be, no matter what.

"So, you tell me what you want to do. Do you want to go home, or should we go back inside for a while?"

"Auntie would be sad if we left early. I don't want to upset her."

That was her sweet girl. Always thinking of other people. Serena pulled her close and kissed the top of her head. "I'm proud of you, Em. I'm happy I get to be your mum."

But Em held back. "Mum?"

"Yes, cupcake?"

"Did you mean what you said earlier, about staying here on Skye, even if you and Malcolm weren't together?"

A note of warning crept into Serena. She should have been more circumspect in her comments. The last thing she wanted Em to worry about was whether her relationship status determined her decisions. "I absolutely did. You and Max and your happiness will always be my first priority."

Em hesitated, then threw her arms around Serena's waist. "Felicity was telling me about the autumn festival at school. And there's a big Christmas program. I might even be able to play piano."

Serena chuckled. "So I take it you've decided you want to stay?"

"Yes!"

Serena smoothed Em's hair and led her back inside, where conversation immediately hushed when they entered. Em wiped her eyes with her sleeve and looked embarrassed at the attention as they rejoined the group on the sofas.

Malcolm came to the rescue. "If I'm not mistaken, not all the gifts have been opened."

"That's right, Auntie, you still have to open ours." Ian stood and retrieved a large cardboard box from the top of the piano. "Sorry we didn't have time to wrap it. We were afraid it might get opened in customs."

Muriel took the box and lifted the flaps, unwrapping layers of paper and bubble wrap to reveal a beautiful carved wooden elephant in traditional caparison, painstakingly painted in bright colors and gold leaf.

"In Hindu culture, elephants symbolize wisdom," Grace said. "We visited Jaipur during Holi, which is the festival of colors. We couldn't resist bringing a piece of it back home."

"It's lovely. Grace, Ian, thank you." Muriel examined it closely, then set it carefully on the table beside her. "I will display it to remind me of you while you're overseas. Though now that Ian is again based in London, I expect to see you two more often."

"I certainly hope so," Ian said.

Malcolm removed a small box from the inside of his coat and passed it to Muriel. "Something to thank you for your hospitality these past months."

Muriel untied the ribbon on the box and removed the lid, her eyes softening. She withdrew a hammered silver brooch in the shape of a thistle. "It's beautiful, Malcolm. I love it. You certainly didn't need to get me a gift."

"You've treated Kylee and me like family, so thank you."

Serena smiled at Malcolm. He did everything right, but it never came off as calculated. He was completely sincere in both word and action. Could anyone blame her for falling in love with him?

"Do you think we should get home?" He nodded toward Max where he lay asleep on the rug.

"Probably." His use of the word *we* seemed unconscious, but it summoned a warm glow to her chest. Serena rose. "Do you mind if we go and get these two into bed?" There she went using the word *we* herself. In that moment she'd have given almost anything to have it be a real *we*.

They said their good-byes, Serena giving hugs to her

brothers and sisters-in-law and her aunt, Malcolm shaking their hands warmly. Then he scooped Max up from the rug and carried him out to the car while Serena and Em trailed behind.

When the kids were safely buckled in, she held him back. He'd neatly diverted the subject away from Em's outburst, but he must have questions. It was time for him to know the whole truth about her past. "Give me half an hour and then come over. There are probably some things you should know."

"You don't have to share anything you don't want to, Serena."

"I know. But it's time." She squeezed his arm, then climbed into the driver's seat. "Thirty minutes."

"I'll be there."

CHAPTER TWENTY-FOUR

HE SHOULDN'T HAVE BEEN NERVOUS. There was nothing
Serena could tell him that would make Malcolm feel differently toward her, but still he felt the twinge of apprehension
as he pulled into his drive, just feet away from where Serena
was putting her children into bed. He walked into his home,
where Kylee was watching television in flannel pajamas and
fuzzy slippers.

"So, how was meeting the family?" she asked in a singsong voice.

Malcolm chuckled and dropped onto the sofa. "It was fine.
What did you do?"

"No homework tonight, so this. Well, I worked on a new
song too, but that doesn't count."

"Can I hear it?"

"It's not done yet. I'll play it for you once I get the bridge right."

Malcolm took a deep breath. "I wanted to talk to you about something. You know your grandmother is in Glasgow. If you're going to uni there—"

"There's no reason for you to come with me and leave Serena," Kylee finished with a knowing smile. "It's okay. I know you're in love with her."

"What? I—"

"Oh, come on, Uncle Malcolm. Girls know these things. I can tell. It's okay. It's only, what, five hours away? Close enough to come home over a long weekend. And yes, Grandmum will be there if I need her. So it's fine. Really."

"You're sure?"

"Yeah, I'm sure." Kylee smiled and gave him a bump with her shoulder. "You keep looking at your watch. Let me guess, she invited you over for more dessert?"

Something in Kylee's tone made Malcolm wonder exactly what she thought he was doing when he went next door for his nightly visit, but there was no way he was going to have this conversation with her. If he'd misunderstood, she'd be too embarrassed to talk openly to him again. And this wasn't really the time to get into the issue of sex and why she should absolutely plan on never having it. At least not while he was still alive and responsible for her. He prayed Nicola had covered all that with her a long time ago. So far he'd been lucky that she was far more focused on music than boys.

"No dessert tonight," he said finally. "I'm stuffed. Just tea."

"Do you want me to wait up?"

"If you want. I'm not sure how long I'll be."

As soon as the hand on his watch ticked off thirty minutes, he pulled on his coat and wandered next door. When Serena opened the door, she looked as nervous as he felt. "I just put the tea on. Come in."

"They're asleep?" He followed her inside and shut the door behind him.

"They are. But maybe we should talk outside. I don't want them to overhear this. Some things children shouldn't know about their parents."

Malcolm retrieved a thick wool blanket off the sofa while she poured their tea, and they went out on the back steps. He wrapped her up in the wool and gave her knee a squeeze of encouragement.

He thought she'd changed her mind until she finally said, "Edward and I were separated when he died."

He reached for her hand, their fingers intertwining automatically. "But Em didn't know that?"

"Not until a few months ago. She goes to school with the daughter of one of Edward's colleagues, and I guess the little girl overheard something she shouldn't have."

"What happened exactly? I mean, what went wrong?"

"Nothing went wrong. I'm not sure things were ever right to begin with." She glanced at him, and even in the dark, he could see her expression was pained. "When I met him, I was twenty-five and a curator at a contemporary gallery in Edinburgh. The gallery often rented out its space for events, and his company held a Christmas cocktail party there."

Her voice softened. "I was taken with him immediately. He was polished and handsome, a little older than the men I had been dating. He flirted with me all night and then, before he left, said that he would like to take me to dinner. He gave me his business card, which I thought was very respectful of him, letting me make the next move. Now I know that was calculated.

"I was young and stupid and I fell hard. I was taken by the fact he was a VP at such a young age and that he got so serious about me so quickly, like some fairy-tale whirlwind romance. I just didn't realize that when he said he wanted a wife and children, that didn't necessarily mean me."

"I don't understand."

"He was ambitious. He knew because he was so much younger than his colleagues, he needed to appear depend-able and settled, responsible. That meant getting married. He met me, learned I was well educated and had extensive connections because of Mum's family. He figured I would make the perfect trophy wife."

"Surely that wasn't the only reason he married you," Malcolm said softly. Maybe marriage was still seen as an alliance in some circles, but he had a hard time believing that any man could spend time with Serena and not fall in love with her.

"I'd like to believe he loved me at some point, but I really don't know. What I didn't realize at the time was that mar-riage with Edward had to be conducted on his own terms. He didn't like the hours I worked at the gallery, so he gently 'suggested' that I would be happier quitting and doing char-ity work instead. I missed my job, but I liked that it left me with plenty of time to paint. But he thought that was a waste of my time. We needed to focus on starting a family, before I got too old."

The picture she was drawing was getting clearer by the second. "Did you have any say in these decisions?"

"Of course I did. At least that's what I thought at the time. He had an argument for every one of my objections, and he had a way of making me feel unreasonable if I didn't agree with him. It took us a while to conceive Em, and I dreaded having to tell him each month that I still wasn't pregnant. Things were getting tenser and tenser between us, as if I were purposely defying his plans. When I did get pregnant, I was so relieved. I thought he would be thrilled. But he only said, 'Finally,' like it was another item on his list that could be crossed off. He started spending less and less time at home, excusing his time at work by saying he had to support his growing family."

"Do you think he was unfaithful to you?" Malcolm asked.

She shook her head. "I don't think so. A mistress would have disrupted his plans." She looked at him, her expression pained. "I don't want you to think that there weren't good times or that I didn't love him, because neither of those are true. I just never knew which man I would come home to—the one who enjoyed spending time with me or the one who saw me as an item to be ticked off his to-do list."

The resignation in her voice stirred up anger. She was such a vibrant, giving person, and now he could see how Edward's control had stamped out her spark. "Did having Em change things?"

"For a while. But she, too, was an item on his list. He knew exactly how her whole life was going to play out, and our future children after that. Except there weren't any more children. For years. It was like because he had no say in that, he became even more controlling. But things were good when he was happy, so I just went along with it. For far longer than I should have."

Serena swallowed hard. Malcolm brought her hand to his lips and kissed her fingers in a show of silent support.

"The final straw was when Em was almost five. She began to get very nervous and insecure. Wouldn't even pick out her clothes without making sure Daddy approved. At first I thought she just wanted his attention because he was gone so much, but then I realized she'd become deathly afraid of doing something wrong.

"And I realized she had learned the behavior from watching me. I had gone along with everything he dictated for my life, but now he was doing the same thing to our daughter. Teaching her to always seek others' approval. So I started putting my foot down. And he lost it."

"Did he . . . hit you?"

"No. But Edward was a master of manipulation. He knew I hated when he was upset with me and that I would do everything to prevent it. So he told me that clearly I didn't care about his feelings or I would take his opinion into account."

"But you didn't budge this time."

"No. Not when it came to Em. As things dragged on and I refused to give in, he must have decided it was time to punish me. He told me he wanted to separate to 'think about what we really wanted out of marriage.' It was outright manipulation. It wouldn't do for him to be divorced. So I told him I thought he should get his own place for a while.

"We intended to tell Em, but we never got the chance. He left on a business trip and came back to his own flat. He had been there only a couple of days when he had a heart attack. His landlord found him after a neighbor complained that his alarm clock had been going off for hours."

Malcolm scanned her expression to gain some clue of her

feelings, but her face was blank, as impassive as her voice. "I'm sorry," he said gently. "Even with your problems, that must have been a shock."

"It was." She turned to him, a film of tears glimmering in her eyes. "The worst part is, I felt relieved. I never wanted to be divorced. I saw how it tore my family apart, how my parents pitted my brothers and me against each other, even unintentionally. But I didn't see a way out. Edward was so obstinate that he would never have given in. And I knew that if I caved, he would never let me forget it. I would have had to spend the rest of my life making up for what I put him through."

Malcolm could hear the helplessness in her voice, but her tears still didn't fall. "Serena, that's all understandable. You were in an impossible situation. Of course you were conflicted once it was over."

"I just wonder if anything would have been different if I'd told him."

He blinked as he realized the one detail missing from the narrative. "Max. Edward didn't know you were pregnant."

"I didn't tell him. I was afraid he would somehow use it against me. But now I wonder . . . would we have worked things out had he known? If he hadn't been alone, if he had been home that morning, he might not have died."

And they might still be married. Selfish as it was, Malcolm hated that thought. Not just for himself but because she'd been so horribly unhappy.

As if she guessed his thoughts, she said, "Maybe our marriage couldn't have been saved. But Em and Max would still have their father."

Malcolm shifted the blanket from her shoulders so he

could wrap his arms around her. "I'm sorry. I know relation-ships can be complicated, but I don't understand how he couldn't look at you and thank God for every day you were in his life."

She lifted her head, her lips parting in surprise at the words, naked vulnerability in her expression. He brushed his fingertips across her cheekbone and smiled. "I think now I understand why you reacted how you did when we first met."

"I may have come on a bit strong. I hated the implication I wasn't capable of making my own decisions."

"Understandable, considering the circumstances. And I might have resented having my authority questioned by a vixen in designer jeans."

"Vixen?" Her eyebrows arched upward.

"Oh yeah. From the first time I saw you, I thought you were gorgeous and sexy and much too good for me."

Serena laughed. "You were so far outside what I was look-ing for, it annoyed me that I found you so attractive."

"Is that right? You probably shouldn't have told me that."

She scooted closer. "And what exactly do you plan on doing about it?"

He shifted her onto his lap and took her mouth with his before she could say another word. But rather than the explo-sive demand of desire, the long, sensual kiss held the slow burn of both passion and promise. It was impossible to deny his feelings had gone beyond the physical. He wanted all of her—heart, body, and soul—forever.

She leaned back, her eyes half-closed. "You have no idea how much I want to ask you to stay."

"But . . ."

She sighed. "But I can't. Or won't. You already knew that, though."

"I did." He kissed her again. "And Kylee's already put me on notice that she's watching me. I'd bet she's waiting up."

"I hate being a good example."

"I hate you being a good example too." He smiled wryly, knowing that wasn't the real reason he would be leaving her on her back porch tonight. He scooped her up as he stood and set her on her feet again. Instead of saying all the things he wanted to say, all the things he felt but didn't want her to think were just a way to get her into bed, he kissed her again, slowly and tenderly. "Good night, Serena."

"Good night, Malcolm."

Reluctantly he stepped off the porch and left her there, felt her watching him as he cut through her garden and stepped over the low fence that separated the properties.

He loved her. He wanted to marry her. It was time to find a ring.

Serena checked on Max and Em after Malcolm left, then climbed the stairs to her loft bedroom. She had expected to feel wrung out and exhausted after telling her story, but she felt fine. If she had been questioning whether she was ready to move beyond the shadow of her past, tonight had answered that in abundance.

She changed out of her sweater and trousers, pulled on her pajamas, and crawled into bed without removing her makeup. She'd been a breath away from inviting Malcolm to stay, but she knew if she had, she would have regretted it tomorrow. Call her old-fashioned, but until she could trust a man enough to marry him, she couldn't trust him with her body and soul. It just didn't stop her from thinking about it. She desperately needed a distraction.

Fortunately there were plenty of other demands crowding her mind. The planning for the hotel's tour offerings, the grand opening of the gallery to the public, her permanent living arrangements on Skye. The latter she was delaying, partly because she loved her current proximity to Malcolm, and partly because she secretly hoped the next time she went shopping for a house, she'd be doing it with him.

True, they hadn't discussed it, but everything she sensed from him was moving in that direction. Given all the complications inherent in dating a single mum with two young children, he wouldn't still be around if he weren't looking for a long-term commitment.

Her phone chimed beside her and she reached for it. A text message from Malcolm: Miss you already. Hope you're asleep.

She replied: Not yet. Was Kylee waiting up?

She was. I'm not sure which one of us is the adult here.

Serena laughed aloud, and she was halfway through a reply of *I love you* before she caught herself and changed it to I miss you. Until tomorrow.

Can't come soon enough.

She put aside her phone and let out a happy sigh. She loved him, and even if he hadn't said the words, she was certain the feeling was mutual. He had once told her to lighten up and take things on faith. For the first time in years, she was beginning to believe love might work out for her in the end.

CHAPTER TWENTY-FIVE

MALCOLM WAS GLAD the hotel guests required little attention for a change, because he could barely keep his mind on
his work throughout the rest of the week. The thought of his
plans for Saturday made him too nervous to concentrate.

He took Kylee's car when they reached Fort William, saying only that he needed it for errands while she was at the
music studio. She had a double lesson today, both her usual
voice instruction and an extra guitar session. She had taken
to heart Glenn's advice to work on her playing technique as
diligently as she did her singing.

He drove directly to a little line of shops on the high street,
close to the dock where the ferry loaded for the trip across
Loch Linnhe, and parked at the curb. A sign painted with
neat white letters identified the shop on the end as Ben Nevis

Jewelers. He climbed out of the car, and his palms instantly turned clammy. It was the only fine-jewelry store within a hundred miles—not a huge surprise considering Fort William was far more of a tourist destination than a place where someone bought an engagement ring—but his research had revealed that the owner was a legitimate designer.

Malcolm braced himself and opened the door to the clamor of bells. Instantly a middle-aged man with graying hair came from the back. "May I help you?"

"Mr. MacTavish? We spoke earlier this week. I'm Malcolm Blake."

"Ah yes, Mr. Blake. Do come in." Mr. MacTavish circled the counter and held out a hand, which Malcolm shook. "You were interested in the design of an engagement ring, were you not?"

Just the words shot a current of uneasiness through Malcolm. He had no idea what Serena would like. The birthday dinner had been the first time he'd ever seen her wear jewelry beyond her tiny gold studs, and he suspected even one of the pair of diamond earrings she'd been wearing was far outside his budget. Was he mad to think she would marry him? And if she did say yes, would she suffer permanent disappointment every time she looked at his ring?

"Sir?" Mr. MacTavish prompted him.

"Sorry. Yes. Engagement ring."

The jeweler looked him over and chuckled. "Come around the display, and we'll discuss what you want for your young lady."

Malcolm followed him back to a small workspace beside a bench stacked with drawers of tools, lights, and magnifying glasses.

Mr. MacTavish gestured for him to take a seat in a wooden chair, then settled himself on a padded stool. "Now, tell me what you're thinking. Style? Stone? Budget?"

Malcolm found himself telling the jeweler about Serena, how she was classic and unfussy but came from a very wealthy family, so he didn't want to feel as if he were competing. He'd seen the enormous diamonds that James's and Ian's wives wore, both undoubtedly bespoke and approaching the cost of an expensive car or holiday home.

"Have you considered vintage?" Mr. MacTavish asked. "Perhaps a sapphire or ruby? Colored gemstones are back in vogue for engagement rings."

"She was once an art curator," Malcolm said. "And she does have an appreciation for antiques."

"Edwardian or art nouveau, then, perhaps. Clearly she likes something with a bit of story to it. Wait here."

The jeweler went into the back for a moment, then reappeared with a black-velvet tray containing several rings. He pulled out a simple round diamond in a platinum band and handed it to Malcolm.

"Pretty," Malcolm said. "But it doesn't feel like her."

The next five rings the jeweler showed him didn't seem right either, though Malcolm didn't know what he was looking for. Finally MacTavish unlocked a drawer in his workbench and withdrew a tiny plastic bag. He came back to Malcolm and shook the ring into his hand. "I just purchased this from a customer this week. It needs some minor restoration work, but the setting is too beautiful to simply harvest the gem."

Malcolm took the ring and held it up to the light. It *was* beautiful and old-fashioned: white gold with an engraved band and floral setting that cradled a brilliant purple stone. "An amethyst?"

"Oh no. This is a purple sapphire. Very rare, far more so than the blue color. They don't require heat treatment to bring out their best color, and they naturally change depending on the light. This particular ring is an art deco piece from the thirties. Knife-edge band, you see, with some lovely engraving. It's missing a prong, and the band is misshapen, but those are relatively minor repairs."

"It's perfect." For a former museum curator who loved the stories behind art, what could be better than an antique ring approaching the century mark? "How much?"

Mr. MacTavish quoted a price that was above what Malcolm had intended to spend but still within reach. He could picture Serena's expression when she saw it. He hoped at least some of the excitement would be about marrying him.

"If you wish, I can complete the work this week while you consider. If I don't hear from you by the weekend, I'll put it on display in the case."

Malcolm looked at the ring a moment longer and handed it back to the jeweler. "I think that's more than fair. Thank you, Mr. MacTavish. I would never have thought to consider vintage."

"My pleasure. Your Serena is going to fall in love with it, I am sure."

His Serena. He shook Mr. MacTavish's hand and stood, feeling simultaneously more settled and more nervous now that a decision on a ring had been made.

He puttered around Fort William while he waited for Kylee to finish her lesson, debating on whether or not he should say something to his niece about his intentions. In the end he decided not to. The ring repairs would take time, and he couldn't take the chance that Kylee might slip. He also wanted to make the moment special, and as of yet, he hadn't thought of a way to accomplish it.

Still, his anxiety must have shown, because the minute Kylee climbed into the car, she scowled at him. "What's wrong with you?"

"Nothing's wrong with me. Why would you think anything's wrong?"

"You're acting really odd. And you keep tapping the steering wheel."

He stopped abruptly. "Too much caffeine. Sorry."

Kylee slanted him a look that said she was unconvinced, but he didn't elaborate. As Malcolm drove, he considered romantic date options for his proposal. The weather was warm, but the stargazing was done for the year. Serena seemed to like the outdoors, so maybe a picnic?

"Something's up," Kylee said when he pulled into the drive of their home. "You were much too quiet. Even for you. You and Serena didn't break up, did you?"

"No! Of course not."

She frowned. "Okay. Good. 'Cause I like her."

Malcolm climbed out of the car and followed Kylee into the house. He was already in the kitchen putting the kettle on to heat when he heard a gasp and a squeal from the next room.

"What? What happened?" He rushed out of the kitchen to find Kylee standing in the hall, her phone cradled in her trembling hands. She looked up at him, her eyes glimmering. For a moment he couldn't tell whether she was happy or upset.

Then she whispered, "I got in. Look."

She thrust the screen at him, and his heart plummeted as he recognized the Berklee College of Music header across the top of the e-mail. It was indeed an acceptance notice, congratulating Kylee for having been admitted.

"I don't understand," he said numbly. "I thought you said it was nearly impossible to be admitted from the wait list. You already committed to Glasgow."

"I'll have to withdraw." She did a little jig in the hallway. "This is incredible. I can't believe Glenn actually did it."

"Wait. What? What about Glenn?"

"Glenn works with a producer who is on faculty at Berklee this year," Kylee said. "He told me he'd send my audition footage and see if his friend would put in a good word for me. I just didn't think he would." She frowned. "I told you all this."

"No, Kylee," Malcolm said quietly, "you didn't."

"Well, I thought I did. This is amazing! But I only have a few more days to accept. I should go log on now—"

"Wait."

Malcolm's word stilled her in her tracks. She turned, a sick look on her face that matched the feeling in his gut. "You said if I got in, we could go. You said we'd both move back to America. I thought that's what you wanted."

"I did say that." And he'd meant it. But he'd put that possibility aside when she was wait-listed. He'd all but made up his mind to stay in Scotland as soon as Serena entered the picture. "Are you sure this is really what you want? You're making a very specific decision if you go to Berklee."

"That's exactly why I want to go. Why would I waste my time on opera when I could study songwriting and music production? I'll have the chance to make all sorts of industry connections. Why aren't you happy about this?"

Malcolm sighed and put his arm around her, gave her a quick squeeze. "I am happy for you, Kylee. Truly I am. I'd just had a completely different plan for how this year was going to go. This is a big decision, moving back to America."

"You don't have to go with me, you know. I'm going to be eighteen. I don't need you watching over me."

He interrupted her with an upraised hand. "You know that wasn't the deal. The only reason your parents even considered sending you to uni in America was because I was a few hours away, in the same time zone. You know they would never agree to you going alone."

"Yeah, well, they're dead. They don't get a say." The bitterness in Kylee's voice took him aback. She turned wet eyes on him once more, now shining with deep hurt. "You're not going to let me go, are you? Because of Serena."

"Kylee, I didn't say that."

"You didn't have to. This is so unfair!" She grabbed her rucksack and raced up to her room, slamming the door so hard it shuddered the entire house.

Malcolm pushed his fingers through his hair, grabbing a handful in frustration. In the space of five minutes, his entire life had changed. Their entire life had changed. He'd been ready to propose to Serena and make a home here in Scotland, and now he found himself having to choose between the two people he loved most in the world.

He went back to the kitchen, where the kettle had long since switched off, and poured himself a cup of tea. What was he supposed to do? On one hand, Kylee had her heart set on attending this school, and he'd vowed to do everything necessary to make her dreams come true. There was no doubt she would get a far stronger start to her music career if she lived in America, especially since it seemed she already had a music-producer contact there. It was impossible to quantify the difference influential connections in the industry could make.

Yes, he could allow her to go by herself, but Nicola had adamantly opposed the idea back when Kylee first broached it, until Malcolm had pointed out that it was only an hour's flight from Baltimore to Boston if Kylee needed him. Didn't he owe it to Nicola to abide by her wishes for her daughter?

He needed to talk to Serena. This wasn't a decision Malcolm could make without her. And yet in her mind, they were just dating. He hadn't yet proposed. He hadn't even told her he loved her. Would she consider moving after everything she'd said about wanting to raise her kids on Skye, give them the island childhood she'd had? Inverness wasn't exactly a bustling metropolis, its population topping out at just over sixty thousand, so if she'd felt it was too city-like, there was no way she would approve of America's East Coast.

He had to think about this first. The minute she saw his face, she would know something was wrong. So he took the coward's way out. He called her.

"Hey, handsome." The sultry lilt to her voice made him feel as if he were somehow betraying her.

He forced himself to sound normal. "Hey, yourself, beautiful. How was your day?"

"Amazing. I cannot wait to show you what I got for the gallery today. And it was a complete random occurrence too. One of those serendipity moments."

"Oh yeah?" He smiled and sat back in his chair, momentarily brightened by her enthusiasm. He loved that excited timbre to her voice, the gleam in her eyes, and for a moment he regretted he hadn't gone to see her in person.

"We were at the bakery in Portree having breakfast, and who should walk in but Máire MacLeod?"

"Am I supposed to know who that is?"

"She's the artist who did the canvas at Davy's that I pointed out to you. I don't know her well, but I invited her to join us and told her about the gallery. She only works on commission these days, but she has two talented protégés she would like to see exhibited there. Our next two slots are booked!"

"Wonderful!" he said. "I love how quickly it's coming together. Maybe we can put together a preview of the upcoming months' exhibits for the cocktail-party launch."

"That's an excellent idea. I can make up a rack card showing the first three exhibits and hand them around at local businesses."

"Perfect. I'll put together some ideas. I'm heading to the hotel in a few minutes."

Serena sighed, but he thought it was a happy sound. "I didn't realize how much I missed Skye or how good it would feel to work with art again, even if it's on a much smaller scale. I love being able to champion artists."

Her enthusiasm drove into his heart like nails, each word a hammer blow pushing them deeper. "I think you should consider exhibiting some of your own work."

"Oh, I couldn't. Besides, the point is to showcase talented newcomers, give them a little boost in their careers. I'm neither."

"You are far more talented than you think," Malcolm said.

"And you are completely biased." A scream split the quiet

in the background. "That didn't sound good. I have to go. See you tonight?"

"I have a few things to help Kylee with. Tomorrow at church?"

"It's a date. Kind of."

Malcolm hung up, more conflicted than ever. She was excited, had a sense of direction for the first time in years. How could he possibly ask her to give that up?

Kylee's door was closed, the thud of bass shuddering the walls, a clear sign she wasn't ready to talk yet. He bypassed her room for his own and changed into workout gear, then grabbed his wraps and gloves and headed straight to the back garden.

He forced himself through a sensible warm-up, the routine too ingrained for him to think about doing otherwise, then unleashed his frustrations on the vinyl surface of the bag. When he'd been in the ring, he'd always fought smart, not angry, but his opponent today didn't hit back. When his energy was finally spent and his muscles had turned to jelly, he grabbed the swaying bag and leaned his forehead against it while he caught his breath.

Boxing out his feelings was usually enough to clear his mind, but not today. He still had no idea what he was going to do.

When he looked up, he realized he had an audience. Not Serena but Kylee, perched on the back step with her hoodie wrapped protectively around her. Slowly he pulled off his gloves and walked over, lowering himself to the step beside her. "Hi."

"Hi." Her eyes were swollen and red rimmed, her expression miserable. "I'm sorry I slammed the door on you."

He nodded in acknowledgment of her apology, but he really had nothing else to say. He braced his forearms on his knees and stared out over the back garden.

"I wish Mum and Dad were here," she said in a small voice.

"I wish they were too."

Kylee remained quiet for a long stretch, then cleared her throat. Her voice sounded thick with unshed tears when she spoke. "I know what you gave up for me, coming back to Scotland. That's why I'm going to Glasgow."

"What?" Malcolm frowned at her, sure he had heard wrong.

"You lost your job and your girlfriend to come back to a place you hate. And now that you're actually happy, you're going to have to leave again. That doesn't seem fair."

They were the very words he'd hoped to hear, but they sounded wrong to his ears. The resignation in her voice, the sadness—she was doing what she thought was the right thing. She was miserable about it, but she didn't want his unhappiness on her conscience. And yet she was the one who had lost both her parents. She was the one struggling after her dreams in the wake of her grief.

"I think you should go to Berklee," he said, aware that his own voice held far more resignation than enthusiasm.

"What?" She blinked at him. "But—"

"It's your dream, Kylee. And you've lost enough. I don't want you to lose this, too."

"I don't know what to say."

"'Thank you' would be a start." He gave her a wry smile and hugged her to his side with one arm. "I love you, you know."

"I love you too, Uncle Mal." She paused. "Can you let go of me now? You're all sweaty."

Malcolm laughed and released her. "Sorry."

"What about work and Serena and all that?" Her expression turned wary again, as if the reminder might change his mind.

"Why don't you let me worry about that?"

"Okay. Wow, I can't believe it! I have to ring Lane!" Kylee jumped up from the steps and dashed into the house, her mobile in her hand before the door even shut behind her. He heard the faint sound of her excited voice trail from inside.

It was the right thing to do. He'd known it the minute he'd spoken the words aloud. It just didn't bring him any closer to a decision on what to do about Serena. He needed to talk to her soon.

But he would wait until after he picked up the ring next Saturday. It felt like an act of faith that everything would be all right. Once he explained the situation and she realized how committed he was to her, they could figure out a way forward together.

CHAPTER TWENTY-SIX

SERENA WAS BEING ANNOYINGLY PERKY, and she knew it. She couldn't help it. It felt as if everything was unfolding with ease, and the upcoming gallery grand opening breathed new excitement into her day. Maybe more excitement than she deserved, considering how her developing relationship with Malcolm made her breathless with anticipation. She was finally where she needed to be.

She woke up early to make puff pastry for breakfast before church, then hustled the children into their Sunday best. Given Max's inclination for finding "just one more thing" to do before they walked out the door, Malcolm, Kylee, and Muriel almost always beat them there. That was fine since they saved her a seat and she didn't have to answer the questions about her love life posed by some of the ladies of the congregation.

True to form, the trio had already claimed their seats in a front pew when she slipped through the door. Muriel raised an amused eyebrow as Serena tiptoed down the row and plopped into the empty space between her and Malcolm just seconds before the service started.

He squeezed her hand in greeting. "Cutting it a little close, don't you think?"

"We had a stuffed-giraffe emergency," she whispered. "Max won't go anywhere without it."

"Oh yeah? Where did you finally find it?"

"The fridge."

Malcolm muffled his chuckle with his fist, which made her grin. Max hadn't offered any explanation other than the fact he'd forgotten where he'd put the soft toy. This in contrast to Em, who used to do head counts of her dolls like a school-teacher supervising a field trip.

When the minister took the pulpit, Serena focused her attention forward, enjoying the fact that Malcolm didn't release her hand, even if it meant her attention wasn't entirely on the sermon. It was almost laughable what a heartsick teenager she became in his presence, but she wasn't going to apologize for it. After a decade of walking on eggshells with Edward, followed by years of thinking she was destined to be alone, she deserved to enjoy being around a man who made her feel this way, someone who let her be who she really was.

The minute the service ended, Muriel kissed her on the cheek and slipped out, ostensibly to get home to start Sunday roast dinner. Serena went to retrieve Max from the crèche and Em from Sunday school, then returned to the vestibule, where they usually met Malcolm and Kylee.

Malcolm was nowhere to be seen, but she spotted Kylee's blonde head in the crowd and led her children to where she was speaking with two older couples.

". . . can't believe it's actually happening. It's been my dream to study music in America for years, but now it's really coming true!"

Serena frowned, sure she'd misheard. Hadn't Kylee said she'd already committed to attending the University of Glasgow? But the girl was still talking.

"We're not really sure when we're going to leave. A lot has to do with Uncle Malcolm's job and how fast he can find a new one. But isn't it great? Maybe I'll actually learn to surf! Do they even surf on the East Coast?"

Serena felt the blood drain from her face. Malcolm and Kylee were moving to America? Surely what she was hearing couldn't be true.

"Are you ready to go?" Malcolm's quiet voice beside her jump-started her heart again, but she knew she must have looked stricken when she turned to him.

"You're going to America?"

The sick, guilty look on his face told her all she needed to know. "Serena—"

"When were you going to tell me?" The ground rocked beneath her feet. Maybe it was the impact of all her hopes crumbling around her.

"Serena, maybe we should talk about this outside."

"Mum, what's wrong?" Em looked up at her with concern and a touch of fear.

"Nothing's wrong, cupcake. Some adult stuff to be discussed. Why don't we get you two into the car?"

Serena guided them from the church on autopilot, too numb with shock to comprehend anything but the fact Malcolm was following. She buckled Max into his car seat with trembling hands, leaving Em to fend for herself. Then she shut the car doors and stepped away to confront Malcolm. "Is it true? Are you leaving Scotland?"

There was that look of misery on his face again. "It's true. The decision was just made. Kylee was admitted from the wait list at Berklee. I had promised her if she got in, I would move with her."

The explanation only made her feel worse. "You knew this was a possibility, and you never said anything? Not even when I started on about permanently relocating to Skye?"

"No. There was almost no chance she would get in, and the fact that this ... miracle ... happened ... I can't deny her this. I didn't even know Glenn was going to pull some strings for her."

"I don't understand." Dread slowly crept in behind the shock.

He looked as if he had been caught. "Glenn asked a producer friend at Berklee to put in a good word for her."

"You used me?" The words spilled out before she could consider them, driven by hurt.

"No." He grabbed her by the shoulders and bent his head down, forcing her to look at him. "I did not use you. I didn't even know about this. Serena, you have to believe me. I don't want to leave you. I love you."

Those three words broke through her daze, but rather than bringing the thrill of joy she had imagined they would, she felt only a wash of sadness. "Somehow I never thought I'd be standing in a car park when you told me that."

He dropped his hands, looking as helpless as she felt. "Can't we talk about this? Somewhere else, somewhere less public? There's more I have to say that I don't want an audience for."

"Yes. We can talk. Just not right now." Without waiting for his response, she walked back to her car and climbed into the driver's seat. The door shut behind her with a hollow thud, sealing Malcolm out.

"Are you okay, Mum?" Em asked in a small voice. "You're crying."

Was she? She lifted her hand and dashed away the tears that had fallen without her knowledge. The words *I'm fine* died on her lips before they could emerge. She wasn't fine, not remotely. "I don't know, cupcake. Right now I'm feeling really hurt."

"Are you and Malcolm breaking up?"

Serena curled her hands around the steering wheel, squeezing hard while she wrestled her voice under control. "I don't know that either, love. But I do know that Auntie Muriel is expecting us for lunch. And I, for one, could do with a giant slice of pot roast." And a time machine so she could go back and warn herself not to fall so thoroughly for Malcolm.

Except she knew she wouldn't have taken the advice.

She spent the drive to Muriel's concentrating on forcing the breath in and out of her lungs, on the tears that needed to remain walled behind her eyes for Max's and Em's sakes. But all the time, questions rolled through her mind. Why hadn't Malcolm told her? Why hadn't she been the first one he called when Kylee received the offer? Had she even figured at all into his decision to pack up and follow his niece to America?

All questions he might have answered for her had she stuck around. But she couldn't look at him without seeing the man who held her happiness in his hands, without hating how quickly and thoughtlessly she'd handed over the power to hurt her again. To hurt them.

She parked in Muriel's drive and let the children go inside without her while she remained in the car, head tilted back against the seat. The front door opened, and Muriel stepped out on the stoop, her expression concerned; then she retreated inside. Serena understood why when she saw Malcolm's car pull up behind her in the rearview mirror. He was alone.

Serena climbed from the driver's seat and waited, wrapping her arms around herself while he walked toward her slowly, like one would approach a skittish animal. When she didn't back away, he put his arms around her and pulled her against his chest. After a moment she wrapped her arms around his waist, hating both the ache in her heart and the realization that she had never felt this safe with anyone else.

"Can we talk, please? I have a lot to explain."

"Let's take a walk," Serena said. "I don't want Em and Max to overhear."

Malcolm tentatively took Serena's hand. She drew a deep breath as they walked down the drive toward a path that cut across the open meadow beyond. "Okay. Explain. I'm listening."

Malcolm told her about the plan that he and Nicola had made to send Kylee to university in America when he had still been living there, how he had promised Kylee that the plan wouldn't change just because he had moved back to

Scotland. When she hadn't been accepted to Berklee, he'd assumed the issue was closed.

"You have to understand, Serena, it never once occurred to me this was a possibility. She didn't even tell me Davy and Glenn were going to help. That's why I never said anything. And I would have discussed it with you, but I wanted to wait—"

"Wait for what?"

He seemed to be gathering courage when he took both her hands and turned her to him. "For your ring to be finished. I meant what I said. I love you. I was planning to ask you to marry me."

For the second time that day, she felt the solid ground beneath her feet shift. "Marry you?" And then she realized what he'd said. *Was planning*. Past tense. "But now you've come to your senses, is that it?"

"No, Serena, no." He swore softly beneath his breath. "That's not what I meant at all. This is why I didn't want to do it this way." He straightened his shoulders and looked into her eyes. "Serena, I want to marry you. Will you have me?"

Serena stared at him. Twenty seconds ago she'd thought he was letting her down easy, and now he was proposing? She couldn't process the change.

"Serena, say something, please."

"I'm sorry, I just—" She gathered herself. "Malcolm, I've thought about this so much, I would have thought there would be no question in my mind if you asked me that."

"But there is." Hurt hung thick in his voice.

"You're not just asking me to marry you. You're asking me to move halfway around the world. To take my children away from their family, from everything they've ever known."

"Do you love me?"

She couldn't lie. "I do. I do love you."

"But it's not enough."

She flinched. "You have to understand what we've been through. For the first time in longer than I can remember, we have a true home. Em loves her school. She's finally making real friends; she's learning to speak Gaelic. And it's clear to me that Muriel needs someone nearby as she gets older. I love you. I really do. But how do I tell them all we're picking up and moving to America?"

He wiped a hand over his face, looking gutted. "There's nothing I can do to change your mind?"

"Could I change yours and convince you to stay here?"

The stricken look on his face said it all. "I can't go back on my promise to Kylee. And I can't let her move by herself. It's not what Nicola wanted for her. I could never live with myself if I put her well-being at risk for my own happiness."

The worst part was, she couldn't even blame him. She blinked back tears, but they blurred her vision and choked her throat anyway. "Is this it, then?" she whispered.

"I don't know." He sounded as lost and broken as she felt. Bewildered at how they'd come to this point. She didn't understand herself. Her world had been turned upside down, and this time there wasn't anyone to blame. It just . . . was. As inexplicable and irreversible as the fact that Edward wasn't around to be a father to her children. At last she had found a man she loved, the one she wanted to spend her life with, but she couldn't marry him.

They walked back the way they'd come, hand in hand, though there might as well have been an ocean separating them already. When they were at Muriel's house again,

Malcolm took Serena's face in his hands and kissed her so tenderly that she wanted to change her mind, say she'd do anything if he didn't leave her here like this. But she didn't. Instead, she just choked out, "I wish it didn't have to end this way."

"Must it?" he asked, his expression pleading.

She bit down on her trembling lip. "For Max's and Em's sakes, it's better that it's a clean break." But that was a lie. It was for her sake. She couldn't stand to see him and know there was no future for them. If she had any hope of getting out of this whole, she needed to face facts. She needed to move on.

"Be well, Serena," he whispered. "Do what makes you happy. I know you're capable of anything you put your mind to."

He pressed one last kiss to her forehead, then climbed into his car. She waited until it was no longer visible down the road before she climbed the steps to Muriel's house.

Her aunt was there in an instant. "Serena?"

"Are Em and Max in the back garden?" she asked hoarsely.

Muriel nodded. Once she knew they were alone, Serena collapsed in her aunt's arms and cried like a heartbroken child.

Serena tried to pull herself together, but even if her gravelly voice and swollen eyes didn't give her away, her children knew her too well not to see that there was something dreadfully wrong. Max climbed into her lap and placed a little hand on each of her cheeks. "Why are you sad, Mummy?"

Serena blinked back a fresh round of tears and forced a smile. "Sometimes even mums have a bad day, monkey."

"Then I'll kiss it better," he declared and delivered a wet smack to her lips.

"That is so much better, Maxie. Thank you." She gave her son a tight squeeze, breathing in his still-baby smell, and she didn't let him go until he wiggled out of her grasp to go play. Em just watched her with mournful eyes. She had to know what this morning's argument meant, why her mum was trying not to cry in Aunt Muriel's lounge. Serena didn't know whether to be grateful that Em didn't ask questions or guilty that her daughter had to worry about her fragility.

She managed to make it through lunch and the rest of the afternoon, baking cookies and playing games with Em and Max at home, all the while praying she would be able to hold in her emotions until she had the house to herself.

But as soon as she climbed into bed, before she allowed herself to unleash her hold on her tears, the soft thud of feet traveled up the stairs.

"Mum?" Em called quietly from the doorway. "Are you awake?"

"I am. Couldn't sleep?"

Em shook her head and crawled under the covers with her. Serena put an arm around her and let the little girl snuggle up beside her.

After a long stretch, Em asked, "You and Malcolm aren't getting back together, are you?"

Serena swallowed the lump in her throat. "I don't think so, cupcake. We love each other, but there are too many things we couldn't work out."

"I don't understand. Why do people keep leaving us? Don't they like us?"

Em's words, her ownership of the situation, was more

than Serena could take. The tears she had held back spilled down her cheeks, accompanied by Em's mournful sniffles. "Oh, my little love, this has nothing to do with you and Max. Sometimes things just don't work out, is all."

"I'm going to miss him and Kylee," Em said, hugging her tighter.

"Me too, Em."

Em drifted off to sleep beside her, but Serena simply stared at the vaulted ceiling of her bedroom. Had she done the right thing? She'd been trying to make the decision that was best for her family. No matter how she might love Malcolm, she'd known him for only a few months. She couldn't risk her children's happiness by moving them halfway around the world any more than he could bring himself to go back on his promise to Nicola and Kylee. This was one of those situations that was nobody's fault, just a matter of bad timing.

In time her heart would come to understand that.

CHAPTER TWENTY-SEVEN

MALCOLM THREW HIMSELF INTO PLANNING. It was all he could do now that the decision had been made. He and Kylee were moving. Serena wouldn't be coming with him.

"What happened?" Kylee asked, wide-eyed, when he returned home.

"Serena and I are over," he said flatly. "I asked her to marry me, and she said no. So you can stop feeling guilty about all this."

"I'm—" she began to protest, then cut herself off. "I'm really sorry, Uncle Malcolm."

"Yeah. So am I. You already put in your letter of intent?"

"I sent it in yesterday, as soon as you agreed." Her voice turned hesitant. "What do we do now?"

"We need to download all the forms and due dates. I think you probably already missed the deadline for on-campus housing, so we'll have to figure out whether we need to fly there early and look for an apartment."

Kylee just stared at him.

"I'm okay, Kylee. We just have a lot of planning to do in a short time. I need to contact the institute and see if they have any openings, and then we'll schedule a trip to get us both sorted. I'll come back and look over the process of renting the house."

"You're not going to sell it?" Kylee asked in a small voice.

"No, Kylee. Your parents left this to you. I want to make sure it's here for you if you ever decide to come back to Skye. When you get older, if you want to sell it, you can."

"It's all just happening so fast."

It was. And he needed it to happen fast, before he could feel the full impact of what he was doing and change his mind. This was the best decision for Kylee's education and for his own career. He'd never intended to stay on Skye, managing a tiny hotel at the edge of Scotland. Once he was back in Baltimore or Boston or Philadelphia, assuming he could get a similar job, he could pick up where he left off, and this year of his life would just be a blip on his CV. A distant memory.

At least that's what he told himself. Serena couldn't be erased that easily from his heart.

Before he could go down that maudlin path, he sent Kylee to her room to print the information packet, then booted his own laptop on the dining-room table. The web surfing took his mind off the implications of his actions as he searched job listings and apartment adverts. But he knew that was simply a distraction from the task that would make this move real.

Moment of truth.

He opened an e-mail to his old boss in Baltimore and started the change in motion.

Bill, it looks like I'm moving back to America.

The hotel looked different to Malcolm now that he knew he was in his final two weeks of managing it. It wasn't a job he'd have ever thought he would hold, but in retrospect, he had enjoyed it. The variety of tasks, the stretches of solitude. Of course, he wouldn't miss the fairly regular complaints of guests about things outside his control, but there would be an entirely different set of annoyances once he was back to an office job: politics, interpersonal bickering, long hours spent staring at a computer screen. He'd have to make a point of getting outside into the fresh air whenever he could.

He never thought he would miss anything about Skye, and now he was walking away with a whole list of regrets.

The host of problems that met him when he arrived was a welcome distraction. An electrical issue in the kitchen turned out to be a loose connection that he easily fixed without needing to call an electrician. Then the hotel's website decided to crash, thanks to an unexpected server update. That took a call to technical support, followed by an hour combing through code before he found the line that was conflicting with the new database software. It was as if God were throwing him challenges ideally suited to his skill set so he didn't give in to the growing impulse to call Serena and beg her to reconsider.

He wouldn't. Couldn't. She'd been manipulated enough through guilt, and he wouldn't be another man who refused to let her make her own decisions. Even if the prospect of being without her hurt with every breath.

When he finally got back to his desk after the last emergency—a leaking drain in the bar's sink—there was an e-mail waiting from his former boss. He opened it and read the terse reply: *Your previous position has been filled, but maybe you'd be interested in this? If so, send me your résumé and apply through the website.*

Malcolm clicked on a link, which took him to a job description for a senior software engineer at the Space Telescope Science Institute. Rather than general systems engineering, this particular position was tied specifically to the Hubble Deep Field program. It was just the sort of thing that had appealed to him when he decided to work in astronomy.

He didn't hesitate as he pulled up his CV from cloud storage and attached it to a reply to Bill. He was already committed, he told himself. Clicking Send would do nothing to change that. But his chest felt tight as the arrow hovered over the button. Given his excellent reputation at the institute, he had a good shot at the position. They would want him to come out for an interview, and once he did, he would be returning to Scotland only to pack and ship their things and rent the house.

He pressed Send.

CHAPTER TWENTY-EIGHT

ONE FOOT IN FRONT OF THE OTHER. One day at a time. The mantras carried Serena through her waking hours now as they had gotten her through the early days after Edward's death, when she struggled with what to tell Em and tried to reconcile the fact that she was going to have another child, completely alone. Even though this wasn't a physical death, the abruptness brought the same sense of grief, the sensation of having her future pulled out from under her, the deep realization of her aloneness. Yes, her children were there, and if anything, her pain reminded her how intensely she loved them, but her responsibilities also reminded her that she didn't have anyone who could take care of her in return.

She avoided the hotel during the daytime hours. It was

painful enough to know that Malcolm was right next door, yet so far out of her reach that he might as well have been in America already. But the opening of the inaugural gallery exhibit was this weekend, and that didn't change just because her heart was broken. She left the kids with Muriel and went to the hotel after she knew Malcolm had handed off responsibility to the new assistant manager, Catriona. She tweaked the positions of the paintings and rearranged furniture. As long as she kept herself busy, she didn't have to think about Malcolm and the hole he had left in her world. She didn't have to examine why she'd let him so thoroughly infiltrate the life she had built for herself and her children.

On Tuesday morning came the phone call she had been dreading. "Hi, Jamie," she said cautiously. She'd avoided talking to her brothers so she didn't have to relive the situation, but there was no chance it wouldn't come up now.

"Serena, I just received a resignation letter from Malcolm. He gave me two weeks' notice. Do you know anything about this?"

She hung her head. "Uh, yeah. He and Kylee are moving back to America. I didn't know what the time line would be, so I didn't say anything. I just assumed he'd deliver it to me."

"Does this mean—?"

"That we're over? Yes." She tried to keep her voice strong, but it caught anyway.

"I knew it," Jamie muttered. "I'm going to kill him."

"No," Serena said quickly. "It was my decision. He asked me to marry him and move, and I said no. Our home is here in Scotland. On Skye."

"Are you sure, Serena? I would have sworn—"

"I'm sure." This time her voice sounded solid. Firm. "I've made my decision. I won't lie and say it doesn't hurt, but I don't regret it. Em and Max are finally settled. This is where we're meant to stay."

"I'm so sorry. I hate that you're hurting again. Especially after all you went through with Edward."

"You knew?"

"Of course we did. You're our sister, Serena. We know when you're not happy. But you would never take any criticism of Edward, and you insisted things were fine. What else should we have done?"

"Nothing. I wouldn't have listened." She hadn't been ready to admit how bad things had gotten, because once she did, she would have had to do something about it. And the choices had been impossible: divorce him against her personal beliefs or let him make her and her daughter miserable.

"Do you need us, Serena? I'm in London, but I could be home by Saturday. Andrea could come out too—"

"No. I'm okay. I promise." The last thing she wanted was to be around Jamie and Andrea, who were the very definition of *blissfully in love*. She quickly changed the topic before he could force the issue. "What do you think about having me take over management responsibilities at the hotel? Max and Em will be back to school in August."

"I think you would be excellent. Are you sure that's what you want to do?"

"What else am I going to do with my time?"

"You could paint."

Somehow the suggestion hurt more than she had ever imagined. "I don't paint anymore." Or at least she didn't plan to. The first thing she'd done when she and Malcolm parted ways was pack up her easel.

"Whatever you want to do, Ian and I will back you up. Just let me know if you need anything, will you?"

"I will. I promise. Love you, Jamie."

"Ditto, Sis. Take care of yourself."

She tried. She really did. At least she went through the motions of living, playing with Em and Max, baking in her wonderful vintage oven. When the day of the opening reception arrived, she moved through it like a shell of herself, smiling and making small talk, introducing visitors to their first artist. This was what she'd been working toward—the thrill of once again doing something in the field she enjoyed—but even when they made several sales, the joy eluded her. Every time the door opened, she looked up, her breath held, hoping it was Malcolm; every time her hopes crashed again.

He had been a part of this, whether he knew it or not. He'd nudged her to take chances, to open up, to trust herself again. Without him, the victory felt hollow.

She picked up the phone and then hung up more times than she could count over the next several days. They were over. There was no future for them. He would be gone from Skye and out of her life for good in only a few days.

Still, she somehow didn't expect to walk into the manager's office one evening and find it bare.

The stupid mug that always sat on his desk was gone, as were the potted plants. And in their place, precisely aligned in the center of the desk blotter, was a thick three-ring binder with a note taped on the cover. Malcolm's barely legible scrawl was visible even from the door. She pulled the note off the binder with trembling hands.

Dear Serena,

You've no doubt heard that we are flying to America, and this is my last day at the hotel. James told me you're taking over, but I've arranged for Liam and Catriona to cover the hours for the next two weeks while you get your feet under you.

I've laid out the procedures I established for ordering, maintenance, and deliveries. You'll find a list of already-approved vendors in the back of the binder. I hope this makes the transition easier.

I wish we could have done this in person, but I think you're right that it would be too difficult. For both of us.

Wishing you all the best,
Malcolm

She ground her teeth, her throat suddenly tight, as she flipped open the binder. With typical engineer thoroughness, he'd laid out his entire procedure in tabbed sections, arranged by day and task. There were spreadsheets with inventory lists, notated with the vendors and the regular ordering dates. Employee schedules. Troubleshooting lists detailing the most common problems she might face on a daily basis and whom to call if she couldn't fix them herself. And each sheet had a file path printed so she could find the electronic copy. In short, he had spared no effort in making sure she had everything she needed to run the hotel efficiently without him.

Serena sank down onto the desk chair, her heart clenched and aching. She didn't know if she was more touched by the gesture or pained by what she had lost. She'd been lamenting the fact that no one was looking out for her, and here he was trying to help her from afar even after she had broken his heart.

He was a good man; he loved her; she loved him. And yet she couldn't have him. What welled up in her now wasn't grief but anger. She leaped out of her chair, stormed from the hotel, and shut herself in her car, where she could let the sorrow and rage pour out. Why? She'd done everything that was ever asked of her. She'd gone to church. She hadn't slept around. She'd married someone she thought was a good man, a Christian. And he had betrayed her by not loving her, not loving their child the way he should have because of some deep insecurity that made him dominate those he was supposed to care for and cherish.

And then, just when she had given up on love, Malcolm came along, someone who was everything she never thought she wanted and every last thing she actually needed. She changed her life's direction, began to believe that maybe God was looking out for her after all. And instead of a lasting love, instead of the happy family she craved for herself and her children, she was once more alone. Shouldering the burdens herself.

"Why?" she whispered, staring up through the window to the sky beyond. "What is wrong with me? Why do You always take everything away?" But instead of the familiar glimmer of light against an ocean of dark, the stars were hidden by perpetual twilight.

It felt symbolic of her life, caught on the cusp of day and night, between happiness and sorrow, always waiting.

She put the car in gear and backed out of the hotel's car park, her jaw clenched and her heart aching. She was merely being sensible. She was doing the responsible thing by putting her children's well-being above her own needs. That's what being a mother meant. But if that was true, why was she so miserable? Why did her heart feel not just broken but irreparably shattered? Was this the lesson she wanted to teach her children, that love wasn't worth fighting for, that it could be discarded out of practicality? That made her no better than Edward.

By the time she reached Muriel's house, she was more confused than ever.

The anger drained out of her as she trudged up the walk to the front door. When she entered, the lights had been turned low and her children were sound asleep on the sofa. Only the kitchen light shone brightly. She followed it and found her aunt wiping down the countertops with a rag.

"Are you finished already?" Muriel asked without turning.

When she didn't answer, Muriel swiveled and then stilled when she took in Serena's tearstained face.

"He's gone," Serena said, her voice wavering. "What if I made a terrible mistake?"

"Oh, sweetheart." Muriel moved to her side and put her arms around her. "I'm so sorry. Is that how you feel? Can't you just . . . go over there and talk to him?"

"I don't know," she whispered. "On one hand, I made the only decision that made sense, and on the other, I feel like it's a huge mistake to let him walk out of my life. Our lives."

Muriel patted the stool at the island, then bustled to the kettle to make tea. Celebration, sorrow, the answer was always a cuppa. If Serena weren't so distressed, the observation would have made her laugh.

"Why do things like this keep happening? Am I that

foolish? Edward seemed so perfect but made me so miserable. Yet Malcolm is Edward's exact opposite . . . and I'm still miserable."

If Muriel was surprised by Serena's admission, she didn't show it. "Seems to me that you just traded one cage for another."

Serena frowned. "I don't understand what you mean."

"We all saw how Edward dictated every detail of your lives. But once you were free, didn't you do the same thing? You kept your life exactly as it was. You could have gone back to work; you could have started painting again, but you didn't."

"So this is somehow my fault because I didn't go back to art?"

Muriel raised an eyebrow, indicating she didn't appreciate Serena's tone, regardless of the context. "No, dear," she said patiently. "I'm suggesting you became so obsessed with giving your children the kind of life they would have had with Edward that you didn't stop to consider whether you should. Then once you decided that Skye was the best place for them, you refused to budge."

Once more, the responsibility for her mess of a life fell soundly in her lap. "Is it so wrong to want to give them stability?"

"Of course not, dear." Muriel softened. "But stability doesn't mean you never move forward. They have a mother who loves them more than anything or anyone else on earth. These things won't change, whether you're in Scotland or America."

Serena fell silent. "You think I should have said yes."

"That's not my question to answer. What does God tell

you? Only you know where He is leading you. If that's Skye, then perhaps you and Malcolm were never meant to be." Muriel poured tea into Serena's cup and pushed it across the countertop.

"I'm not sure God's paying attention anymore. Or if He is, He's staying pretty quiet."

Muriel reached across the counter and took her hand. "Serena Marie, you need to stop blaming God for all the heartache in your life. Until you do, you will never hear His voice over the sound of your own hurt."

Serena jerked her gaze up, shocked by the statement. "I don't—no! That's not true."

Muriel stared back, unyielding, though there was compassion in her expression. She squeezed Serena's hand one more time. "I love you, Serena. Whatever happens, I'm here to support you."

Tears brimmed on the edge of Serena's lashes, and she blinked them away. As soon as she finished her tea, she woke Em and carried Max to the cold, quiet car. The entire way home, she turned Muriel's words over in her mind. Was her aunt right? Serena had felt distant from God, but she'd been blaming Him and not herself. As if all the things that had happened—her parents' divorce, her unhappy marriage, Edward's death—were His doing and not simply a result of circumstances and bad choices. As if He hadn't held up His end of a deal.

And somewhere along the line, she'd decided she could do better herself. Oh, she taught her children to pray, but besides her family's health and safety, had she really sought out God for anything?

The answering nudge to her spirit felt uncomfortably like conviction. Along with a whisper: *It isn't too late.*

Then a surprising request surfaced, especially since she wasn't the lay-out-the-fleece sort: *Please give me some sort of sign.*

As she turned up the road to the croft house, she impulsively passed her home and slowed in front of Malcolm's house. The windows were dark, and the drive was empty. They were gone.

It was a sign, all right. Just not the one she'd wanted.

CHAPTER TWENTY-NINE

THE PARLOR WAS PACKED with people, both hotel guests and locals. Serena stood to the side, watching the event but not mingling. Selma McCann, the artist whose canvases were on display this month, had that part under control: she chatted easily with the guests, her expression as bright as the line of silver hoops that edged her left ear. Serena smiled, basking in the sensation of a job well done.

To say her idea had gotten off to a rough start would have been an understatement. After the initial gallery launch, she'd been so buried with work at the hotel that she'd had to rush to complete the next exhibit on time. Now she was glad she had. Selma pointed the man she'd been talking to in her direction, and Serena put on a friendly smile as he approached. Selma's first sale.

By the time they were finished for the day, two of Selma's eight paintings had sold. It might not have been the curation work to which Serena had once been accustomed, but somehow this gave her even more satisfaction. At nineteen, a young artist had made her first sales and gotten the encouragement she needed to continue with her art.

Even so, Serena was glad when the reception ended and she could grab a few minutes of quiet while she cleared abandoned appetizer plates and straightened the brochures and information cards on the rack. For the thousandth time in the past six weeks, she felt a wash of sadness at Malcolm's absence. He would have been proud of what she'd accomplished, she thought. She just wished he could have been here to see it through to the end.

Well, she wished for a lot more than that. But in the past month, the anger and the grief had faded into a sort of gentle resignation, even acceptance. Yes, she'd loved Malcolm. She loved him still. But she had to accept that perhaps it hadn't been the right time for them, that her true purpose for coming back to Skye was so she could shed her decades-long history of hurt and distrust.

She took the remaining plates to the kitchen, then strode back to the storage room, her mind already whirling with the other items on her to-do list. The housekeeper would come in to do a quick cleaning, and the sold paintings would need to be carefully packaged so the guests could take them when they left. First, however, she had to select new paintings to take their places and rearrange the remaining pieces in a way that showed them to their best advantage. Carefully she sorted through the paintings in the stack leaning against the back wall, choosing them more for their themes, sizes, and colors than any artistic merit. She had plenty to choose from, and the fact they were her own work no longer gave her pause. She'd forgotten how many paintings were stashed in the attic of her house in Nairn, wrapped to keep them from prying eyes, all but forgotten. Now they played a supporting role to other artists in her little gallery. She was comfortable with that. She didn't need the acclaim or the validation to prove she was a great artist, because she wasn't. It was enough to put them out there, to acknowledge that part of her existed, and it was okay if it wasn't her identity. Because it was her choice.

Now that she'd admitted that to herself, the pile of paintings in the storeroom just kept growing, fueled by the art supplies and easel propped in the corner of her front lounge at home. Painting had become her respite, a way to pour out her feelings as she once had, something of a visual prayer. She'd forgotten how she felt God's presence when she painted, as if He chose to communicate with her in a medium she was guaranteed to understand. Even if she could barely stand in front of the easel without thinking of the first time she had shown Malcolm her artwork, she recognized that too as an answer to a silent prayer. Without his little nudge of encouragement, she might have succumbed to that critical inner voice that had smothered both her creativity and her spirit.

Still, whatever she might have gained from the experience, six weeks was not enough time to erase love. And she could finally face the truth: she'd made a mistake in not fighting harder for her future with Malcolm, in not trying to work things out. Somehow. Any way they could manage.

Slowly she removed a rectangular piece of cardstock from

the reception-desk drawer, where it had been stashed for the past month. It was a pastel version of the Callisto painting, drawn on one side of a heavy postcard, the other side already addressed to Malcolm in Baltimore. She just hadn't been able to bring herself to send it. She still didn't have the words to adequately express her feelings. But maybe it didn't need to be complicated. The truest words were often the simplest.

She took out a felt-tip pen and scrawled a message on the back side before she could talk herself out of it.

I miss you. I love you. Serena.

She put a stamp on the corner and dropped the postcard into the basket of outgoing mail on the front desk, the pounding of her heart nearly as strong as her urge to take it out.

Instead, she went back to the storeroom for a second painting. When she returned, a man was standing in the gallery examining the details of one of Selma's charcoals.

"That one is sold, but the one next to it is still available if you fancy landscapes."

The man straightened and turned, and her heart nearly stopped. "Malcolm?"

He smiled uncertainly. "Hi, Serena."

She stared in disbelief. His hair was a bit longer, his face clean-shaven, making him look younger and even more handsome than she remembered. Was he really standing there in the hotel parlor, or was she at home in bed, dreaming? It wouldn't have been the first time her imagination had summoned him in her sleep.

He shifted uncomfortably under her stare. When she didn't speak, he moved to her and took the painting from her numb fingers. "Let me help you with that. I assume you're replacing the pieces that have been sold?"

He held the painting up, taking in the swirl of colors against the dark-blue background: a woman, chained with threads of stardust, looking with longing across a star-bright sky. "Wait. This is Andromeda. Like your Callisto."

Serena nodded dumbly, using the time to find her voice. "What are you doing here?"

He carefully set the painting down against the wall. "Is there somewhere we could talk?"

"Yeah, I . . . Let me get Catriona. I brought her in to help while I worked the art reception." Feeling unsteady on her feet, the thrum of blood whooshing through her ears with each heartbeat, she went back to the manager's office to let the woman know she was stepping out.

She followed Malcolm out the front door, and he led her across the car park to the meadow alongside the hotel. The green field was now studded with summer wildflowers that swayed in the cool breeze blowing off the sound, brilliant bursts of white and yellow and purple. The whole time Serena stole glances at him, trying to reconcile his presence beside her with the fact she'd thought she'd never see him again.

"You lost the beard," she said finally.

He ran his hand over his smooth chin. "It was time for a change."

"You've gone all clean-shaven and professional now that you're a software engineer again?"

"Something like that."

"How's Kylee adapting to Boston?" If she kept talking, kept asking questions, maybe it would keep the answers from hurting so much.

"She's doing well. She starts classes next month. She stayed behind while I came back to deal with the house and ship the rest of our things."

So he wasn't back for her. Thank God she hadn't yet sent off that postcard. Serena forced down the spike of pain and made her voice strong. "I'm glad you came by, but I should finish up inside now. It's good that things have worked out so well for you two."

His hand shot out to grip her arm, and her traitorous heart did its customary leap the minute his fingertips touched her skin. "That's the thing. They really haven't."

"I thought you got your job back. The one you wanted."

"I did." Malcolm took a deep breath and pulled her to face him. "Everything fell into place. I got my job back—a better one, actually—and rented a house. We went to Boston to look at apartments and roommate listings, but everything was too expensive or too rowdy or got rented out from under us. I was starting to get worried that we'd moved there just to have no place for Kylee to stay.

"And then one Sunday, Kylee and I happened into this church in Boston, one we randomly picked as we walked by. And who should we meet there but the Mitchell family, originally of Edinburgh, now Boston residents. They just happened to have a daughter who is a sophomore at Berklee."

The slow, steady creep of understanding came over her. "Someone to show Kylee the ropes?"

"More than that. They have a vacant apartment over their garage. The daughter wanted to live there, but they also needed the rent. So now Kylee has a roommate."

"And a Scottish family to look out for her."

"Exactly. Completely opposite of the situation we were seeking, but it was an answer to prayer."

He paused for a moment and took her hand. Her heart gave another leap at his touch. "Here's the thing. The whole time, I knew I was doing the right thing in helping Kylee reach her dreams and making sure she was looked after. And when we met the Mitchells, I realized that just because Kylee is supposed to live in America doesn't mean I am."

Serena caught her breath, her free hand going to her chest in a vain attempt to loosen the sudden tightness there.

"Serena, I love you. I've been miserable without you. I couldn't figure out how to reconcile my responsibilities with the feeling I'd just made the biggest mistake of my life. And now I know it was because I was only supposed to get Kylee started on her way and let her go. My place is here with you."

Serena just stared, unable to form words. Tears welled in her eyes and spilled down her cheeks. "I don't know what to say. I'd resigned myself to the idea that we weren't meant to be, and now—"

"Say you love me, that you'll forgive me for leaving you. Say you'll marry me." He reached into his inner pocket and pulled out a ring, holding it between two fingers so that the stone glinted in the sunlight.

Her eyes rose to his face, and the earnestness and love there took her breath away. She realized then that she had no need for fancy words or an elaborate proposal. It was all just window dressing for the fact that after all her tears and loneliness and doubt, God had heard her after all. He had brought Malcolm back to her.

"Yes," she said simply. "Yes, I'll marry you."

He slid the ring onto her finger, then threaded his hand

through her hair and bent to kiss her—gently, sweetly, and with such tenderness that the tears returned in force. When they parted, she held out her hand to admire the ring—an old-fashioned white-gold band with the most unusual purple stone she'd ever seen.

He followed her gaze and smiled. "There's a story behind this one. This is the ring I had picked for you, but I never went back for it. I didn't expect that it would still be there when I returned to Scotland. But the jeweler had misplaced it and never completed the restoration work, so it hadn't been put on display. It was waiting there for me when I got back. Some coincidence, huh?"

"I don't believe in coincidence anymore," she said, stretching up on tiptoes to steal another kiss, her heart full. "Some things are just meant to be."

SERENA STOOD AT THE EDGE of her property, looking out across the sweeping expanse of green where it disappeared down to the edge of Loch Eishort, the brilliant blue of the water reflecting an unusually sunny July day. They had been in this home on the far tip of the Sleat Peninsula for more than six months, but she still sometimes found it hard to believe she was back for good. Even harder to believe that she and Malcolm had been married almost an entire year.

"Getting inspiration for another painting?" As if her thoughts had summoned him, Malcolm stepped up behind her, slid his arms around her middle, and pressed a kiss to the side of her neck.

She leaned back against him, soaking up his familiar, solid presence. "Just thinking how much I love this place."

"Is that the only thing you were thinking about?"

His lips were working their way down her neck to her shoulder.

She smiled. "We have guests, you know."

"Do we? I'd not noticed."

She laughed and turned around in his arms so she could kiss him full on the lips. "Did you ever think that we would end up here?"

"Kissing in the back garden? Or married with two kids and a dog?"

"Kissing in the back garden is a given. But you're mistaken. It's three kids. Or soon it will be."

He frowned in confusion for a moment, and then his eyes widened. "Are you serious?"

A bubble of nervous laughter spilled out. "I found out this morning. I'm pregnant. About six weeks."

He picked her up and gave her a squeeze, then put her down quickly. "Sorry, should I not have done that? Did I hurt you?"

Serena laughed again at his concern. "I'm not breakable, I promise."

"But how? We were so careful because we agreed there were too many risks." Even though Malcolm had admitted he would like a child of his own, they'd both been concerned about what a pregnancy would mean for her, considering she was now forty. Somehow that had seemed so old when she'd had Em nearly ten years ago, but she felt younger, happier, and healthier than she'd ever been. She attributed that to her husband and their peaceful life on Skye.

"Sometimes God has other plans, I suppose. It wouldn't be the first time He's decided to surprise us, would it? You're going to be a father."

"I already am a father," he said softly. "I was perfectly content with Em and Max and Kylee. But this—this is wonderful news."

She sighed happily and lifted her face for another kiss. She'd known he'd be thrilled, and even though she felt a quiver of nervousness at the prospect of starting over with a baby, it was a gift. This time around, Malcolm would be with her every step of the way.

"We should probably go in now before everyone wonders where we are," she said. "And I should start getting ready for the party."

Malcolm took her hand, and they walked together up the slope to their sprawling home. The Ord house was another blessing that had fallen into their laps. After they'd eloped the previous September and spent a week's honeymoon in Cornwall, they came back to Skye and immediately began searching for a new home together. Kylee's Breakish house was leased for the year, and Serena's home in Nairn was on the market, but even if they'd not been, she and Malcolm had decided they needed a new start together. Serena had been thinking of a modest little croft house that they could fix up together, but when this whitewashed five-bedroom home had become available, they'd fallen in love with it.

It didn't hurt that it was situated on the water with views of Black Cuillin and the Isles of Rùm and Canna. Not only did it have enough bedrooms for the children and guests, including Kylee, but it also contained spaces for Serena's art studio and Malcolm's home office, something he'd put to immediate use when he'd started his own business. Contract software engineering, he'd told her, could be done anywhere with an Internet connection. Working for himself also gave him the flexibility to spend afternoons on the project he and Serena had just begun, an after-school program that offered classes in their areas of special interest: boxing, art, and astronomy.

Malcolm opened the patio door for Serena, and they stepped into the windowed conservatory they used as a dining room, its twelve-person table large enough to accommodate the family that always seemed to congregate on free weekends. Right now, it was decorated with streamers and balloons and a big paper banner that said, "Happy Birthday, Mara." Serena had already set the table with pink flowered paper plates and matching plastic cups.

"Where is everyone?" Malcolm asked with a frown.

In answer, a round of laughter rang out from the front reception room. They followed the sound and found Serena's family gathered on the large overstuffed sofas, Jamie and Andrea on one, Ian and Aunt Muriel on the other. Grace was kneeling in the corner, the ever-present camera in her hand, snapping photos of the three children standing stock-still in the middle of the room. Or at least Em and Max were motionless. Mara was wiggling with typical one-year-old enthusiasm, grasping one of Kylee's fingers for balance. The teen looked absolutely smitten with her baby "cousin."

"Simon says . . . hop on one foot." Jamie grinned as Em and Max started hopping. It took Mara a second to catch on before she started jumping in an adorably awkward two-footed hop. "Simon says, turn in circles. Stop."

Em and Max froze, but Mara kept on spinning, helped along by a grinning Kylee.

"Mara wins!" Jamie said, scooping up his adopted daughter and smothering her in kisses. She laughed delightedly while Em and Max groaned over their loss. "Uh-oh, someone needs a nappy change."

"Here, I'll take her." Andrea held her hands out for her little girl, but Jamie just bent down and kissed his wife's nose.

"I have it. I'll be back straightaway."

Andrea watched her husband and daughter with an expression just short of beaming and then fell back against the sofa. "All right, you two. Are we playing for second place?"

Serena let out a happy sigh. Maybe it was the emotion surrounding her own news, but having everyone together in one place filled her heart to bursting. The house never felt more like home than when it was the center of a family gathering, even if it still felt strange to take over the status of hostess from her aunt. She plopped down between Muriel and Ian on the sofa and kicked her feet up on the padded ottoman.

"How are you, Sis?" Ian slung an arm around her shoulders in an affectionate hug.

"Good. Having fun?"

"I am. Grace won't sit down and relax, though."

"I heard that," Grace called. "And this *is* relaxing." But she rose and perched on the ottoman across from him. Ian tugged her forward by the strap of her camera and stole a kiss, earning him a smile from his wife in return.

Jamie came back into the room, swinging a giggling Mara by the arms. "So, I think there's a birthday girl ready for cake and presents. What do you say, Serena?"

"I think that's an excellent idea." She hoisted herself up from the sofa, and she couldn't help but think about how difficult that was going to be in a few months, when she had a baby bump to maneuver around. She'd been so intent on the birthday party and the need to break the news to Malcolm that she hadn't let herself dwell on what that meant. The first thrill of excitement shot through her at the prospect.

The whole assembly moved to the dining room and adjacent kitchen, Muriel and Em following Serena to help move the cake and punch to the table while everyone else took their seats. As they filed in—the whole extended family that would be growing even more in the future—Serena felt tears well up again.

"You okay?" Malcolm whispered in her ear, putting his arms around her.

"Blasted pregnancy hormones," she whispered back, but she smiled through her tears.

It was impossible not to feel grateful when she looked back on how much her life had changed since coming to Skye more than a year ago. She had felt alone and disconnected, gripping what she had so hard that she couldn't grasp the blessings God had for her future. And now the center of her universe was a home built of love and laughter, all proof that the greatest gifts were the ones that could never be planned.

A Note from the Author

ONE OF THE MARVELOUS THINGS about the Isle of Skye is its northern latitude, which produces a state of perma-twilight throughout much of the summer but sometimes makes it hard for authors to work stargazing opportunities into books whose time lines stray past spring. Peak stargazing in the Highlands and islands ends in late April rather than the first week of June as I've implied in the story.

For travelers wishing to see this spectacular location for themselves, I highly recommend a trip in mid- to late April, when you can enjoy both the stargazing and the beginning of the spring warm-up. You won't regret it!

Discussion Questions

1. Throughout the book, Serena struggles with insecurity and self-doubt over her choices. Why do you think that is? How have her past experiences affected how she feels about her abilities and worth? Have your past relationships—both platonic and romantic—colored the way you think about yourself?

2. Serena feels guilty about wanting more from her life beyond motherhood. Do you relate to her need to have something of her own? In what ways is this important to her becoming a whole, thriving person?

3. Malcolm takes great pride in his work. However, he gives up his dream job for someone else not once but twice. What does that tell you about what he truly values? How do you think his childhood experiences might have shaped what's important to him?

4. In Serena's mind, art, faith, and passion are intertwined—when she lost one, she lost them all. Why do you think

that is? How do you think those three things might be interrelated?

5. Muriel tells Serena that until she stops blaming God for her heartaches, she will never hear His voice over the sound of her hurt. Do you think this is true? What examples can you give from your own experiences?

6. Malcolm has a habit of defaulting to humor when he's uncomfortable or at a loss for words. He rarely speaks of his faith openly. How might his behavior and choices be a better gauge of his beliefs and values than his words? Give examples.

7. How does Serena's attitude toward God change from the beginning of the book to the end? What events contribute to that transformation?

About the Author

CARLA LAUREANO is the two-time RITA Award–winning author of contemporary inspirational romance and Celtic fantasy (as C. E. Laureano). A graduate of Pepperdine University, she worked as a sales and marketing executive for nearly a decade before leaving corporate life behind to write fiction full-time. She currently lives in Denver with her husband and two sons, where she writes during the day and cooks things at night.

CHAPTER ONE

AT LEAST THEY COULDN'T FIRE HER.

Andrea Sullivan propped her elbows on the bar and buried her head in her hands. How had things gone wrong so quickly? One minute she'd been on the verge of closing a half-million-dollar deal. The next, she'd nearly broken her hand on the jaw of a client who thought her company's offerings extended to favors she had no intention of delivering. Three years of working her way up the ranks toward VP of Sales all down the tubes because one man couldn't keep his hands to himself.

No, her company certainly wouldn't risk an ugly public legal battle. They didn't have to. Her boss had other, more subtle means of showing his displeasure.

As punishments went, Scotland was a big one.

"What's so terrible about Scotland?"

Andrea jerked her head up and met the bartender's gaze. Had she said that aloud?

The man's eyes crinkled at the corners as he ran a towel along the polished mahogany surface of the bar, evidently amused by her slip. Round faced and topped with a thinning mop of dishwater-blond hair, he looked as stereotypically English as the London pub in which he tended bar.

She let out a long breath, her shoulders slumping. "Scotland's cold, it's miserable, and the food is horrible."

"Oh, it's not so bad as all that, is it?" His expression turned from amused to sympathetic. "Take in some countryside, tour a castle or two, maybe some high street shopping . . ."

"This is a business trip. Trust me. My dream vacation involves sunshine and umbrella drinks on the beach, not rain and fog in some backwater village."

If she'd only managed to keep her temper in check, she'd have been spending the next week in the tropics with the promise of a fat commission and a guaranteed promotion, not serving time in Scotland babysitting a celebrity client who suddenly wanted to dabble in the hotel business.

James MacDonald.

She'd never heard of the man. Then again, she didn't own a television. She spent so much time on the road, she wasn't even sure why she owned an apartment. She seemed to be the only one on the planet, however, who hadn't heard of the Scottish celebrity chef. Half a dozen restaurants, four cookbooks, his own television show. Even her taxi driver had been able to name MacDonald's three London restaurants without hesitation.

Andrea toyed with her half-filled wineglass, watching the golden liquid slosh around the bowl. "I should be on my way to Tahiti right now, not sitting in a pub drinking a rather mediocre glass of wine."

"That's because you go to Paris to drink wine," a deep male voice said over her shoulder. "You come to London to drink ale."

Andrea straightened as a man leaned against the bar beside her. He was tall and broad-shouldered, dressed in a pair of dark slacks and a business shirt, the collar unbuttoned and sleeves rolled up to show off muscular forearms. Dark hair worn a little too long, brilliant blue eyes, handsome face. Handsome enough she took a second look and immediately wished she hadn't been so obvious about it. His grin made her heart do things it was certainly not intended to do.

She couldn't prevent the corners of her mouth from twitching up in a smile. "Now you tell me."

He glanced at the bartender. "Get me a 90 Shilling, and whatever light's on draft for the lady." He looked back at her. "We can't have you leaving London thinking that pathetic chardonnay is the best we have to offer."

"That's very thoughtful." She offered her hand. "I'm Andrea."

"Mac." He held her hand just a moment too long while he studied her face. Her stomach made a peculiar little leap. She quelled it ruthlessly and drew her fingers from his grasp while he slid onto the barstool beside her.

"Now tell me why you're sitting here instead of on what sounds like a brilliant holiday in the South Pacific."

Because my temper finally got me into more trouble than I

could talk my way out of. Aloud she said, "I'm doing research on the owner of this pub."

"Ah, the illustrious Mr. MacDonald. Brilliant chef, but not the full quid from what I hear." The sparkle returned to those devastating blue eyes, and she had the feeling she was the butt of a private joke.

Andrea couldn't pass up the opportunity to gather some local gossip. She plowed onward. "You know him?"

"That depends on why you're asking. Is it business, or is your enquiry of a personal nature?"

"Business. I'm supposed to meet him in Inverness tomorrow, and I'm looking for a little background."

"Are you always so unprepared for meetings?"

Andrea bristled. "Of course not. I only got the call from my office a few hours ago. I'm now fortifying myself for a long night of web browsing back at the hotel."

"I can see that. Well, I'd say this pub is a pretty good reflection of him. Comfortable, slightly sophisticated. Best selection of locally brewed beers in England and some truly inspired food."

Andrea looked around. Typical decor, lots of wood and brass, dim lighting. Stained glass and leather accents. Upscale but not uptight. Welcoming but not sloppy.

"Middle of the road," she murmured. "But that still doesn't tell me much about the man."

"And why do you need to know so much about him?"

The bartender returned with Andrea's drink and poured Mac's from the bottle into a glass, watching them as if they were his evening's entertainment.

"My job requires rapport," she said. "I can't convince someone we're right for the project if I don't know what he's looking for. I can't win him over if I don't know which buttons to push."

"Hmm." He sipped his ale, his eyes dancing over the rim of the glass.

Was he laughing at her? "What?"

"I've just never heard a woman worry about which buttons to push when she's wearing a skirt that short and heels that high."

Heat crept up Andrea's neck and into her cheeks as she tugged down her suit skirt. It wasn't as if she were wearing a miniskirt. The length was perfectly modest when she wasn't sitting on a barstool. The heels were admittedly less conservative, but she wore them for height, not for looks. Then she realized he was watching her with a satisfied smile. She had taken the bait. Who exactly did he think he was?

She stilled her fidgeting and fixed him with a direct stare. "I could close a deal in jeans and tennis shoes. I just don't like being unprepared. Besides, I'm used to dealing with hotel groups with hundreds of properties, not celebrities with nothing better to do than play innkeeper."

"So MacDonald's a dilettante?" He swiveled on the stool and leaned back against the bar, arms crossed over his chest. Repressed laughter flashed in his expression.

"Frankly, I don't know the first thing about him. I've never seen his show, I certainly don't cook, and I can't fathom why anyone with a successful career in London would want to open a hotel on the Isle of Skye."

"Now that just sounds like bigotry. We Scots have an overabundance of national pride."

Andrea's cheeks heated again. How could she not have noticed? His accent, while refined, had a distinct Scottish burr. She was really off her game if she had failed to pick up something that obvious. Still, he had needled her about both her clothing and her professionalism, and she had to pry the apology from her lips. "I didn't mean to be rude."

He waved a hand in dismissal. "You've got bigger problems if you know so little about your client. Though you'll do fine if you avoid the pejoratives about his native land. I do think you have one thing in common."

"What's that?"

"You both think work is a terrible reason to cancel a trip to Tahiti."

A reluctant smile crept onto her face. "I can drink to that."

"*Slàinte*, Andrea." He clinked his glass to hers, took a long pull of the ale, and hopped off the stool. "I should get going now. I would suggest you do the same, Ms. Sullivan. You've got a long day ahead of you tomorrow."

She blinked at him. "How did you—"

"Night, Ben. Her drinks are on the house."

"Night, James."

Mac—or the man pretending to be Mac—winked at her and sauntered out of the pub.

"That was . . . He was . . ."

Ben seemed to be fighting a smile. "Mr. MacDonald, yes. I daresay that's the first time not only has a woman *not* fallen all over him, she's actually insulted him to his face."

Andrea's heart sank to the soles of her Jimmy Choos. "I think I'm going to be sick."

"I wouldn't worry too much. I rather think he liked you."

Right. She glanced back at the door, but James MacDonald had already gone. Why, oh why, did this happen now? She had to hook this account if she had any hope of getting back into her boss's good graces, and now she'd be spending the next few days trying to placate a celebrity ego.

She'd never been particularly proficient at groveling.

Andrea hopped off the stool and reached for her purse before she remembered Mr. MacDonald had taken care of her bill. She found a couple of one-pound coins in her change purse and set them on the bar as a tip, even though Ben had done nothing to signal her impending disaster. Would it really have been so difficult to give her a shake of the head, a raised eyebrow? But of course he'd stay out of the matter when his boss was involved.

"Thank you, Ben." *For nothing.*

"Good night, Andrea." He slipped the coins beneath the bar and added, "Don't think too badly of Mr. MacDonald. He's a good man, beneath it all."

Andrea forced a smile and hiked her handbag onto her shoulder, then escaped onto the dark London street. At nine o'clock on a Sunday evening, traffic had tapered off, and the usual haze of diesel fumes faded into the musty scent of damp concrete. She made a left and strode toward the Ladbroke Grove tube station, irritation speeding her steps.

How many times had she lectured her junior account managers on the importance of maintaining professionalism at all times? Every contact was a prospective client or referral. She'd just proved her own point in a particularly embarrassing manner.

Not that she excused James MacDonald for his role in this debacle. She knew his type. Wealthy, good-looking, famous. He expected women to fall at his feet, and God forbid one had a mind of her own. She'd probably be dodging his advances for the next three days while she tried to convince him she was more than a pretty face. He was lucky she hadn't smacked him for commenting on her clothing in the bar.

Truthfully, she hadn't been in much shape to do anything but put her foot firmly in her mouth. It had been years since she'd let a man rattle her, and it had taken only a smile and a lingering handshake to do it. Heaven help her.

She only made it a few blocks from the pub before the stiletto pumps began to rub blisters on her heels. She gave up on her plans of an indignant walk to the tube station and raised a hand to the first black cab she saw. She climbed into the rear and gave the driver her destination.

She could salvage this. She'd spend the rest of her evening with her laptop, finding out everything she could about the man. From here on, she would act with the utmost professionalism. She hadn't gotten this close to VP through years of seven-day weeks and grueling round-the-clock hours to blow it now. Her boss may have given her this assignment as some backhanded punishment—after all, it had been years since he'd wasted her on a barely five-figure deal—but there had to be some sort of cachet to landing a celebrity client like James MacDonald. Surely she could turn it into bigger accounts. But first she had to repair the damage she'd done with her big mouth.

The cab pulled up beside the imposing Victorian brick edifice of the Kensington Court Hotel. Andrea paid the driver and climbed out with a wince, once again regretting her choice in footwear. She limped into the richly decorated lobby and rode the lift to her fourth-floor room.

The lush carpeting muffled her footsteps to a whisper when she let herself in. She certainly couldn't complain about her accommodations. She had stayed in the hotel dozens of times over the years, and each room was impeccably decorated in its own style. Her current space featured an enormous tester bed, framed by blue silk brocade draperies that spilled from a gilded corona above the headboard. She gingerly eased off her shoes, sank onto the luxurious mattress, and heaved a sigh.

She was tired, and not the kind of tired a good night's sleep in a fluffy bed could solve.

She lay there for a long moment, then threw a glance at the clock and calculated back five hours. Her sister should just be getting supper ready in Ohio. She pulled her cell phone from her pocket and dialed.

Becky answered on the fifth ring. "Andy! Why are you calling me? Aren't you supposed to be on a plane right now?" Something sizzled in the background, punctuated by a child's scream.

"Did I call at a bad time?"

"No more than usual. I'm frying up some chicken for dinner—Hannah! Leave the cat alone!"

Andrea smiled. Becky was almost eight years older than Andrea, and she had three children: a nine-year-old son and three-year-old twins, a boy and a girl. "I can call back later—"

"David! Don't hit your sister! I'm sorry, what were you saying? Aren't you supposed to be on your way to Tahiti?"

"Change of plans. Michael booked me a consultation with some celebrity client while I'm here. I'm flying to Scotland tomorrow."

"And you're okay with that?"

"I'd rather be in Tahiti, for sure."

"No, I meant—"

"I know what you meant. I'm okay. What's one more, right?"

"Oh, I don't know, the difference between a luxury vacation and a padded room, maybe?"

Andrea chuckled despite herself. Even from Ohio, Becky couldn't resist the urge to mother her. "It's my job. What am I going to do, say no?"

"That's exactly what you say. 'Michael, I've planned this vacation for over a year. Find someone else to do it.'"

"I know." The smile faded from Andrea's face. Had it not been for the disastrous outcome of her last appointment in London, she would have said exactly that. She'd gotten away with plenty of attitude in the past based on her unmatched sales record, but in this business, she was only as good as her last deal. "I'll be fine. Really. I'm meeting the client in Inverness tomorrow, and then we're driving to Skye. I should be back in New York on Wednesday."

"Maybe you should take a few days off while you're in Scotland. Your vacation is blown anyway."

"I don't think that's such a good idea. I'm staying at the client's hotel."

"Who's the client?"

Andrea paused. "James MacDonald."

The squeal that emanated from the speaker belonged to a teenage girl, not a thirty-eight-year-old mother of three. Andrea held the phone several inches from her ear until she was sure her eardrums were safe.

"And here I thought your job was completely boring!"

"Strictly business, Becks. I've got less than two days to put together a proposal, and he doesn't seem like the easiest client to deal with. It's going to be a long trip."

"I bet you don't even know who he is," Becky said reprovingly.

"Oh, I know who he is." *A self-absorbed celebrity with the sexiest smile I've ever seen.* She yanked her mind back from that precipice before she could slip over. "I need to do some research for my meeting now. I'll call you from Skye."

"All right, have fun," Becky said in a singsong voice. Andrea could practically hear her grin from four thousand miles away. "I expect an autograph, by the way." \

Not likely. "Love you, Becks. Give the kids a kiss for me."

Andrea clicked off the line and pressed her fingertips to her eyes, trying to calm the urgent thrumming of her heart. The last thing she needed was to think of her client in anything but a professional fashion. Men like MacDonald were predators—any sign of weakness and she'd never be able to shake him. She knew all too well what could happen if she succumbed to an ill-advised attraction. She'd been there once, and she wasn't going back there again.

"Strictly business." The steadiness of her voice in the quiet room reassured her. She took a deep breath and levered herself up off the bed. Enough procrastinating. She still had work to do.

Andrea slipped out of her suit jacket and skirt, hung them carefully in the closet, and ensconced herself in a luxurious hotel robe. Then she chose an obscure Dussek piano concerto from her phone as mood music and dragged her laptop onto her legs.

James MacDonald chef, she typed into the search box, and waited. Page after page of results appeared: restaurant reviews, interviews, television listings. Andrea clicked through to his official website first and quickly read through his bio. Born in Portree, Isle of Skye, schooled in Scotland. Completed a degree in business at the University of Edinburgh, followed by culinary training at Leiths School of Food and Wine in London. A long list of assistant and sous-chef positions at some of London's most prestigious eateries culminated in his first restaurant, a gastropub in Notting Hill. That first location was quickly followed by smaller, more focused restaurants in Knightsbridge and Covent Garden, then Cardiff, Edinburgh, and Glasgow.

Last year he had been invited to prepare his take on traditional English food for the prime minister. A few months ago he had been named a member of the Order of the British Empire for his philanthropic work with at-risk youth.

She blinked at the screen. Wonderful. She'd just insulted a member of a British chivalric order. That was a distinction not many women could claim.

Andrea moved on to the newspaper articles, all of which called him the standard-bearer for nouveau-British cuisine, then scanned a Wiki page listing each of his six restaurants. All of them had received starred reviews in the Michelin Red Guide. The Hart and the Hound, the flagship pub she'd just visited, received one of only a dozen two-star ratings in Britain.

She should have bypassed the wine and ordered dinner instead.

MacDonald couldn't have accomplished all that by age thirty-five without a sharp mind and plenty of talent. Somehow that just stirred up her irritation. She'd half-expected to find evidence he had simply ridden his looks and charm to success, but every detail pointed to hard work and sacrifice. For heaven's sake, the man had even established a vocational cooking program for secondary-school dropouts.

"The perfect man," she muttered. "Just ask him."

She scrolled through the search results until gossip sites began to appear. Photos of MacDonald with a string of beautiful women—models, actresses, dancers—at exclusive parties and club openings. So he was that sort. Never with the same woman twice.

Great. Her hand still hurt after the encounter with the last wannabe Don Juan. Now she had to spend the next three days trying to get James MacDonald's signature on a contract while keeping things strictly professional. The fact he'd already turned her into a blithering idiot once didn't bode well for her quick thinking.

But she'd manage. She had to. She hadn't come this close to achieving her goals just to let a man get in her way.

TYNDALE HOUSE PUBLISHERS IS CRAZY4FICTION!

Fiction that entertains and inspires

Get to know us! Become a member of the Crazy4Fiction community. Whether you read our blog, like us on Facebook, follow us on Twitter, or receive our e-newsletter, you're sure to get the latest news on the best in Christian fiction. You might even win something along the way!

JOIN IN THE FUN TODAY.

 crazy4fiction.com

 Crazy4Fiction

 @Crazy4Fiction

CP0021